SUBMERGING INFERNO

BRANDON WITT

DSP PUBLICATIONS

Published by
DSP PUBLICATIONS

5032 Capital Circle SW, Suite 2, PMB# 279, Tallahassee, FL 32305-7886 USA
http://www.dsppublications.com/

This is a work of fiction. Names, characters, places, and incidents either are the product of author imagination or are used fictitiously, and any resemblance to actual persons, living or dead, business establishments, events, or locales is entirely coincidental.

Submerging Inferno
© 2014 Brandon Witt.

Cover Art
© 2013 Anne Cain.
annecain.art@gmail.com
Cover content is for illustrative purposes only and any person depicted on the cover is a model.

All rights reserved. This book is licensed to the original purchaser only. Duplication or distribution via any means is illegal and a violation of international copyright law, subject to criminal prosecution and upon conviction, fines, and/or imprisonment. Any eBook format cannot be legally loaned or given to others. No part of this book may be reproduced or transmitted in any form or by any means, electronic or mechanical, including photocopying, recording, or by any information storage and retrieval system, without the written permission of the Publisher, except where permitted by law. To request permission and all other inquiries, contact DSP Publications, 5032 Capital Circle SW, Suite 2, PMB# 279, Tallahassee, FL 32305-7886, USA, or http://www.dsppublications.com/.

ISBN: 978-1-63216-347-9
Digital ISBN: 978-1-63216-348-6
Library of Congress Control Number: 2014944943
Third Edition March 2015
First Edition published by Brandon Witt, January 2011.
Second Edition published by Dreamspinner Press, August 2013.

Printed in the United States of America
∞
This paper meets the requirements of
ANSI/NISO Z39.48-1992 (Permanence of Paper).

For CNH
Who gave me love, happiness, and heartbreak
—without whom this novel would not exist.

CHAPTER ONE

BRETT WRIGHT

THE coffin looked almost child sized. It could have appeared smaller than it was due to how far away I was hidden, but I was willing to bet she had chosen a kid's coffin. I couldn't help but chuckle at the thought, however disrespectful it might be to laugh at a funeral. It's not like it mattered. He was dead. He couldn't hear.

I could picture her at the funeral home, wringing her hands and pacing back and forth. She wouldn't have cried. I was sure she still hadn't. It might be weeks before she cried, if ever. No matter how lonely she would be without him, she wouldn't let her emotions betray her faith that her husband was in Heaven. Still, she would have felt guilt-ridden at the prospect of burying him in a child's coffin. Grandpa had always been self-conscious about his tiny stature. However, he had been equally concerned with never spending a dime more than absolutely necessary, no matter how many millions of dimes he had to his name. Apparently, his frugalness had won out. As much as I wished I could just feel angry, a twinge of guilt tightened my chest, knowing that she had gone through all of this alone.

The obituary Sonia had shoved in my face yesterday as I went out for a swim had simply said that Marvin Alexander Wright had died at home at the age of seventy-five from colon cancer complications, and that he was survived by his wife, Beverly, his daughter, Jessica, and his grandson, Brett. It hadn't bothered to say if it had been a long battle or if there had been much suffering. Maybe he had already been sick when he disowned me two years ago. I found it odd that the obituary had mentioned my mother. Her name hadn't been brought up more than a handful of times in my entire life. It seemed presumptuous to assume Jessica had survived him. We had all taken for granted that she was dead. The thought that she had somehow seen the obituary and was now somewhere close by, secretly watching the service, made the hair on the back of my hands stand up.

A warm gust blew the veil back over Grandma's simple black hat. She reached up and quickly pulled it back into place. Even from this distance, I could see she had gotten smaller, a feat that I wouldn't have thought possible. She didn't look sick, though. Considering the speed with which she had readjusted her veil, it didn't seem like she was any worse for the wear.

I had arrived less than ten minutes ago, and I was already antsy to leave. The longer I stayed, the greater the chance someone would turn in my direction. Standing between the ancient pine and the shelter of a gothic-inspired tomb, I felt fairly camouflaged, but a man my size tended to draw attention. Plus, there didn't seem to be any point to staying. I knew I wasn't going to suddenly change my mind and run, bawling like a baby, to Grandma's arms. She would be fine. She was tough, and I was certain the other women of the church would make sure she wasn't alone for long periods of time. I was ready for the day to be over, and it wasn't even two in the afternoon.

Today had been weird. Actually, the past two weeks had been weird. At first, I thought I was having eye problems, seeing strange things floating off in my peripheral vision. This morning, however, it was a lot more than just seeing something. The feeling that I was starting to go crazy was only heightened by the fact that I was hiding in a graveyard in the middle of the day.

I glanced again at my grandmother. Despite everything, I still loved her, and I hated that I couldn't be there for her right now. She had sided with him, though, when he'd made it abundantly clear that I wasn't welcome in their home until I turned from my vile ways. Even if I'd been willing to, he'd never be able to count me as his grandson again. I hoped her God, the one I used to believe in, would be able to help her not feel alone.

After walking the half mile to where I had strategically parked my car, I slipped in and floored the gas. My tires squealed in protest. I quickly jerked my foot off the pedal and hoped the sound hadn't carried to the funeral service. Surely not.

As I wove around Torrey Pines Drive, I couldn't help but remember how much I had once loved it here. The cliffs in La Jolla were still my favorite place in the world, at least on days where there weren't a million San Diego tourists ruining the serenity. Everything else here, though, now left a bitter sensation in my gut. The gorgeous West Coast mansions, the exclusive shops, everything. Everything except the ocean. No matter what memories came flooding back, the ocean could never be tainted.

THOUGHTS of the morning and the implications of my grandfather's death occupied my mind during the twenty-minute drive back to my quaint little bungalow in Hillcrest. Without realizing it, I had parked, gotten out of the car, and had my key turning in the front door. Before I felt the lock click out of the way, the door flew open, and Sonia accosted me. Her strength never ceased to amaze me. I marveled at the power in her tiny body as she wrapped her arms around my neck and forcefully pulled my head down nearly a foot so she could kiss my cheek.

"Oh, Brett, sweetie. How ya doin', hon?"

I pulled some of her long strands of black hair out of my mouth. "Aside from having my head nearly pulled off, I'm doing good, thanks."

As if not hearing me, or maybe *because* she heard me, she squeezed her arms tighter around my head, and my ear folded uncomfortably. In one swift move, she grabbed my hand and pulled me through the door.

"So, tell me all about it. Was it a beautiful service?"

I gave her an exasperated look. "Sonia, I told you I wasn't going to actually attend the service." I tossed my keys on the Craftsman table by the door. They bounced and hit the picture of Sonia as a little girl with a hideous dog. "I keep telling you I'm gonna break that picture if you leave it there."

She ignored my attempt at a subject change and followed me into the living room, where I had already stretched out on the couch. "You didn't even say anything to your grandmother?"

"Sonia, don't start, okay?"

"But, Brett, she really needs you right now." She pushed my feet off the end of the couch and sat down cross-legged.

"You've never even met her. She'll be fine. She's a strong old cookie." I swung my feet back up and plopped them in her lap. I waggled my eyebrows. "As long as you're there…."

She rolled her eyes and once again swiped my feet to the floor. "You could have at least taken your shoes off first."

"I thought Chinese girls were supposed to be subservient."

"And I thought big, strong, macho men weren't supposed to be afraid of their grandmothers." She stuck out her tongue.

In spite of myself, I laughed. "I'm not afraid of her."

I looked at Sonia, momentarily paused in my defense by a sweeping rush of gratefulness to her. Whether brought on by the events of the day or simply being tired and sentimental, the truth was I loved this girl more than anyone in the world. There wasn't anything I couldn't tell her. I had barely graduated college when I had been kicked out of my grandparents' house. I didn't have a job and barely had any money. Answering her online ad for a roommate, I almost left when I saw how nice her house was. I knew there was no way I could afford it. She told me her parents had put a huge down payment on the house for her twenty-first birthday and that she just needed someone else to help with the small monthly payments. Small for San Diego, at any rate. She let me live there rent-free for nearly three months until I started getting paychecks from my job as a lifeguard—one more decision my grandfather never would have understood or supported. It wasn't like he contributed to the cost of my bachelor's in psychology. I failed to see how my choosing to "go another direction" would affect him. Sonia, on the other hand, supported my decisions. Immediately, it felt like we had known each other our entire lives.

"Did you at least wait till they had left so you could put some flowers on his grave?"

"Nah." I flicked my hand, waving her off. "I'll go back some other time." She opened her mouth, getting ready to respond, but I cut her off. "So you're not going to believe what happened when I went swimming near Blacks Beach this morning."

As I knew it would, the mention of the ocean caught her attention. "Brett, I've never understood why you are so careless. You're going to drown."

I shrugged. "It's only a few miles. I never swim out far enough that I can't see land." That wasn't exactly the truth, but I figured I didn't need to worry her any more than I already did.

Her voice rose slightly. "I don't care! That's never safe! Especially with what's been going on lately with your eyes when you're in the water. What if you get disoriented? What if you get startled by something and hit your head and pass out?"

I let out another laugh. "What am I going to hit my head on in the middle of the ocean? A shark?"

Her eyes narrowed. Sonia's fear of sharks was beyond irrational. She couldn't even get in a swimming pool unless accompanied by someone else. "That's not funny."

I grinned at her.

She gave me the finger. "So what did happen? Could you tell what you were seeing?"

"I've told you, there is nothing there to see. It's in my mind. I'm going nuts! I need to see a shrink or something."

"No argument there."

"Shut up."

"Really, what did you see?" She leaned forward and placed both hands on my knees.

I couldn't suppress a shudder. I had always lived in the water. I felt safer in the ocean than I did on land. The fish and sea animals always swam with me, and it was never a problem. I had even received scholarships to college by joining the swimming team. The training to be a lifeguard almost wasn't fair to the others who were trying to get the job—it was like they were competing against a fish. Never once had I felt a moment of fear or trepidation in the water, until lately. "I didn't see anything different, just the same stuff. Flashes of faces and arms, once in a while something that looks like a gold fishtail. But today...." I shuddered again and took a deep breath. "Today, I felt something."

Sonia's violet eyes grew impossibly wide. "You *felt* something?" Poor girl, she would never go into a pool again after this conversation.

"Yeah, at first I thought I was feeling some stray seaweed or something—light little touches on my arms and back, sometimes my stomach. Each time, I stopped swimming and looked around in the water, but I never saw anything."

She shuddered at the mention of looking around in the water.

"I kept swimming, but I started heading back in. I was only a few hundred feet from shore when something grabbed me."

With a little yelp, Sonia shrank back into the cushions of the couch. Her voice was barely audible. "What was it?"

"I don't know. But—and I know this sounds crazy—but it felt like… like a hand."

"A hand?" The absurdity of it seemed to make her momentarily come out of her fear. She had probably been expecting some huge sea monster's tentacle or something. "Like a human hand?"

"Yeah. Around my ankle." I glanced at the floor and then back up to her. "And that's not the weirdest part…." My voice trailed off, and my gaze once again returned to the floor.

She leaned forward once more, her hands clutched in her lap. "What? What happened?"

I shook my head. "I caught on fire."

She cocked her head. "You caught on fire? Under the water?"

"Yeah. I think so."

"But, sweetie, that's not possible." Her voice took on a soothing quality, as if comforting a child after a nightmare. "And, even if it were, you're fine. You're not burned."

"I know, I know. Maybe that's the wrong way to say it, but it was like I was on fire. I was completely surrounded by flames. I'm pretty sure even the water around me got warmer." It was my turn to try to sink into the couch cushions. "And, even crazier, is that I think it came from me."

She gawked at me, her hair making curtains over her cheeks and falling nearly to her waist.

I shrugged again. "What?"

"Brett, I don't think you should go swimming for a while. You need to relax. You're seeing things in the water, your grandfather just died—you've got to be stressed like crazy." Her expression went from deadly serious to playful in a flash. "Plus, how long has it been since you've gotten laid? Two years? That's gotta do something to ya!"

I whipped the cushion from behind my back and chucked it at her head. "It hasn't even been five months!"

"Oh, *honey*, if I had to wait five months, I'd be feeling things grabbin' for me too."

"Right! Like you could make it a week!"

She got up and headed to the kitchen. On her way, she tossed her hair, glanced back over her shoulder, and batted her eyes. "Just 'cause you're not interested, don't mean there isn't a line of other gorgeous men lined up around the block."

"Don't I know it!"

I heard her open and close the refrigerator, no doubt drinking out of the milk carton again. After a second, she poked her head back around the corner. "I'm on tonight at Rascals. You should come in. See if we can't fix that dry spell you're going through. Shouldn't take me too long to get a hunk of a man like you hooked up."

I scowled at her.

"What?" She tried to look all innocent and failed utterly. "You know, you're getting older. Almost twenty-five. After that, things start to droop and sag. Get it while you can, sweetie."

"I'm not even twenty-four yet! Quit trying to make me as old as you."

Sonia gasped in mock horror, and she walked back to the couch. "I'm gonna go get ready for my shift. You should go take a nap or something. I'm worried about you." She twirled some of my blond hair in her fingers. "You'll come by tonight?"

I nodded.

"Good." She headed down the bright hallway to her bathroom and then turned back around. "And, Brett? Don't go back into the ocean for a while, unless someone's drowning, okay?"

CHAPTER TWO

WE'RE almost equals, Sonia and I. Truth be told, I'm prettier than she is, and we both know it. Pretty isn't the right word. We're polar opposites. She is one of the rare Asian women blessed with curves a supermodel would envy. She dresses the part. Every eye follows her as she glides from table to table, taking orders and delivering both accelerated heart rates and food. She is the definition of femininity, and not in the "afraid to touch worms" way.

Likewise, no matter what my grandpa said, I am the quintessential male. At six feet, three inches, I tower over most men. There's not an ounce of fat on my body, never has been. The muscles that encase every inch of me make it seem like I spend all day, every day, in the gym. Looks can be deceiving. I never work out, never have. I swim constantly, but that's not for exercise; that's just because I love it. I'm sure most people who know me secretly hate me. I can eat whatever I want, however much I want, and the only change that can be seen is an increase in the amount of muscle mass.

Due to my accelerated metabolism, even alcohol never affects me. The few times I intentionally set out to get drunk with friends in high school, I discovered that no matter how much I drank, I was never able to get wasted or even buzzed like everyone else.

I'm not sure where I got the genes I have. Both of my grandparents have dark hair and eyes and are tiny and sort of mousy in appearance. In all honesty, they are unattractive in almost every aspect. I saw a few pictures of my grandmother before my mom was born. While she wasn't beautiful, she had some attractiveness about her, which she rapidly lost. I've only seen two pictures of my mother. One where she was a raven-haired little girl, looking extremely uncomfortable in an Easter dress. The other, she was no more than twelve or thirteen. While pictures can be deceiving, she appeared to be twice as gorgeous as Sonia is at nearly twenty-five years old. However, even she had dark hair and eyes, in contrast to my blond hair, blue eyes, and fair skin.

Sonia always gives me a hard time about being a prude. I hardly think I deserve that title. Although, compared to Sonia's standards.... I'm an insatiable flirt, and I like sex as much as the next guy. However, it almost always comes with complications. Why didn't I call the next day? Do I want to go out again? What do you mean you don't want a relationship? It's not you, it's me… blah, blah, blah. Just makes life too complicated. Something I don't need any more help with. I may have the slightest tendency to be moody and indecisive. Maybe. The last thing I needed or wanted was a relationship, even the illusion of one. However, after the insanity-inducing swim and the funeral from afar, I couldn't help but think Sonia's plan was pretty good.

SOMEHOW Sonia managed to miss seeing me come in and take a seat in her section, allowing me to settle back and enjoy watching her work the room. Rascals was a bright, colorful, loud restaurant and bar combo, most of which opened up to the outside. Combining that with the tiki torches and the décor made it seem like every night was a party at the beach even though the beach was miles away.

When she finally saw me, her bright smile increased to brilliant as it became genuine. She waved and delivered meals to a couple more tables before she came over. "Hey! I was beginning to think you were gonna bail. It's almost ten."

"Yeah, sorry, Sone. I fell asleep. Just woke up twenty minutes ago."

"Well, sweetie, you've had a rough day. If I were you, I probably wouldn't wake up till next week." Her voice already seemed strained. Between the music and everyone talking, it was loud enough that you had to yell everything in order to be heard.

"You gonna make it? You've still got four more hours to go. Your voice sounds painful."

"Five hours, actually." She rolled her eyes dramatically. "Remember that new kid, Troy, we hired a couple of weeks back? Well, he came in stoned off his ass tonight. Who do you think they made fire him? And, who do you think has to stay late to clean up?"

"Aw, I'm sorry. I was thinking we could watch a scary movie when you got off work."

She shook her head and gave me a crooked grin. "No, you weren't. I know that look in your eye. You didn't come here for a cheeseburger."

I dipped my head sheepishly. "You know me well. But while you're at it, a double cheeseburger sounds great. And a Cherry Coke. Oh, make it a triple, actually, and throw on some cheese fries, 'kay?"

"You make me sick. You know that?"

"Nah, you love me."

"Well, duh!" She waltzed over to a table on the other side of the room, somehow managing to give a smile, friendly word, or flirtatious wink to every person on the way.

IT WAS getting close to midnight by the time I finished the burger, five Cherry Cokes, and a second large order of cheese fries. Sonia hugged me good-bye, shoving the tip I left her back into my pocket, as she always did.

"Why still alone? Most of the good ones are gone already. Want me to go pick one out for ya?" She started to point openly to a table by the front door.

I jerked her arm down. "Cool it, Sone. We don't all have to be as outwardly inviting as you are." She threw up her hands in mock offense as I leaned closer and lowered my voice. "Eye contact's been made. We'll just have to see how it plays out. You picked the right one, though. Good job."

She patted my cheek. "I know what my baby likes. Give me a second to get the check over there before you go. You don't wanna make it where I don't get paid, right?"

"Okay. See ya at home?"

"Of course." She gave me one of her trademark winks. "If you make it home tonight, that is."

I WAITED until I saw Sonia take the credit card receipt and a pen back to the table, then got up and walked out the door, making sure to keep my gaze straight ahead. I was already starting to regret this, even though my mind was made up. The last thing I needed was a random hookup to worry about in the morning.

I made a show of staring up at the stars on my way to the car, trying to slow my gait. My car was only a block away, and even with my stargazing, it didn't take much time before I had put my key into the car door.

The tap on my shoulder didn't startle me. I'd heard the footsteps following behind. I managed to make my voice sound casually surprised as I turned around. "Oh, hi."

"Hi." He looked down nervously, his voice wavering with insecurity. "I, uh, thought we had a moment back in the bar." He glanced up at me, then lowered his gaze again. "Sorry if I misread you."

He was rather adorable. I could tell he was a lot younger now that he was away from the noise and lights of Rascals. I had thought he was older than me, but now I guessed he had to be barely twenty-one. He ran a hand over his military-cut dark hair as he turned sheepishly away.

I reached out to grab his elbow faster than I meant to. More desperately. "No, no. You didn't misread things. I thought you were cute."

He turned back around, daring to meet my eyes this time, a shy smile breaking across his face. "You did?"

"Yeah." I let go of his elbow, and he immediately looked doubtful again. "I'm glad you followed me."

He raised his hands in front of his chest. "Oh, I wasn't trying to follow you. I'm not trying to stalk you or anything crazy like that. I was just—"

I interrupted him. "I know. I didn't mean it like that. I'm glad you're here."

"Oh." He smiled again. He really was a beautiful boy. "Sorry. I'm a little nervous. I'm new at this."

Great. Apparently my luck at picking guys hadn't changed in the past five months. I liked to flirt, nearly as much as Sonia, but most of the time, I'd rather let the other guy make the majority of the moves, at least in the beginning. It seemed this time was going to have to be different. "So, were you wanting to get together or something?"

He might have been shocked at my bluntness, but to his credit, it didn't scare him off. He just nodded.

"Cool. You got some place we can go?" I never bring guys back to the house, at least not those I'm only planning on seeing once.

His gaze fell to the ground again. "I… um, live with my parents."

Kiss of death. Maybe it was that he seemed so vulnerable. Maybe it was my five months of celibacy. "Well. We could go swimming."

He looked up at me in surprise. "Swimming?"

I offered my most innocent smile and shrugged. "Yeah. Swimming. The beach is really beautiful this time of night."

The boy peered over his shoulder as if expecting to see his parents running down the street toward us. "Won't the water be cold?"

"Nah, not with me there."

He just nodded.

I motioned to the passenger side of the car. "Get in."

He only hesitated a moment. At first I thought he was going to change his mind, do the smart thing. His gaze roamed over my shoulders and up to my lips before he dashed to the other door.

He didn't say anything all the way to the beach. I put my hand on his knee, and that seemed to calm his nerves. Even so, I was fairly certain he was trembling the entire way. By the time I turned off the car and slid my keys under the visor, he had managed to stop sounding like he was going to hyperventilate.

A warm breeze met us as we got out of the car and started walking toward the beach. It was an unusually clear night, and stars filled the sky. I couldn't have planned it better if I had been trying.

We stopped a few yards from the shore. His voice sounded shaky again. "There's nobody else here."

"That's the idea. That okay?"

His tongue darted out and licked his lips. It was too dark to see his eyes. "Yeah. I guess so."

I tried to make my voice sound soothing. I don't think I succeeded. "I won't hurt you. We don't have to do anything you don't want to do."

He just nodded. I took a few more steps toward the incoming surf, then turned back around when I realized he wasn't following. "You coming?"

His hands were shoved deep into his cargo shorts, making him appear even younger. "Where are we going?"

"Well, we came for a swim. I'm going to the water."

"I didn't bring any trunks."

I hated having to do this much work. "Me neither."

I turned away from him and started to walk toward the ocean. I kicked off my flip-flops, pulled my shirt over my head, and dropped it to the ground. The moon was behind us, and I knew it was lighting up my back. I couldn't help but feel pleasure knowing he was watching me. A few feet from the reach of the waves, I let my pants fall. I stepped out of them and kept walking without turning back to him. As soon as my toes slid beneath the water, I felt all the emotions of the day start to drain out of me. I kept going until the water was just above the tops of my thighs. I turned to face him, crossing my arms in front of my chest.

He was still where I had left him. He waited a few moments before finally taking tentative steps in my direction. He had almost made it to the edge of the water before he stopped to slip off his shoes and shirt.

"Are you sure it's safe out there?"

I thought I heard his voice catch. "Yeah. Trust me." I let my arms fall to my side and dipped my fingertips into the water.

He glanced around before finally sliding his shorts over his hips and stepping out of them. I couldn't see his features with the moon behind him, but his silhouette looked skinnier than I was expecting.

He gasped and jumped back like a little kid when the waves hit his feet. "It's freezing!"

"You can do it. It's not cold out here."

To my surprise, he only hesitated a second or so before he launched himself toward me. He made it a couple of steps before falling and disappearing below the surface.

I started to move forward, but he came up, sputtering and gasping. He stood there in shock, the gentle waves lapping just above his knees.

With a sigh, I closed the distance between us and put my hands on his arms. "You okay?"

I could hear his teeth chatter. I took a step closer, and when he didn't draw away, I wrapped my arms around his back.

"Oh, it's weird." He sounded more himself. "The water almost feels warm now."

"Told ya." Although he was thin, I was pleased by how firm he was. I let my hands fall across the smooth muscles of his back and gradually came to a stop below his waist, resting on the curve of his ass.

"Wow." He traced his right hand reverently across my chest. From the feel of him against me, he wasn't cold any longer.

We stood there for several minutes, our hands exploring and breaths quickening.

When his fingers moved from running across my chest hair to following the path below my belly button, I took his hand and pulled him toward the shore.

We made it nearly out of the water before I fell on top of him in the sand. The waves caressed our ankles. He pulled me down to him, our stomachs slick against each other. My mouth met his. His lips were warm, and I could faintly taste the beer he'd had at dinner. As I slipped my tongue into his mouth, I let myself get lost in the sensations, the feel of him lightly throbbing against me, his fingers sliding over the curve of my ass, the embrace of the waves as they traveled up to our hips.

I pushed away the doubt. It didn't matter if I would regret this later. His back arched, pushing his body closer. My worries about Grandma being alone dissipated as I sank my tongue deeper into his mouth. All I felt was his skin, the water steaming around us, the pressure of my hips on his. The feel of him writhing against me.

It took several seconds for the sounds to register, for them to break through the trance of the moment. It wasn't until I felt his teeth clamp around my tongue that I realized something was wrong.

With a flash of anger, I yanked my head back from the pain. He was pounding his fists on my chest. His face was bluish gray, his eyes bulging, nearly rolling back into his skull. His body convulsed as he gasped, trying desperately to suck in air. I threw myself off of him and rolled him over onto his side toward me. His skin seemed to be on fire. When I lifted my hand from his arm, it left a white indentation, which quickly flushed to a pink, then to a scalding red that matched the skin around it.

His choking gave way to a flood of seawater rushing out of his mouth. Every convulsion brought with it a new gush of fluid. Again and again his body caved in on itself, a never-ending torrent emptying from him. I watched in stunned terror as his body finally slowed and came to rest. I reached out and touched my fingers to his throat, afraid he was dead. He screamed in agony as I felt for his pulse. He managed to jerk himself backward.

"Get the fuck away from me!" His raspy voice sounded like his throat had been torn to pieces. "What the hell are you trying to do to me?" As he scurried backward on his elbows, I could see that blisters were starting to form all over his body—even as some of them were ripped open by the sand and began to ooze.

I reached out toward him and started to move closer but stopped when his frenzy increased, the pitch of his hysteria hurting my ears.

"Stay the fuck away, you psycho! Trying to drown me! Fuck!" He winced as he raked himself over the sand. He glanced down at his skin, just now taking in the welts forming over him. He looked up at me, the fury in his eyes replaced by fear. "What did you do? What the fuck are you?"

I leaned closer to him. "I'm sorry. I don't… I don't know what happened. Here, let me—"

"Stay the fuck away!"

I started to stand so I could go over to him.

"Get away!" His screaming was unbearable. "Go away!"

I hesitated, uncertain. Then ran.

CHAPTER THREE

"WAKE up, sweetie."

I felt something warm on my back, making caressing circles. I tried to shrug it off.

The soothing motions on my back ceased, instantly replaced by a more forceful shaking of my shoulder. "Brett! Wake up!" The shaking increased. "Or at least put some clothes on."

"What?" I sat up straight and barely caught the afghan before it slipped off me and onto the floor. I pulled it closer, secured it to my body, and shot a look around. "What's going on?"

Sonia sat down beside me, causing my balance on the cushion to shift. "You tell me. I've been trying to wake you up for the past five minutes."

Gradually, my brain cleared enough to let the pieces begin to fall together. "Why am I in the living room?"

"That's what I'd like to know. I came out here after getting ready, and here you were on the couch"—with a sly grin, she let her eyes glance down my body—"naked as a jaybird. You're lucky I didn't take pictures to try to sell at the bar before I covered you up."

I ran my hand over my face, trying to block out the light. In a wave, the events on the beach came crashing back on me. With a groan, I sank into the cushions. "Shit."

"What?" To her credit, Sonia sounded more worried than curious. "What happened last night? I didn't get back until after three, and you still weren't home." She placed her hand lightly on my chest. "I take it things didn't work out so well last night?"

My stomach tightened as the boy's burned skin flashed behind my eyes. "No. It didn't go so well."

"Well, what happened?"

I opened my mouth to tell her but then stopped. What was I going to say? I nearly drowned a guy while I was kissing him, then boiled him? "I don't wanna talk about it. Okay? Sorry."

"It's okay. You sure you're alright?"

"Sure. Sure."

She leaned over and pressed her lips quickly to my forehead. "Well, when you're ready to talk about it, I'm here for you." She stood up and looked back down at me before giving me a quick wink. "Actually, I won't be. I'm going in to work right now. I switched Alice for her early shift. I'm going out with Derek tonight."

"Huh?" I was trying to remember the boy's name. Had I even asked, or had I just taken him to the beach, not caring who he was?

"I said, I've got a date with *Derek* tonight!"

"Oh. That's good."

A flicker of annoyance on her face quickly gave way to concern. "Are you sure you're okay? I say I've got a date with Derek tonight, and all you say is 'that's good'? I've been trying to get him to work up the nerve to ask me on a date for weeks!"

"I'm sorry, Sone." I shook my head. "Don't mind me. That's wonderful. I hope you have a great time."

She cocked her head at me and started to walk toward the kitchen.

"Hold up! You said you're going to work *now*? What time is it?"

"Noon. I get off at seven. Don't wait up for me, though. If things go my way, I won't be home tonight." She slipped into the kitchen. "Want some grapefruit juice?"

"Nah. Thanks." I gingerly sat up and leaned forward to retrieve my pants. I glanced under the coffee table and felt under the couch. "Hey, Sonia! Where are my clothes?"

Her voice was muffled behind the sound of running water. "I don't know. Maybe you took them off in your room before you crashed on the couch."

I wrapped the fabric tighter around my waist and stood up. I felt like I could lie back down and sleep for weeks.

My clothes weren't in my room. After checking the laundry basket, I slipped into my trunks and went out to my car. I half expected to see a huge dent from sideswiping another car during my blind night drive. Thankfully, the car seemed to be intact, but my clothes weren't anywhere inside.

"You okay?"

I jumped at the sound of her voice.

"Whoa! Easy boy." Sonia paused by my side. "Would you like me to cancel on Derek? I can come home after my shift tonight. You seem like you might need some company."

"No, no! I'm okay, just lost in thought I guess. You go. Have a great time with your new boy toy."

Her eyes narrowed as she studied me more closely. "Are you sure you're going to be alright?"

"Yes, Sonia." I gave her a quick hug and directed her toward her cherry-red Miata. "Now go away. Thanks for not taking any incriminating pictures this morning."

She ignored the comment. "Well, if you change your mind, just text me. I'll be happy to come home."

After watching her zip her tiny sports car out of the driveway, I returned to inspecting my car. I couldn't find any hint that something had gone wrong on my drive home, other than not finding my clothes. I guess that was enough proof. If something had happened, I would have woken up in jail for reckless driving and indecent exposure.

With a sigh of relief, I checked the drop-drawer and found my wallet resting safely inside as always. Nothing to link me to whatever happened on the beach, as long as I hadn't told the boy my name either, that is. If I'd left my clothes there, surely that wouldn't cause me any problems. I hadn't killed him. What were they going to do? DNA tests on my T-shirt?

The thought made me run back into the house, throw on a tank top and tennis shoes, and hop into the car.

THE traffic-infested drive to the beach felt like it took hours instead of the actual forty minutes. I replayed every scene of the night before over and over in my head, trying to examine each detail, searching for a clue that would shed light on what had transpired. No matter how I tried, I couldn't find an angle that would let me place some of the blame on the boy, whatever his name was. None of it seemed to be a setup. He didn't steal anything, except maybe my clothes. He didn't try to hurt me. It didn't seem like he had been faking the choking, not that a person could fake gallons of water erupting from their body, and there was no way he could have made his skin blister.

Still, there had to be an explanation. He could have swallowed all the water while we were kissing—the waves came up, and I didn't notice. Maybe he'd swallowed the water when he tripped entering the ocean. Perhaps he'd had food poisoning, and his vomit had only looked like water in the moonlight.

Try as I might to hold on to some scrap of hope, each explanation sounded more ludicrous than the one before. Even if I could somehow explain away the water, I couldn't come up with even a remotely plausible scenario that would allow for his skin to cook and blister. None except that I had somehow caused him to simultaneously drown and boil at the same time. I wished that sounded as crazy as the other possibilities, but when I combined it with what had happened during my swim earlier in the day, I could feel how right the thought seemed.

It was me. I had done it. Somehow I'd filled the boy with water and heated up his skin. As much as it seemed insane to even consider such thoughts, I couldn't find any other equation that made sense. And if it was me, how did I do it? I had somehow managed to have sex with other men before and not mutilate the guys. What was different? Maybe it was him, or at least the combination of him and me. Some chemical reaction between the two of us. I tried to make myself believe it, that I wasn't doomed to potentially murder the next guy I thought was hot. But if a specific reaction between the two of us were somehow possible, then why didn't I experience a similar outcome? Surely both of us would have been affected.

Squinting through the glare as I turned the car to face the sun, I pulled down the visor. The beach was relatively deserted, which was surprising at the height of the day. There was a woman jogging, her black lab prancing joyously through the surf, an old man and what appeared to be his granddaughter picking up seashells, and a couple of others lying on beach towels.

I parked the car in the same spot as the night before and wandered down onto the beach. I wasn't exactly sure where we had been, but I figured it had to be in a fairly straight line with the car. My heart sank as my gaze swept out toward the water. Nothing. There wasn't anything more than a few limp strands of seaweed littering the beach. I couldn't even see any footprints that didn't belong to the girl who had just jogged past. That thought gave me a tiny surge of hope. Maybe the tide had come in and washed away not only our footprints but my clothes as well—pulled them out to sea, far enough to not be incriminating.

I decided to walk along the beach, in case the clothes had washed back to shore farther down. I went over a mile in each direction. Nothing. I even checked several yards of sand where I thought we had been, thinking there might be scorch marks or some sign of what had caused the boy's injuries. After I paced the same patch of beach several times, I began to notice a few people watching me warily. I probably looked more than a little crazy, wandering back and forth over the same bit of sand, continuously muttering to myself and raking my hands through my hair.

Sheepishly, I returned to my car and leaned against the hood, staring out at the calm greenish-gray water. So what if I couldn't find my clothes. So what if the boy had taken them. What could he prove? Who would possibly believe his story? At best, they'd think he was just some little twink who had gotten drunk, managed to scald himself, and stolen his trick's clothes.

It was too much. All too much. I should leave and go hang out with Sonia at Rascals. Maybe find another cute boy and let him occupy my mind the rest of the afternoon.

I shuddered at the thought. What if I hurt him too? What if it were worse the next time?

Without realizing what I was doing, I ripped off my shirt, threw it through the driver's side window, and ran full speed back down the beach, oblivious of the stares of the people watching as the crazy man returned.

As always, as soon as my bare feet touched the water, the rest of the world disappeared. The water rose past my calves, then up to my thighs as I ran through the waves, each step taking me closer and closer to tranquility. Within seconds I was up to my waist. I paused, letting the warmth of the water envelop me, the ebb and flow of the tide coursing like a pulse through my veins. With a groan, I pushed off the sand with my toes and dove under the surface.

The instant my head was submerged, the peace of the moment was shattered. I could feel eyes on me. I knew I wasn't alone. I knew whatever was there was watching me, and I knew it was close.

This time, I didn't see flames or light, but I felt the water bubble and boil around me. I heard myself bellow an angry scream before I realized that my head had broken above the water. I surged back toward the beach, making the water spray in all directions. My knees were just above water level when I felt something snag my left foot. I nearly fell.

I shoved my hand below the water and felt it close around something at my feet. With another yell, I yanked it up, expecting to see my attacker. It was several seconds before my brain could register what I was holding. I kept trying to make it into some type of fish or tentacle, some ripped-off appendage of a sea monster. I blinked at it and bugged my eyes before the item took shape.

It was a flip-flop. My flip-flop. One of my neon-green flip-flops that I'd had on the night before. I heard myself suck in a breath. With a mix of panic and relief, I shoved the shoe in my mouth and plunged my hands back in the water, feeling across the sand, desperately trying to find the mate. Back and forth, moving closer to the beach and then a little farther out toward the deep. I found nothing besides clump after clump of seaweed.

"Dude! You okay?"

Startled, I turned back toward the beach.

"Are you okay?"

It was a man on the shore, maybe one of the people who'd been lying on the towels. At first, I looked around me, trying to see who he was talking to, feeling even more stupid when I realized he was obviously addressing me. Who else would he be talking to? There wasn't anyone else yelling and splashing around in the water.

"You need me to call somebody?"

I waved him off, feeling my face redden. I straightened my back and took the flip-flop out of my mouth. Feebly, I glanced around one last time and then walked out of the water and marched straight up to my car, refusing to tear my gaze from directly in front of me. I got to my car, tossed in the shoe, and left the beach, cursing myself for coming back in the first place.

I PARKED several blocks away, on the other side of the golf course, and slowly walked around Torrey Pines. I knew I wasn't actually going to talk to her, but I thought maybe I would be able to view her from a distance. There wasn't really a specific reason I wanted to see her, but for some reason, the thought of being close to Grandma was comforting.

While not as big or modern as the other houses in the area, the brick home Grandpa had built remained stately and a little imposing—bland yet immovable, just like he had been. It didn't have a specific California feel to it, but it was generic enough to blend in without offense. The pine trees that grew en masse around their home and the rest of the neighborhood were ancient and had grown massive and gnarled.

It had to be past three in the afternoon. Typically, Grandma would be at the church helping the pastor's wife get the lesson ready for the next adult Sunday school class. Maybe with the death of her husband she would be off her typical routine. On the other hand, there was a distinct possibility that she had stayed at the church all week, throwing herself into her God and her religion.

I approached the house from the north, the side with the attached garage and no windows for her to see me from. I noticed an unfamiliar car in the driveway. A baby-blue Ford Contour. It was possible that she'd purchased a new car since I'd seen her, but I doubted it. Grandpa ran their cars into the ground before he would consider trading them in, plus this car's color was in stark contrast to Grandma's love of browns and oranges. She must have company.

To my surprise, disappointment shot through me. I definitely wasn't going to be able to talk to her if she had someone else there. Had part of me intended approaching her? Did I really think she would want to see me now that Grandpa was dead? True, it hadn't been her who had cut me off from the family, but neither had she ever convinced Grandpa to change his mind about me.

While Grandpa had never been affectionate or overly kind to me, I had expected Grandma, with her devotion to the scriptures, to be the one to overreact when I announced I was gay. And she had reacted, with much tears and weeping. Pleading with me to fight against it so I could save my soul—as if I hadn't been trying for years. However, not once did she act angry or disgusted, only heartbroken. It was Grandpa, who adamantly refused to even darken the door of a church his entire life, who had declared me vile and less than a man, barely human, who told me never to speak to them again as long as they lived. No qualifying, no exceptions in case I changed my mind, nothing. Just never again.

At the thought of him, I felt a pang of guilt that I didn't feel any sorrow for his death. I hated that Grandma was alone now, but I couldn't bring myself to feel a minuscule regret. I wasn't glad he was gone. I simply couldn't seem to make myself care either way.

As I traced one of the few blond bricks that broke up the otherwise dirt-red-toned wall, I realized that if one of the neighbors saw me, they probably wouldn't stop to ask questions. They would pick up the phone and call the police or, worse yet, my grandma, and let her know there was a giant prowler scoping out her house. The thought made me step closer to the front of the garage, where the largest clump of pine trees offered more shelter.

Now that I was here, I had even less of a clue about what my intentions had been in the first place. Even if she let me in the house and told me she wanted to join the gay pride parade, that still wouldn't help me come any closer to figuring out what was happening to me. If the thought of me being gay had left her heartbroken and convinced of my damnation, a confession of nearly drowning and cooking another man during foreplay would hardly have a positive effect on how she saw me. It would definitely negate any hope of a future reconciliation. Besides, even if she miraculously managed to evade a heart attack, there was no chance she would be able to offer any insight into my situation.

"Thanks again for coming to me, Judith. I couldn't find the energy to fix myself up today." I stiffened and stupidly flattened my back against the garage at the sudden sound of my grandmother's voice, as if there were any chance all six foot three inches of me could melt into the wall.

"Oh, Beverly dear, no need to thank me. It was my pleasure to get to see you." I heard the screen door click shut. How had I managed to miss hearing it open? "However, I really wish you would reconsider about coming to church with me next Sunday. You should stay home and relax, give yourself some time to heal."

"Nonsense. I promised Pastor Johns that I would help you lead this series on holiness, and I am not going to break my vow."

"Beverly, my husband would understand. He tried to come here with me today, but I told him it would be better for us to just have women time."

As I calmed my breathing, I worked up the nerve to tentatively peek around the corner. Luckily, the large bush planted beside the garage door provided protection while still letting me get some glimpses through the leaves.

Grandma and a barely recognizable Judith Johns walked slowly down the porch and toward the Contour. I hadn't seen the pastor's wife since before Grandfather had kicked me out of the house. The years had not been kind. She used to be a rather large woman—the kind for whom her size actually made her seem sweeter and more approachable. She must have lost over a hundred pounds. She was rail thin and appeared to be on the verge of breaking with every step. Her gaunt, gray skin gave away the sickness that seemed to flow off her.

Grandma, nearly a foot shorter at a few inches less than five feet, seemed to tower over her friend. Although I could see the exhaustion in her eyes and the sag of her face, she looked as healthy as she ever had. If it weren't for all her wrinkles and age spots that splattered abundantly over her face and arms, she would have appeared well under her nearly seventy years of age.

Once Judith had unlocked her car door, she turned to Grandma and took her hand. "I can't tell you how crushed I am that Marvin never came to believe in Christ. After all the prayers over the years."

Grandma patted her hand comfortingly. "Well, we'll never know what happened the last few days when Marvin was unconscious. Possibly he was able to pray and make things right before he died. I have to believe it. I don't think I could stand it any other way."

Judith simply nodded. She opened her car door and started to get in, but paused and turned once more to face her friend. "I must say, I was surprised not to see Brett at the funeral yesterday. I know things never really got repaired between you three, but I thought he would have the decency to show his respect."

I felt my hands clench at the judgment in her voice. I seriously doubted she had any true *respect* for my grandfather. More than once, he had told her exactly what he thought of her God and suggested that her husband should get a real job and stop conning people out of their money with the promise of salvation.

"Now, Judith, don't put the blame on Brett. He doesn't even know his grandfather was sick." Her voice broke, and she let out a long breath. "Much less that he died."

Judith gaped at her. "You didn't tell him?"

Grandma raised her chin in a small show of defiance. "Marvin made me promise not to contact Brett about how sick he was. Not that I know how he expected me to get a hold of him. He thought he got rid of Brett's phone number."

Judith cocked her head. "He didn't?"

"Brett sent me a birthday card shortly after Marvin asked him to leave. Marvin threw it away. If he knew that I got in the trash and tore out the phone number and address Brett sent, he never let on." She looked off into the distance, as if attempting to search me out. "His place is over in Hillcrest."

I thought I saw Judith shake her head in judgment upon learning I lived in the "gay neighborhood."

"I drove by there a couple of times, hoping to see him. I never have. It looks like a nice little house, though."

"But surely he didn't mean it. You should have called Brett. No matter what choices the boy has made about his life, Marvin was still his grandfather."

Grandma stiffened and peered up, straight into her friend's face. "I will not go against my husband's dying wishes. Besides, it seems Brett has moved on with his life. I haven't heard anything else from him since that card. For all I know, he may have moved to another house or have a different phone number." She wiped at her eyes. I couldn't tell if she was crying or simply removing a hair from her vision. "I don't want to disturb him, anyway."

The roughness of the bricks pressed through my shirt as my back leaned into them. The thought that my grandmother had gone against my grandfather enough that she had actually driven into Hillcrest to see where I lived was nearly beyond comprehension. I had never heard her utter one word of disagreement against him my entire life. It didn't matter that he didn't believe in God. She still followed the letter of the Bible, that the man is the head of the household. Even when he kicked me out of the house, she hadn't said anything against him, only stood in the kitchen sobbing.

Judith reached out and embraced Grandma before finally stepping into her car. "I love you, dear, and really, if you don't feel up to it, just call me. I can handle Sunday school on my own."

CHAPTER FOUR

OLD TOWN San Diego is my favorite place—aside from the beach, of course. It should be called Old Mexican Town. Actually, Old Tourist-Trap Americanized Mexican Town. As cheesy as it is, I love it there. There are tons of touristy shops, an open-air market "town square," and several Mexican restaurants featuring homemade tortillas and tamales. Everything is bright, loud, and cheerful. Even in the off-season, Old Town is always filled with people—the perfect place to go when you want to be alone and unrecognized without actually being by yourself.

I was finishing up a plate of beef and chicken fajitas at my favorite restaurant, Taberna de las Brujas, when I felt my cell phone vibrate. I fished it out of my pocket, having to rise up uncomfortably in the booth. It was Sonia. A couple of hours ago, after I had gone back home and cleaned up, I had texted her, with no response.

She said she was on her date with Derek and was in the bathroom of the restaurant, and that she would most definitely not be home, unless I needed her. I wrote her back, telling her to have a good time and that I would be okay. I nearly added *try and not set Derek on fire after you get him naked* but decided that would freak her out and ensure she would come home to be with me. Part of me wanted that. The thought of going home to an empty house filled with nothing but my worries about what was happening and my new guilt over my grandmother seemed like too much to bear. Having Sonia home wouldn't help, anyway. She wouldn't stop pestering me until she got me to tell her everything that was going on, and she would know if I was lying. For some reason, I still couldn't bring myself to tell Sonia about what had happened at the beach.

I could always go to Rascals. Even if I didn't plan on taking another guy home, I could still flirt and distract myself with whoever was there. As quickly as the thought occurred, I dismissed it. The last thing I needed right now was another encounter with a guy. Sadly, I realized I didn't even want to go to the beach. Actually, I wanted to stay as far away from the ocean as possible. It was a new sensation, and one that made me uncomfortable in my own skin.

"You look like your world is crashing down, *amigo*."

The voice tore me out of my obsession, and I turned toward it. "Oh hi, Ricky." It was Ricardo Medina. He and his wife owned the restaurant. I came here so often that they knew me by name. They were a friendly couple, occasionally not charging me for the meal since I was such a regular.

Ricardo let out a growl. "I told ya to quit calling me Ricky. Who do you think I am, Ricky Ricardo? What next? You want me to sing 'Babalu'?" Everyone called him Ricky, and he did this little speech with everyone, all the time, often ending it by calling his wife over and doing his best impression of "Lucy, you got some 'splainin' to do!"

I forced a grin at him. "I know, I know. The food was great tonight, Ricky, as always."

He puffed out his chest, his fists on his narrow hips. "Well, of course. Like it could be any other way." He winked at me and slid into the bench across from me. "Seriously, Brett, you look awful. You doing alright?"

"Yeah, Ricky, thanks. I'm fine. Just a lot on my mind. Just needing to handle it on my own, you know?"

"Yeah, I know." He reached over and snagged a grilled pepper off my plate and popped it in his mouth. "You're lucky Christina's not here. She wouldn't leave you alone until she got the truth out of ya."

I smiled and shook my head. "I know she wouldn't. Where is she tonight?" I glanced around the room, as if finally taking in my surroundings. "Come to think of it, I haven't seen Peter and Saul around tonight either."

"She took the kids up to her folks. Her mom wanted her help making some empanadas for a special order at the bakery. The boys decided they'd rather go hang out with their grandpa than help their old man wait tables."

At the mention of "grandpa," my stomach tightened a little. "Can't say I blame them. I'm sure that's more fun. The last time I was in here, I couldn't believe how big they've gotten. How old are they, anyway?"

I noticed his chest puffed up again, this time unintentionally. "Peter's eight and Saul's gonna be five in a couple of weeks."

"They're really good-looking boys. You should be proud." Truth be told, the whole family was near physical perfection. Ricky had to be pushing forty, but he had a physique that men ten years younger would covet, and his wife was no different.

His grin broadened. "Speaking of good-looking boys…." He leaned closer and said in a mock whisper, "Christina's been dying for you to meet her little brother, and he happens to be here tonight. She'd kill me if I didn't introduce you two."

The volume of my voice rose more than I intended it to, and I held out both of my hands in front of me. "No way, Ricky. Not tonight. I really need to be by myself. The whole reason I came here was to—"

Ricardo interrupted before I could continue. "How old are you anyway, Brett?"

I rolled my eyes. "Twenty-three."

He clapped his hands. "That's perfect! Finn is twenty-five. Not too old for you."

"Finn?"

"*Sí!* Finn. Christina's brother." Ricardo was already sliding out of the booth. "I'll go get him. Hold on."

My hand snaked out and grabbed hold of Ricardo's forearm. "Please. Don't. I'm really not up to it tonight. Rain check, okay?"

Ricardo held up his hands, shrugged, and gave a fake groan. "Oh, Brett. What are you trying to do to me here? I'm not gonna get in trouble with the wife because you don't want to meet a pretty boy. He looks like his sister…." He paused and then grimaced and shook his head. "Except like a boy, not like his sister." He put his hand on my chest and lightly pushed me against the back of the booth. "Stay here. I'll get him. Just say hi. Dinner's on the house!"

Before I could offer any other protest, he was gone. I cursed to myself. I should have gone home, dealt with whatever thoughts came, maybe tried to drown or set myself on fire in the shower.

I considered getting up and walking out. I could leave a twenty on the table and be done with it. I had made it abundantly clear that I didn't want to meet his brother-in-law. No matter how much he resembled his sister. What kind of sales pitch was that, anyway? Christina was beautiful, but I didn't want a boy who looked like her.

If it hadn't been for how much I loved coming to Taberna de las Brujas and how much I liked the Medinas, I would have left. However, surely I could suck it up and make small talk with this *cute brother* and be done with it.

I slid my plate away, not hungry any longer, and nervously tapped my fingers on the table. It seemed to be taking forever. Maybe the brother-in-law was putting up as much resistance as I had. Maybe he would win.

The bell that chimed as the front door of the restaurant opened caught my attention, and I glanced up. Immediately a hostess came up to the man who entered, but he waved her away with a flick of his hand. As she stepped aside, he stared directly at me. I stopped breathing. As far as I could tell, everyone else in the restaurant quit moving. No sound was made, no clatter of dishes, no scrape of fork on plate, no buzz of speech. I didn't move. Didn't even blink.

He wasn't overtly good-looking. Not unattractive, but not handsome. He was tall, although shorter than me. He was fairly lanky, possibly even skinny. He had on grungy clothes—black shirt, brown pants. Actually, his clothes weren't grungy, they were filthy. He had red hair. I've never been attracted to red hair. He had green eyes. Emerald-green eyes. Clear as glass. Bright and shiny as glass. I couldn't tear myself away from his eyes. I wanted to, but they held me, denying me the right to choose. Making me feel naked, uncomfortably so. The hair on my neck and arms stood up, and my skin prickled. I felt myself harden down the leg of my pants.

A hand came down on my shoulder, and I jumped, my eyes at last tearing themselves away from the man at the door.

Ricardo laughed. "You really are nervous, aren't you, Brett?"

I forced my eyes toward his voice, but I seemed unable to focus on him.

"Brett, this is my *maricón* brother-in-law, Finn."

"Honest to God, Ricky, you can be such an ass." I assumed the voice came from the man beside Ricardo, but I wasn't sure. My gaze had returned to the man at the door.

"Sit down, Finn! You can thank me at your wedding." I felt him squeeze my shoulder. "Now, you boys have a good time getting to know each other. Finn, I'll send out some sopaipillas. I told him dinner's on the house."

As Ricky walked away, Finn crossed in front of me and slid into the booth, momentarily blocking my view of the stranger's eyes. His rushed, nervous voice passed in a blur as I craned my neck to reconnect with the gaze. "I'm sorry about my brother-in-law. He means well. I've heard for months from him and my sister that I simply had to meet this guy Brett who always comes into the restaurant. As I'm sure you noticed, they don't really take no for an answer. We can have some dessert, and then you can be on your way, and we can tell them we tried. Again, I'm sorry. This is truly embarrassing."

I had never seen eyes like his before. I had never seen green of the like before. I thought I saw his lips move, and I glanced at them. Not overly thin, but not really exceptional either. Lips were always one of the first things I was attracted to, and his weren't that impressive. I felt him force my eyes back up to his.

I heard someone talking to me, asking me if I was okay, if I wanted him to leave me alone, but the voice didn't seem to matter. Only his eyes mattered. They blinked, and for a moment the green was cut off from me.

Their absence was a physical pain in my stomach, causing me to groan. Then they were back. I let out a sigh of relief.

The eyes grew in intensity. Feeling myself leave the seat, I began moving toward the man. The path from the booth to the front door was endless and agonizing. Each step a force of will.

At last I reached him. I felt him take my hand. He turned around and led me out the door.

As we walked, he didn't look at me again, though I wanted to cry out to him, beg him to stare at me, for him to gaze into my eyes. I followed the pull of his hand, the glow of his wavy red hair in the moonlight.

I wasn't sure how far we walked, whether it was half a block or miles.

I WAS facing a brick wall, one hand on the gritty surface, the other curled around the edge of a dumpster. I felt the tepid breeze pass over my back and my ass. I knew I was naked, though I couldn't remember undressing.

An arm circled around my chest from behind. I felt fingers glide over my hair and wrap over my forehead as they pulled my head backward. A body melded to my back, the pressure pushing my chest, stomach, and hips against the cold metal of the dumpster, nearly as cold as the body moving against mine.

As he moved, I felt him throbbing on my ass. I tried to utter an objection, but it was strangled before it could leave my throat. I heard him let out a groan as, with one swift movement, he thrust into me.

The world came rushing back. I could see the dumpster clearly, painted black and covered in rust, I could see the moon glaring in the cloudless sky, I could feel him slam back into me again, I could feel the pain. I let out a scream and shoved off the dumpster.

The man grunted as I whirled around, my fists ready to pummel his face into nothingness.

His eyes met mine. The moonlight made the emeralds blaze. I could see each different shade and fleck as they twinkled around his pupils. I saw my hands reach out to him, trace the faint muscles in his hairless chest, traveling down his stomach. I heard my voice, hoarse and pleading. "More."

His eyes narrowed as he smiled. I lay down on the ground, the walls on each side of the alley towering above me.

He took his place on top of me. Every part of my skin that touched his burned cold. His eyes continued to pierce mine as our lips met and his tongue filled my mouth.

Finally, he blinked again, and we parted. My eyes closed as I felt his lips and tongue move down my jaw, over my Adam's apple, and across my chest. I gasped as I felt him nip playfully at my nipple. He laughed and leaned up, his eyes once again finding mine.

My breath caught as he filled me, only the slightest pain as he entered.

He smiled. A beautiful smile. Teeth brilliant white, nearly glowing.

His lips returned to my throat, their pressure increasing from a gentle caress to something more demanding. His thumb and fingers wrapped around my chin and pulled it over to my right shoulder.

I screamed when I felt his teeth sink into me, part in agony, part in pleasure. Another thrust. He sank deeper into my neck.

The rhythm of him surging into me as my blood flowed into him washed over me. Lost in the tide, in wave after wave coursing through my body.

The orgasm increased with each draft of blood. Again and again I felt the release of my body—groin and neck, coursing into him as he did in me.

My hands clutched his shoulders, trying to both tear him from me and pull him closer, deeper.

My bellows were drowned out by louder, more agonized screams. I felt his teeth pull out of me, leaving me hollow, aching. My eyes opened to search for him.

A blur, he stood above me, flames engulfing his shoulders and moving up to his face, setting his hair ablaze. The stench reached my nose, and I managed to pull myself backward on my elbows.

His screams grew louder and louder. He fell against the opposite wall, causing the bricks around him to crack and crumble. Throwing himself to the ground, his body began to writhe, rolling this way and that over the trash. Here and there, little scraps of paper and plastic began to glow and catch fire.

I couldn't tear my eyes off of him. I could see his flesh blacken and crack. His hair was completely gone, and his face was being eaten away. With every thrash, the fire on his body lessened. Finally, after what seemed an eternity, the fire was gone.

He crawled over to the wall and dragged himself up. He stood over me—the lower half of his body porcelain white and pristine, the upper looking like charred wood.

My eyes found his, no longer emerald, only empty black holes. For a moment, I thought he was going to smash my face with his foot.

He turned and took off, staggering and stumbling down the alley.

CHAPTER FIVE

FINN DE MORISCO

LONG ago I lost count of the bad dates I've been on and the number of horrible setups that have been thrown at me by friends and family. None of them, regardless of their ultimately shabby endings, started off as poorly as the one my brother-in-law dredged up.

I was utterly humiliated when Ricky dragged me over to the customer he and Christina had been wanting me to meet. I'd heard often enough about the hot blond who ate at Taberna. My sister had even called me at home once when he'd come in. I'd counted myself lucky that, despite my frequent trips to the restaurant, I hadn't landed on the same time as him, considering how much they'd reported he came. I knew it was just a matter of time—I'd only hoped it wouldn't be as bad as I feared.

Much to my chagrin, I felt my heartbeat speed up as Ricky pulled me closer to the booth the man was sitting in. Even my palms got instantly clammy. This guy was hot! Hotter than any man I'd ever seen in real life. I was torn between running back through the kitchen doors and giving Ricky a hug.

Any gratitude I felt toward my sister's husband vanished at his introduction. Calling me a *maricón* in front of any potential date would have been bad enough, but in front of this perfection of male masculinity? It was enough to kick him out of the family.

With such a bad beginning, I thought there was a chance that things would get better. It was a safe bet things couldn't get much worse.

How wrong I was. Not only wasn't the male model interested, he didn't even acknowledge my existence. Even as I spoke, he craned his head around me, searching out the front door.

Granted, I've never considered myself the most beautiful man in San Diego, but I can typically at least get a *hello* out of someone.

I couldn't say that my past relationships had gone so well—gave too much, got too little. Came out a little damaged. From what I hear, that's just part of the dating game. We all get a bit beat-up and battered. Neither my heart nor my ego had escaped unscathed. I knew full well I shouldn't take a stranger's rejection personally, but it felt a bit like I'd been shat on once again.

By the third attempt at starting a conversation with this too-good-to-talk-to-anyone-not-as-pretty-as-himself guy, my hurt feelings morphed into anger. I'd just pushed off the tabletop with my hands, lifting myself out of the booth to tell Mr. Brett Wright to go fuck himself, when he stood and nearly ran toward the front door.

I crashed back down in the booth, deflated. My anger exited to make room for self-loathing once more. In wonderment, I twisted around, the wood squeaking under my weight, and watched his retreating muscular form.

Then I saw him, a thin redheaded guy standing by the hostess booth. Brett was making a beeline for him.

For him? No matter what my insecurities, I knew I was better looking than that skinny dude. He seemed like he hadn't showered in weeks. The only remarkable thing about him was his eyes. And really, were green eyes all it took to impress Brett?

I whipped back around, too disgusted to watch. Maybe he had a fetish or something—he liked the grungy look. I shuddered. If that's what he was into, more power to him. Gross. I liked a manly scent, but that's a whole different ball game.

I picked up a piece of chicken off the fajita skillet and took a bite. Dodged a bullet with that one. No need to have a date with someone who thinks their shit doesn't stink and has a thing for guys who do.

Still, Brett's hotness factor was astronomical. I didn't need to marry the guy. A hot date, a fun night together—that wouldn't be too bad. I could put up with his arrogance long enough for that.

Pathetic! I shook myself. What was my damage? What kind of self-respecting guy thinks like that?

I eyed the heaping carafe of sour cream, dunked the chicken in deep, and shoved it into the shredded cheese on the side of the plate. I took a huge bite, then sank back into the hard booth with a sigh. Cheese. Better than a man any day.

No big deal. I hadn't planned on a date tonight anyway. I'd just return to my original plan. Grab a bite to eat here—I glanced down at the plate; hell, I'd eat *his* dinner—then head over to the bakery and try out a new recipe idea I'd been playing around with. If it worked out, I could do it for the special in the morning.

Before I reached for another strip of chicken, the dirty stranger's green eyes again rose unbidden in my mind.

I let out a gasp and nearly tripped as I threw myself from the booth and took off in a sprint for the front door. I had to shove a few patrons out of my way, but most saw or heard me coming and stepped aside. Their cries of indignation were lost even before the front door closed behind me.

Those damned eyes! How had I not realized the guy had been a vampire? Even if I hadn't seen his eyes, the fact that a man that looked like Brett was entranced by such a scrub should have been clue enough that something was amiss.

Before I realized I no idea where I was going, I'd run nearly two blocks from the restaurant. I stopped abruptly and forced myself to pause and look around. Other than a few people who were still gawking at me, wondering why I'd torn through the crowds only to stop and stare, no one even seemed to notice there was anything out of the ordinary. They continued to talk and laugh, wait in lines outside of bars and restaurants, and peruse shop after shop. Twinkling lights draped in the ancient trees overhead gave a soft, romantic light to the scene. Trumpets and guitars sang out over the crowd, making it impossible to hear anything.

For a moment, I searched for the vampire. There were scores of people roaming through the streets, and at least half a dozen had red hair. Then I realized it was Brett I should be searching for. He was the one who would stand out. There wasn't one other person in Old Town who could be mistaken for him.

Even so, he was nowhere to be seen. If what I knew about vampires was true, I didn't have much time, and I'd already wasted too much sitting in the booth. I should have gotten to Brett before he'd even made it to the door instead of getting all butt-hurt.

I shook the thoughts away. Hindsight wouldn't help me find Brett and the vampire. Closing my eyes, I forced myself to take a couple of deep breaths. As much as I could, I let the outside world fade away. Within a few seconds, the noise of Old Town receded to the level of a muted television in the background. Once I was certain I was as centered as I was going to get, I cast my senses around me.

Again I began with the vampire foremost in my mind. Focusing on his dirty appearance, his red hair, his green eyes.

Nothing.

I waited, pushing my senses further.

Still nothing.

With a groan of frustration, I opened my eyes, and the world rushed in with a torrent of sensations. Of course I couldn't find the vampire. The monster was dead, after all. No heartbeat, no pulse. No sign of life other than his victim's blood coursing through his veins.

Chiding myself, I slammed my eyes shut once more. It took longer to get centered this time. Both my annoyance with myself and my fear that I wouldn't find him hindered my attempts to block out the world.

I could see Brett clearly in my mind. His California blond hair. Gorgeous face, porcelain skin. Huge shoulders. Dusting of golden chest hair visible in the V of his button-down.

The countless people around made locating anything nearly impossible. Too many heartbeats. Too many thoughts and desires. Too much pain. Even worse, I had nothing to go on about Brett other than his physicality. As striking as he was, his body wasn't who he was. It wouldn't help me find him. I had no idea what he was like. I didn't even have the timbre of his voice to give me a clue to his inner being. Still, I needed to find him. I had to try.

Using all the strength I had, I opened my eyes once more while keeping my senses spread out around me. Everything was dimmed, as if looking through a filter. Even the sounds from the crowd and band were heard as if from a distance.

I glanced up and down the main strip of Old Town. I tried to see the space like a vampire might. Like a predator who needed some amount of privacy.

There were endless side streets and alleyways. Too many to check. Too many to even walk by. The thought brought on a panic that nearly caused me to lose my focus, and I paused once more until I regained the strength I'd had previously. I couldn't think about all the different streets, all the possibilities. I had to work with what I could do. Again I looked in both directions on the main street. I knew that southeast led to the entrance to the highway. No way the vampire would head toward the Five. He'd take his victim as far from people as he could.

Feeling somewhat encouraged, I headed off in the opposite direction, which was still in the heart of Old Town, but the farther the road went, the more it delved into the residential neighborhoods that surrounded the tourist trap.

Still focused on a revolving image of Brett's face and perfect body, I made my way slowly down the sidewalk. Even the picture I had in my mind was already fading. I'd only seen him for a matter of minutes. As pretty as he was, his appearance had begun to morph into a stereotypical conglomeration of male features.

How long had it been since he'd left with the monster? Five minutes? Ten? I was willing to bet it had been at least ten minutes, probably more. How long did it take for a vampire to kill a person? I doubted it took all that long. Brett was a pretty big man. Maybe that would buy him some time. I cursed my sheltered upbringing. If Mom and Dad hadn't protected us from every little thing, maybe I'd have a chance at finding Brett in time.

Again I shook off the unneeded thoughts. My fear brought a spike of inspiration. I may not know anything about Brett, but I did have an idea how he was feeling. At least I did if the vampire wasn't controlling Brett's thoughts and emotions.

I let my terror flow freely. It was so intense that I had to wait as my body adjusted to functioning under such stress. When I'd regained control, I refocused my senses, this time searching for fear, for pain, for anything that might tell me something traumatic was happening. With so many people behind me in Old Town and around me in the surrounding neighborhood, there was a good chance there could be several people having such emotions. Surely none would be as strong as the terror a person would feel while being bitten by a vampire

A few more minutes passed before I felt a surge of fear. It was coming from somewhere in front of me. I couldn't tell where exactly, but it was there, and it felt strong enough to be caused by a vampire. Maybe.

No sooner had I picked up my speed than the fear abruptly stopped. It was so sudden that it caused me to halt where I was. It had been him. He'd been terrified, and then he died. I was too late.

So what? Even if he was dead, I needed to find him. I took off in a jog in the same direction from which I'd felt the fear cease. I wasn't sure what I was going to do when I found him. What if the vampire was still there? The only good that would bring was giving him one more snack.

A new rush of fear surged over me, and I started running. This time I was certain. He was still alive, and he was still somewhere in front of me. I was going the right direction. No doubt. It was getting stronger. The fear was so intense I was sure it came from someone being killed. Surely there wouldn't be someone else suffering such a fate at the exact same moment.

Again the fear stopped, as surely as if someone had closed a door on it. The thought of his death was quickly pushed aside by another surety that both gave me hope and caused my terror to increase. The vampire wasn't letting him feel his fear. He was making him feel something else, or nothing at all. While that meant he probably had a little time left, I was scared to even imagine what could be happening to him.

I tore off, running full speed, the sound of my shoes shouting as they smacked against the uneven sidewalk.

Forcing my senses further and further from me, I kept running, the haze around me building. I barely dodged low-hanging branches and hardly kept from falling over uneven cracks in the cement. I glanced down every driveway and alley I passed, but saw nothing.

Pain and terror crashed over me again, nearly crushing me to the ground.

I'd gone too far! I felt him behind me. I wheeled and sprinted back the way I'd come, Brett's agony increasing with every step I took. After passing one of the alleys I'd crossed by earlier, I felt his sensations drift behind me once more. Momentarily confused, I dashed back to the alley and looked down. Nothing.

Another spike of pain.

I was on the wrong block! I rushed down the alley, slipping on some sort of ooze beside a dumpster but managed to keep from falling. Exiting on the other side, I slowed, getting another read on his feelings. When I was certain, I veered to my left and broke out into a full run once more.

A scream cut through the night. Pure terror and anguish laced the sound. Wave after wave of emotions washed over me. His fear was increasing to a level that was nearly impeding my ability to move.

Once again, like being doused by a bucket of cold water, his terror vanished, leaving me empty.

I was close. I knew I was. There was no way his feelings could have been that strong if he was still a long way off.

I rushed on to the next alley, slowing as I neared its entrance, and peeked in. Nothing.

Running again, I tore down the next block, slowing a few feet from the next alley opening.

I glanced in and nearly started running again, but halted as the scene halfway down the alley under the solitary streetlamp took form in front of my eyes. It took a moment to make sense of it.

They were facing away from me. All I could see were bare feet and a scrawny ass pointed in my direction, moving in a disgusting motion. The events formed in shocking clarity as the vampire reared up, his back illuminated in the yellow light. From somewhere below him a jet of blood spewed out like a fount of glistening rubies.

I fell back, a scream rising in my throat as my eyes blurred with hot tears of anger. I was too late. Mere moments too late!

Paralyzed, I stared as the vampire lowered himself once more toward Brett's lifeless form. Unthinking, I took a step forward, ready to rush at him.

My scream of fury was cut short as Brett's hands shot up and clasped the vampire's shoulders.

Again I paused in a wash of confusion. Then joy took its place. Brett was alive. I'd made it in time.

I started forward again, only to be thrown back as the vampire burst into flames.

I stared in dumb awe as the creature, screaming in high-pitched agony, threw himself from Brett. He landed against the opposite alley wall. Its crumbling bricks exploded with dust, the particles glistening in the blazing fire.

Still screaming, the vampire fell to the ground. His body twisted and beat against the pavement, stirring up the trash around him, small fires breaking out, then quickly suffocating.

I couldn't force my body to move, not that I'd have known what to do anyway. Finally the flames died, and the monster crawled back to the wall and pulled himself up to a standing position.

I couldn't suppress a gasp. The skin on his face and upper body was charred away, blackened and revealing huge portions of his skull and bones.

He lurched toward Brett, who was still lying on the ground. He looked like he was going to stomp on him or smash in his head, killing him one way or another.

The thought allowed my body freedom once more, and I tore down the alley. I'm unsure if I yelled. Not certain if the vampire heard me coming or not. Regardless of the reason, he swiveled away from me and faltered down the alley.

For the briefest of moments, I considered following him. Surely in his state I could catch up. However, even injured as he was, I knew it would take no effort on his part to kill me. As I approached Brett, all my attention was drawn to him, anyway.

His eyes were closed, and for a moment I thought I was too late, that he'd died in the last few moments. Then his chest moved slightly, and relief flooded through me.

He was a mess—a gaping wound on the side of his neck still seeping blood. His naked body was covered in the crimson liquid. Claw marks were scattered over what I could see of his chest, stomach, and upper thighs.

To my surprise, I didn't hesitate. I'd been indecisive too often tonight, and it had cost him. No more.

I moved behind his head, slipped my hands under his armpits, and dragged him to the side of the dumpster, close enough that he was mostly covered in shadow.

I turned and dashed forward a few feet, my hand already digging in my pocket for the keys to the Chevy. Then a thought hit me, and I rushed back to Brett. I checked to make sure there were no other people around and then knelt beside him, once again making sure he was breathing.

When I saw that he was, I placed my hand a few millimeters over the skin of his chest and drew all my focus to the blood covering him. As I drifted my hand over him, the blood pooled into streams and poured off his body, accumulating in the cracks of the concrete. Once his body was clean, I found his clothes discarded on the other side of the dumpster and wrestled him into them.

As much as I could, I averted my eyes from his body—focusing on his face and the pulse at his neck. From what I'd seen, the last thing he deserved was a stranger taking the opportunity to inspect his body. There was nothing sexy about his abused form or how close he'd come to death. Nor the fact that he might not have suffered at all if I had been a little quicker to realize what was going on.

I rearranged him once more beside the dumpster so anyone wandering by would think he was just a drunk sleeping off too much tequila. The chances of anyone coming this far from Old Town were slim anyway, and anyone living around here probably wouldn't be making a late-night trip to put out the garbage.

Once again I tore off down the alley, running as fast as I could back to my truck.

CHAPTER SIX

BRETT WRIGHT

"WHAT were you thinking? How could you bring it *here*, to our house?"

"What should I have done? Leave him there to die?"

"*It's* a demon. It wouldn't have died."

"You don't know that. That doesn't even make sense."

I could tell the voices were angry. They should have been loud, but they seemed muffled, a long way off. I wanted to open my eyes, but even the thought sounded too exhausting. I just wanted to rest. A flash of irritation shot through me—couldn't they tell someone was trying to sleep? Whatever their problem, couldn't they take it elsewhere?

"Get back in the truck and go dump it somewhere else. Take it back where you found it."

"Mom, seriously. You weren't there. I don't think he's a demon. If he were, the vampire would have been obliterated."

I must have fallen asleep on the couch again, and Sonia was playing one of the stupid movies she was always making me watch. I tried to turn over to reach for the remote control, but as I did, I felt a rip at my neck. My eyes shot open, wide-awake, as the pain made me gasp. I tried to sit up, but the motion caused me to lose my balance, and I tipped off the edge, my hand coming down to stop my fall.

When my hand came into contact with a floor mat, I realized I wasn't on my sofa. I glanced around, the motion once again causing me to grimace in pain. I felt like I had fallen down a couple of flights of stairs. Every muscle was throbbing and on fire. I took in the glove compartment in front of my face, the stick shift gouging into my side, and the steering wheel at my feet with a Chevy emblem in the middle. My eyes shot up toward the windshield. The moon was barely peeking out from behind a cloud.

Tentatively, I lay back down and tried to calm my breathing enough that I could figure out what was happening. It only took a few moments before I saw the charred monster above me, his hollow eyes bringing back everything. I shot up in the seat, once again crying out at the pain that caused my vision to go dark for a second. I heard the female voice gasp, and I looked out the windshield to see two figures staring at me.

I grabbed the door handle and shoved with all my weight. It flew open, and I crashed to the ground. The gravel from the driveway cut into the palms of my hands, but before I could feel the injury, I shoved off the ground and began to lurch forward, away from the two figures, away from the truck, away from the talk of demons and vampires.

My legs gave out before I had taken my second step. Maybe I had been in an accident. My muscles were screaming at me in fury.

"Wait!" I heard the male's voice behind me and feet running in my direction. "You're going to hurt yourself. Please, stop. Everything's okay!"

I took off again, this time on my hands and knees.

"Stay!" This time it was the female voice, harsh and commanding.

My body froze, one bloody palm stretched out, unable to go any further.

"Mom, don't! You don't need to!"

"Be still!" I heard a crack, and then nothing else.

WITH a groan I opened my eyes, expecting to see the gravel, possibly the inside of the truck again. Instead, there was a white ceiling fan circling above me. I blinked, waiting for my vision to return. When I opened them again, the fan was still there. My gaze left the fan and followed around the small, square ceiling and made its way over the walls. I was in a tiny bedroom. The walls were pale lavender, with a wallpaper border of pink and blue pansies halfway down. Translucent blue curtains framed a small window. A dim shadow of a tree swayed gently outside. It appeared to still be night. What if it were a different night? How long had I been unconscious? The thought brought a rush of panic. I started to move to the window, but I couldn't. My body didn't seem to be responding to directions. I tried again. Nothing. I didn't feel so much as a muscle flex. I glanced down to see what I was tied up with, only to realize I couldn't even move my head. I rolled my eyes down, trying to see my body. It was the strangest sensation I had ever experienced. I almost expected to not see anything where my body should be. I had no awareness of my arms or legs, and I couldn't feel myself taking breaths. I felt like I was a floating brain with eyes. Thankfully, as my gaze traveled down, I could see everything was still attached. I couldn't see anything binding me. I looked like I was just lying on a bed.

Again, I told myself to sit up. Nothing happened, not so much as a twitch. Maybe I was paralyzed. Something that thing in the alley had done to me! No, that was earlier. I had been in a truck—I almost got away. Maybe whoever had been outside arguing had hit me and broken my back. My heart sank at the thought. That had to be it. I was paralyzed. I wouldn't ever walk again. Never swim. I wouldn't be able to defend myself if they came back.

When they came back.

In desperation, I peered over at my right hand, which was sprawled out away from my body, palm up on the bed. I focused all my concentration on my little finger, telling it to move, to curl. Nothing. It felt like my body should be trembling with effort, sweating with the intensity of will. Nothing.

I could feel the rage building up inside of me, felt it come rushing toward the surface, ready to release in a scream of agony.

Nothing.

Even my mouth had given up control. I tried to speak, cough, clear my throat. Nothing.

A feeling of claustrophobia enveloped me. At least the part of me that could feel. The room shrank smaller and smaller around me, the bed closing in upon itself. I was clawing the inside of my mind, trying to find some way out. I slammed my eyes shut. It was the only control I had.

Gradually, after several minutes, I began to calm down, attempting to force myself to take in the situation. Try to see what I could do to prepare for whoever or whatever came back for me.

I looked around the room, hoping to find something I could use as a weapon, even though I had no idea how I would be able to use it if I found one.

The room was strange. It appeared to be a little girl's room, or an old woman's. However, there were posters of sports figures plastered on the lavender walls and small action figure toys on top of the dresser and desk. I narrowed my eyes in an effort to see them better in the dim light. They weren't the normal superhero-type action figures. They were gruesome. A wide array of monsters, most dripping with blood. A mummy, werewolf, ogre, two-headed Cyclops, and many others I didn't have names for, the majority with large fangs and talons, some with dismembered arms or legs hanging from the mouths. Most of the time, such toys would have been only mildly interesting to me, but combined with the prissiness of the room and all that had happened, the sight of them made me shudder—or would have, if my body had been able.

I forced myself to look away from the hideous toys to search the rest of the room. There was a stack of what appeared to be old yearbooks in the corner by the dresser. Next to them were a baseball, glove, and bat. *Perfect*! A momentary thrill shot through me until I remembered I couldn't use the baseball bat very effectively while frozen in place.

I continued to search the room, but found nothing more helpful than a few plastic trophies and a lightweight teal dumbbell set.

It made me nervous not being able to see behind me. Since I was in a bed, the chances were good that I was against the wall, but what if I wasn't. There could be anything there, just waiting. Waiting for what, I wasn't sure, but the thought made me glad the monster toys were within my eyesight. Also, I realized I hadn't seen a door, which meant it must be behind me. I wouldn't be able to see whatever came through it.

Mentally, I shook myself. I was thinking of these things as *whatevers*. There had to be an explanation for everything. Yeah, some guy had definitely sucked my blood in the alley, but you heard stories of people doing sick stuff all the time. It didn't mean there were actual vampires, no matter what my kidnappers wanted to call them. And so what if they said something about demons? They were probably crazy, or just being dramatic. People at the church always spoke about demons when I was growing up. The stories they told used to keep me up at night straining to see the glow of red eyes peering from my closet.

Those days were past. It wasn't going to help anything if I let myself get freaked out over things that didn't exist. I'd broken my back; that was all. Or my kidnappers had broken my back. Either way wasn't good, but it didn't mean they were demons. If there really were such things as demons, they probably didn't have pastel paint and curtains.

Still, if I had a broken back and was paralyzed, there were no guarantees that *whoever* had captured me was going to do anything better to me than the scenes the toys depicted on the dresser.

Then, out of the blue, it hit me. I couldn't talk! If I had broken my back and could still see and move my eyes, then I should be able to talk. I would be paralyzed from the neck down. That wouldn't affect my speech. Whatever it was, my back wasn't the problem. I brightened at the possibility. I would be able to walk again. To swim.

Following that train of thought led me to the conclusion I was drugged. That had to be the explanation. It would all wear off. Then I could escape out the window and call the cops. Even if it was a couple of stories high, I could manage that. No. There would be no jumping. My eyes found the baseball bat again. As soon as I could manage to move, there were a couple of heads I was going to bash in first, and then I'd call the cops. I felt like I had been unconscious for a long time, so surely the drugs wouldn't last much longer. Soon, I'd be able to—

A soft creak broke my thoughts, and I could see light flow into the room from the left side of my peripheral vision. I slammed my eyes shut. Better to have them thinking I was still unconscious from the drugs. Then maybe they'd leave again, giving me time to get my body back.

The floorboards creaked as my captors made their way around the bed, and I felt a hand press down gently on my chest. I felt breath on my face. It was a good thing I was paralyzed, or I would have jumped. As it was, I was impressed I didn't fling my eyes open.

"I can't believe you're still unconscious," the male voice from earlier whispered a few inches from my face. "Mom swore she didn't use that much force. I guess you just needed to sleep." He exhaled, his breath smelling like cinnamon. "I don't know what we're going to do with you, but it would sure help if you could wake up and give me some assistance explaining this. The others are going to be home any time, and it would make it easier if you weren't sleeping."

The pressure lifted off my chest, and his steps made their way across the room. As he walked away, I cracked open my eyes just enough to see where he was. His back was to me, and he stood in front of the desk. I let my eyes open the rest of the way, certain I could close them should he turn around.

He appeared to be a little shorter than me, and his tight green T-shirt showed off a muscled back and thick tan arms. Tousled black hair reached most of the way down his neck. "God, Caitlin, you always were a bit of a freak," he muttered as he picked up one of the more gory toys.

As he inspected the figure, I realized I could see most of his face in the mirror over the desk. He was extremely good-looking—light caramel complexion, thick neck, squared jaw, full lips, smallish straight nose. His honey-colored eyes met mine in the reflection. He let out a gasp.

"You're awake!" He turned around, still holding the toy at chest level. "I've been so worried about you. I was afraid that…." He made his way nearly to the bed but paused suddenly midstride, cocking his head to one side and narrowing his eyes. "Did you drink any of his blood?"

I felt my eyes grow wider. *Drink his blood?* The guy in the alley, or was there someone else I couldn't remember? What kind of question is that? Why would I possibly drink someone's blood?

The man turned the toy over in his hands and began to pace in a small circle between the foot of the bed and the dresser, muttering to himself. "Even if you did, surely, it wouldn't have had an effect so quickly. But if you did, then it will probably happen before the night's over. I wish I understood how this works." He glanced back up at me, his voice almost irritated. "Well, did you?"

I could feel my face get warm with anger. I wanted to scream at him. Did I look like some blood-guzzling freak? Was *I* the one who had drugged someone and put them in a strange bed? As it was, my mouth didn't move. I thought I started to feel some of the heat going through my body. I was vaguely aware of my arms at my sides.

"Oh. I'm sorry." The man looked down sheepishly. "I forgot, you can't answer that, can you?" He came and sat down on the bed and put his hand tenderly on my left forearm. "Okay, I need you to stay calm. It will take me a little bit longer than normal since Mom is the one who secured you. Just give me a couple of minutes, and you'll be able to move around and—"

"Oh no, he won't!" A short dark woman swept into the room and smacked the man's hand that reached out toward my face. "What do you think you are doing?" Her voice was shrill, and she pointed a finger in my direction as she bellowed at the man. "First, you bring this demon here, expecting me to care for it, and now you're just going to set it loose so it can kill us and then wait around for your father and sisters to get home? I thought I raised you better!"

The man's face flushed, but his voice remained calm. "Mom, come on! You know he's not a demon. If he were, you wouldn't have been able to even get him to stay on the ground, much less float him up here and put him in bed."

Did he just say *float* me up here?

I didn't have time to consider it before the woman began yelling and waving her hands dramatically. "We are going to wait for your father to get home. He will decide how to handle this mess. I swear to the good Lord that you are going to be the death of this family! You need to learn to take care of yourself and quit worrying about everything that crosses your path! Thank goodness your sister and the kids left before you dragged this thing in!"

"Mom! Enough!" This time his voice was loud, and it caused her to stop her ranting. "Look at him! Does he look like a demon to you?"

She glanced over at me and then back to her son. "Yes!" She nodded emphatically, crossing her arms over her chest.

He let out a slow, deliberate breath. "You are just being stubborn. He isn't big enough to be a demon, and you know that."

"Look at his face!"

"Yes, Mom. I can see his face. So what?"

"It's perfect!"

"I can see that, Mother, but that doesn't mean he's a demon. Since when do demons come in normal human size?"

"He's big enough! You don't know. You've never seen one. I have!" She whirled around toward me, thrust out her index finger, and touched my lips. "You tell us! Tell us you're a demon."

"You're both crazy!"

It took a second to realize I had spoken the words aloud and hadn't simply thought them. As soon as I did, however, I tried to throw myself off the bed. If I was fast enough, I could take out the son before the mother could respond. My body, however, didn't so much as flinch. I couldn't feel anything other than the heat slowly making its way down my legs. The drugs must be starting to wear off. The angrier I got, the more I could feel.

I moved my mouth, slowly opening and closing. "I can talk."

The woman rolled her eyes. "Of course you can talk. Don't play stupid with me. That won't get you anywhere. I promise you, I'm no fool."

The man looked at his mother and then back at me. "I don't think he's playing, Mom." He reached down and placed his hand below my knee. "Brett, are you feeling okay? Do you remember—?"

"How do you know my name?" As soon as I asked, I felt stupid. It's not like it would have been that hard to search my wallet when I was unconscious.

"What? You don't remember me?" He moved closer to the head of the bed, but his mother placed her hand on his arm and stopped him.

His response made me pause. I looked at him closer. I couldn't draw a name to match his face, but I guessed it was possible we had gotten together at some point. He was most definitely my type. The dark hair, tan skin, thick muscles, even the faintest hint of a hard little belly under his T-shirt. Is that what this was? Some twisted retribution for not calling him back the next day?

"Wow! You *really* don't know who I am, do you?"

"Listen, if I did something to upset you or hurt your feelings, I am sorry. I'm sure I didn't mean to, but this isn't the way to handle things. You could have just called or something. If it meant this much to you that we get together again, we could've—"

"Brett, stop!" The man cast an embarrassed glance toward the woman before returning his imploring gaze to me. "It's Finn! From the restaurant?"

"Who?"

I thought I saw a flash of hurt pass over his eyes. "Taberna de las Brujas. I didn't realize I was so forgettable. My brother-in-law was trying to set us up."

His mother made a disgusted sound in her throat. "That reminds me. Don't let me forget to teach Ricardo a lesson! Trying to set up my boy with a demon!"

"Ricardo? Is he here?" Finally, someone familiar.

"No, we haven't called him. Mom just called Dad. He would know how to help you more than Ricky."

"We were on a date tonight?"

"No, you were at the restaurant, and Ricky came and got me to introduce us. You don't remember meeting at the restaurant?"

Flashes began to break through the fog. "Oh! I remember Ricardo telling me about Finn. About you. Then he went off to find you. Then this red-haired guy came in with these green eyes and...." I closed my eyes, trying to visualize the restaurant. "That's all I remember. Until the alley." I squeezed my eyes tighter in an attempt to block out the memory. It didn't work. I felt my fear, terror. Then a flash of pleasure, followed by guilt. Fury exploded, burning away every scrap of arousal. Fury at what had been done to me. Fury that I hadn't killed the fucker. Fury that I was still helpless and at the mercy of strangers. That I'd traded my prison in an alley for one in a bedroom!

"The vampire." The mother stepped between Finn and I. "How did you set the vampire on fire if you are not a demon?"

"Lady, why do you keep calling me that? I am not a demon. There's no such thing!" She started to interrupt, but I cut her off, every ounce of my anger spewing forth in her direction. "There's no such thing as vampires either, so could you give it a rest! And while we're at it, give me something to get these drugs out of my system. I'm not staying here another moment!"

Her face crunched into a disgusted expression, her temper attempting to match my own. "You're on drugs?" She turned to Finn, her voice rising. "He's on drugs! Ricardo not only set you up with a demon but a drug dealer! Your sister sure picked a winner when she married that idiot!"

"Mom, come on. Don't be like—"

"For the last time, there is no such thing as demons, and I am not a drug dealer! The only drugs I am on are whatever you gave me to make it where I can't move!" For the briefest of moments, fear began to set in once more. Eagerly, my anger burned it away.

She narrowed her eyes and gave me a hard stare. I glared right back. After several moments, she looked back to Finn, her voice a mixture of surprise and begrudging surrender. "He's not lying. He truly thinks we drugged him."

Finn seemed as bewildered as his mother. "Do you really not know? How is that possible? You set that vampire on fire with your bare hands. I saw you."

"You saw me? You were there?" My system was about to overload. One second I felt anger, then fear, then anger again, and every bit swallowed up in helpless confusion. It was bad enough to think I'd not been able to defend myself, let alone know that the entire thing had been witnessed by someone else. "What? You saw something you liked? Didn't get the date your brother-in-law promised you, so you thought you'd drug me up and take your turn!"

The man's hands flew up, as if warding off punches. "Whoa, not at all. I had only just found you. I rounded the corner into the alley, and there you were. Both naked. He was on top of you. Blood everywhere." He shook his head and wiped a hand over his eyes, letting out a strangled sound, like he was trying to regain control of his emotions. He forced his gaze back to mine, a pleading expression in his eyes that made me feel even more uncomfortable. "I thought I was too late, that you were already dead, but then he burst into flames right where your hands were. I'd never seen a spell like that. Hell, I've never seen anything like any part of that. I had no idea what to do. Then you did whatever spell that was, and got him off you before I could even take in what was happening. I'm so sorry. I swear, if I'd have realized—"

"It wasn't a spell." Finn's mother placed her hand on his shoulder, and her voice grew gentle. "You always want to see the best in people, Finn, you always have. This time, it's gotten you into trouble. You know spells don't work like that. We don't have that kind of power. The only thing that could have burned him like that is a demon. I can't say I understand it. I agree with you. A demon should have completely burned the vampire to ashes. I don't blame you for trying to help after witnessing what happened. No one deserves that. No one." She eyed me cautiously. "Regardless of the circumstances, he's a demon. And now he's here, under our roof."

I looked back and forth between them. They were serious. Crazy or not, they believed everything they were saying. Plus, he had seen me set the guy on fire. How was that any less insane? I returned the mother's stare. The insanity of it all, stripping away the anger, leaving me tired and empty. "How is it possible? How did I set that guy on fire?"

She simply stared at me, her brown eyes slowly moving back and forth, searching mine. At first they were still hard with anger, but slowly that anger began to give way to confusion.

This was all too much. All of it. The things in the water. Hurting that boy at the beach. Getting raped in the alley, and someone drinking my blood. Setting the man on fire. I was losing it. I was either developing some bizarre strain of schizophrenia, or I was becoming something else. Something like the monster toys on the dresser. As a tear leaked out of my eye, the woman placed her hand on my cheek, giving a slow, decisive nod. "I'm going to release you bit by bit. Don't try anything. If you do, you won't be leaving this bed. Understand?"

The last thing I could do was understand any of this. I stared at her numbly.

She lifted her left hand, reached over my body, and slowly ran it down the length of my right arm. Sharp tingling sensations started in the skin and slowly trickled toward the center of my arm, leaving a warm itch in their wake.

"Move your hand. Slowly." She stood and backed away from the bed.

I raised my arm and squeezed my hand into a fist several times in front of my face. As part of my body regained control, the original feeling of claustrophobia came over me again. Desperate to get out of the bed, I reached over and grabbed my left arm to move it out of the way. It didn't budge. It was like it had been melted onto the bed.

"Give it time. I will release the rest of you." Her eyes held mine once again. "You'll stay calm, not go after anybody?"

"Mom! Really, I don't think that's necessary."

"Be quiet, Finn!" She leaned in closer. "Well, Brett, do I have your word?"

I nodded frantically.

"Very well, then." She repeated the process, gently tracing down my left arm with the palm of her hand. The tingling and itching started anew. Once more she waited for several seconds, gauging my every movement and reaction. Finn didn't interrupt her again.

It felt like hours by the time she had repeated the process on my neck, right and left legs, and finished with her hand pressed on my chest. I groaned as the sharpness pulsed through my body with each beat of my heart. Just as the itching flamed over my skin like thousands of fire ants, she placed a hand over my forehead. "Don't scratch. Give it a moment. You'll be fine."

Gradually my skin cooled, and my breathing returned to normal. She nodded in satisfaction.

"Can I get up now? Please."

"Of course, Brett. Slowly, though." The switch in her tone from interrogator to motherly was disconcerting, but a welcome change.

I groaned again, this time in pleasure, as I cautiously sat up, stretched and swung my legs over the side, then stood.

Tension filled the room as we all stood there, each waiting for the other to make a move, to show their intentions.

Finn grinned at me encouragingly but then returned to looking serious. "So, back to my question. Did you?"

"Did I what?"

"Drink any of his blood?"

"No. I don't think so."

"Good." Finn's mom nodded once more. "You'd know if you had."

"Why? Besides being gross, why else would it matter if I drank some of the guy's blood?" Despite my internal turmoil, I couldn't restrain my curiosity.

Finn's grin broadened. "Well, we don't need any newly raised vampires running around the house."

"Why do you keep calling him that? He wasn't a vampire."

"Why not?" It was Finn's mom's turn to grin.

"Because there is no such thing as vampires!"

"Oh? Well, then what about witches?"

"Of course not."

"Are you blind, boy? What do you think just happened in here?"

I opened my mouth to reply, but I didn't have an answer. What did I think happened? How had she held me down without any ropes? And if I was drugged, how did she release the effects one body part at a time? "I don't know. What did happen?"

"Well, let me put it this way." She thrust out her hand at me. "I'm Paulette de Morisco, and I am a witch and a baker." I only stared at her hand, which she then used to gesture over to Finn. "And this is Finn de Morisco, a warlock and my son."

My gaze continued to pass over them, one to the other and back again. Other than being obviously amused with themselves, they seemed to be quite serious. "Let me get this straight. You're telling me that the owner of my favorite restaurant tried to set me up with his magic brother-in-law?"

"Warlock, actually." Finn winked at me. I could tell he was still nervous, but he seemed to be trying to put me at ease. Although how that was supposed to happen when they were telling me they were witches, I had no idea.

"Ricardo is a warlock as well," Paulette interjected, "just not a very good one." Finn glared at her reproachfully.

Just keep playing along. "Okay, fine, the restaurant is owned and operated by a warlock, I got set up with another warlock, and then I got... uh... taken by a *vampire*?"

"Pretty much." Finn moved over and sat on the edge of the bed. "Honestly, I'm a little confused why you're having such a hard time grasping this when you have the power of fire."

Power of fire. "And what does that mean? Why do I have the power of fire, whatever that is?"

Paulette let out a little laugh. Now that she had lost most of her defensiveness and wasn't holding me prisoner on a bed, she looked like a normal, mildly plump, fiftyish housewife, albeit one with long black hair and nearly flawless skin. "Well, I would guess it is fairly clear what the power of fire means. *You're* the one who set the vampire on fire."

"And by vampire, you mean...?"

"Vampire." Finn held up his two index fingers to his mouth and pointed them down as he wiggled them. "Sharp fangs, undead, only come out at night, drinking blood."

"That's what I was afraid of." Despite myself, it was starting to seem a little less crazy and even more terrifying. I turned my attention back to Paulette. "And what does all this make me?"

She smiled a sweet smile, although her dark eyes still had a hint of nervousness about them. "I'm not sure, dear."

"Hello?" A voice sounded from somewhere else in the house, causing me to jump.

"Oh, that must be my husband. I didn't hear the car pull in."

CHAPTER SEVEN

"STAY here," Paulette commanded as she brushed past me out the door and closed it behind her.

I glanced over at Finn. He attempted a smile, but it faltered and he refocused on the floor. With Paulette out of the room, everything felt a little less real. If it weren't for the muffled raised voices from outside the bedroom and the throbbing in my neck, I probably could have pretended that nothing strange had happened. Maybe it was just wishful thinking and not wanting to have to consider the implications of everything that was going on.

My gaze traveled down Finn's body, since he wasn't looking. He really was beautiful. Without his mother in the room, he seemed more self-conscious. I couldn't help believe that he'd done everything he could do to save me. "I'm sorry that I don't remember you from the restaurant."

His gaze flitted up at me, his cheeks flushing. "It's okay. I hear that vampires make it hard to concentrate on anything else around you." A little laugh escaped. "Actually, it kinda makes me feel better. When I sat down at the booth, you wouldn't even acknowledge that I was there. It wasn't till you got up and walked off that I realized you were looking at someone else. By the time I saw him and realized he was a vampire, he already had you through the door."

At the mention of vampire, my hand, of its own accord, gingerly covered the wound on my neck. "Yeah, it was impossible to look away. I've never felt like that before." At the mention of him, even now, his green eyes seemed to float in front of my face, and I could feel his cold skin on mine. Scenes from the alley flashed behind my eyes.

"You okay?" I felt a hand on my arm and glanced down. Finn had moved closer.

"Yeah, sorry." I forced myself to focus on Finn's face, trying to replace the emerald eyes with the kind, warm brown ones in front of me. There were rings of yellow, nearly gold, around his pupils, which seemed to cut through the brown of the iris in a pattern, almost like a star. "Uh, so, you've had to deal with vampires a lot, huh?"

He shook his head. "No, not hardly. Mom and Dad would point them out to us when we were kids, so we would know the telltale signs. I see one from a distance from time to time, but they leave us alone for the most part. Tonight was only the second time I've been so close to one."

The conversation was making me nervous. "So, this is for real, this whole vampire, witch thing?"

Finn gave me an apologetic smile. "Yeah."

"And your mom's a witch and you're a... warlock?"

"Yeah."

"So that means your dad is a...?"

"He's a warlock too."

"Okay." I took a deep breath. I felt like a fool even having this conversation. Part of me wanted to laugh at the ridiculousness of it all, but part of it felt right. Kind of like when I finally admitted to myself that I was gay. As much as I wanted to fight it, as much as I did fight it, some place inside of me felt completed, at peace. "So I'm one too, then. Aren't I?"

"One what?" His voice sounded apprehensive. "A vampire?"

"No!" I brought my suddenly raised voice back down to normal. "No, I think I would've figured that out on my own when I was drinking people's blood. I'm a warlock too, right?"

Finn shook his head.

There was a sharp increase in the volume of the voices outside the room. We both looked toward the door. I made out a few curse words from a female voice I didn't recognize.

Finn groaned. "Shit, what is she doing here?"

"Who?" The tone in his voice made my pulse begin to race. I wasn't typically this easily set on edge, although considering the evening's events, I cut myself some slack. "Should I get out of here? Go out the window?"

"No, she's not *that* bad." He laughed. "Well, not quite. It's Caitlin, my sister. This is her old room, but she doesn't live here anymore. She must have still been at the shop with Dad when Mom called."

"She's a witch too, then, I guess?"

"Yeah. All my sisters are. Runs in the family, you know."

I nearly asked how many sisters he had, but then realized I didn't really care. "You said you found me in the alley, right? That you saw me set the... the vampire on fire?"

Finn nodded.

"What happened to him? Did I kill him?" A shot of hope darted through me at the thought that maybe I'd managed to destroy the fucker after all.

"No, he got the fire out. He looked horrible, over half of him burned away, but it takes a lot more than that to kill one."

I remembered his charred, eyeless face as he stood above me and cringed. "Then what happened? Did he come after you?"

"He took off down the alley. He didn't even notice I was there. At least I don't think he did. I thought you were dead, but when I got closer to you, I could see you breathing. You were just unconscious. I ran and got my truck, loaded you up, and brought you here. The rest you know."

I wasn't really sure what to say. "Thanks, I guess. For helping me."

He shrugged it off. "All I did was bring you here. I probably should have taken you back to my place. If I'd thought about it, I would have. Mom always overreacts at first." More yelling from somewhere else in the house made its way into the bedroom. Finn grinned. "Another thing that runs in the family."

"Your mom seems to believe that I'm not going to try to kill all of you now, at least."

"Oh yeah, she does. She's really good at reading people. She was just afraid, I think, not knowing what you are. It's obvious you're not a warlock, your fire wouldn't have been like that, and she's right, you do look like a demon, at least from what I have heard about them, anyway...."

"I do? How? Is there a mark or something on me that I can't see?" I glanced down at my hands—half expecting to see "666" glowing up at me like a stamp under black light.

"Well, not exactly. All the stories I have heard about demons say"—his gaze darted away nervously once more—"that demons are the most beautiful creatures to walk the earth."

We both jumped when the bedroom door flew open. Paulette, her face flushed and her voice breathy, leaned in through the doorway and beckoned us to follow her. "Come on, boys, I think I've finally gotten your sister calmed down enough for us to have an intelligent conversation."

Finn raised his eyebrows at his mother. "What's she wanting to do?"

Paulette rolled her eyes. "She wants us to call the Vampire Cathedral."

Finn snorted. "Right! 'Cause we have them on speed dial!"

I lowered my voice as I looked at Finn. "What's the Vampire Cathedral?"

Finn attempted a smile and shook his head. "Don't ask. You don't wanna know."

"It doesn't matter. Come on downstairs. They're waiting in the living room." Paulette turned and left the room, assuming we would follow.

Finn fell in line behind his mother. As we walked down the hall, we passed a few more bedrooms. The doors were open, but the lights were off, so I couldn't see any details other than the outline of beds and other pieces of furniture. At the end of the hallway, we came to a staircase and made our way down.

It appeared that the downstairs was all one massive room. At the foot of the stairs was a large rectangular wooden table with several spindled chairs around it. In the center of the table, sitting on a doily, was a cake platter with a mostly eaten chocolate cake. The right side of the room was a long, open kitchen. The countertops were a lime green, while the tiles and painted wood were a pale yellow. It could have looked retro. However, even from a distance, the age of it was apparent, even though it was all spotless and pristine. The entire room was papered in a blue-and-white floral pattern that was clearly from a different era than the kitchen décor but still obviously dated.

The only space not covered in the passé wallpaper was the left side of the room, several feet in front of the dining area. Here, there was a sunken living room with orange shag carpet. Dark wood paneling covered the walls. Under different circumstances, I'm not sure I could have kept my reaction to the room unnoticeable. However, after merely a glance around the room, all my attention was focused on the three people occupying the recessed space.

The tension was palpable. No one said a word. There was a handsome man, who I would have placed in his midfifties, perched on the edge of a brown recliner. I assumed this was Finn's father. His face was tight, but he attempted a smile when my eyes met his. Although they weren't identical, it was easy to see that Finn got most of his physical features from his father.

Close to him, seated on the couch next to a window, was a very pretty woman. She had long mahogany hair that fell past her waist and gathered around her on the sofa cushion. Her olive-green eyes were wide, and she glanced away when she noticed me observing her. Her delicate fingers were tipped with long rose-colored nails and shook as she folded and unfolded them in her lap.

The only commotion in the room came from a short, thin woman pacing back and forth in front of the barren fireplace. She was wearing a skintight black minidress. Her hair was spiky and had been dyed black with red-and-orange streaks down the middle. Her dark eyes glared at me in fury. I suddenly found myself starting to sweat under her gaze.

Paulette and Finn had taken the three steps down into the living room and left me standing above them all, trying to figure out what to do.

"Come on down, Brett. Take a seat." Paulette motioned toward one of the cream-colored chairs, which looked like it had been brought over from the dining room set. Finn sat down on an identical one next to it.

After another second's hesitation, I moved down the stairs and sat, feeling utterly exposed.

As she made her way to sit next to the woman on the couch, Paulette patted the man in the recliner on his shoulder. "This is my husband, Wendell de Morisco." He didn't say anything, but smiled once more and nodded. I wasn't sure what I was expected to say, so I simply nodded back.

Paulette motioned toward the long-haired woman next to her. "This is my youngest daughter, Cynthia." Cynthia did not look up at me but kept her eyes firmly focused on her nails. Paulette continued, undisturbed. "Of course, you already know my oldest daughter, Christina, from the restaurant. She and Ricardo aren't aware of what all has happened this evening. I didn't want to wake the boys, even if I had known it was going to be a family meeting." At this, the pacing woman let out a disgusted sound and muttered something under her breath. Paulette sighed and motioned toward the fidgety woman. "And this is our middle daughter, Caitlin."

At the sound of her name, the breath the woman seemed to be holding broke free in a streaming wave. "Seriously, Mother, don't you think this is all a little ridiculous? Why are you wasting time with formal introductions when we need to get this over and done with?" Caitlin didn't take her eyes off me as she addressed her mother. "You can tell by looking at him what he is."

"Shut up, Caitlin. You're being a bitch." Finn sneered at his sister, his expression equal parts angry and bored, as if this were a typical sibling disagreement. "If Brett were a demon, do you really think any of us would be sitting here discussing it? We'd be burned to a crisp already."

"And what if he's biding his time? You're just excited to have a cute boy in the house."

"Just because *you* don't know what to do with a hot guy, Caitlin, doesn't make him a demon!"

"Enough!" Paulette clapped her hands with more force than I would have thought possible. I could have sworn I felt a rush of wind reverberate from her as her hands came together. She glared at her daughter. "Before I brought him down here, we agreed we would talk calmly and rationally." She turned to Finn. "And watch your language, and try to remember neither of you are teenagers anymore."

"Mom? Can I go up to my room? I don't really think you need me to help figure this out." Cynthia's voice was soft and birdlike as she addressed her mother from where she had sunken into the couch.

"Oh, grow a pair, Cynthia!" Caitlin snarled. "You're twenty-seven years old. Act like it!" No sooner had the words left her mouth than her hand raised to cover it, as if she'd shocked herself with her words.

"Stop it!" Paulette raised her voice, cutting off her daughter. "Caitlin, you don't live here, so you are free to go. But if you choose to stay, you will control your tongue. And, Cynthia, by all means, if you can't handle this, you can leave." Her voice didn't sound cruel when she addressed Cynthia, and it was clearly laced with concern.

As if she had been suddenly cut loose, Cynthia popped out of the sofa and half ran, half skipped out of the living room and up the stairs.

Ignoring Caitlin's renewed muttering, Paulette addressed me. "Brett, I made a mistake, and I am sorry. I overreacted. If I had listened to Finn and talked to you first, I would have realized you weren't a demon. I wouldn't have called Wendell in such a tizzy and caused all this drama. We aren't going to hold you captive. You are free to go whenever you wish."

She paused as if expecting some response, but once again, I had no clue what to say. What would I do if I left? Go back to Sonia and tell her to watch out for vampires, demons, and witches?

"Wendell and I talked it over, and you are welcome to stay here for tonight, if you would like. You've had a rough evening and received a lot of new information."

Wendell broke in, his voice deep and nearly as soft as his youngest daughter's. "Paulette said that you don't know what you are. We thought you might have some questions that we can help with."

Questions? Hell, yeah, I had questions! What do I do now? What if the vampire comes back? How did all this happen? How did I almost drown a boy by kissing him? How do I wake up and get back to reality? "What am I?"

"Well, you're obviously not a warlock," Paulette said matter-of-factly, like I should already know. "As we've already said, the fire Finn described was much too strong to be from a warlock, plus it came out of your hands."

"So warlocks don't control fire?"

"Hell yes, we control fire." Somehow, I had already forgotten about Caitlin. A small ball of flame appeared in front of my face, bobbing up and down as if it were suspended on a string. I flinched back, trying to avoid it, nearly tipping over the chair.

"Cut it out, Caitlin!" Finn growled. With a wave of his hand, the fire evaporated into a puff of smoke. He turned to me. "What Mom means is that the fire came out of you. Out of your body. You didn't just call it to you. It was part of you. Witches can't do that."

I narrowed my eyes, trying to understand. All the while, I still felt none of it could be real. Although that was impossible, considering I'd just seen a woman pull fire out of the air and her brother extinguish it with a flick of his wrist. "So, you're saying I have fire in me, and you guys, witches and stuff, have to do magic to make it appear."

"Sort of, dear." Paulette smiled encouragingly. "However, there is no such thing as magic, at least not in the truest sense. Magic is making something from nothing. We can't do that. Everything we do revolves around the elements, around what is already here in nature. We call it to us, or have it do what we request. Nothing more. And only some of us can use fire. It depends on the individual witch or warlock. We are blessed, however." She reached over and patted her husband's knee affectionately. "Our bloodline is strong. There are only a few areas we cannot take advantage of, although each of us is stronger in certain areas than others."

"Paulette, I don't think the boy needs a lesson on warlocks and witches." He returned his gaze to me. "I have a theory, and there really isn't an appropriate way to test it, but I think Paulette wasn't too far off in her initial assumption."

I felt my throat constrict. "You mean, you think I am a demon after all?"

He ignored my question. "Were you raised by your parents, my boy?"

"Yeah, always. My.... Oh. Actually, I guess I wasn't. I was raised by my grandparents, my mom's folks. I just always thought of them as my parents."

Wendell nodded slowly. "Are you similar to them, physically?"

I laughed unintentionally. "No, not at all. In fact, it was always a sore spot with my grandfather. He was so tiny. The more I grew, the more jealous he became." I stopped, suddenly realizing where he was going. "Do you think they weren't my real family?"

He put his hand out as if to stop me from going too far. "Now, slow down. I don't know about that. But they weren't your parents, so it doesn't really change anything."

"Dad, there's no way that could be." Finn's eyes were wide. "If that were true, he'd be only once removed. He would have killed us instantly."

"Not necessarily, Finn. If these people weren't his real grandparents, say they adopted him from somewhere, he could be further removed."

I glanced back and forth between Finn and his father. Once removed from what? "Wait. What are you saying? Why would I have already killed you? You don't think my grandparents are my real family? They have pictures of my mom and everything, pictures of me as a newborn. They have to be my family."

"Slow down, Brett. This is just a theory. I can't explain it all, but it does make sense. The way you look, your size, your affinity with fire. You're most likely part demon. The question is, how much?"

"I told you we should call the Vampire Cathedral!" Caitlin had taken a seat on the couch after her sister had left, but now got back up and took a step closer to me. "He's dangerous and shouldn't be here." The hate in her eyes was shocking. It was almost a physical force. I looked closely at her for the first time. Her pacing and spiky hair had been distracting. Seeing her now, full in the face, she radiated a fierce beauty, her caramel-brown skin, pouty lips, straight, brilliantly white teeth, huge wide-set eyes. Eyes that were nearly as unusual as Finn's. Eyes ready to tear me apart.

My gaze was locked with hers so intently that at first I didn't realize Finn and Paulette were both screaming at Caitlin. I blinked, and Finn had thrown himself out of his chair at his sister and knocked her to the couch. Paulette rushed to me and hit my arms again and again with a pillow.

I glanced down to see the pillow extinguish the last bit of flame from my skin.

"Oh, Brett, are you okay? We'll call an ambulance. Let me just—"

"Paulette!" For the first time, Wendell raised his voice. "Look at him. Look at his arms."

She glanced down and then gasped, covering her mouth. She then stared at the charred pillow in her hands, as if to make sure. Her eyes rose to mine. This time, some of the fear that was there in the beginning was back. "You're fine. Not even a hair singed."

"I told you! I told you!" Caitlin yelled from underneath her brother.

Even Finn's eyes widened, the warm brown darkening in apprehension.

I held up my arm and twisted it in front of my face. There was some residue from the fire on my skin, but no damage. Nothing. If anything, that area of skin appeared fresher and more rejuvenated than it had before. Had I always been fireproof?

"Calm down, calm down. That doesn't change anything." Wendell turned his attention to Caitlin before looking back at me. "And you're very lucky this was the outcome, Caitlin. What if you had been wrong and burned him for real?"

I returned Wendell's gaze. "What? What does this mean?"

"Only a demon can't be hurt by fire. Even vampires and witches and warlocks can burn." He looked back to his family. "It doesn't change anything. Like Finn said, if he were a full demon, he wouldn't be confused about it, and we would be dead already."

CHAPTER EIGHT

It had been a rough night, and I was exhausted. Even after Caitlin had stormed out of the house shouting about how her family had signed their own death warrant, everyone else was tense. It seemed that Paulette had been fine with the idea of having a partial demon in her house—in theory. Once confirmed, however, it appeared to be more of a concern for her. She hadn't resorted to incapacitating me on the bed again, but she seemed ready to fly into action at the slightest scent of danger.

Cynthia didn't come out of her room the rest of the evening.

Even Finn looked on edge. One moment I would catch him staring at me with a sort of dazed expression when he thought I wasn't watching, and the next he was finding excuses to leave the room and be away from me.

Only Wendell seemed at ease. In fact, he seemed rather excited at the thought of having a demon in the house. He kept asking me to show him how I call my fire. I don't think he really believed me when I told him that I had no idea how to "call my fire," and that the whole thing was new to me as well.

I'm not completely sure why I stayed. I guess the thought of going home knowing Sonia was staying over at Derek's didn't sound all that appealing. Not that I was sure I wanted to see her anyway. How do you tell your best friend you're a demon? Knowing there was a pissed-off vampire out there, possibly looking for me, didn't exactly make me want to be by myself either. How do you face your best friend and tell her you've been raped, that you've nearly been killed? How do you not? She was the person I wanted to talk to the most, but the thought of actually doing it made me want to curl up in a fetal position in the corner.

I went up to bed before Finn and his parents. They had me sleep in Caitlin's room. I wasn't sure that was such a great plan, given her reaction to me, not that I was sure I even wanted to sleep in the same bed I had been confined to earlier.

As soon as I closed the bedroom door, I went over to the gruesome action figures, intending to cover them up with my shirt. Once there, however, a morbid sense of curiosity came over me. They were worse than I had been able to see. Nearly every one was covered in blood. Most had arms and legs missing. It appeared that most of this mutilation had been done after they were made. I could see knife marks where their limbs had been removed. The blood looked like red paint, or possibly nail polish. The thought of Caitlin's enjoyment of torturing her little monsters was more disturbing than the actual toy abominations themselves.

I lay in bed wide-awake, my mind torn in a million directions. I wanted to fight the idea of being a demon, the idea that there were actual demons at all, not to mention witches and vampires. I couldn't argue with it, though. In a bizarre way, it made too much sense.

It was the notion of being adopted that finally made things click into place. It would explain why my grandfather was so distant and why he was so quick to disown me at the end. I was never a part of him. I was sure he resented having to spend money on food and clothing for a child that wasn't his blood when he could have been putting more into savings. I guess it showed how loving my grandmother truly was. She never treated me as anything other than her own, at least until she was forced to choose, her husband and church or her grandson.

But if they weren't my grandparents, then where had I come from? Was the beautiful girl in the picture really my mother? Maybe they had adopted her as well. Maybe she had been made up from some old pictures they had found somewhere to make me feel like I had a mother.

I dismissed that notion before it was fully formed. She had been real, and she had been their child. The pain my grandmother felt and the anger of my grandfather were genuine. Those hadn't been for show. Maybe they had adopted me from someone once their daughter ran away—replacing one child with another. If so, where would they have found a demon baby?

Several times that night, I got out of bed, stood naked in front of the dresser mirror, and inspected every part of me. Nothing looked different than it had the day before. There were a couple of bruises here and there, but those were from the vampire, I was sure. They were already going away. I had always been a quick healer. Even the bite marks on my neck were starting to fade. Quick healing. One more demonic sign? What other things that I'd always taken for granted would be signs of my demon heritage? Other than healing remarkably fast, I found nothing else unusual. Every part of me looked human. Even my size. Sure I was a big guy, tall, tons of muscles, but I had seen plenty of guys just as big dancing at the gay clubs.

It did seem to explain several things, like why I was never cold, maybe even why I could eat whatever I wanted and never gain weight, why I never had to work out to maintain my muscles.

The fire had come from me when I was under the water. I felt some semblance of relief that I hadn't been going crazy. It didn't explain what was in the water with me, however. Were there water demons? Had the vampire been stalking me? Could they even swim? I told myself to remember to ask Finn when we got up the next day. It even explained how I nearly boiled that boy at the beach, although I didn't understand what any of this had to do with nearly drowning him.

I seemed to have more questions than answers when I finally dozed off a little before dawn.

"GOOD morning!"

I groaned.

"Brett! Good morning! You awake? It's almost ten."

Resentfully, I opened my eyes. I blinked several times at the shirtless man standing above me. "Huh?"

"Time to get up."

"Oh, right." I huffed. "I almost forgot where I was." I rubbed my eyes roughly and then got a closer view of him. "Wow. You look good." In my head I could hear Sonia laughing at me—even vampires and demons couldn't keep me from flirting. Apparently, a few hours of sleep had me feeling back to normal. Relatively.

Finn took a step back, his face flushing pink. He had on a pair of low-slung yellow sweatpants. His hands came up to cover his hard little belly, causing his chest and shoulder muscles to ripple. "Hard to keep this off when you work at a bakery."

"Nah, keep it. It suits you." I stifled a yawn. "You work at a bakery?" He looked more like a firefighter or construction worker than a baker.

"Yeah, it's my mom's shop. I do most of the baking." He took a step closer to the door. "I've got breakfast going downstairs, if you want some."

"Sure, be right there." I gestured toward the floor. "Would you hand me my jeans?"

His face managed to turn a darker shade of red as he bent down and picked them up. His gaze stayed on the floor as he handed them to me and quickly left the room.

I chuckled to myself as I got out of bed and slipped into the jeans. I was feeling surprisingly cheerful this morning, all things considered. Maybe being a demon was going to be a good thing after all.

Finn had bacon, scrambled eggs, and a pan of huge cinnamon rolls out on the table when I walked down the stairs.

"Apple or grapefruit juice?"

"Apple. Thanks."

He set the juice in front of the plate closest to where I was standing. "Well, have a seat. Don't want the rolls to get cold." He'd put on a white sleeveless shirt, highlighting the gold of his skin. Maybe I'd teased him too much.

I sat down in the chair, intending to apologize for being so forward with him in the bedroom, but he spoke up before I could begin.

"I'm really sorry about last night. All of it, Caitlin, my mom keeping you under a spell, even Cynthia acting so weird. And I'm sorry I got a little freaked out after you didn't get burned by the fire."

I shrugged. "Whatever. You pretty much saved my life last night. I'd say you're entitled to be freaked out. I sure was."

He plopped the center roll onto my plate. "*Was?*"

"Yeah. I mean, I still don't really get it, and I imagine there's a lot I don't know, but I think I'm okay. It kinda explains some stuff, ya know?"

"Sure." He sounded unconvinced. He changed the subject. "So, what are you wanting to do today? Do you want me to take you back to San Diego, or do you think you need to stay here for a while longer? My folks said to tell you that you are more than welcome." He blushed again. "You can always stay at my place for a bit too, if you need."

"Thanks, I might. I'm not really sure what the smartest thing to do right now would be. I should call Sonia and make sure that.... Wait. Did you say take me *back* to San Diego? We're not in San Diego right now?"

He shook his head, his mouth full of food.

"Where are we?" I didn't much care for the panicked sound in my voice. Maybe I wasn't quite as okay with everything as I thought I was.

Finn swallowed. "Encinitas, it's only about half an hour away."

I nodded. Encinitas was just a few miles north of San Diego, but I hadn't spent much time there. "You scared me there for a second. Thought I had been kidnapped."

Finn grinned. "I thought about taking you to Kansas, but figured you'd probably rather take your chances with a vampire."

My throat constricted at the thought of the vampire, but I forced myself to laugh. "You are correct, sir. Still, I don't know what the point of me staying up here would be. I should probably get home and get out of your way. I've already caused your family enough stress."

"It's not a problem, really. Caitlin's always like that, and Cynthia has a hard enough time getting her nerve up to take people's orders at the bakery. You might as well stay." He added hastily, "In case you have any more questions, or something."

I smiled at him. "Cynthia works at the bakery too?"

"Yeah, we're all pretty close." He poured some more juice into my glass. "So, who's Sonia?"

I raised an eyebrow at him, tearing my gaze from his flexing triceps as he moved to set the pitcher back on the table. "Hmm?"

"You mentioned calling someone named Sonia. Is she your girlfriend or something?" His voice went up hopefully. "Your *sister*?"

A laugh escaped even as I tried to hold it in. "What! You think your brother-in-law not only set you up with a demon but some straight boy on the down low?"

He grinned sheepishly. "Well, you never know…."

"Breathe easy there, Finn. Sonia is my roommate. My best friend."

His face continued to redden as he simply nodded. His gaze returned to his plate.

We fell into silence, simply enjoying the food. It was wonderful. I wasn't sure if I was that hungry from the night before or if Finn was that good of a cook, but either way, I was beginning to feel downright happy. Which, actually, made me a little nervous, all things considered.

After several minutes, I caught Finn staring at me, his fork suspended in midair. "What? What is it?" I asked, expecting some type of flirty comment.

"Oh, sorry. I wasn't trying to stare. It's just…." He put his fork down and leaned forward. "It's just that I can't get over it. You are so obviously demon that I can't figure out how I missed it to begin with, or how Ricardo and Christina missed it all those times you were in their restaurant."

I wasn't sure if this was a compliment about my appearance or not. "You mean because of how I look."

Finn tilted his head. "Yeah, that for sure, but more than that. Everything, really. How smoothly you move, how perfect your posture is, everything. Human, but a hundred times human." His voice turned questioning. "But yet…."

"Yet what?"

He let out a breath and leaned even closer. "Yet, you are too much demon, nearly completely different from us, but you're not trying to kill us. You're even pleasant and nice."

"You're making me sound like some kind of animal you expected to kill you but turned out to be a puppy."

He shook his head. "No, nothing like that. I'm sorry. I forget you don't know anything about this. We're part demon too."

I felt my eyes widen. "Who?"

"All of us. Witches."

I felt a little flash of anger. "Then why all the theatrics last night? Your sister was ready to kill me."

He put out a hand to slow me down. "Not like that. It's like comparing a Neanderthal with a modern man. They're the same, but two different species."

"I have no idea what you're talking about."

"It's like this." He took a deep breath. "We, witches, all descended from demons, but we're talking a *minimum* of twenty or thirty generations ago. We're not really even comparable. It's how pure our blood is that determines the amount and type of power we have, but no matter how diluted our blood becomes, we still are demons in the purely technical sense."

I squinted my eyes and shook my head. "I still don't get the difference."

"Brett, demons are like minigods, terrible gods. Nearly indestructible. In fact, the only thing that can kill a demon is another demon, or an angel, but same thing, really."

"Wait, what? Demons and angels are the same thing?" A flash of Grandma telling me that the angels watched out for me when I was a kid went through my mind. "There are real angels too?"

"Demons are so violent," he continued, waving off my question. "Pure evil. They like nothing more than the torment of others. That's especially true of demons with the power of fire. They tend to be the most vicious—not that there's really a harmless pussycat in the bunch."

The good feeling I'd had when I woke up was quickly going away. "Okay, so what does this have to do with me—you were saying that I'm too much demon?"

"Well, it's obvious you aren't very far removed, generationally speaking, from a demon. Everything about you. Caitlin's fire didn't touch you at all. Even a demon many generations removed wouldn't get seriously hurt by someone else's fire, but they would have some type of injury, even if it was only their hair that got burned. But with you, nothing happened. I don't even think you noticed you were on fire."

I just looked at him, feeling sick to my stomach.

"But you're not dangerous, or at least not homicidal."

"Oh wow, thanks! I'll put that on my resume for my next job, 'not homicidal, I won't eat the customers'!"

"Brett, I didn't mean it like that. It's just that you shouldn't be able to control your bloodlust if you were only a few generations removed from your demon ancestor. And you don't seem to be very far removed. But here you are, as cordial and human-acting as any witch or warlock I have ever met. I'm blown away by you, that's all. I can't figure you out."

I didn't know what to say, so I focused my eyes on my plate and began to shovel in the remainder of the food.

CHAPTER NINE

WE HADN'T been in the car for more than five minutes when Finn put on his blinker and took a right turn into the parking lot of a strip mall.

"Here we are!" he announced, flourishing his hand toward a row of indistinguishable stores.

"Wow, that was fast. You live on the same street as your job?"

"No. *I* live several blocks over, but Mom and Dad have always lived on Encinitas Boulevard. They bought this place in the early eighties, before I was born. Wanted to be close to home in case something happened with one of us kids. Don't know why they worried about it. We were never home by ourselves. They put us to work as soon as we could walk."

I looked sideways at him as he pulled into the parking space farthest away from the shops. "You've worked at the bakery all your life?"

He shrugged. "Yeah, from time to time I would help Dad at his store, but mostly I stayed at the bakery. Besides, the bakery has a backroom they turned into our playroom and classroom, so it was more fun there, more toys." He turned off the ignition.

"You went to school at the *bakery*?" I asked, incredulous.

"We were homeschooled." He took in the bewildered look on my face. "What? Did you ever see any little kids in your school levitating their pencils across the classroom or juggling fireballs? All witch kids get homeschooled. We can't take the risk of a kid who's not in control of their powers accidentally using magic in public. There's not a big castle away from the rest of the world to go to school like in *Harry Potter*. Although that really would have been great."

"So you never went to school?" I guess I sounded rather daft, but I was having a hard time picturing Finn as the product of homeschooling. I'd always pictured them as freaks who couldn't fit in a normal society. However, on second thought, maybe that's exactly what Finn was, as well as myself. I just hadn't realized it. Demon blood? Sounds a lot more freakish than being homeschooled.

Finn's eyebrows creased in an expression of annoyance. "You make it sound so weird. Lots of people are homeschooled. Besides, many witch kids go to public education when they enter high school. By that time, most of us have a handle on how to control and hide our powers." He shrugged again. "I didn't want to. I waited and went to culinary school for college, focusing on pastries, of course."

"I'm sorry, Finn. You surprised me. You just seem so normal. I never expected that."

Finn only looked at me. Stared at me, actually, and for a second, I started to feel uncomfortable with the intensity of his gaze. Suddenly, I was aware of the seat belt beginning to grow tighter across my lap and chest. I glanced down. The black vinyl was slowing snaking its way across my lap, through the locking clasp, up over my stomach and chest, and disappearing deeper into its slot on the car wall. Almost instantaneously, the pressure began to make it hard to breathe. I wrapped my hands around the seat belt at my chest and pulled it away from my body. It continued to slide slowly through my fingers. I clenched my fists tighter and pulled with all my might. The seat belt quit moving but refused to give any slack. I looked back over to Finn to ask for help, but he was still staring at me.

After another couple of seconds of my muscles burning with the strain of holding the seat belt still, Finn blinked and a half grin cut across his face. "Oh, I'm not normal, Brett. Don't kid yourself about that." He winked at me, his cheerful mood returning. I heard the click as the seat belt came unfastened, and my arms flew forward as the pressure vanished, retracting the excess out of its compartment in the wall. Finn chuckled.

I wasn't sure I found the situation so humorous.

Once the seat belt was safely back where it should be, we got out of the car and started walking toward the strip mall.

Maybe I shouldn't have taken Finn's offer to stay with his family longer. After breakfast, I had hopped in the shower in Caitlin's room and put on the clothes I had worn the day before—Paulette had washed, dried, and folded them while I'd been asleep. While I had been getting ready, Sonia had sent a text saying that she was going to spend the morning at Derek's before reporting for her shift that afternoon and that she'd tell me all the details when she got off work. Since she was busy and I wasn't really sure what I was going to tell her, if anything, when I saw her next anyway, I decided I would spend the day with Finn and his family. Maybe try to figure out some more of what all this meant.

I was starting to reconsider, however. My emotions kept flip-flopping. One moment, I was fine with all the changes that were going on, and they felt welcome and right. The next I was being suffocated by a seat belt and reminded there was a whole other world I wasn't aware of, even though I was part of it. Maybe it would be a better idea to go home, try to forget it all, and hope that this new world would stay as oblivious to me as I had been of it.

"You've got to try one of my mom's shredded chicken and spinach empanadas. They're her specialty."

Finn's voice brought me back to the moment, and I tried to focus on him and shake off the feeling of anxiety that was starting to build. "Ah, yeah, sure. That sounds good."

We were only a few feet from Finn's car, but he stopped and tentatively touched my arm. "Brett, I'm sorry about the seat belt. I was trying to be funny. I wasn't trying to freak you out. It's not like I've ever talked about any of this stuff to someone who wasn't already a part of it."

"It's okay. I don't know... it's just a lot to take in." I resumed walking. "I'm fine."

Finn took a couple of quick steps to catch up with my larger strides. "Well, I am sorry. I'll warn you before I do something like that again." His voice sounded guilty, which annoyingly sparked the same emotion in me for making him feel that way.

"So which are your mom's and dad's shops?" There were probably ten to twelve little stores, each one connected, making a wall of glass that stretched the entire block, each with a lit-up marquee-style sign on top with writing in black letters, save one.

Finn pointed to the middle of the stores. "The one on the right is my mom's, obviously, and the one on the left is Dad's."

Now that I looked closer, it was obvious which stores they were. Their signs were the only ones in Spanish. "So, Panaderia is your mom's store?"

Finn suddenly grinned again, making me feel a little better. "You don't speak Spanish at all, do you?"

I shook my head.

"You really are a gringo. You don't know about witches or demons, and you don't know Spanish. I thought *I* was sheltered!" He pointed to the sign on the right and then to the one directly to the left. "Mom and Dad are both pretty literal, I guess. Panaderia means 'bakery,' and Dad's store, Mascarada, means 'masquerade.'"

"Masquerade? Your dad has a party store?"

Finn laughed again. "Not exactly. It's a costume shop, where you can rent outfits for Halloween or special events, that kind of stuff."

Before I could respond, he pointed to the store next to Mascarada, the only store with a different style sign. This one said "The Lair" in bright red neon. "That's Caitlin's store. The candle shop that was next to Dad's went out of business a couple of years ago, and Caitlin took over the lease."

It was only then I noticed that the windows under the sign were painted black. From the little I had seen of Caitlin last night, and from what I had guessed about her from the toys in her room, none of this surprised me. "What's The Lair? An S and M shop?"

Finn chuckled. "Good guess, but Caitlin's not quite as literal as Mom and Dad. It caters to the goth, drag, and cross-dressing communities. Lots of clothes and jewelry and makeup, that kind of thing. She's also a makeup artist, and she operates her business out of there."

Before I could ask what kind of makeup he meant (I couldn't quite picture Caitlin selling Mary Kay), we had reached the doors of the bakery. The bell chimed as Finn opened the door, and I followed him through.

As soon as I stepped into the shop, I heard a gasp and a metallic crash. I glanced over just in time to see Cynthia flush crimson before she whirled around—her long hair flying as she escaped through a doorway behind the counter.

Less than a second later, Paulette rushed into the bakery through the same door Cynthia had used to make her getaway. "What in the world, Cynthia? I swear you get more...." She glanced down at her feet, and the volume of her voice rose about three octaves. "You dropped the pan dulce all over the floor! The whole tray is ruined! I spent all morning working on that dough, and now...." She glanced up and saw Finn and me in the doorway. "Oh," she murmured. "Brett's here. Why *wouldn't* you drop all my sweet breads on the floor?" She let out a stream of breath from her nose, wiped her hands on the front of her apron, and curved her lips into a smile. "Good morning, boys. It's about time you two got out of bed."

"Long night, Mom."

"Well, you weren't the only one up half the night, but somehow I managed to get here at four to prepare for the morning rush *and* the lunch crowd."

"Sorry, Mom."

Pausing, I inspected the shop. Everything was white—the walls, the countertops, the tables. The space was small and bright enough that it managed to look cheerful and clean instead of institutional, as it easily could have. Of course the smell and sight of the huge case full of row after row of assorted pastries, most of which I had never seen before, gave the space an automatic homey feel.

Paulette came around the counter and gave her son a quick squeeze and a peck on the cheek. She eyed me hesitantly for a second and then seemingly made up her mind. She reached up and wrapped me in a firm hug. "Good morning, Brett. I hope you slept well."

"I did, thank you, Mrs. de Morisco."

"Good gracious, boy. Call me Paulette. I held you captive on a bed for hours. I think we can move past formalities at this point." After giving my cheek two swift pats, she moved back behind the counter and began picking up the spilled pastries as she continued speaking. "You'll have to forgive Cynthia. She's always been a bit... fragile, but it's been worse the past several years. She seems to be near a nervous breakdown at the moment, even more than usual."

She turned her attention back to me. "Did you get breakfast, dear? Feel free to pick out anything that appeals to you. You don't even have to choose something off the floor."

"Oh no. Finn made cinnamon rolls this morning. They might have been the best I've ever had."

Paulette raised an eyebrow at her son. "So you have the energy to get up and make rolls for the good-looking demon boy, but not for your loyal customers who depend on you every morning, do you?"

Finn just groaned and continued sweeping.

I felt my eyes go wide at my newly acquired nickname. I hoped that was a good sign.

Paulette gestured toward a nearly empty glass counter on the other side of the cash register. "Every morning, Finn fills it with cinnamon rolls and croissants, and ham and cheese rolls at noon. None of which customers were able to purchase today." Her voice rose again, this time more in gentle teasing than in anger. "And I suppose that there won't be any fruit tarts or marzipan chocolates for this evening's customers either, will there?"

"Probably not, Mom."

"Just as I supposed."

He grinned at his mother. "Besides, you are always complaining how my creations aren't staying true to our culture."

Paulette scoffed. "Well, you have to do something to pay off the loans from that fancy New York pastry school."

It was my turn to raise an eyebrow at Finn. "You went to culinary school in New York?"

"I told you I went to public school for college."

"Yeah, but *New York*?" I had never even been out of San Diego.

"Never mind the mess." Paulette took the broom and dustpan from her son. "I'll make Cynthia clean it up, if I can get her to stop shaking. Take Brett over to see your dad's shop, and let me get back to work. And don't go through the back door in the kitchen. I'm sure if you run into Cynthia, it will be the last we'll see of her for a week."

"Okay, okay. Hold on." He reached into the glass case and pulled out a huge golden brown turnover. "First, I promised Brett one of your chicken and spinach empanadas."

CHAPTER TEN

MASCARADA was as overflowing with stuff as Panaderia had been absent of clutter. As we entered to the familiar door chime, I could hear Finn's dad shout out a welcome from somewhere in the back, assuming we were customers. The lighting was dim, and there was a musty smell I couldn't place. I couldn't even see the back of the store—it was like entering a maze. Werewolf, zombie, and dead-president masks hung from the ceiling. Wigs, makeup, and fake blood overflowed from haphazardly placed cabinets and display cases. Styrofoam tombstones and cauldrons littered the floor. Here and there the path trailed off to another gruesome section. If Finn hadn't told me it was a costume shop, I would have assumed we had entered a haunted house in the midst of getting ready for Halloween night.

I turned to Finn. "This is your *dad's* store?" It was hard to picture Wendell, who had seemed so quietly analytical the night before, responsible for such a conglomeration of gruesome items.

"Yep. He loves it. It's like his playground." He pointed to one of the trails that seemed to shoot off toward the right. "That way leads to the back, to the costume area, which is where Dad spends most of his time."

"This isn't the costume area?"

"Nah, this is just stuff for Halloween and gag-gift kind of things. It's crazy busy during October, but doesn't do much the rest of the year. The costume shop is where most of the business comes from."

The store seemed to be overly crowded with things that would only sell once a year, but I didn't say anything and started heading down the path he had indicated.

I hadn't gone ten steps when a black object came flying at me out of a cluster of clown masks hanging from the ceiling. I let out a yelp and jumped back with my hands in front of my face.

From behind, I heard Finn burst out in laughter.

I turned around and glared at him. "I thought you said you were going to warn me the next time you used your powers on me."

Finn wiped at his eyes. "I didn't use any powers. That's straight from the Frightmare Production Company."

I returned my attention to the thing now suspended in air, blocking my path. I stepped forward, embarrassingly cautious, and gave it a closer inspection. It was just a black cape. A cheap plastic skeleton gazed blankly back at me as I peered under its hood. Standing in front of it, it was easy to see it was simply impaled on a rod that was hinged to something behind all the clutter.

Finn was still laughing, although not quite to such a ridiculous degree. "Last year, we had a guy in here. He was just a little bit smaller than you, actually. He screamed higher than any girl ever has. After jumping back about twenty feet, he reached out and snapped the thing right in half. Took Dad three months to get another one in. He thought it was the funniest thing he had ever seen."

"Seems like a good way to scare off your customers."

"Nah. People get a kick out of it. Anyway, most of the people who come back every year remember it's there. They enjoy it as much as Dad when a newbie happens to wander by." He reached past me and pushed the skeleton by the rib cage until there was a slight click, and it was safely hidden behind the masks once again.

"Ya know, I've kinda had a rough day or so. You think you might be a little gentler with your humor?"

He reached out and patted my chest, leaving his hand there briefly as he gazed into my eyes. "Come on now. You're a big boy. You can handle it." He turned abruptly. "This way."

I followed Finn down the winding path, which seemed to go on longer than I would have thought possible. The store was a lot bigger than it appeared from the outside, much bigger than the bakery had been. The farther in we went, the less gruesome the merchandise. Plastic scythes and swords gave way to fairy wings, wands, and wigs with long strands of what looked like Easter basket grass intermingled in the curls.

Abruptly, we came to an arched doorway with blocks painted around it, making it seem like an entrance to a castle. As we stepped through, everything changed. Every wall space was covered in mirrors, the lighting was bright, and the ceiling was painted soft purplish-gray. From wall to wall, the room had row after row of costumes. Above each aisle hung signs labeling what you would find there: Medieval, Shakespearean, Roaring Twenties, Fairy Tale, Rock Star. It seemed that every possible time period and theme was accounted for. I felt my jaw go slack in amazement. "Did you guys use magic to make this place fit in here?"

Finn rolled his eyes. "We are capable of doing things without magic, you know, and don't let Mom hear you say *magic*, or you'll get 'the m-word lecture' again." He made quotation marks with his fingers. "The store makes an L shape. This section is directly behind the bakery, which didn't need as much space, so Dad remodeled." He smirked at me. "Using hammer and nails, *not* by wiggling his nose." He gave me a crooked grin. "At least not entirely."

"Well, hi, boys!" Wendell stepped out from one of the aisles behind me, causing me to flinch. I never used to be so jumpy. I was going to have to get a hold of myself. "Sorry, there, Brett, wasn't trying to startle you."

"It's okay, Mr. de...." He gave me a look, and I faltered momentarily. "Sorry... Wendell. It seems I'm a little bit on edge."

"Finding out you're a demon can do that to a man, I imagine."

It seemed to me they were all a little too casual using the word *demon* so often. I glanced around. I hadn't noticed any customers, but they would have been easy to overlook in such a place.

"Don't worry yourself about that. There's nobody here right now. The beginning of summer is always slow. Gives me a chance to get everything back in order."

"Are most of your customers other witches and warlocks?" That would explain his seeming lack of concern for other people hearing.

"Oh no, not all. Most of my business is through schools and small theater companies needing costumes and props for their productions. Although, since Caitlin's started making a name for herself as a crackerjack makeup artist, there have been a few independent film-type people come in and get stuff for their movies."

I couldn't help but be impressed. "Really? They rent your stuff for movies?"

Wendell swelled nearly imperceptibly with pride as he answered. "Well, not very many, and none you have seen, I would imagine. They're all low-budget kind of deals. Are you into horror movies?"

"No, not really."

"Ah, that's too bad." He looked somewhat deflated as he gave up hope of listing off a movie I might have seen. "Caitlin specializes in wounds and creating monsters with makeup and prosthetics. So far, those are the only movie people that have been in." He held up his hand and crossed his fingers. "But let's keep hoping some of the others hear about us. That'd be quite a break."

I could see what Finn had meant. His dad's face lit up as he talked, and his eyes gazed far away as he envisioned outfitting a major motion picture. Finn caught my eye and grinned as he waved a hand playfully in front of his dad's face. "Dad. Earth to Dad."

Wendell gave himself a little shake. "Oh, sorry. What can I do for you boys?"

"I wanted to show Brett around. I didn't think it was a good idea for him to be by himself today."

His dad nodded. "Smart. You don't want to leave him alone in case the vampire comes back."

I stiffened. "What? You think he's coming back?"

Finn cut in. "I just meant that Brett's been through a lot finding out about all this and thought he might need some time to adjust to being part demon."

Wendell's face reddened. "Oh sure, of course. That makes sense."

I held up a hand. "Hold on. Why do you think he's coming back? Is that how vampires are—once they take a drink of somebody, they don't leave them alone until they kill them?" The thought shouldn't have surprised me. Why hadn't I even considered that?

For a moment, Wendell seemed at a loss for words, but then started, "Well, not necessarily. You see, it depends on which type of—"

From a distance, a chime interrupted, causing all three of us to freeze. Had the vampire followed me here? My eyes flitted between Finn and Wendell, trying to judge their reaction. Then I realized it was daytime. I didn't need to be worried. Yet.

"Dad?" Like the bell, the voice was far away. "Are you in the back? I ran out of latex sponges. Do you have any?"

Finn and his dad let out sighs of relief simultaneously. Wendell grimaced. "What's wrong with me? It seems you're not the only one who's jumpy, Brett. Come on, boys." He motioned for us to follow him as he shouted out. "On my way!"

As we made our way back toward the front of the store, Finn whispered, "It's just Caitlin. Maybe it would have been better if it had been the vampire."

I almost stayed behind but took a look at the endless rows of costumes. Despite myself, I couldn't help imagining the vampire lurking behind each one, and decided to take my chances with Caitlin. Within a couple of steps, I had caught up with Finn and his dad. Along the way back through the Halloween portion, we took a turn and ended up in a section of vintage Hollywood monster masks I hadn't noticed before. As we rounded the next corner, I saw Caitlin, the red streak in her hair even more spiky than it had been last night. She stood at the counter beside the cash register.

She had started to speak to her father when she noticed me. Her eyes narrowed. "What's he doing here?" Her voice was a growl.

"Don't be rude, Cate." Wendell's voice was firm. "Brett is our guest. He's welcome here."

Her lip rose in a snarl. "Since when did this family become demon lovers?"

"Cate, really, that's enough."

She turned to Wendell, her face softening. "Seriously, Dad! This is insanity. He's going to get the whole family killed."

"We covered this last night. If Brett were a typical evil demon, we would all be dead already." Finn's smooth face creased in anger.

"God, Caitlin, you need to get a girlfriend already. It's been too long since you got laid."

Her snarl returned as she addressed her brother. "Shut up, Finn. Mind your own business. You know that's not what I was talking about. The big oaf is obviously about as dangerous as a defanged poodle."

I knew I should have been offended, but it didn't really seem worth the effort. I stepped around Finn and stood in front of her. "Do you mean the vampire?"

She craned her head up to gape at me, her face showing surprise at me speaking to her. Her narrowed eyes shot back and forth rapidly, searching my face, as if realizing for the first time that there was an actual person in front of her, not just some thing that was causing her a nuisance. Gradually, the corners of her mouth relaxed, and she spoke with a gentler tone, but her eyes stayed hard. "Yes. I mean the vampire. Or vampires."

"*Vampires*? Plural?" Once again, I was embarrassed by my simplicity. I hadn't thought in terms of multiple vampires being after me. It had been bad enough to consider the one in the alley.

Finn reached out and turned his sister toward him. "Come on, Caitlin, do we really need to do this?"

"You weren't going to tell him?" She snorted. "I thought I was the one who was being rude to him."

I looked away from her toward Finn. "Tell me what?"

Finn sighed and slowly forced himself to meet my gaze. "I hoped you wouldn't need to know." He glared at his sister. "I still do, but it seems that's not going to be an option any longer."

"What? Just tell me already."

Wendell interrupted. "Brett, the deal is"—he gave me a rather helpless expression—"we don't know which type of vampire attacked you."

I stared at him, confused. "Which type? How many types of vampires can there be?"

"Two. Just two."

Just two. Like one wasn't enough. My brain seemed to stop functioning. I was sure I should ask something, but I didn't understand enough to even form a question.

I felt a squeeze on my hand. I glanced down. Finn's hand had found mine. He pulled it a little closer to himself. At any other time, I would have felt pleased by the gesture.

"Brett, I'm sorry. Maybe I should have told you this morning, but I didn't want to worry you. We don't know what kind it is, so I didn't think I needed to give you anything else to stress over until we knew for sure."

"Which is why I wanted to call the Vampire Cathedral last night. If they were in charge, then we could have turned him in and been done with it." Caitlin's last words tapered off until they were almost imperceptible. She glanced up at me and then away quickly. "Sorry, but it's what needs to be done." She actually did look sorry.

Finn's grip tightened as he turned on his sister. "How evil can you be? You want to turn him over, just let them take him? Let them kill him?"

Caitlin's voice rose again. "And what do you want to do? Keep him as your boyfriend till the whole mess of them shows up and kills us all? Either way the end is the same. The only question is if we get to live or not."

I pulled my hand free of Finn's and stepped closer to Caitlin once more. "Tell me. What are the two types of vampires? Why am I dead either way?"

Again she seemed surprised to see a person, demon or not, in front of her. For the fist time, she didn't have anything to say. She cast her gaze down at the floor, flushing.

I waited for a few seconds, staring at her. Finally I gave up and turned to Finn and his dad. "Well?" I was pleasantly surprised to hear my voice sound firm. Everyone talking in circles was starting to irritate me "You might as well just tell me and get it over with. I want to know what I'm up against." I glanced at Caitlin and then back. "Whether or not you turn me over to the Vampire Cathedral."

Finn sighed. "We're not going to turn you over to the Vampire Cathedral. You don't need to worry about that."

"Either way, I need to know."

Wendell interrupted, "Why don't we go over to Paulette's? We can sit down and talk it over with some coffee and pastries."

I shook my head firmly. "Just tell me."

The three of them stared at the ground, each other, the Halloween crap around us, everywhere but at me. Less than a minute ago, Caitlin had been ready to turn me over to die, and now she couldn't even look at me. I felt my face flush as I began to get more agitated. "Finn!"

He gazed up at me, his eyes wary.

"Tell me about the two types of vampires. Which one do you think attacked me last night?"

He nodded. "Fine, but I still say you don't need to worry about it until we know for sure. I guarantee you. It was just your run of the mill solitary vampire. Nothing to worry about."

Caitlin's voice rose once more. "You don't know that."

Finn ignored her, holding my eyes with his. "Most vampires are like stray dogs. They wander around by themselves, never staying in one place too long, and taking a meal from wherever they can find it. They are pretty much like what you would have seen in movies: only come out at night, sleep during the day, not thinking about much more than drinking people's blood, and always on the lookout for the next source. It's not going to be a big deal. From what I've been told, most of the time they are gone before you can even track them down. They're not gonna care if they only ate someone halfway. They will just move on to the next person in line."

Out of the corner of my eye, I saw Caitlin open her mouth to argue, but Wendell reached out and put his hand over hers, silencing her.

"So, if this thing that bit me is one of those, you think he will just let it go and forget about me?" I wanted to feel hopeful, wanted this to be the case so I could move on with my life. Forget about vampires, forget about demons.

Finn shrugged. "If that's the kind of vampire he is, then yeah, he probably will. Although he may hold a grudge for burning him. They have a propensity for vengeance."

Caitlin spoke up, ignoring her father's protests. "And if he isn't a *typical* vampire? What then?"

"Really, Caitlin, do you think the Vampire Cathedral is going to send one lowly vampire out to kill the offspring of some demon? They're not that careless. If it had been them, Brett wouldn't have gotten away, and I probably wouldn't be alive today either."

I broke in before they could continue. "So if one kind is just a *regular* vampire, whatever that is, then what's the other kind?"

It was Wendell's turn to play teacher. "You see, Brett, that's a little harder to explain, at least to someone who wasn't really aware of other races besides human." He reached over and pulled a pair of fake fangs out of the box of novelty items by the cash register and began turning them over with his fingers. Abruptly, he realized what he was doing, tossed them over to the side, and then leaned his elbows on the glass counter. "The other type of vampires are the royal family...."

I couldn't stop myself. As soon as he said "royal family," I let out a loud belch of a laugh. "The royal family? Are you kidding me? I think I would have noticed if it had been Prince Charles or Queen Elizabeth who had attacked me last night."

Wendell's eyebrows creased in confusion.

"Not that royal family, Brett," Finn interjected, "*our* royal family."

"You guys have a royal family?"

Catching on, Wendell let out a little chuckle, which quickly fell flat. "The royal family is what everyone calls them. Actually, they are just called the Royals. Who knows what they actually call themselves, if anything. They are the self-proclaimed rulers of our kind."

"Your kind? You mean witches and warlocks?"

He nodded. "Yes, but not just us, all of the nonhuman races."

I let that sink in for a moment and then involuntarily lowered my voice. "You mean there are more out there than witches, demons, and vampires?"

This time, Wendell did laugh. "My goodness, boy, yes! I forget that you really know nothing of the world that you live in. There are werewolves, fairies, nymphs—"

I held up both my hands. "There are werewolves?"

"Of course there are werewolves, not to mention—"

"Stop! Please. It's too much. I don't think I need the entire list of what's out there." I kept feeling that nothing new could surprise me, but every few moments, there was something I never really dreamed existed. Surely there had to be some way to rewind to yesterday, never give into my craving for Mexican food, never go to Old Town, never follow some stranger into an alley. While I was at it, even go back far enough to never have taken that boy to the beach.

By Caitlin's demeanor, whatever pity for me she might have been feeling had washed away, and she was back to seeing me as the thorn in her family's side. "We're getting a little off track here. Do you wanna know about the Royals or not?"

I nodded.

"Fine. Here's the down-and-dirty, then. The Royals don't have to sleep all day like their disgusting little cousins. They can walk around in the daytime and not get so much as a sunburn. They're also stronger than most regular vampires, which shouldn't even be feasible, and they never do anything alone. Which means, if you were attacked by a Royal last night, then there has to be another, or several, around."

I started to ask a question, but she cut me off with a wave of her hand.

"And if they were Royals, then they won't give up. They will hunt you down, leaving no stone unturned, no accomplice unkilled, until you are found. They don't leave loose ends, and they don't change their minds. Which all means that every second you stay here is another second that you are leading them closer and closer to our family and to our deaths."

"Way to be dramatic, Cate. Nothing like overdoing it." Finn gave his sister a look of disgust.

"Say what you want, Finn. You know as well as I do that I'm right."

They continued to bicker back and forth, but I couldn't concentrate on anything they were saying. One second I was picturing an army of werewolves and vampires slowly closing in on us from outside the costume shop, the next I could see myself morphing into my true demon form, whatever that looked like. Then I was back in the alley, the vampire overpowering me, his teeth glinting above me as he started to burn. "Wait!" For a second, I was sure I had found a loophole. "Why would the Royals be after me? I've never done anything to them. I didn't even know they existed. Hell, I didn't even know I existed. At least, not really."

"Unfortunately, that's not all that uncommon." Wendell offered me a sympathetic smile. "Well, it is in your case, since you clearly have a large amount of demon blood in you, but for those who only have trace amounts of other race's blood, they sometimes don't know it either. Many times, they are killed before they know anything."

My heart sank again. "Why? Why are they killed if they don't know anything?"

Finn shrugged once again. "That's why they are called the Royals. Several centuries ago, many centuries ago, actually, the sun-walker vampires, or the Royals as we call them now, went off on a crusade to rid the world of half-breeds. They hunted down werewolves, witches, and any human hybrids that resulted from humans mating with pure bloods—the offspring of fairies, nymphs, demons… really, any combination that you can come up with."

Wendell broke in. "In truth, so much time has passed that it is hard to know what is fact and what is legend, but the end result is the same. Some mixed species were killed off, and others were greatly reduced. Even species that weren't mixed species, but couldn't pass as human, were exterminated as well. Demons' offspring, and thus witches and warlocks, were so numerous that killing them all was too daunting of a task for the Royals, who are relatively small in number. At some point, and there are no real records of when and why, witches were determined to have separated so greatly from their demon ancestors that we had become our own race, a pure race. Obviously, this was just to save face, but nevertheless, here we are."

Finn glared at Caitlin. "Which brings us back to the fact that there is no way the Royals were trying to kill Brett last night. They don't kill half-demons."

She sneered back at him. "If you're so sure about that, then why are you not willing to contact the Vampire Cathedral?"

"Hold on." Although I was on information overload, I thought I was slowly starting to catch on, or at least understand who some of the players were in this fucked-up game. "What's with the Vampire Cathedral? Is it some other type of vampire?"

Wendell spoke before either of his children could respond. "The Vampire Cathedral is where the Royal Family lives. It's some kind of forest in Central America. They have lived there for the past couple of centuries."

I looked at Caitlin. "And you want to call the Vampire Cathedral to check and see if they sent someone after me, right?"

She met my eyes with a steady, unapologetic gaze. "If they didn't, then there's nothing to be worried about."

CHAPTER ELEVEN

THE ride back to San Diego was silent. Finn was still fuming over the argument he and Caitlin had gotten into when she continued to insist they call the Vampire Cathedral. I couldn't tell if he was angrier with his sister or if he was more embarrassed that she might try to turn me in.

For my part, I was lost in my ponderings. If it really was the "Royal Family" after me, how had they discovered what I was when I didn't even know? Maybe what I did to that boy on the beach had somehow alerted them. And how did whatever had been with me in the water the past few weeks correlate to all of this? It was too much to simply be coincidence. Somehow they had to tie together. I doubted there was a scuba diving team of assassin vampires. The thought did cause a brief moment of amusement.

Part of me wondered if Caitlin didn't have the right idea. If they were really after me, I didn't have any chance of actually surviving anyway, especially if they could be out during the day. There would never be a time I was safe. For some reason, the thought of being attacked during the day seemed less frightening. Plus, if I knew they were coming, the whole situation would be a lot less stressful. If it was going to happen anyway, I might as well call them myself and make an appointment. *Excuse me, Vampire Cathedral? Yes, I was wondering if you were trying to kill me, and if so, could you show up around four thirty this afternoon? Just ring the bell and walk on in, the door will be unlocked. If I happen to be in the bathroom, please wait. I won't take long.*

"What's so funny?"

The sound of Finn's voice caused me to stiffen. I glanced over at him in confusion. "What?"

Finn glanced over at me, his eyebrows furrowed in concern, and then he turned back to the interstate. There was never a time when the Five wasn't teaming with traffic. "You were laughing."

"I was?"

"Yeah, although I can't imagine what you could possibly find funny right now, with my bitch of a sister wanting to get you killed." Angry, definitely angry.

I cleared my throat. "Oh, it was nothing. I was just daydreaming." I wondered if he would get mad at me as well if I told him I was beginning to think Caitlin might be right. "Do vampires have to have your permission to come in?"

It was Finn's turn to be confused. "Huh?"

"You know, to come into your house. Like in movies, before the vampire can come in your door, some stupid idiot has to accidentally invite them in."

Finn shook his head. "No, that's only a wives' tale. They can go anywhere they please."

Of course they could. "Do you know much about how the Royal Family kills half-breeds?"

His knuckles turned white as he tightened his grip on the steering wheel. "Not exactly. I know they normally don't fail the first time, and I've never heard of them failing the second. But honestly, most of what I know is stuff from the past that my folks and grandparents would tell us kids. I haven't really ever heard about it happening in my lifetime. Why?"

"I was wondering if him having… if what happened last night was normal. You know, the way he lured me into the alley, and… what he did after."

Finn gave an embarrassed grimace and then shrugged. "I don't know if there is a normal with vampires. They are known to be seductive creatures, so I guess what happened in the alley would fit their standards." His face blossomed to a rosy shade of brown.

"Way to end my five-month dry spell, huh?"

"Dry spell?" He turned to look at me, his face flushing deeper. "You?"

"Yeah, it had been a while." I felt a momentary flash of guilt as an image of the boy standing naked in the waves surfaced in my mind. I forced it away. Nothing had happened. Boiling someone definitely didn't count as sex. "My roommate, Sonia, has been giving me a hard time for being a prude lately."

Finn's right eyebrow rose skeptically, but he didn't object. After a couple of seconds of awkward silence, he turned back to me, his voice sounding a little sheepish. "I don't think getting raped counts as ending a dry spell."

I stared out the windshield, flashes of the night before threatening to take over. "I suppose not. I can't figure out what to think about it. I didn't want it." I whipped toward him, suddenly desperate for him to believe me. "Really. I didn't want to be with him. I tried to fight. I just couldn't. One minute…." My voice was low enough that I wasn't sure he would even be able to hear me. "I've never felt anything like it. It hurt a lot, but… felt good too." I could feel my face start to burn. Once again, images from the alley made their way into my mind, seemingly blocking every other sight from my eyes. His smooth white chest above me. His green eyes locked with mine. The burn of his cold skin. The throb of him inside me. The drafts of my blood leaving me. His release. "I didn't want him, but then I would feel like I did. Like I'd chosen to be with him. Like I wanted to be with him. But I didn't."

Finn took his gaze off the highway. His voice was soft and warm. Somehow he found the balance between being gentle and not offering pity, which I appreciated. "From what I've heard, that's normal. And, as sick as it sounds, kinda lucky. They don't always make it that way, but it helps keep their victims from calling out and drawing attention. If you hadn't been in a public place, he probably wouldn't have made you feel that way. He would have wanted to hear you scream. He would have drawn out the pain." He paused again for so long that I thought he'd finished speaking. He was looking determinedly at the traffic, but his tone was firm. "I'm not trying to assume how you're feeling, but if it were me, I imagine I'd be wondering if some part of me had made it happen or wanted it." Again, he looked at me, his eyes hard and definitive. "Don't let yourself go there. That's part of the evil he did.

Nothing you did caused it or wanted it. You don't have to convince me, or anyone else that knows anything at all about vampires. It's Vampire 101. It's part of their power. Part of their evil."

We drove in silence for several more minutes. There'd been another thought plaguing me, one I'd not even let fully form in my mind. Maybe it was Finn's warm tone that made me feel like I could trust him. Really trust him. Maybe if I didn't say it, I was going to explode. "I've always been careful. Always. Never even slipped up once. I've been too scared to." My eyes burned, and I slammed the lids shut. A tear rolled down my right cheek, luckily on the side Finn couldn't see. "Do you think… is there a chance…." My throat tightened, suffocating my words.

Still keeping his eyes focused in front of him, Finn reached his hand over, placed it on mine, and held it firmly. "No. There's no chance. You're not sick. Vampires are dead, and in some weird way their blood and… everything else, is pure. You're not gonna get an STD."

More tears slid down my face, this time over both cheeks, and fell in hot, heavy drops on my lap. "Even…."

"Even HIV. Nope. As horrible as it was, and as sick as he was, you don't have to worry about any of it."

I tried to nod, and maybe I did. Relief flooded through me, leaving me weak. With all the other mix of emotions around the events, it was strange to add a sense of happiness. I could face the rest. I had to. I didn't know if I'd be able to face being sick. That would have been too much. I had several friends who had the virus, so somewhere deep within me, I knew I would figure out how to deal. But I was so glad I wouldn't have to.

What seemed like centuries later, Finn's voice broke into my thoughts, cutting through the turmoil. "You ready to go? We're almost to the Washington exit. That's how we get to Hillcrest, right?"

Chapter Twelve

"My car!" I smacked my forehead with my palm as we turned onto my street. "I completely forgot!"

"Huh?"

"I left my car in Old Town last night. Actually, I guess you left it there when you loaded me in your truck."

"Oh, of course. That makes sense."

"I'm sorry to ask this, Finn, but could you run me by my car before you go back home?"

He nodded. "Sure. That's easy. Besides, I was kinda hoping that—"

"That's odd." I didn't mean to interrupt him, but Sonia's red Miata in the driveway caught my eye as we got closer to the house. It was well after two, when her shift was supposed to start at the bar.

"What's odd?" Finn glanced around quickly, as if looking for something ominous.

"Just that my roommate must be home, and she should be at work already." I gestured to the car in the driveway. "The restaurant is only a few blocks away, but Sonia *never* walks." I turned my attention back to Finn. "Is it okay to stop and check on her real quick, to make sure she's okay before we go get the car?" Maybe it was the craziness of all the changes happening in my life, but I began to have a sinking feeling. Something felt wrong.

"Yeah, of course. Besides, I'd like to meet her." Finn pulled into the driveway by Sonia's car.

I jumped out before he had time to put it in park, and was already headed toward the door.

"Hey, Brett! Are you okay?" Finn's voice sounded alarmed. I sped up and reached out for the door. I heard the truck door slam and Finn's footsteps running to catch up with me.

As I turned the handle, the door swung open. Unlocked. Sonia never left the door unlocked. "Sonia!" The sound of the fear in my voice only made my panic increase. I rushed into the living room expecting to see furniture scattered all over the floor. Everything was in its place. It didn't look like anyone had been here since I had left yesterday evening.

I tore off through the kitchen and into the hallway. "*Sone!*"

"Good God, Brett, what the hell's the matter?" Sonia popped her head out of the bathroom door, a baby-blue towel wrapped turban-style over her hair and a white one clutched over her breasts.

I was so surprised for her to actually be standing there that I didn't trust what I was seeing. "Sonia?"

A mixture of annoyance and concern flashed across her face. "Brett, I swear this had better be good. You about made me fall in the shower!"

I stood there looking dumbly at her. "I'm sorry. I... I thought, I thought.... You're okay?"

"Of course, I'm okay. You're starting to scare me. Are you okay?"

"Yeah, it was just that the door was unlocked and...."

"I got home from Derek's a few minutes ago. I'm kinda in a rush, and I...." Her eyes widened as her gaze traveled past me.

I whirled around, ready to fight.

Finn held up both hands. "It's me. It's just me."

My fists dropped to my sides, and I let out a groan. "I don't know what is going on with me lately."

Finn gave me a sympathetic smile and then looked at me expectantly for a few seconds. Finally, he rolled his eyes playfully and turned to Sonia. "Hi! I'm Finn, a, uhm, friend of Brett's."

"Oh. *Oh!*" Sonia offered one of her brilliant smiles, readjusted her grip on the towel with her left hand, and shot out her other one in Finn's direction. "Hi, Finn. I'm Sonia." She turned to me and narrowed her eyes before returning to Finn. "If you'll give me a second, I can put on some clothes and come meet you properly."

Finn grinned and nodded. Sonia ducked back into the bathroom and closed the door with a light click.

Finn stood there with his arms crossed and one eyebrow raised—a look I was already beginning to expect from him. I shrugged and shook my head. "I don't know. I had a feeling." I shrugged again. "I have no idea what's going on. I think I should go back to sleep. Maybe I'd somehow wake up and it would be two days ago."

Finn started to nod and then stopped. "Why *two* days ago?"

"Never mind. Sorry for all the dramatics." I walked past him into the kitchen. "I'm starving. Want a sandwich?"

I HAD only taken one bite of my sandwich when Sonia walked into the living room. She was wearing her default outfit: black hooker boots, black miniskirt, white wifebeater, and a black bra showing from underneath. Her long raven hair was still wet and hung in slick tendrils around her, making damp spots all over her wifebeater.

"Wow! Brett didn't tell me you were a model!" From anyone else, it would have seemed like a cheesy line, but the awe in Finn's voice attested to his authenticity.

Sonia beamed and grinned at me. "Oh, I like him. Good choice. I really like him."

I felt my face flush. "So, just getting back from Derek's, huh? That must have been some night."

Her face softened peacefully as she answered. "Yeah, it really was, but not in the way you're thinking. Not in the way I was planning either. Finn here has gotten a better view of the goods than Derek did.

We stayed up all night, driving around the city, and then talking at his place. We went and got lunch, and I lost track of time."

I scoffed. "Seriously?"

"Seriously!" She nodded happily. "I tell you, Brett, I have never felt like this with anyone before. It was sure worth waiting on him getting up his courage to take me out."

"Wow, Sone. That's wonderful! You two will make beautiful part-Chinese babies."

She swatted my arm. "Shut up!" She turned her attention to Finn. "And where did you find this one?"

I started to say "Don't ask," but Finn spoke up quicker. "My sister and her husband own Taberna de las Brujas in Old Town. My brother-in-law set us up last night."

"Oh, I love that place. Ricky is so nice!"

Finn nodded ruefully. "Yeah, everybody says that."

Sonia tossed her hair over her shoulders, spraying little droplets of water around the room. "Well, I hate to have to rush, but I'm already late, so I need to get out of here. Finn, it was really great to meet you. I hope I get the chance again soon." She reached out, offering her hand.

Without missing a beat, Finn bent down and wrapped her in a bear hug. "You too, Sonia. Congratulations on your successful date last night."

"Thank you!" She held his gaze as she pulled away. "I like you already, but if you hurt my man here, I hurt you. Got it?"

Finn chuckled. "Got it."

As Sonia turned and gave me a hug, intentionally whipping her wet hair around on my face, she pulled me close and put her mouth to my ear. "He is beautiful. Good job, sweetheart."

With that, she turned and rushed toward the door. "See you after work, Brett. It's a short shift. Love ya!"

"Love you too, Sone."

CHAPTER THIRTEEN

"So, I was thinking." Finn's voice was tentative. He had been quiet throughout lunch, and even now, he didn't look directly at me, but kept his focus on the plate he was drying. "I already told Mom not to expect me back at the bakery until tomorrow, and since we need to go pick up your car anyway, we might as well hang out for the rest of the day." He rubbed the dishtowel quicker on the already dry plate. "I mean, I'm sure you must have a lot more questions about everything. Unless you have other plans or stuff you need to do."

His nervousness was both endearing and rather off-putting. It felt like weeks had passed since I had woken up in his truck last night. Part of me felt like we had known each other for months. The tension in the room quickly reminded me that, no matter what had happened since we'd met, we'd only known each other less than twenty-four hours. Truth be told, though, I didn't want to spend the afternoon by myself, and I was more than a little okay with being with Finn as long as possible. Although, every time I let myself notice his muscles or his smile, the burned boy's face flashed behind my eyes. The last thing I should do would be to spend more time with Finn.

"Uhm, yeah, that sounds great." I handed him a glass, forcing him to put down the plate. "Did you have something in mind?"

"Not really. You know, get your car, go to a movie, grab some dinner, go to the beach, go swimming, whatever."

I peered at him quizzically. "Swimming? Why swimming?"

The tone of my voice made him glance up from drying the dishes. "Just an idea, I don't actually care what we do. I like the beach, and it's a gorgeous day out. I'm fine with anything."

I felt my eyes narrow. "Can you read… I mean, can witches and warlocks read minds?"

"Yeah, some can. No one in my family. It's not where our strengths lie. Why?"

"I was just wondering. It's funny that you should mention swimming. I love to swim more than about anything, that's all."

Now that we were talking about it, the need to be in the water became almost a physical necessity. My skin felt dry, the air thin and gritty. I hadn't realized it, but I'd not been in the water, except for the few moments searching for my clothes yesterday, and I actually hadn't swum since the day before that. I couldn't even remember the last time I had missed my nightly swim. "Let's go swimming. Right now." I plopped the silverware I was rinsing back into the sudsy water.

"As in now, now?"

"Yeah."

"Don't you want to go get your car first?"

"No, it's fine. We can get it later tonight."

Finn grinned and shook his head, dumbfounded. "Okay, then, let's go now. I haven't been swimming in La Jolla for a long time. Wanna go there?"

At his words, I felt some of the tension loosen from my body. "I haven't been swimming with the seals in La Jolla for weeks! That sounds per…. Oh wait, no. Not there. I have family that lives in La Jolla. My grandmother. With the luck I've had the past couple of days, she'll be sitting there on the shore waiting for me. I don't think I could handle that today." Then another thought hit me. "Plus, I haven't exactly called in to work the past couple of days. Probably shouldn't show up to simply go swimming."

Finn stood there, mouth open, seemingly missing most of what I had said. "Wait, you're telling me that you go swimming with the *seals*? Often?"

I shrugged. "Yeah, sure. They're a lot of fun."

"Wow. That's crazy. They're not scared off by you?"

I'd never really thought about it. I had always swum with the seals, sea turtles, whatever animal happened to be present at the time. "No, why would they be?"

He let out a snort. "Okay, this I've gotta see. And if you don't want to do it today, that's fine, but seriously, wow!"

I'm not sure why his reaction bothered me, but it did. "You look almost as shocked as when your dad said I was part demon."

"Well, yeah, I guess I am. I've never met anyone who could swim with seals like it was a normal everyday thing. And, now that you mention it, that's doubly true since you're part demon. Animals should shy away from you."

"Really? Because I'm part demon?"

"Yeah, animals always recognize a predator, and demon blood, unless it's extremely diluted like it is with witches and warlocks, definitely sends out a predator vibe."

"Well, cats and dogs don't like me. When I was a kid, Grandma got me a little golden retriever puppy. We kept him for about a week. He'd never quit crying and growling when I was in the room. I think I cried for the next month. I'd wanted one so badly." It was mind-boggling how finding out my heritage was making so many pieces fall into place.

"Yeah, that makes sense. Still, I'd think it would be the same for all animals, sea life and fish included."

"Not that I've noticed." Nearly every time I went swimming, I was surrounded by some type of sea life—most often schools of fish, but sometimes dolphins and rays and larger animals.

"I'm surprised no one has found this strange before me. Your friends at school never thought it was odd?"

"I've never really swum with anyone in the ocean before. It's always kinda been my 'get away from the rest of the world' time."

"Oh." He glanced down at the dishtowel in his hands. "Well, we don't have to do it now. I could let you go swim on your own."

"No, don't be silly. Let's go."

He patted his pockets as if looking for something. "I just thought, I don't have swimming trunks."

The voice of the boy telling me the same thing two nights ago echoed in my ears, but I shoved it away. "It's okay. I've got several pairs. I'm sure one will fit you."

BY THE time Finn drove us to Mission Beach, it was nearly six, and I was already starving, despite the sandwiches. The beach was especially crowded, which would typically make me choose to go somewhere else, but given the events of late, I figured this time it might be a good problem to have.

"If I'd been thinking, I would have stopped by the grocery store and picked up some burgers or something to grill after we swim." Finn's stomach must have been growling as well.

I peered around him to see what he was looking at. There was a family with four little kids sitting around a portable grill cooking hot dogs. "Yeah, I'm not sure if we're allowed to have fires on this beach. I'd say they'll be lucky if the beach patrol doesn't pass by and make them put it out. Good thing I'm off duty."

"It would be worth the risk, I say." Finn rubbed his stomach. It seemed he was already becoming less self-conscious around me. I wanted to reach out and do the same, but I figured that might be a little too soon and make him revert back to trying to hide it. "You're hungry already too?"

He grinned. "Always. Plus, I haven't had my quota of pastries today. I'm gonna have sugar withdrawal here in a bit."

I laughed. "Well, I'll try not to keep you out in the water too long. Don't want you to pass out and get carried out to sea."

"Oh, well, you could just call one of your seal friends to come get me."

"How about a great white, instead?"

WE PLACED our blankets out of reach of the surf. Finn bent down and dug a small hole under one of the corners of his.

"What are you doing?"

He looked up and gave a crooked smile. The sun glinted off the golden brown muscles that rippled over his shoulders and upper back. I tried to keep my eyes focused on his. "I always bury my truck key. Don't want it to get lost."

"You know, those trunks have a little pocket in them."

"What? If it falls out in the water are you gonna have a little hermit crab hunt it down for me?"

"Fine. But don't blame me when someone moves our towels and you can't find your key."

He shrugged. "Hasn't happened yet." His hand shot out and smacked me in the stomach. "Race ya!" Before I could respond, he was off, tearing across the sand. He made a little waving motion with his hand over his shoulder. "Last one in over their head is a demon!"

Within five paces, I caught up to him, our feet now covered in the lapping waves. "You were saying?" I managed to get out between breaths.

Finn raised his left hand, making a flicking motion with his fingers. I felt my knees and elbows lock, and before I could even think of trying to steady myself, I dropped like a fallen tree face first in the shallow water. I landed hard on my stomach and felt the wind knocked out of me. Before I could get my breath back, a small wave hit me in the face. I felt my joints unlock. Sputtering and spitting out water, I hopped up and glanced around.

Finn was in front of me, the water already over his waist. He turned around and waved at me. "What's taking you so long?" With that he plunged himself under the water.

By the time I reached him, he was standing again, his dark hair plastered and dripping. "That was you, wasn't it!"

He raised both his hands, declaring innocence. "What? I never said we couldn't use spells."

"Oh right. What did you want me to do? Set you on fire?"

"Well, if you're ever going to, this would be the place to do it. Fire demons can't do much surrounded by water."

"Really?"

"Of course not. What would you expect them to do, set the water on fire?"

"Well, yeah, actually."

Finn shook his head. "Don't get me wrong. Put a fire demon in water, and he's still a demon, and if he's looking to kill you, you'll die, just not with fire." Finn cocked his head to the side, his eyes narrowing as he peered at my face, his voice taking on a softer quality. "Are you okay? You look kinda worried all of a sudden."

"No, I'm fine. Trying to take it all in." If fire demons couldn't use fire in water, then what did that mean about me? Had Wendell been wrong? And if I wasn't part demon, then what was I?

"Are you sure you're okay?"

"Yeah." I glanced around, trying to shake it off. There were scores of people around us. "Let's swim out farther. Are you okay with that?"

"Sure, I'm not afraid of water."

"Sonia wouldn't even come out this far. She's terrified of sharks."

Finn gave me a little smirk. "I don't really want to come face to face with one, but if I do, at least I have Aquaman here to talk the shark into eating someone else."

"Shut up!"

I WAS surprised as we swam out farther. I didn't feel like anything was watching me. Even swimming underwater, I didn't see anything out of place or feel things touching me. I didn't even see the normal amount of fish that typically would have been swimming with me. That was standard when I was lifeguarding, because there were too many people around, but it didn't seem like just being with one other person should scare them off. Or maybe I was somehow different after the vampire bite.

Although the absence of ocean life was somewhat disconcerting, it was a relief to not feel the alien presence with me. I pushed that worry from my mind.

The ocean worked its magic. Even the new worries about fire demons being extinguished in water didn't concern me. All I felt was the warm fluid surrounding my skin and the distant currents whispering to me. I stayed under, diving deep, coming close to the surface, and diving again for quite a while, until I remembered Finn was with me, and was probably freaking out somewhere above. With a few swift kicks, I broke the surface.

Finn was only a few feet away, treading water. From the look on his face, he had most definitely been worried. "You really are Aquaman! You were under there forever."

"Sorry, got lost in the joy of it all."

"You weren't kidding when you said you loved swimming, were you?" He swam closer to me, stopping less than an arm's length away. He inspected me closely, his eyes wide.

"What? Is there something wrong?"

He continued to stare, openmouthed. "No, it's just, well, I don't see how it could be possible."

A tinge of anxiety crept in, despite the healing effect of the saltwater. Had I burst into flames while I was diving and didn't notice?

Finn reached out toward me, stopping shy of touching my face. "It's just that you are somehow more beautiful now than you were before."

I felt the tension leave my body once more. "Oh please. Come on!"

"No, really. It's almost like you glisten out here or something. You're radiant. Like your skin is covered with mother-of-pearl." With that, his fingers touched my face, tracing down the skin on my cheek and then moving to do the same on the other side.

My skin tingled wherever he touched, and my breathing started to become shallower.

Still treading water with his other hand, he moved his fingers down my neck and followed the path of my collarbone, over my shoulder, and then lower, beneath the waves, making patterns on my chest.

I could hear his breathing grow faster, felt it on my face as he drew closer. His hand, which had been treading water, was now secured behind my neck as he relied on me to keep us both afloat. His other hand now lay flat against my chest, slowly caressing each curve. It passed over my stomach and circled around to my back, pulling him closer, until he was pressed against me. "It's so warm next to you."

I barely had time to make sense of his mumbled words before his lips were on mine. I felt him pull at my lower lip and heard myself groan.

His lips were soft but hungry. Not your typical "let's-get-it-on" kiss. Deeper. More tender. Captivating.

"No!" I shoved him away. Hard. He flew backward in the water several yards, flailing his arms to keep from going under, a look of pain on his face like I had just backhanded him.

I shouted again and then dove beneath the surface and took off for the shore.

CHAPTER FOURTEEN

I SAT on the beach towel, my arms wrapped around my knees. I guessed it had been nearly fifteen minutes since I returned to shore. Had I swum in that much faster than Finn, or was he just mad and not wanting to see me?

I started to get up to search when I noticed him slowly wading through the receding tide. He was a silhouette in front of the first orangish-pink rays of sunset. His shoulders were slumped, and he kept his eyes focused on the ground.

He paused at the water line, glanced up at me waiting for him, and then glanced back down, his face reddening in the fading light. He took a deep breath, attempted to square his shoulders, and picked up his speed. He didn't look at me when he arrived at the towels. He squatted down, lifted up the corner of his towel, and stuck his hand in the sand, digging for his key.

"Finn, listen, I...."

"No, don't." He still wouldn't raise his eyes to me. "You don't need to say anything. I'll take you to your car." His voice was emotionless, flat. He pulled the key out and automatically wiped it off on his wet swim trunks, leaving a streak of sand behind.

"Finn, please, let me explain. You don't understand."

"You don't need to say anything, Brett." He lifted his head and tried to look at me, but the moment his eyes met mine, they darted away. "I'm sorry. I wasn't trying to... well, I guess I thought that... I don't know what I thought."

"*You're* sorry? I'm the one who should be apologizing."

He shook his head. "No. I'm the one who kissed you. I shouldn't have done that. I guess I was reading into things." He paused awkwardly.

"I *wanted* you to kiss me." The depth of emotion in my voice surprised even me.

Finn's face jerked up, and he cocked his head at me quizzically. "You wanted me to kiss you?"

I just nodded.

"Then, why did you… what was wrong?"

I hesitated. I wasn't sure if I really wanted him to know. It was bad enough thinking I was a demon. What might he decide I was after hearing this? It would guarantee he would never kiss me again. Who could blame him?

He started to stand back up, but I reached out and pulled him down.

"Okay, listen." I glanced at him to make sure he was going to stay and then turned away. "Everything has been strange lately. Maybe it was just the part-demon stuff and maybe it wasn't, but I was starting to think I was going crazy."

He started to say something, but I cut him off. "A couple of days ago, my grandfather died, and it brought up a lot of my old 'family issues' crap."

Finn's face took on the countenance appropriate for when someone's puppy gets run over by a semi. "Oh, Brett, I'm so sorry."

I waved him off. "Anyway, in the whole mix of everything, I decided I was going to go end my five month celibacy streak." I glanced at him to make sure he was going to be okay with this. He gave me a forced, yet encouraging, smile. "This guy and I went swimming at the beach a couple of nights ago. We were lying on the sand and… well, you know."

He smiled again, less enthusiastic this time.

"Well, somehow, while I was kissing him, he started to drown, but I didn't realize it."

"Wait. He started to drown? Were you in the water?" He forgot his reluctance in discussing my hooking up.

I shrugged. "Kinda, but not really. I mean, the waves were lapping at our feet, but our heads were never underwater or anything."

"Well, maybe some of the water just seeped in and he choked."

"No. I thought about that too. He coughed up gallons, Finn. I mean buckets of water. I don't even know how he could have that much in him."

Finn thought for a moment and started to speak. I cut him off again. "That's not all." I'd been unable to look directly at him, but now I held his gaze. I needed to see his reaction. "Finn, the guy's skin was like it had been boiled. It was bright red and had blisters everywhere."

Finn's eyes bugged slightly, but other than that, he gave no reaction. I could see the thoughts whirling through his mind. After several seconds, he asked, "What happened next?"

"He was screaming at me to get away from him." I looked down at my lap. "So, I did."

Hesitantly, I glanced back at Finn, who was deep in thought. He sat there, a puzzled expression on his face, his brow furrowed. "Say something."

He leaned forward. "Were you mad or something?"

"No. At least I don't think so." I gave him a moment, then rushed forward. "I went back the next day. I couldn't find any sign of him, so I guess he's okay."

Finn didn't seem overly concerned about the boy. "So, are you thinking you somehow filled him with water while you were kissing?"

"I don't know. That's all I can come up with. What do you think?"

"I'm not sure. That's all that really makes sense... not that it actually makes sense."

"Have you heard of other demons that drown people or something? Maybe I'm a mix between two demons."

Finn shook his head emphatically. "No, I've never heard of a demon with power over water." He looked up as he had a new idea. "Did you happen to mutter anything strange, or think something?"

"What? You mean like a spell?"

"Yeah, I guess so."

"Finn, I don't even know any spells. I didn't even believe in them until last night."

"I know. It's...." He let out a deep breath. "It's just that, if you didn't, then it means that the water came from you, like your fire does. That it's a part of you."

With all the other crazy things that had happened, that didn't seem so surprising to me. "Yeah, so?"

"So, I've never heard of anyone who has the power of fire *and* water in them. The two don't mix."

"Do you think it's a bad thing?"

"I don't know, Brett. I bet Dad would have some ideas, though."

"Finn, I really don't want to have to tell that story to your dad. It was bad enough having to tell you."

Finn gave a look that meant he was having another thought. "So, out there in the water just now, when you shoved me away... you did that because you...."

"Because I didn't want to hurt you. You even said the water was warmer by me. What if I got carried away and hurt you too?"

His eyes softened, and a smile played at the corner of his mouth. "So, you mean that it really wasn't because you didn't want to kiss me?"

"God, no, Finn! I already told you that. What if I wanted it too much? That was the problem." The turn of our conversation hit me. "I tell you about burning and nearly drowning some hookup, and you want to know about kissing me?"

Finn shrugged, ignored my implication, and paused for another second before continuing. "But, you've... kissed... other guys when you weren't in the water before, right?"

"Sure."

"And you haven't burned or drowned any of them, right?"

"Right."

"Then, I think we'd be okay." He started to lean forward.

I put my hand on his chest. "Finn, no. I'm sorry. We can't. I don't want to hurt you. I'm not going to take that chance with you."

I could see him trying to decide if he should give up or press on anyway. He let out another breath. "Fine. But I think we should talk to my dad."

WE WERE just finishing up the Taco Bell we'd gotten when we arrived at Old Town. Finn had mentioned eating at Taberna de las Brujas, but the idea of Ricky and Christina making a big deal about us being together sounded exhausting, and I was sure they had talked to Paulette or Wendell, and the last thing I needed was more questions about being part demon. Truth be told, I wanted to stay in Old Town as briefly as possible. If the Vampire Cathedral really was out to get me, I didn't need to make it any easier to find me.

"Did you park by the restaurant?" Finn popped the last bite of his MexiMelt in his mouth, crumpled the wrapper, and tossed it in the paper bag.

"No, I parked several blocks away, beside a little neighborhood park."

Finn gave me an inquisitive sideways glance.

"I was in the mood to walk around and think last night, plus I didn't want to have to fight for a spot in the lot or have to pay for parking somewhere else."

He chuckled. "Cheap *and* an impatient driver. Guess it's good to know that up front."

"Up front? Were you planning on proposing tonight or something?" *Shut up, Brett! Flirting like that is stupid—in every way.*

In a way that seemed very uncharacteristic, he gave me a wink. "Ya never know. You come very highly recommended."

"Uh…." I searched for something clever to say, but nothing came to mind. It was true that I liked the other person to make the move, but this was a little too much.

He smacked my chest. "Breathe, boy, breathe! Gesh! I'm just giving you a hard time. I can't even get you to kiss me, let alone think about proposing!" He raised his eyebrow. "Besides, what makes you think I'd want little demon babies running around setting everything on fire?"

"Ouch. That's a little below the belt, don't ya think?"

He patted my knee. "Lighten up, Brett, lighten up. Where do I turn, anyway?"

I wasn't sure why his joke about demon babies had hurt my feelings, but it had. "Just take a right up there." I pointed to the next stop sign. "It's after that block, at the very end, by the corner."

Finn rolled through the stop sign, his tires giving a little squeal as he rounded the corner.

I gestured to the right. "Right up there."

He slowed down as he neared the end of the block. "You mean… *that* one?"

My breath caught in my throat. I stared stupidly at my car as Finn pulled his truck to a stop in front of it, halfway on the sidewalk and half in the street.

I didn't say anything as I got out of the truck. I took a couple of steps toward my car and then stopped.

Finn came up behind me and placed a hand on the middle of my back, his voice warm and low. "You okay?"

I didn't reply. I finished the distance to my car, put my hand out slowly, and barely touched it to make sure it was real.

There were four parallel lines that cut through the sides, making a ring around the car, the metal jagged and ripped on every edge. All six windows had been smashed and lay inside and around the car in clumps and shards. Each tire was flat and had a single gash several inches long that matched the ones on the body of the car. Even from where I was standing, I could see the seats had been shredded as well, yellow foam bursting from the black vinyl.

"Wow, he really did a number on your car. I'm really sorry, Brett." Finn's voice by my ear caused me to jump.

"He?"

"Yeah. What else do think could do this?"

I puzzled at his words for several seconds, feeling rather slow when I finally caught on. "The vampire!"

Finn walked closer to the car and leaned down beside the passenger door. He put out his hand and inserted his fingers into the four slits down the side. "I don't know of anything else that could do this, except maybe a werewolf or a full-blood demon, but that seems rather improbable, given you were attacked by Mr. Fangs last night."

"You think he did that with his *fingers*?" I gaped with renewed shock at the torn metal. "It looks like ripped paper."

"Well, it probably wasn't much harder than that for him. Vampires are crazy strong. I don't think you get it. There's a reason the Royal Family was able to declare themselves the rulers."

"Oh shit!" I whirled around Finn and ran to the other side.

Finn jumped up as I shouted, his fists up and looking around frantically. "What? Do you see him?"

I threw open the driver's side door, reached in, and ripped down the visor. My keys fell to the floor. "Oh thank God!" I bent down and scooped them up. Then another thought hit me, and I reached through to the other side and yanked open the glove compartment. I shoved my hand in, tossed papers aside, and pulled out my driver's license. I let out a long stream of breath I hadn't realized I was holding.

"What is it?" Finn asked from behind me.

I turned and showed him the key and ID. "For a second, I thought he'd found out where I live. Sonia...."

"Oh. Yeah." He narrowed his eyes at me. "Are you telling me you leave your keys and wallet in the car?"

"Just my keys and ID. I carry cash in my pocket. I've never worried about it. This car's too old for anybody to try to steal."

He took my driver's license and turned it over, inspecting it. "You're lucky he was only wanting to destroy something." He shrugged. "Not that I can blame him, I guess. If you'd burned my face off, I'd mess up your car too." He motioned to the ID. "Good picture, by the way. I didn't realize I was two years older than you. Twenty-three, you're just a baby."

I snatched my license back. "Whatever." Now that I knew Sonia was safe, the car didn't seem like such a big deal. "I think I might need a ride back to my place, if you don't mind."

Finn laughed. "Ya think?" He peered through the broken window into the backseat. "Did you see what he did to the steering wheel?"

I gazed in from behind him. The steering wheel was sitting in the backseat, cords and wires dangling, making it look like a severed head. "Wow." For the first time, I was beginning to comprehend what a big deal it was that I was able to get away with my life the night before. "When do you think he did this?"

"Dunno. I doubt it was last night. Even though there aren't a lot of houses around here, it seems like someone would have heard something, and even if they didn't, surely someone would have called the police when they brought their kids to the park today and saw this chaos."

The thought of the vampire being here recently gave me a chill. "What do we do? Should we call the police?"

Finn shook his head. "Do you really want to try to explain this? Do you have insurance?"

"Just liability. It wouldn't cover any damage to my car."

He grimaced. "Then I think you're kinda screwed. I know a couple of cops who are in the family, so to speak. I can call one of them."

"You mean they're gay?"

Finn laughed. "No, they're warlocks. I'll just have to say 'vampire' and they'll get it—no questions asked."

While Finn stepped away to call, I went through the car and got the few papers and items I needed to keep. Everything else that could be traced back to me I threw into a garbage can in the park.

IT TURNED out the policeman Finn had called was a friend of his dad's. Officer Torres seemed fairly suspicious of me until Finn told him about the situation with the vampire. Given the circumstances, the cop told us he would have my car towed to the junkyard without filing papers, to avoid unanswerable questions. He wanted us to leave before the tow truck got there. He would pass it off as random vandalism to a stolen car. He wiped off the VIN number with a pass of his finger as he muttered some language I couldn't understand, and then melted the license plates so they were unrecognizable.

A FEW hours passed between finding the car and pulling into the driveway beside Sonia's Miata.

"Finn, why did you tell the cop that I was a warlock?"

Finn sighed and turned his body so he was facing me awkwardly in the front seat. "I don't know if he would have been willing to help if he knew you were part demon."

"Oh. Demons are kind of the lower class on the totem pole, huh?"

Finn tilted his hand back and forth. "Kinda, but not in the way you think. It's not so much he would have looked at you like you're dirty or anything. He just would have been afraid of you. You've got to remember, full-blood demons are like wild animals at times. They live to kill, and those that are only removed by a few generations aren't much better."

"I'm not sure if that's any different. I guess you're saying I shouldn't put 'Brett Wright, Demon Extraordinaire' on my business cards, huh?"

He smiled softly. "Probably not the best idea." He opened his mouth to say something else, then changed his mind. Before I could say anything, he spoke again. "Do you think you're gonna be okay tonight?"

"Yeah, I will." At least until I lie down to sleep and have a chance to start thinking about everything again. "Finn, I don't think I've thanked you yet. You and your family have done so much for me, last night and today. You didn't even know me."

"That seems kinda strange to me that I didn't know you yesterday. It doesn't feel like that. So much has happened that it feels like we've known each other a long time."

"Yeah, I was thinking that earlier, actually. You and your family are completely amazing... well, except for Caitlin, and I'm sure she's good too, if you're not a half-demon."

"Nah, not really. That's just Caitlin." He hesitated once again, his mouth opening and closing, his face growing redder. "I'd like to see you again," he blurted out suddenly.

"I'd like that too. After all, I bet I'll have a lot more questions about all this demon, witch, vampire stuff." *Why'd I say that?* I knew that wasn't what he meant. While I like the other person to do the pursuing, I don't typically play hard to get or get all nervous.

He shook his head. "That's not what I meant, although that's good too. I just mean...." He cleared his throat. "I like you, Brett. I'm sure you hear that all the time. You're gorgeous. Demon gorgeous, for crying out loud! You're smart, funny. I know you could get any guy, but I'd like us to go out sometime."

"We've been out all day." Dammit, why was I doing this?

Finn's face flushed a deeper red, making his typically golden skin look dark brown, and his gaze dropped to his lap. "Yeah, you're right. I'm sorry." He reached over to grasp his seat belt, which he'd taken off when we parked. "Let's just say, I'll see you when I see you, then. You can always pop into the restaurant and—"

Without thinking, I leaned over, grabbed his chin, pulled it up so he faced me, and covered his lips with mine.

At first, he stiffened in surprise, but after a moment, I felt him relax, slip his hand behind my head, and pull me closer. His lips were soft but firm, and his tongue tentatively touched mine, lightly caressing the tip before sinking the rest of the way in, filling my mouth with a faint taste of cinnamon.

I'm not sure how long the kiss lasted, but I had to suck in breath several times before he finally pulled away, his brown eyes bright and wide.

"Yes." I took another breath, trying to breathe normally again. "I want to see you too."

He leaned over and gave me another firm kiss, then pulled his head back slightly, whispering so I could barely hear him. "See, I'm not on fire."

I grinned. "Yeah, and you're not drowning either." He slipped his hand into mine. "Must just be a water thing."

Another eyebrow arch. "Yeah, maybe, but I'd be willing to try an experiment sometime."

The thought caused me to shudder. "I don't think so." We looked at each other for several moments, both pleased with the turn of events. "Would you like to come inside and say hi to Sonia before you go? She'd love that."

"Sure, you bet." He gave my hand a final squeeze before letting go and hopping out of the truck.

As we walked up to the door, I started to feel self-conscious again. It had been so long since I'd had more than a hookup that part of me was a little apprehensive of where this could lead.

Finn, apparently, wasn't feeling any such thing as he hummed quietly behind me while I fished the key ring from my pocket. "I still can't believe you leave your keys and driver's license in your car."

The key slid into the slot. I turned the handle and swung open the door. "Yeah, I guess now I'll have to...." My voice trailed off as I stepped through the door.

"Oh no." Finn murmured behind me.

Furniture was scattered everywhere—chairs overturned and slid out of place, lamps lying on the floor, shattered. There was a hole in the wall where the hallway led out of the living room.

For several moments, all I could do was let my gaze follow the destruction of the room. Everywhere I looked, there was more broken or out of place. The kitchen table that sat on the far end of the living room, right outside the kitchen, was split in half. One of the chairs had been thrown through the sliding glass doors that led to our tiny backyard.

I turned to look at Finn, who started to reach for me. "Come on, Brett, let's go outside."

My brain finally snapped back into place, and I reeled away from him and flung myself into motion. "Sonia!" I tore off through the living room, hopping over debris. "Sonia!"

"Brett, don't!" I heard Finn's voice, but it sounded miles away.

As I ran past the kitchen, I glanced in. It seemed to have been spared from whatever had happened. I could see the bread and meat on the counter, and an open mayonnaise bottle with a knife sticking out of the opening. "Sonia! Sonia!"

I didn't pause by the bathroom. I rushed through the hall, past my bedroom, and came to a stop outside Sonia's door.

I stood there, staring at the door handle, expecting it to somehow turn on its own and let me into the room.

Finn grabbed my shoulders as he caught up with me. He tugged firmly. "Brett. Brett, come on. Follow me outside. You don't have to do this. Just come with me."

I shrugged off his grip, grabbed the door handle, flung open the door, and stepped through without another thought.

As soon as I was in Sonia's room, my feet stopped moving. I stood there, hands limp at my sides, jaw slack, eyes wide.

The sheets had been ripped off her bed, which sat at an angle in the far corner of the room. Her dresser and chest of drawers were both turned over, the closet's doors were ripped off, and clothes were scattered all over the room.

Blood covered everything. The bed seemed to be the source—all of it splattered out from there, streaking the walls in such a way that it looked like a child had used red finger paint to smear the rays of the sun. Splatters of blood plastered every surface, dotting the overturned furniture, pooling on the hardwood floor, and soaking into the fallen clothes.

CHAPTER FIFTEEN

FINN DE MORISCO

EVERY so often I was certain that Brett recognized me. His eyelids would open, brilliant blue eyes would lock onto mine, and I'd think he was back with me. Each time, though, their gaze was dull—the empty eyes of a zombie. Sometimes they would stare at me, unblinking, for minutes at a time. At others, it was only moments.

The first couple of times, I would get excited, go to him, and begin talking—asking him if he was okay, what he needed. Soon, I simply just stared back.

Once in a while, he would shout out, nearly causing me to have a heart attack every time. Soon, however, even that became commonplace.

Before they went to Sonia and Brett's house, my folks came over, not long after I'd gotten Brett to my place. I'd begged Mom to erase the memories from his mind, or at least make them far removed so he could face them easier. She handles the psyche much better than I. No sooner had she touched his temples than she pulled away, flicking her hands, having received a shock. It seemed, even in a comatose state, demons had power to protect against outside forces.

Most of the first night was a blur. Having realized too late what Sonia's room would show, I kept my focus on Brett, only taking in small aspects out of my peripheral vision.

He'd been fairly easy to coax out of the bedroom and down the hall.

Once we reached the entryway, however, he lost control. I don't know if it was leaving the house that set him off, or if it was the picture of Sonia with a white dog by the door that he'd noticed.

Without warning, he slammed his fist into the wall, turning the drywall into powder, and then he threw himself into the opposite wall and crashed into a hunched-over position on the floor, flames engulfing his body.

I was helpless to do anything but watch as his clothes burned off and he convulsed over and over, crumbling further against the floor, retching violently, each spew devoured by the flames before it reached the floor. The wall behind him charred and smoldered, but I was able to keep it from being consumed until his energy was spent and he lay curled naked on the charred hardwood floor, tendrils of steam wafting off his skin.

After hurrying away, I found his bedroom and grabbed some clothes out of the pile by his bed. It seemed his eruption had used up his resistance, and while he didn't help, he didn't fight back as I clothed him and then led him outside through the rain that had begun to fall and into my truck.

He didn't speak on the way to my place. I tried to explain the situation to Dad on the phone as quietly as I could. I kept glancing at Brett, unsure how I would handle it if he burst into flames again while we drove down the Five. He didn't. He just sat hunched over, his forehead pressed against the window, his eyes wide and haunted, staring at nothing.

He surprised me by not resisting as I led him out of the truck, into the house, and to my bedroom. I got him undressed and into bed.

He lay there, a constant and silent stream of tears coursing over his face, soaking into the pillow.

After my folks left to meet some of the others at Brett and Sonia's house to start the cleanup process, I slipped into my sweats and cautiously got into bed next to him. As I slid over to him and wrapped my arms around his chest, forming myself to his back, I could hear

Caitlin in my mind, screaming about lying with a demon who was going to use me as kindling.

Though I couldn't see his face, it seemed that, as long as I was holding him, the tears stopped and his breathing turned deep and slow, giving him what I hoped was a dreamless sleep.

Sleep was the furthest thing from me as I waited for him to explode into flames and for the vampire to burst into the bedroom. Guilty for the pleasure I took, I thought back to our kiss in the truck, to the feeling I'd found something I hadn't hoped for in a long time.

I WOKE to a tapping on my shoulder.

Groggily, I attempted to roll over to see the tapper better but found my right arm trapped under Brett. Carefully pulling it out from under his head, sharp tingles coursed through my forearm as blood rushed back into the veins. I shook it harshly as I turned over, then swiped some of the hair out of my eyes.

Cynthia's face was bright red, and her gaze was cast down, firmly not looking at her shirtless brother and the demon who had been in his arms. If it had been Caitlin, the flush on her face would have been from anger and disgust at such a sight. With Cynthia, however, it was much more likely from the intimate position she had found me in. Although older than me, Cynthia had always been shy, almost to the point of being handicapped. That predisposition had been magnified by an assault that happened to her. She hadn't even kissed a guy, let alone been in bed with one, before the assault.

I could only imagine how long she had stood there, trying to get her nerve up, before she managed to attempt to wake me.

"Hey, sis."

"Hi, Finn." Her soft brown eyes glanced up to meet mine before focusing back on the floor. "I wanted to let you know that everything is done at *his* house." She made a timid gesture toward Brett's back.

With a glance back to make sure Brett wasn't awake, I swung my legs over the edge of the bed and bent down to pick up my shirt and slip it over my head as I stood. I motioned toward the hallway. "Come on. I don't know how much he can hear, but just in case...."

Cynthia followed me to the hall, leaving the door cracked behind her, finally able to look me in the face.

"Why didn't you call to tell me? You didn't have to come over here."

She gave an insubstantial shrug. "I wanted to check on you in person. I was worried. I wanted to know that you were okay. You and… Brett."

Before I could comment about her using Brett's name, she rushed on. "So, are you okay? We couldn't find any sign of his roommate."

"Sonia."

"Yeah, Sonia. There was nothing besides blood. Everywhere."

"That's what I figured. If he had left a body to find, the vampire would have made a spectacle out of it."

"It looked like she must have put up a huge fight." She shuddered and wrapped her arms around herself. "I can't imagine what she went through—and to think she didn't even know anything about vampires. To her, it must have been like getting attacked by a nightmare. Do you think the vampire…?"

I didn't have to ask what she meant. When I'd been able to pull my thoughts away from Brett, that was all I thought about. "Let's pray not. I'm gonna assume the best."

"Are you going to mention the possibility to Brett?"

I shook my head and draped my arm around her, pulling her close as she reached up to wipe tears from her eyes—always the most sensitive one in the family.

It didn't surprise me that Cynthia had felt the need to come over. Despite the family being overly cautious with her, she really did have a deep core of strength, and she was always fiercely loyal to her family. Especially me. Caitlin and I had always fought like cats and dogs, Christina and I always had the most fun together, but it was Cynthia and I who were the closest. Maybe because we were the two youngest, or maybe because in some ways we were the most alike. She had always been my confidant, and I had been hers.

"You're probably right, but still, to think of her having to fight for her life in her own home, never knowing what was going to happen to her." She suddenly wrapped her arms around me, pulling herself in close. "Are you truly okay?"

"Of course, Cyn. We didn't even see the vampire. We got there after it already happened. We were never in danger."

"What about Brett?" She pulled herself away and took a small step back to look up into my face.

"He's not responding. I stayed up with him most of the night. I didn't even realize I'd fallen asleep until you woke me up. He hasn't responded to anything. I guess it might be shock or something. He's completely shut down."

"Do you think you're safe here? If the vampire can find Brett's house, why couldn't he find yours?"

That thought had been on my mind the night before as well. "I'm not really sure how he found their house. My best guess is that he'd been stalking Brett for a while before he attacked him the other night. I'm sure we're fine here. There's no way he can know where we are. If he'd been watching when we got to Brett and Sonia's house, he would have tried to kill us then." I wasn't completely sure that was true, but it was what I had decided made the most sense.

"I think it would be a better idea if you came back to Mom and Dad's. We are safer if we all stay together."

"No, we'll be fine, sis. Really. Besides, I can take care of myself against a vampire."

She gave me a skeptical look.

"Well, between Brett and me, I'm sure we could do some major damage. Maybe even kill him."

"I doubt that. Even if that were true, Brett's nowhere near able to fight a vampire as he lies there sleeping."

I couldn't argue with that logic, so I didn't bother. "We'll be fine."

Cynthia started to protest, but I cut her off. Some of my thoughts from the long night lying wide-awake next to Brett came back to my mind like a compulsion. "I have a favor to ask."

Her brows furrowed as she somehow sensed she wasn't going to like my request. "What?"

I cleared my throat, knowing I was about to test her to the limit. "I need to go do some stuff for a while, and I was wondering if you could stay here with Brett. I don't want him to wake up by himself."

She stared at me, her mouth hanging open. "Are you kidding?"

I shook my head.

She closed her mouth and licked her dry lips. Her hands trembled as they played with her long hair. "Stay here with Brett? In the bedroom?" Her voice went high and cracked.

I nodded.

I could tell her mind was whirling, darting from one hideous possibility to the next, and then her narrowed eyes rose to mine. "Wait a minute, where are you going?"

I shrugged. "I just need to get out of here for a while. It's been a long night, and I need some fresh air."

She gave me an exaggerated eye roll. "You're gonna have to do better than that. There's no way you'd leave him just to go get some fresh air." She crossed her arms over her chest. "You're up to something."

I should've known better than to try to pass it off so casually. She knew me better than that. However, there was no way she'd let me out of her sight if she knew what I really wanted to do.

I let out my breath, like I'd been caught and was giving up the truth. "I want to go get some personal stuff for Brett. We left everything at the house, so he'll need everyday items when he wakes up—toothbrush, deodorant, all of that. That way it will all be ready for him when he wakes up." I couldn't suppress a twinge of guilt. I hated lying to her.

Cynthia narrowed her eyes, as if trying to see through me. If anyone could, she'd be able to. "I can go to the store and get whatever he needs. That way you don't have to leave."

"Please, Cynthia." The pleading in my voice wasn't for her benefit. It was real. "I need to get out of here for a bit. I've been lying here feeling completely helpless."

With a sigh, she nodded. "Fine."

"Thanks, Cyn!" I wanted to go check on Brett and give him a kiss before I left, but didn't want to give Cynthia any time to change her mind. Instead, I pulled her close for a quick kiss on the cheek and took off before she could offer any more objections.

The drive to Encanto would normally have taken a little over forty minutes, but thanks to low traffic and not caring about speeding tickets, I made it in less than half an hour.

A GUY I'd dated right out of high school had lived in the Emerald Hills portion of Encanto. The relationship had started off well enough, but after a couple of months, his true colors started showing through. Jake had been charming at first but had turned jealous, controlling, and a bit abusive by the end.

I thought I'd never have any reason to be thankful for the time I'd spent with him, but it was to him that my thoughts drifted the night before as I lay by Brett, trying to figure out what options we might have besides waiting to become the vampire's next infusion.

The majority of the time I spent with Jake had been at his house. Most of my memories of Encanto revolved around the hot tub on his back deck, which was where we ended nearly every night. It had great views of downtown San Diego and the Coronado Bridge. I was young, and at the time it had all seemed romantic.

However much I liked to pretend that I had no idea what Jake was really like at the beginning, I never took him home to meet my parents. I'd known what they would say. Jake never had any qualms about "persuading" humans to do what he wanted. He rarely paid for any of our dates, instead compelling people to believe he'd already paid. While I was never fully comfortable with it, there was a certain thrill to watching him use our powers in ways I'd never seen before.

Jake took me to The Square toward the end of our relationship. I lasted less than an hour before I made him leave. He had torn me up and down for that—he thought I was ready, thought I was tough enough, thought I'd loved him enough. Manipulative asshole.

The Square was in one of the rougher parts of Encanto. When he first described it to me, I was desperate to go. He told me stories about werewolves and vampires and other witches all living and partying out in the open. The thought of a place where supernaturals could gather, unafraid of what the Vampire Cathedral would think, was intoxicating.

It lived up to its name, bringing to mind photos I had seen of town squares in the Midwest. One square block—each of the four sides facing what looked like an old courthouse. For the most part, it resembled a ghost town, save for the multitude of bars. You could feel the evil in the place. There were humans everywhere, drawn by free drugs and alcohol. Most of them looked homeless, but here and there were high-school-age kids who had come to party. Whether or not they realized those around them weren't typical people, I wasn't sure. Maybe they were too engrossed in the thrill of the place to notice until it was too late, or maybe they just didn't care.

My final straw was when I noticed what I thought were two guys making out by the restroom in the corner of a bar. When I took a couple of steps closer, the man facing me raised his head. His eyes shone red, and blood covered the lower part of his face as he snarled in my direction. The huge, gaping wound on the boy's neck was the kind from which I knew he wouldn't recover.

I WASN'T sure where The Square actually was, but I was fairly confident that if I found Jake's house, I would be able to locate it without too much trouble. My only real concern was that it would be a wasted trip. I wasn't sure whether The Square had any activity during the daylight hours. If not, I had no idea where to turn.

I'd decided last night that I had to find the vampire. Take the fight to him. Well, not so much a fight—I knew which one of us would win in that scenario. However, if I could find where he slept, the outcome might look a little different. I wasn't entirely sure if vampires did sleep during the day. Did they sleep buried in the ground? In coffins? Surely not.

Vampires hadn't been a huge part of my education—at least not your run-of-the-mill vampires. The Vampire Cathedral had been the only real exposure I'd had, and that hadn't been extensive either—especially since they could be in the sun, and thus obviously didn't have to sleep all day. My education didn't help me at all.

Of course, there was the issue of what I was going to do once I found him. While I probably could defend myself enough to not get killed, that was about all I could boast, despite what I tried to tell Cynthia. What was I going to do if I knew I couldn't kill him on my own? Ask him nicely to leave my boyfriend alone? Boyfriend? I guess it would have to be "leave the hot guy I kissed alone." I shoved that train of thought from my mind. That was the last thing that would be helpful.

There had to be something more to this that I was missing. That we were all missing. It was true vampires loved to torment and decimate their victims before they finally killed them. Play with them until the vampire got bored. But that was only if it was easy, not if they had to go to all this work. Plus, that didn't make sense with Brett. He wasn't your normal vampire victim. He was part demon. Even vampires weren't brazen or stupid enough to play cat and mouse with them, at least not more than once. There could be a chance it was all to get revenge for burning his face off, but that didn't feel right either. And, honestly, did it really matter why? All that mattered was that the vampire had made his intentions very clear, and neither Brett nor anyone around him was safe until the vampire was either dead or had his attention focused on other things.

I almost missed Jake's house. It was the fire hydrant that caught my attention. Someone had painted it a yellow and lime-green camouflage motif. I'd forgotten about it, but it stood out like a beacon on the otherwise nondescript street. Jake had hated it and always said he was going to repaint it one day so he'd have something less distracting to see from his front porch. Just like everything else he talked about, it seemed he never found the gumption to do anything about it.

The house seemed drab and worn down. While it wasn't falling apart, a shroud of grayness seemed to have descended on it. Whether it had always looked like that, or it was my perception of who lived there, I wasn't really sure. Not knowing if it was still Jake's house, I kept driving down the block. The last thing I needed was to see him, especially when I was in a vampire-fighting kind of mood.

After pulling up to a curb a few blocks away, I put the truck in park and cautiously got out. My nerves were on edge. I felt a little stupid to be so jittery with the sun shining so brightly, but I couldn't help continuously glancing around me, unsure if I was checking for tagalong vampires or for Jake. An amused smile crept onto my face as I pictured some old woman watching me from her curtained window as she saw some crazed Hispanic man wandering down her street. Of course, considering Jake might still live here, it probably wasn't anything she wasn't already used to.

I figured I'd be more likely to find The Square on foot than in the truck. Jake and I had walked from his house. It seemed that if I let my feet take control, they might just lead me in the right direction.

After ten or fifteen minutes, I realized my plan wasn't working. I was fairly certain I had never been this far east before. I started back in the direction I had come, trying to determine when things began to look familiar again. I wasn't going to do Brett any good if I spent all day walking around Encanto checking out the different neighborhoods and alleyways.

How easy could it be to hide a whole square block devoted to supernaturals? It should stand out like a beacon. If nothing else, the magical vibe—yes, Mom, I said it, *magical*—should be detectable to other supernaturals. The thought made me stop in my tracks and glance around, this time to see if anyone noticed how stupid I had been. Of course there would be a vibe I could detect, magical or otherwise.

What kind of warlock was I, anyway? Caitlin's voice rang in my mind, answering that question for me.

I wasn't exactly sure what I needed to do. Most things that my mother refused to call magic came as naturally as breathing. I didn't need to think about them; they just happened. This was different.

I walked over to a large tree at the edge of someone's yard and leaned my back against the thick bark. I slid down until I was resting on the ground, legs crossed under me, my hands spread wide and flat in the grass. I closed my eyes and focused on feeling the core of my being in my chest. Letting the connection to the earth build in my consciousness, I felt it grow heavy. Gradually, I let it flow from me and seep into the ground, feeling it shoot out and around, a thin disc coursing in waves ever wider. It made me feel both small and connected at the same time. I could feel the energies from the people living in the houses around me, the life force of the animals as they scampered across the ground or from tree to tree. Here and there, small sharp peaks shot through me as my core came into contact with a soul that was unusually pure or dark—very few who weren't human, and nothing that would suggest anything out of the norm.

It could have been mere moments, or it might have been hours. I was only aware of the ever-expanding circle of lives coming into contact with mine.

When I finally connected to The Square, it was as if something had sucked all the air from my lungs and begun contracting my rib cage and skull. Intense heat surrounded me, steam gushing over me. I pulled back, trying to withdraw into the relative safety of my body. Instead, my throat began to constrict, and my eyes burned.

The pressure continued to build and build. Each moment now seemed an eternity, each increasing the pain to a new level of agony. It was as if there were claws digging into me and pulling me ever deeper into darkness.

With all the strength I could muster, I let out a yell and jerked backward, trying to force distance between myself and whatever it was that had hold of me. With the sound of snapping and a loud scream, I contracted back into my body with a force that slammed me into the trunk of the tree, my head smashing with such force that my vision was stolen from me.

Slumping to the ground, I lay there, forcing myself to drag in ragged breath after ragged breath. Every part of me hurt. I felt scorched, like my skin was blackened and cracking.

A few moments later, still trying to breathe, I forced my eyes open. Blinking them rapidly, trying to wipe away the blurriness, I inspected my arms. They seemed fine. Despite the feeling, they looked healthy—maybe more flushed than normal, but definitely not burned.

When I was convinced that I was indeed alive and not charcoaled, I sat up. The sudden motion caused me to gasp in pain and once again lose my breath. Probing my side gingerly with my fingers, I discovered the snapping sound must have been a couple of my ribs breaking. I lifted up my shirt and saw the left side of my body was already turning a dark shade of purple.

Slumping back against the tree, I let my eyes close as I attempted to breathe normally and get my racing heart under control.

I wasn't entirely sure what had transpired. I'd never experienced anything of the like. Something had a hold of me. Not just the part of my psyche I had sent out searching, but me, my body, my mind. I also wasn't sure how I got free of whatever it had been. I'd been too panicked to cast a spell or a curse. It had been a gut reaction, fight or flight—and it was most definitely flight.

The burning in my eyes was slowly dissipating, and with it, things gradually began to come into focus. It seemed like there should be people around me. Surely someone in the houses had heard me screaming. Had it all been in my head? Glancing around, nothing had changed, not even the grass. I expected it to be charred and burned away, but it was as lush and green as when I'd sat down.

Maybe it hadn't been an actual presence, nothing alive. It might just be an alarm system of sorts, a type of curse meant to protect the location of The Square. But even so, why would they need protection? I knew exactly where it was now. There was no way I'd ever have trouble finding it again. Its location would be burned into me for the rest of my life.

The thought sent a shudder through me. If it had been an actual entity, could it now find me as easily as I could find it? That possibility made getting away from where I was take on the utmost importance. I shoved off the ground but only made it to a half-slouched position before my breath caught and the pain sent me crashing back into the tree. I yelped. Somehow, I'd managed to forget about my ribs.

Groaning, I moved my fingers over my ribs, gingerly exploring each one. Cynthia was much better at healing than I, but I could make do until I got back to the house.

Laying my right hand flat on the ground once again, I focused on the energy in the earth and splayed my left hand across my ribs. Closing my eyes, I went inside my body and traveled to the ribs. I focused first on the swelling and sent the fluid to be reabsorbed, then zoned in on the broken ribs and encouraged the splintered fragments to grow together and solidify.

When the majority of the pain had subsided and things seemed mostly back to normal, I withdrew from the wounds. I knew they were weakly mended and would easily crack again, but it should be enough to help me function until Cynthia could do her thing.

Chapter Sixteen

Sure enough, it was easy to find The Square. Too easy. It could be an advantage if the internal homing device only worked one way, but that didn't seem too likely. If whatever it had been was intending to protect The Square, the last thing it would do would be to make it where I was more aware of it while it had no knowledge of me. However, why hadn't it struck out at me yet? Vampires were bad enough, but the thought of having something unnamed possibly stalking me made me even more nervous. My uneasy feeling continued to grow. I had probably set out on a fool's errand. One that didn't even have a defined destination. Hunting for a specific vampire during the day, entering a known demonic area—anyone with half a brain would have turned around and gone home. But what was I going to do there—watch Brett suffer whatever dreams were tormenting him and wait for the next time the vampire chose to attack? At the very least, this gave me the illusion of doing something to help Brett.

The neighborhood continued to get worse and worse as I neared The Square, each block growing more worn down and drab—the darkness seeping out like a fungus.

There was no physical indication that I had entered The Square. No neon-pink sign like at Hillcrest. No warnings or caution tape. One minute I was in a nondescript, broken-down residential neighborhood on Forest Street, and the next, as I crossed Imperial, I was in the southwest corner of The Square—the tumult of vile energy announcing the vortex of evil.

After my experience under the tree with the entity, I was expecting to have a horde of demons fall upon me and rip me to shreds. Nothing happened. Nothing so much as even an electric shock or an unusually strong gust of wind. Feeling a fool, I cracked open my eyes to glance around me, realizing that, in anticipation of an onslaught, I'd squeezed them shut—not summoning surrounding energy to help me fight back, not casting out my senses to determine what was coming my way. Nope, just closing my eyes and cringing. Warlock my ass.

Maybe I had been in sensory overload on my first visit, or maybe it was because it had been at night, but The Square wasn't as ominous in appearance as I remembered. True, compared to the neighborhoods on the outskirts, it was even more rundown and sinister looking, but it was better than what I'd expected. There was still an abundance of empty storefronts, but a bookstore, restaurant, and a couple of stores were dispersed among the bars.

While the marble courthouse in the middle of The Square was larger and more imposing than I remembered, I wasn't all that surprised it didn't stick out in my memory. There was nothing overly memorable about it. The only adornments the building could boast were a carved lion's head in the center of the overhang, etched words that scrolled around the top of the marble wall, and massive, crumbling columns spaced about every ten feet or so. Even the small sweep of steps leading down from the entrance was in disrepair—stray weeds and struggling saplings shoving through the cracks here and there. The few windows that weren't covered in cardboard from the inside were cracked or gone altogether. A small forest of trees surrounded most of the massive courthouse, obscuring it from view.

A movement from behind the courthouse drew my attention. A tall, thin man—at least, it moved like a man—exited a bar in the far northeast corner. Stumbling, he turned to his right and moved out of sight, the courthouse blocking my view. I waited for him to reappear on the other side, but after several more moments, I assumed he had entered another one of the bars.

Other than the oddly skeletal man, there were no other living people to be seen. Part of me would have felt less exposed if there had been a crowd of people to blend in with, but at least this way, I'd see whoever might decide to come in my direction.

Unsure of what to do now that I had arrived, I continued walking down Forest Street, glancing around at all the buildings in The Square. Either painted above the doorway or on signs hanging from the tattered awnings, each store had a simple name. The first I came to was empty, but the following said BOOKS, and the next BAR. Peering in both of the windows of the bookstore, I couldn't see anyone moving around, but could see row upon row of bookshelves in the shrouded room. BAR's windows were painted over in black. The lot that followed was empty and charred. Whatever establishment had been there had not been rebuilt after it had burned down. The store flanking the scorched lot read PORN. These windows were filled from floor to ceiling with large screens, each showing scenes that had never before come into my imagination—many of which I was sure were illegal. The last store on the block, before The Square wrapped around onto Nogal Street, was another empty building, its storefront windows gone entirely.

Having walked the one block allowed me to scope out all corners of The Square. I counted six stores that were labeled BAR—no other differentiation than that. Besides the BOOKS and PORN, there was also RESTAURANT, DANCE, HEAD SHOP, and GIFTS. The idea of a gift shop in The Square caused me to laugh out loud rather abruptly. The sound of my voice startled me. This time, I began to gather energy around me as I prepared for who, or what, I might have just alerted to my presence.

Still no one moved. I was by myself.

Maybe I'd assumed once I got here the answer would pop out—the next move obvious. However, I was more confused than ever. I'd spent so much of the afternoon searching, there wasn't all that much time left until sunset. So much for finding the lair of the vampire during the day. Still, there had to be something here. Something.

Maybe this was how it should be. Maybe I needed to be here after sunset. Hell, maybe the vamp would show. It could be my lucky night. Not sure if that would really count as luck or not.

I shoved my hand into the right pocket of my jeans and pulled out my cell phone to call Cynthia. She'd be worried that she hadn't heard from me yet, and would get even more so when I told her I wouldn't return as soon as I'd anticipated. Running my finger across the screen, the option menu lit up, telling me it was later than I'd originally thought. Holding my finger over Cynthia's face on my contact page, I waited for it to dial.

Nothing.

I held the phone to my ear. Silence.

Another glance at the home screen informed me that I had no service. I let out a sigh. Imagine that. No service in a place of evil. Who'd have thought?

At the moment, I was rather irritated with my parents. Even though they wanted to protect all of us from the darker side of our society and from the more dangerous species, it might have been advantageous for them to have at least taught us what we needed to know in order to defend ourselves against whatever might come our way. I was beginning to feel like Pollyanna being dropped off at the beginning of a horror movie, with no other tools but her ability to play the "Glad Game."

After taking another few glances around, trying to get some type of sign, I finally decided to go to the store marked GIFTS, partly because I couldn't imagine what they would sell and partly because it seemed the least daunting.

Still not encountering anyone as I made my way down Nogal Street, and after passing two of the other bars, I took a steadying breath and pushed the door open. A chime sounded, the same as at Dad's store. What had I expected? The calling of ravens or women screaming?

Pausing for a few moments, I held the door open, waiting to see what would come out to greet me. When no one came, I let the door swing shut on its own.

Honestly, the store wasn't anything like I'd expected. It was clean, well lit, and much more organized and feng shui than Dad's. Items were displayed on bamboo shelves and cabinets along the walls. A glass counter made a large square in the center of the store—merchandise exhibited within and a cash register on top. A large fish tank seemed to be taking up most of the expanse of the rear wall.

Stepping further into the store, I walked over to the glass counter. Glancing through, there didn't seem to be much different here than at a lot of the tacky gift stores at the mall. Most of the case was taken up with resin statues and figurines. The ones in front ranged from unicorns and fairies to ornate dragons and knights on black horses. I bent to inspect a glittering black unicorn. The memory of Caitlin's mocking voice caused me to redirect my attention. My unicorn fascination was far more shameful than her fetish for mutilating monster figurines, or at least that was her assertion.

As I walked around the case, the figurines took a darker turn. Devils, monsters, and scenes of people being tortured replaced the lighter and more fanciful. I bent once again to inspect. This was much more up Caitlin's alley.

"Can I help you find something, dear?" The scratchy voice above me caused me to shoot up from my crouched position beside the case.

Turning, I saw a short, thin woman. Her mouth settled into a hard line. I must have been gawking at her without realizing it. "There's no reason to be rude, boy." Her hands subconsciously smoothed out the top part of her skirt.

"Oh no. I'm sorry." I tried to quit staring, but I couldn't tear my eyes away from her as I spoke. "I just wasn't expecting…."

"What?" Her voice became a short staccato, even raspier than before. "A witch?"

I continued to stare at her, all the time trying to focus on something else in the room, but every time my eyes attempted to look elsewhere, they were drawn instantly back to her. She wore a full-length black dress with black lace poking out in ruffles from the hem of her long sleeves and skirt. On top of her head was one of the tallest, most tattered and pointed "witch hats" I had ever seen, long stringy gray hair hanging limply underneath. She'd applied an obviously fake wart to the side of her left nostril and held a ratty wooden broom in her hand.

She leaned closer to me, her hand shooting out to close over mine where it was gripping the counter. "Don't let the outfit mislead you, warlock. You try anything funny in my store, I swear I'll make it where you can't…." She let out a gasp as her black-contact eyes met mine for the first time. "Oh, I'm sorry." While still gravelly, her voice took on a less menacing tone. She let go of my hand and took a step back.

Unclear what had caused her sudden change of attitude, I waited—not sure if she expected me to do something or if she was getting ready to make an offensive move.

When she continued to simply stand there, her eyes downcast, I addressed her cautiously. "I'm sorry. I wasn't trying to offend you. I wasn't expecting a witch to dress so, well, so much like a witch, I guess."

She lifted her eyes from the floor but still refused to meet my gaze. "It's just part of being here in The Square. The *humans* expect it." I could hear the distaste in her voice.

Looking past her ridiculous costume, which most witches would refuse to wear on principle, it was easy to see the older woman wasn't any more like the witch from storybooks than my mother was. I was even willing to bet the gray hair hanging around her face was sewn into the hat, hiding her real hair underneath.

I almost asked her why her attitude had changed with me, but then decided I'd better not press my luck. It would be more helpful to simply get her on my side somehow. "Well, I'm sorry that you have a boss who requires you to wear that. Although I guess it's the same as having to wear a crazy getup for fast-food restaurants and those pretzel places with the bad hats."

For a split second, I could see the anger shoot through her once more, but she quickly stuffed it back down and gritted her teeth. "*I* own this store."

"Oh. Sorry." I glanced around, trying to find some other topic, something that might make it easier to lead into a conversation that could offer some details about Brett or the vampire. Drawing a blank, I turned back to her. "Do you mind if I look around?"

She opened her mouth to reply but was cut off by the chiming of the front door.

I turned around to see who had entered. It was a human couple. A goth girl, probably in her late teens or early twenties, with her computer-geek boyfriend, who looked ready to turn around and flee as he caught sight of the "real-life witch" talking to me. The girl, on the other hand, let out an elated squeal and rushed toward a section of vampire paraphernalia—books about vampires, blood-scented candles, fake teeth—dragging her hyperalert boyfriend along with her.

Muttering something about wishing she could show her new patrons a real vampire, the witch left me at the counter and headed over to the couple.

In her absence, a feeling of purposelessness washed over me again. What did I expect to find here? Sure, I'd seen a vampire here for all of five minutes when Jake had brought me years ago. Sure, this store was owned by an actual witch, costume notwithstanding. So what? I might as well take a break from the bakery and walk over to Mascarada. At least Dad had actual supernatural items in his store. It wasn't just a dumb tourist trap. Maybe all this was a lure to get humans to come play on the dark side, all the while giving a select few supernaturals money and occasionally providing a vampire with a meal or two.

I'd spend a few more minutes in here, maybe try another store or two, and then be on my way. No matter if trying to find the vampire helped me feel like I was doing something, it was definitely more useful to be home soothing Brett than being here at this messed-up Disneyland.

Wandering in the opposite direction of the most mismatched couple of the year, I headed to a section comprised of different weaponry. Although there were a few toy guns and grenades and such, the majority seemed to be of the medieval theme—plastic swords, maces, axes. Most were cheap replicas that were obviously nothing more than children's toys with noticeable plastic seams and acrylic jewels. However, there were a few that were fairly convincing fakes. A lightweight metal sword had the head and body of a dragon for the hilt, its tail swirling around to form the guard. In fact, the longer I browsed through the weapons section, the more I found that were real, many of them looking like actual ancient weapons, as opposed to reproductions. I accidentally grazed my arm on the head of a morningstar club, its sea-urchin-like spikes easily slicing through my skin, leaving a small line of blood.

"You need to be more careful around here, young warlock." The witch was back at my side with a malevolent smile on her face, her eyes still refusing to meet mine. "Don't let the attempts to appease the masses fool you." Without warning, her hand shot out, and her long, deep purple nails scraped against the cut, removing the blood and healing my skin in its wake.

I stood frozen, expecting her to raise her finger to her lips. Instead, her eyes flashed toward mine for the briefest of moments as she wiped her nail on the inside of her high lace collar.

"Did you not expect there to be genuine among the fake? Sometimes the best place to conceal the exceptional is amid the counterfeit."

Glancing over, I saw the couple perusing T-shirts and backpacks with the emblem of the stone lion head and "The Square" in blood-red text embroidered on them. "Like a genuine witch hiding in a witch's costume." I was disheartened to hear the tremble in my voice.

"Obviously." This time, when she reached for me, she did so slowly, giving me time to pull away if I chose. Gently, she took my left hand and turned it up within hers. Then her talon-like nails traced and swirled over the lines in my palm. "Now tell me, warlock, you didn't come here to play with plastic swords. What is it you seek?"

"I'm...." *What do I say to this woman?* Obviously, I couldn't trust her, but I knew I was out of my league if I hoped to trick something out of her. "I'm not sure."

"Come, come now." She was bent over my hand, the top of her pointed hat hitting me in the face as her nail began to trace the lines more slowly and deeply. "You didn't come here to play games any more than you did to play with my toys. What is it you seek?"

"A vampire." I hadn't consciously chosen to tell her, but now that it was out, it flowed. "I am looking for a particular vampire. I'm not really sure where to start. Do you have any idea how to find one?"

This time, when her eyes met mine, they held on, not darting away. "*A* vampire? *Really?*" She cocked her head at me, all at once resembling a crow. "A solitary vampire is why you think you are here?"

I nodded stupidly.

She shifted to peer at me from the other side. Her gaze probed deeply, her fingers never ceasing to follow the lines in my palm.

She let out a harsh chuckle. "Fine, then. A vampire. You're here to find a vampire." She dropped my hand without preamble, and her fingers reached out to caress the morningstar that had wounded me.

"Yes. What can you tell me about them? Can you tell me where to find them?"

She began walking away from me, and I followed.

Her path was bringing us closer to the human couple. Seemingly uncaring, she began to speak, her craggy voice steady and clipped. "Vampires. You can find them here, but you already know that." She gave a dismissive flick of her hand. "Disgusting creatures, really. Shouldn't exist." Her volume increased, as if she were yelling at someone across the room. "At least we haven't had any of those dammed Royals prowling around lately."

She paused and glanced at me over her shoulder. "Are you wanting to become one?"

I shook my head.

She nodded. "Fuck one?"

"No!" I hadn't expected that.

"No, thought not." She let out a wicked chuckle. "You're already fucking something much more dangerous than a lowly vampire." She grinned. "Or at least, you will be."

She had to be talking about Brett. I could feel my heart pounding against my ribs. I was unclear if it was responding to her knowledge of Brett or her veiled promise of what lay ahead in our future.

I turned to face her, suddenly not caring if the human couple heard us any more than she did. "You obviously can either see into the present or the future. You know things about me. You'll also know what it is I need to know. Where do I find him?"

"The vampire?" Her voice was mocking.

I leaned closer to her, refusing her the opportunity to turn away. "You're right, I'm not here to play games, so quit playing with me. Tell me what I need to know. Where do I find the vampire?"

Not looking at all concerned, she shrugged. "A lone vampire's location is not what you need to know."

"Then what is it I need to know?" It was my turn to grit my teeth.

She offered another noncommittal shrug. "I won't answer what isn't asked."

I struggled to keep the frustration from my voice. "I know compared to you I am young in my power, but I'm not new to it. Quit. Playing. Games."

She broke into a crooked smile. "You may be young, warlock, but your power is greater than mine. I also know you won't use it against me, so don't bother with the attempted intimidation."

I continued to glare. She was right. We both knew I wouldn't actually try to hurt her, but I had no idea why she thought my power was stronger than hers. I couldn't read palms or tell the future. Of course, maybe she couldn't either. It could all just be some messed-up mind game she enjoyed.

She reached up and gave my cheek a quick smack, causing me to flinch back from the sting. "Trust me, boy, I'm not the one playing games."

Our attention was drawn by another shrill squeal. "Frank! Look, a sea dragon! I love sea dragons!"

Glancing behind, I could see the goth girl once again pulling the geek (Frank, apparently) along behind her toward the fish tanks on the back wall.

I turned back to the witch, but she was already stepping away from me. "We're done, warlock. For now. Why don't you check out my fish selection for sale before you show yourself out."

I started to move after her but then thought better of it. It was clear any *help* I might receive from her this evening was going to be shrouded in vagueness and would be no use at all.

Uncertain why I listened to her, I closed the gap between where she had abandoned me and the wall of fish.

Upon closer inspection, I realized the wall was indeed one giant fish tank. It was divided into thirteen narrow vertical sections, stretching from floor to ceiling. I hadn't really given it more than a glance before, but it was beautiful. The water seemed more like a crystalline gel than fish water, particles refracting rainbow light sporadically.

"Frank! Look at this octopus! I've never seen one such a gorgeous red before!"

I followed her gaze. Sure enough, the octopus, compacted into one of the rear corners of the tank except for a couple of its tentacles that reached alluringly toward the couple, was a shimmering ruby red. Glistening yellow spots were scattered randomly over the gemlike skin.

Mesmerized, I stepped closer to the octopus's section of the tank. The tentacles reaching toward the humans whipped back to entangle within its mess of arms. The flawless crimson skin paled instantly to a dull gray, nearly allowing it to disappear against the rear glass of its enclosure.

Goth girl looked over her shoulder at me, an annoyed expression on her mousy countenance. "It doesn't seem to like you very much."

"Sarah!" Frank-the-geek-king turned to me nervously, probably expecting to see another witch. His eyes narrowed, but he must have determined that I was harmless. This time Sarah was the one to get her arm pulled. "Come on. Let's get outta here."

She shot another longing glance at the wall of fish. "Fine. You promised we could go dancing. Can we go dancing?"

Frank eyed me once more. "Sure. I don't wanna stay too long, though. I've got shows recording at home."

Sarah let out a soft whine. "Just great. Just what I was looking forward to after a night of dancing."

"Come on." He gave her a sterner glare than I would have thought him capable of and led her to the door.

Watching them exit, I realized the sun had set since I had entered the store. Maybe the witch was wrong. Maybe I would find him tonight. True, I still had no idea what I'd do then, but that didn't matter at this point—I'd wing it.

I turned back to the octopus, which was still a lackluster gray. A flicker of movement caught my eye. The sea dragons were in the adjacent column. Moving over slightly, I peered in at them. I'd seen them at aquariums before, but could never quite get used to them. They never appeared to be real. Their lightning-shaped bodies and countless leaflike projections made it seem impossible for them to be living, much less to have the capacity to swim.

The largest one glided inelegantly toward me. Its body was striated in the typical yellowish-brown, but its leafy projections were a vibrant blue. It was nearly a foot long, dwarfing the others. I leaned closer, mesmerized. Its emerald-green eyes followed mine. I stared at it. It stared back.

Unconsciously, my hand rose to press against the glass. The sea dragon glanced at my hand, then returned its gaze to mine, coming closer.

"No." My voice was so low, I couldn't even hear myself. "No. It can't be."

After a few more moments, I tore my gaze from the dragon. With a quick glance, not seeing the witch, I rushed from section to section, peering just long enough into every column to confirm my suspicion. Why would she have wanted me to see this?

Without another look, I dashed across the store, nearly colliding with a shelf full of crystal balls. Avoiding them, I made it to the door and through it without checking over my shoulder.

At first, I didn't even take in the growing crowd on the sidewalk, nor the lamps that had ignited all over the square. I couldn't believe what I had seen.

The witch wasn't selling fish for collectors' aquariums.

Every specimen in there was a magical creature. Not only was it against our laws to capture or traffic in supernatural animals, especially in public, but these were ones that had been believed to have gone extinct eons ago, or to have never existed at all.

CHAPTER SEVENTEEN

THE growing number of people milling about The Square, as well as the soft lighting from the old-fashioned gas lamps that enclosed its circumference, should have helped calm my nerves. At night, The Square had a nostalgic charm about it. My mind was too overwhelmed by what I had seen in the gift shop to allow the environment to have an effect on me. I was already halfway across the other block before I realized I was walking aimlessly and that this was the last place a person should be caught unaware. When I finally came to a halt, I was in front of DANCE.

A girl bumped into me in her rush to get in the dance club. She didn't bother to acknowledge my presence. Stepping out of the way, I took a second to look around and regain my bearings. The increase of people in The Square was exponential. There were a few witches and warlocks here and there (none that I recognized, of course), but the majority were everyday humans, most obviously comfortable, like they'd been here before, but a few glancing around nervously. The windows around The Square were lit up, except for the ones that were boarded over or painted black.

Part of me felt silly for rushing away from the witch and her wall of fish. I hadn't been in any imminent danger. The discovery of such specimens alive—not only alive but for sale out in the open—well, the implications were too significant to even begin to comprehend. Few humans, if any, would notice anything overly special about the fish. Maybe they'd think they were brighter or bigger or more unusual, but there was little danger of anyone getting suspicious. I'd pretty much decided I would head back to Brett after the gift shop. However, if such things were right there, out in the open, in the first place I'd gone into, what else was this place hiding?

I was now facing the rear of the courthouse. The building was even less impressive from this side. Turning my attention away, I tried to determine my next move. It looked like most of the traffic was going into the dance club. As I turned to enter, a thin redheaded man caught my attention from farther down the block. I felt my heart start to pound. I couldn't be sure, I'd only seen the back of him as he walked through the door, but he triggered the memory of the vampire as he'd turned and led Brett out the door of the restaurant.

Okay, what was I supposed to do? Walk up to him and ask him why he was stalking Brett? I was fairly certain I could defend myself against him, at least enough to not get killed, but I also knew there was little to no chance of killing him on my own either. If nothing else, maybe I could follow him, figure out where he slept during the day.

Blood rushing, I headed back down the direction I'd come. I slipped in through the door the redhead had gone through. I was in a bar. It took only a millisecond for my eyes to adjust to the dark. The room was long and narrow. The glass bar, made up of two-foot-square glass blocks, took up most of the west wall. The blocks were backlit by a deep red glow, giving the room a false sense of muted warmth.

There were only eight to ten people in the bar, including a beautiful, scantily clad witch, her long blonde hair reflecting back the red light behind her as she shook a martini shaker.

I did my best to only pause for a moment. I'd done a bad enough job of blending in at the gift shop. The Square had humans and supernaturals alike who came and went as they pleased. Why couldn't I simply be one of them? There was no reason to act out of place, except for whatever had nearly captured me when I'd been under the tree.

After another quick scan of everyone and not seeing the redhead, I walked over to the bar, where the blonde bartender was now leaning intimately toward a burly man across from her. I could have sworn the man's black eyes flashed over toward me before he whispered something to the witch. I chastised myself for being so paranoid.

Despite obviously seeing me sit down at the bar, the witch continued her conversation, never acknowledging my presence. Jake had gotten our drinks when we'd come here before. I wasn't sure if there was a protocol I was missing or if I was just supposed to yell rudely at the staff. It was The Square, after all. Instead, I waited, feeling awkward sitting there with nothing in my hands.

There didn't seem to be much special about the other patrons. Over half were a group of humans, all of whom seemed to be more out of place than I felt.

A witch and warlock couple toward the back of the bar were mostly obscured by the back of their booth, which appeared to have been made from the frame of an antique canopy bed. Every so often, bits of their tense conversation rose to a decibel allowing me to get an idea of the topic. That, along with the witch's tears, made it seem like it was nothing more unusual than your everyday lover's quarrel. She felt he'd shown too much interest in the bartender. Apparently, he'd always had a thing for blondes….

The two women toward the front of the bar had a supernatural feel about them. They weren't witches, but I couldn't tell what they were. The final patron was directly across the bar from me at the other end, his willowy frame hunched over his drink in a declaration of defeat. I stared at him for a couple of minutes before his bloodshot gaze lifted and gave me a reproving glare. I hadn't been able to figure out what he was until I saw his eyes. It took everything in me not to gasp. If you hadn't known the signs, you'd probably not notice. His eyes were just a little too big for his face, slightly larger than human or witch eyes. More noticeable was the crystalline quality they possessed. Despite the multitude of red veins running through them, his eyes appeared cleaner—more unpolluted—than anyone else's I'd ever seen, a true sense of what eyes should look like. A fairy.

Fairies have one of the lowest populations of any supernatural species. I'd heard of them—Mom and Dad had a great story of one they'd met on their honeymoon in Hawaii—but I'd never seen one for myself. From what I knew, most fairies were mostly harmless, more obsessed with beauty and playing tricks than anything else. However, there were accounts of some who were anything but harmless pranksters—initiating wars, mass murders, all types of devastation that humans never knew they were being manipulated into performing. From his rather disgusting physical appearance and the hate in his eyes,

I felt it was safe to assume he was the kind who would take pleasure in performing the role of puppet master in such a conspiracy.

The fairy's eyes darted to his left, away from me. Following his glance, I saw the redhead emerge from somewhere near the rear of the bar. Maybe the restroom. On his arm was a young girl, maybe fourteen, *maybe*. Her eyes were glazed and never left him as he led her through the bar. There were fresh bite marks covering her neck, blood making a slow stream into the collar of her filthy baby-blue T-shirt. Following the trail of blood, I saw a small assortment of deeper bite marks on her forearm.

I'd been right about the redhead being a vampire, but it wasn't the right one. Brett's vampire had appeared to be a little younger than me. This one seemed to have been changed in his early fifties. His face swiveled to me as I made to get off my barstool. His upper lip curved in a silent snarl, exposing his fangs in a warning.

Not sure what I was going to do next, I took a step toward the couple, planning on trying to paralyze him. I knew the spell worked easily enough on witches. I'd used it on Caitlyn more than once, but I wasn't sure about vampires. Seemed like a good time to find out.

"Whatever you're thinking about trying, kid, I wouldn't." I felt a viselike grip on my left elbow, the strength of it stopping me where I stood.

Turning, all I could see was a beer logo across a gray T-shirt straining over a massive chest. Moving my eyes upward, I met the black eyes of the man who'd been sitting at the bar. Werewolf. How had I missed that tiny detail?

I glanced back toward the vampire. He'd already exited the front door. I could see him still leading the girl away from the bar windows. Again, I made a motion to move toward them.

"Maybe I didn't make myself clear before, boy. Leave them alone." He didn't attempt to hide the growl in his gravelly voice.

I could feel my face flush in anger as I turned and glared back up at the werewolf. "If I don't do something, he'll kill her."

He gave an unconcerned shrug. "Part of coming to The Square. She shoulda stayed clear." His gaze passed over my head as he followed their path through the window. "Can't blame him. I was thinking of having her as a little snack myself."

I made another motion toward the door, only to be jerked back more forcibly. "Dude, come on. I need to help her."

"No." His eyes leveled with mine. They were solid black, no differentiation between the pupil and the iris. "You don't. This happens all the time here, whether you're here or not. You don't know if he will kill her or just use her. Either way, even if you did save her, she'd only be back tomorrow."

To my disgust, I couldn't find a reasonable argument against his logic. This was what went on here; it was part of it. If I was going to be distracted by every person who made their choices and took the risk of coming here, I'd never even have a chance at helping Brett. Not that a girl that young could really make her own choices. At least not responsible ones. Still, I was sure there were lots of teenagers that came here. I couldn't change that.

"Come on back to the bar." He was already leading me back. "It's easy enough to get into trouble your first time here. You don't need to go searching for it."

"It's not my first time here." I cringed inwardly at the defiant teenage tone in my voice.

"Really? Might as well be." He settled back onto his barstool. I followed his lead. "Does your dad know you're here?"

That was the last thing I expected him to say. "My *dad*?"

"Yeah, I doubt Wendell would be too pleased." He paused and gave a cockeyed look. "You are one of Wendell de Morisco's kids, right?"

I stared at him, dumbfounded. "How do you know my dad?"

A crooked grin cut across his chiseled face, giving his craggy features the smallest hint of boyishness. "He comes here all the time. One of the regulars. Right, Marina?" He thrust his chin toward the bartender. She only rolled her eyes.

"He… h-h-he comes in here?" My worldview was beginning to crumble.

Letting out a howl of a laugh, he brought his hand down hard on the bar top, causing Marina to give him a sidelong glare. "Nah! I'm fuckin' with ya, kid. Your dad wouldn't come within a hundred yards of this place."

"Oh" was all I could manage to get out.

He took a huge draft of his beer. "I go into your dad's shop from time to time. He helps me out on stuff. He's a pretty cool guy."

That made more sense, but still, picturing Dad being on a first name basis with this werewolf was off-putting.

"The name's Farvin." He didn't put out his hand.

"Finn."

"Oh sure, yeah. I've heard him talk about you before. You, ah… *bake* or something, right?"

"I work in Mom's bakery, yeah."

He seemed to not find it necessary to acknowledge any more on the subject of baking. Turning back to Marina, he cast his heavily muscled arm over my shoulders. "Bring a beer for my man here, wench."

"I told you the next time you call me that, Farvin, I'm spittin' in your drink." She gave him a scowl but poured beer from the tap into a frosted mug and slid it over.

As he pushed the beer toward me, he kept his arm across my shoulders, his heavy bicep flexing against the back of my neck.

"Farvin, uhm… I'm not sure if I'm reading you right, but I'm sorta seeing someone." Nothing like putting the cart before the horse.

An eyebrow rose quizzically, and then he jerked his arm away with a shake. "Awww, fuck. A fag? Really? Wendell didn't mention *that*." He cast a withering glare at me. "Not that I blame him."

It had been years since I'd been called that. I'd almost forgotten the sting, like getting backhanded. I slid off the barstool. "Screw you, asshole. If you didn't—"

He pushed me back onto the stool with a light shove. "Come on now. Don't get your panties in a bunch. I know you witches are fine with whatever the in thing is at the moment. Werewolves? Well, we don't put up with that kinda stuff, but whatever, man, your deal, not mine."

In thing at the moment? Was this guy for real? "Listen, Farvin, it's obvious I'm wasting your time here. I think it would be better if I—"

He raised his massive hands in a surrendering gesture. "Relax, man, relax. Besides, I'm curious what one of Wendell's kids is doing at The Square. Gotta be a good story behind that." He leaned a couple of inches closer, his lowered voice sounding even more like a growl. "You came here for some of the back rooms, didn't ya? I know they've got some stuff for *your kind*." By "your kind," I didn't think he meant warlock.

"Back rooms?" My face gave a genuinely blank expression.

"Oh." His eyebrows furrowed together. "Guess you're more like Wendell after all. If you're not here for the back rooms, then what are you here for?"

"Well, I'm not exactly sure where to find what I'm looking for. Maybe these back rooms would have it."

"Nah, if the back rooms had what you were wanting, you'd already know and would have come here with them in mind." He gave another scowl. "So, what? You lose your *boyfriend* or something?"

I ignored the disgust in his voice, remembering that I had to do whatever I needed to do to help Brett. I must have been insane to think this guy had been hitting on me. Still, he knew my dad, and that had to mean something. Maybe he could help. "Actually, yeah, kinda. He's got this vampire following him, seems like he's stalking him. Killing people he loves, that kind of thing."

His scowl deepened. "Sick fuckers. Nothing worse than vampires. Not any better than a bunch of cockroaches." He took another deep guzzle and emptied the glass, then swiped his arm across his mouth, leaving traces of foam in the thick black hair on his forearm. "It's the only bad thing about this place—having to share it with the likes of those freaks." At least there seemed to be something he hated more than *fags*.

"Yeah, can't say I'm too fond of them at the moment either." I motioned out the window toward the path the vampire had taken with the girl. "He's the reason I came in this bar. He looked like the same vampire. Tall, redheaded. Wasn't him, though."

His gaze traveled over me, giving me the once-over, another grin cracking his face. "And your plan was to what? Do some spells? Ask him to leave your boy toy alone?"

I couldn't help it as my chin thrust out defiantly. "Actually, I wasn't completely sure. I guess the best case scenario was that I'd find him and follow him so that I'd know where he slept during the day."

He nodded, as if granting his approval, grudgingly. "Not too bad, actually. You've got guts at any rate, planning to try to kill a vampire. Not that I'd expect any less from one of Wendell's kids. Even if he is a queer."

Not knowing if I should take his words as a compliment or another insult, I just sat there, staring at him.

"You missed one vital aspect to the old vampire hunt, though."

"Did I?" My voice was expressionless, fully expecting some gay-bashing punch line.

"Yep, the one thing vampires and werewolves have in common. The *only* thing."

I didn't even try to keep the sarcasm out of my voice. "And what's that, Farvin?"

He leaned closer, this time the growl in his voice clearly intentional. "Just so you know, Wendell's kid or not, the next time we speak, if you continue to have such an air of disrespect when you address me, you'll find out how good your witchy spells are against a werewolf."

Without waiting for a reply, he leaned back, his voice returning to his normal baritone pitch. "You can't ever follow a werewolf, or a vampire, without their knowledge. I guess it's the shared predatory instinct. We always know when we're being tailed."

He got up and slid his glass across the bar. "Marina, I'll be back to pick you up by the time you're done. I'm going out for a run." She flipped her long hair over her shoulder as she gave him the briefest of glances.

Turning back to me, the quiet snarl once again returning, he leaned closer. "If you weren't Wendell's kid, I'd sit back and enjoy the show. If there's a next time, if I get my druthers, I will." He turned to go but then swiveled back for one last comment. "But I'll give you one more helpful hint. Get out of here, kid. Staying here will just get you deeper in shit than you already are, trust me. Tell your dad hi."

I SAT there for another fifteen or twenty minutes, intentionally nursing my beer. I'd been surprised by how the bar had filled up during our talk. The two women of unknown origin were still there, but the small group of humans and the quarreling witches had given way to a larger mix of human, witch, and vampires—none of which matched the one that attacked Brett.

Eventually, I decided to take Farvin at his word. There was nothing left at The Square for me tonight. I needed to go home. I needed to be with Brett.

CHAPTER EIGHTEEN

Cynthia must have heard me pull into the drive, as she met me at the door. The hair around her face was plastered to her damp skin. Her concerned relief passed in an instant, giving way to uncharacteristic anger.

"Where have you been?" Her voice was hushed but shrill as her emotions got the best of her. "You've been gone for hours. Hours! I had no idea what to do. No idea if you were safe or not. I tried and tried to call, but it kept going straight to your voice mail! Getting him stuff at the store does not take that long."

My mouth opened, attempting a response.

"Don't even try it, Finn Christian de Morisco! If you even think of telling me that you were getting stuff for Brett, I swear I'll put a binding spell on you that you won't break out of for the next week! I was just getting ready to call Mom and Dad if you—"

I cut in, my voice rising momentarily above hers. "You didn't, did you?"

Her arms folded tightly across her chest, her voice hissing through her gritted teeth. "Didn't *what*?"

"Didn't call Mom and Dad."

She rolled her eyes. "Of course, *that's* the part you're worried about. Never mind all my worry. How I was afraid you were dead. Never mind that I had to put Brett out twenty or thirty times! All you care about is—"

"Put Brett *out*? What do you mean?"

"His hands kept catching on fire. Over and over again. I'd barely get the sheets repaired and there he'd go again. I wasn't sure what I was going to do. Finn?"

I rushed past her and into the bedroom before Cynthia had time to leave the doorway.

Brett lay on his back in a tangle of sheets, scorch marks evident here and there on the fabric. His clothes were rumpled and damp with sweat. His blond hair lay in wet tangles over his head, his closed eyes puffy and red above his grimacing lips.

Cynthia squeezed my shoulder supportively as she stepped up behind me. Her voice returned to her soothing cadence. "He's been like this almost since you left. Tossing and turning. Crying, calling out. Catching fire."

"What's he calling out?"

"Not words. Not most of the time, anyway—sometimes I'd hear Sonia's name or yours once or twice—mostly angry shouts or yells, or, even worse, these anguished sobs. I've never heard anything like it. He sounded like a dying animal."

I glanced out the window. "The neighbors?"

She let out a sigh. "I am capable of a muffling charm, you know."

"Right." At least one of us was remembering she was a witch. I gazed back at his beautiful face, twisted in agony. At his matted hair. "Does he have a fever?"

"How would I know, Finn? He's a fire demon. What's the normal body temperature for a fire demon?" She gave him a look most reserved for small children, not demons. "I don't think he's actually sick. I think he's just hurting, and if you'd been catching fire all day, you'd be sweating too."

I walked over to the bed and swept his hair off his brow, feeling silly as I glanced up, remembering Cynthia was in the room. "I'm sorry, Cyn. He wasn't like this last night or this morning. I couldn't get anything out of him. If I'd have known, I'd never have asked you to stay with him." Guilt washed over me. How could I have left him when he needed me here? Just to make myself feel useful? And for what?

She watched as my fingers trailed gently down his cheek and then over his shoulder. "It's okay. I hated seeing him in so much pain and not being able to do anything. I tried every comfort and sleep spell I could think of." Her gaze passed back and forth between Brett and me several times.

"What?" I could feel my face flush under her gaze.

She took a few steps forward and sat on the opposite edge of the bed. "It's just that... well, he's better."

"Well, it's only been a minute or two."

Her eyes met mine, direct. "No, you don't understand. It has been constant. Even when his hands weren't bursting into flame, his body never stopped writhing. He never stopped groaning and calling out."

"Huh." I looked away from her stare and gazed at Brett's face, which did seem a little more relaxed. The expression couldn't have been described as peaceful, but he did seem more at ease. "That's strange. I wonder what changed."

She let out a little laugh. "Well, isn't that obvious?"

I looked at her quizzically.

"You, silly. You." She leaned forward and took hold of his hand. "He's better now that you're here. You soothe him."

I didn't answer her, but the thought gave me pleasure. What if she was right? Maybe he really was better now that I was here. Maybe he did need me in some way... care about me....

"And no, Finn. I didn't call Mom and Dad. I was going to give you about twenty more minutes."

I gave her a brotherly smile. "Thanks, sweetie. I'm sorry I put you through this today."

She shrugged. "Well, at least I can say that I know how to extinguish a fire demon now. One that's unconscious, at any rate."

A little laugh escaped. Only Cynthia could evoke laughter from me right now. I looked at her, at my quiet and reserved sister. At my passionate and loyal sister. "I owe you huge, Cyn."

Her long mahogany hair cascaded as she shook her head. "No, you don't. The only thing you owe me is the truth."

I glanced up at her, both of my hands wrapped around Brett's protectively.

"Seriously, Finn. Where were you?"

We stared at each other in silence. Each waiting on the other to bend.

"I can't tell you." My voice was quiet. I was surprised she was able to hear me.

The crease between her eyebrows deepened. "What do you mean you can't tell me?"

I gave a guilty smile. "Well, let's just say I went vampire hunting."

Cynthia's eyes nearly bugged out of their sockets. Her mouth moved silently for several moments. I thought maybe I'd actually rendered her speechless. Then her lips formed a begrudging smile. "Only you would try to find a murderous vampire. In the middle of the day, no less."

"Can you think of an easier time to kill a vampire?"

Her eyes closed as she suppressed a shudder. "I should have known better than to let you be by yourself today"—she glanced at the digital clock beside the bed—"or yesterday, to be more precise."

I gave her another sheepish grin.

"Did you have any luck?"

My head drooped. "No. Nothing. I don't know any more about who this vampire is or where to find him."

"Well, I can't say I'm surprised. I'd be concerned if you had any idea where to start looking for a vampire."

I sidestepped that comment and did a poor job of stuffing the guilt of lying to Cynthia. She deserved better, but she didn't deserve to be stressed out by learning of The Square's existence, let alone what happened there. I resorted to diversionary tactics. As true as they were, I hoped it would steer us away from the chance I would accidentally slip up and say where I'd been. "That's exactly it, Cyn! We need to be better prepared. We should know where to find a vampire if we need to. We have no idea what's really out there."

She started to object. I cut her off. "We don't. We aren't prepared for all the evil in the world. Not only vampires. We're descended from demons. We are one of the most powerful witch families. We, the six of us—nine if you include Ricky and the boys—should be a force to be reckoned with. Instead, we are bakers and restaurant owners, costume shop proprietors and makeup artists. We have no idea what all is out there, and even less how to really protect ourselves and those we love."

We sat in silence, both of us lost in our thoughts. By the distant haze behind her eyes, I knew she was reliving her nightmare as clear as if it had happened yesterday.

After a time, I attempted to stretch out closer to Brett, as he seemed more restless. As I lay back, I gasped and reached over to clutch my ribs.

Cynthia narrowed her eyes in suspicion. "What is it? What did you do?"

I sighed. "Let's just say, I may not have found a vampire, but I still managed to hurt myself."

Her brown eyes widened again. "How?"

"Might have broken some ribs."

"How in the world did you break your ribs?"

I gave a noncommittal shrug and didn't meet her eyes. "Just trying a spell that didn't go so well."

"What kind of spell was that?"

"Cyn, please! Can you just help me out here?"

She glared at me, but she came around the bed and moved her hand to tenderly replace mine on my ribs. "Well, truthfully, it serves you right for putting me through so much worry today."

Without another word, she closed her eyes, and I could instantly feel her inside my body, a warm, soothing, balmy wave of power. Heat radiated outward from my ribs, a not unpleasant tingling pulsating around them. Within minutes, Cynthia's eyes opened, tired and worn. "You'd done a pretty good job on them yourself."

I nodded at the compliment. "I've never been strong at the healing side of things like you."

She neither denied nor acknowledged the truth of the statement. Instead, her gaze wandered from my fingers intertwined with Brett's, traveled over his body, and came to rest on his face. "What about him?"

I steeled myself, unsure where she was going with her question. "What about him?"

"What are you thinking? Are you hoping for a relationship?"

I shrugged. A gesture I knew didn't convince either of us. "I really like him, Cynthia."

"He's beautiful." Her eyes returned to me. "Of course you like him."

"Well, yeah, he is. But it's more than that."

She waited, smiling gently.

"He's such a mixture of confidence and bravado and quiet uncertainty. Like this little kid inside the body of a huge man." I felt foolish as my eyes got moist. "I don't really know what it is. I just feel… feel… well, I feel safe with him. At home. And I want to protect him, all at the same time."

"Oh, sweetie. At home? You barely know him."

From anyone else, such a comment probably would have earned a snappy retort, but not from her. "I know. I know. I can't describe it. And if someone else was saying these kinds of things about a guy they'd barely met, I'd call them a fool, but it's true, Cyn. It feels right. Like I might actually have everything I've always dreamed of but never dared to really hope for."

She gave me a sympathetic look and kissed me on the cheek. Her voice was hushed. "I love you, little brother. If you'd gotten yourself killed today, I'd have killed you."

With that, she slid fluidly off the bed, padded to the door, slipped through, and closed it behind her.

Curling up, my body fitting tightly into Brett's, I vowed to not leave his side again for any reason until he woke up.

CHAPTER NINETEEN

BRETT WRIGHT

I DON'T remember leaving my house or getting into Finn's truck. I'm not sure if I checked the bathroom or my room to see if I could find Sonia's body. I don't remember if I tried to clean up the blood or turn the furniture upright. I vaguely recall Finn's voice speaking in hushed panic into his phone as the truck sped us into the night, but the words are unintelligible in my memory. I remember seeing my reflection in the rain-splattered truck door window with every streetlamp we passed, my face slack and dull, the eyes of a stranger.

I WAS in a bed. The lights were off, but there were a few small candles flickering across the room. Often, I was aware of hands rubbing my back, pulling blankets around me, arms circling me, and a body pressing into my back. Other times, I knew I was alone. I must have passed out at some point, for the next thing I knew, there was light shining through the drawn curtain. I looked at the white comforter wrapped around me, traced the small stitches that made swirling patterns that circled in on themselves before shooting off to make more dandelion tufts whirling through an imaginary breeze on the surface of the fabric. The soft whiteness of the bedspread captivated my world.

After a time, I realized that the voice imploring me to eat and the hands I sometimes felt against my skin belonged to Finn. Without thinking of it, I knew I was in Finn's home, in his bed. I didn't look around. I saw nothing of the room, outside of the eddies of the blanket. I didn't feel the pressure of Finn's body as he got in and out of the bed. Occasionally, I would notice that the window was dark and the candles were lit once again. I'm sure I had to have gotten up to use the restroom, but I don't remember ever leaving the safety and warmth of the blankets.

I knew that if I stood up, if I lifted off the blanket, if I unwrapped my arms from around my torso, that my chest would rip open, my heart crush into thousands of pieces and fall out in a cascade of ashes onto the floor. I couldn't even see her face in my mind. I couldn't remember the exact hue of violet of her eyes, the shimmering of her hair, or the curve of her lips as she smiled. I couldn't even think her name. All of my consciousness was centered on the gaping hole slashed through my core. Breathing felt like more effort than I was able to give, yet somehow each breath was followed by another one, each ripping the hole deeper.

The candles had been lit and extinguished at least two different times when I felt a tear leak out of my left eye and make its way across the bridge of my nose and down my right check. I heard a deep, guttural moan and felt my throat crack. After the bed creaked, I felt the arms once again circle around and a hard body press into my back, warm breath against my neck. The sobs wracked my body until it felt as if not only would my heart splinter, but my entire being would fragment, every particle splitting and ripping asunder.

It would seem that the tears were finished, that there were no more that could possibly come, when a fresh wave of agony would overtake me and the tears would pour out again, putting to shame the ones that came before.

In time, not only did her name return but so did her face, her contagious laughter, the playful sarcasm in her voice. Each breath I exhaled spoke her name. Each thought another reminder of what I had lost. Sonia wasn't just a friend. Nor was she only family. She was the one person who had stood by me through everything. The one who had given me strength to face life on my terms, the one who loved me when the rest turned their backs.

She was gone. It didn't make any sense. I couldn't imagine a world without Sonia. I couldn't imagine me without Sonia. The fact of her existence was as sure as the sun rising each day. She couldn't be gone. It simply wasn't possible. There was no choice but for the universe to fold in on itself and return her to her proper place.

The past couple of times I saw Sonia started replaying through my mind. Her excitement over Derek. Her thrill of finding someone who she thought she could start something real with. Derek! What about Derek? What would he be thinking? What would he do when he found the house in shambles, her blood everywhere?

With a shake of my head, he flew from my mind, Sonia too powerful to be kept out. I saw her eyes twinkle at me as she took in Finn for the first time. Saw her float through the room at Rascals, delivering beer and cheeseburgers. Heard the concern in her voice as I talked to her about the strange things happening in the ocean as I swam.

The hole in my chest ripped deeper as I realized I would never be able to tell her about the new world I had discovered. The new me. She would never know that I was more than I appeared to be. Never know that there was magic. Never know about all the amazing things we never thought really existed. With bitterness, I realized that wasn't true. She did find out that there were creatures that were out of our fairy tales, out of our nightmares.

She died not knowing I was a demon. She died without knowing there were vampires, at least until it was too late. She died without knowing she was in danger just by knowing me.

In an instant, the hole burst fully open. Unlike what I'd expected, however, my heart didn't spill out. It didn't crumble. It exploded. Anger, like I never knew I could have, coursed through me. I felt my skin grow hot, felt my body convulse in rage. I swept the blanket off of me and pushed myself out of bed. I caught a brief reflection of myself in the mirror as I crossed the room to the door. It was enough to make me pause. I could see the steam wafting off my bare chest and shoulders. However, it wasn't my smoldering skin that caught my attention. My eyes shone like blue flames. Even in my state of mind, they caused me to stop and take in a breath. For a moment, I felt a stab of fear. Those eyes weren't human. They didn't look real. They didn't look from this world. They were alien. They were terrifying... they didn't matter. I tore my gaze away from the mirror.

The front door was visible from the bedroom, and I rushed toward it, swiping the keys off the back of the sofa. I didn't pause to close the door as I threw myself into the driveway, tore open the door to Finn's truck, and jammed the keys into the ignition. The truck roared to life and peeled out, tilting precariously as it turned into the street.

I had driven several miles and had somehow gotten to the Five before I realized I had no idea where I was going or where I had just been seconds before. After a time, I remembered that Finn had said he lived close to his parents, so I had to be in Encinitas.

I had to find the vampire. I had to rip him into pieces. Stamp his emerald eyes into the dirt. Burn him until he was nothing more than a pathetic pile of ashes in the street that I could piss over.

For a split second, my mind asked, *then what?* I shoved that thought aside before it had finished forming and felt the rage begin to overtake me again. I had no idea where I should start looking for him. I closed my eyes and gripped the steering wheel tightly, seeing if I could get a sense of where he was.

It was the smell and the sound of sizzling that made me open my eyes, not the blaring of horns from the cars around me on the highway. Instantly, I saw black smoke rising from the steering wheel. I pulled my hands off it. As I did, thin inky tendrils clung to my palms. On the steering wheel, there were deep impressions of my hands. I was melting the steering wheel. For a second I couldn't think what was happening.

I hit the window button with my elbow and shoved my hands out into the breeze, steering with my knees.

Calm down, calm down. You're not doing her any good like this. Save it for that fucker, to melt his face off. Breathe, breathe. After several moments, I returned my hands to the inside of the cab and tenderly touched the steering wheel. I didn't notice any more smoke, so I took that as a good sign.

I realized I was heading back home. My stomach dropped as I thought of walking through the doors. Could I handle being back there? It didn't matter. I had to handle it. Period. I had no other idea of where to begin searching for him. I doubted he just stayed lurking around the alley in Old Town, but if I couldn't think of anything else, I'd go back there too. Maybe there would be some clue at the house, something he dropped, something Sonia had ripped off of him. The thought made me cringe. Maybe she'd found a way to leave me a clue.

Turning into Hillcrest, I realized that it was daylight. I hadn't thought about it, but unless the vampire was part of the Royal Family, he wouldn't be out in the daytime. The thought made me breathe easier. I hadn't even been aware that I was partly afraid I would find him at the house. On the one hand, it was all I wanted. The sooner, the better. The sooner, the quicker Sonia could be avenged. But what if I couldn't win? What if, despite everything, he did that ridiculous voodoo with his eyes, and I followed him around like a housetrained puppy? For a moment, I considered going back to Finn's. Maybe warlocks were immune to whatever powers of compulsion vampires had.

No, this was my fight. I needed to be the one to avenge Sonia. I would be strong enough. I had to be.

I SAT in the driveway, staring at the house. Sonia's car was still parked where it always was, the red paint sparkling like candy in the sun. The house was quaint and charming as always. If things had not been happening like they had been recently, I would have thought I had made it all up, that I would walk in and the house would be just as it always was, that Sonia would be inside talking on the phone or getting ready to go to work, that there weren't demons, that I wasn't a demon.

I knew better. If anything, seeing Sonia's room the other night had made it clear that I not only knew I was a demon, that there were parts of my past I couldn't even imagine, but that nothing in my life would be the same again, ever.

With heavy feet, I made my way to the front door. I started to reach in and get the keys out of my pocket, but my hand couldn't find its way into the pocket. I glanced down. I'd forgotten. I only had on the sweatpants Finn must have put on me. My bare feet stuck out of the folds of fabric at the bottom. I glanced around to see if anyone had noticed me standing half-naked on my doorstep. I couldn't see anyone. As I turned back, I positioned myself so I was hiding the doorknob. I had never tried anything like this before, but after everything else, I didn't question it. I took it firmly in my hands, gave it a sharp twist, and felt it crack. I felt a twinge of disappointment as, with a gentle pull, the door handle slid out into my hand. I guess part of me had been hoping I had made it all up, that I couldn't smash a doorknob as easily as crushing popcorn.

Taking a deep breath, I pushed open the door, steadying myself against seeing our home broken and desecrated.

I stepped through and stared in bewilderment. For a split second, I thought I had broken into the wrong house. There was nothing out of place. The chairs were back in a standing position around the kitchen table, which was no longer split in half. There weren't any papers or broken glass scattered over the floor. Even the hole in the wall was gone. I walked over to it, cautiously touching it with the tips of my fingers. It hadn't been patched or freshly painted. It was just whole, like it had always been.

Glancing into the kitchen told me the same story. Not only was nothing out of place, but it had been cleaned up. The constant pile of dishes in the sink was gone, the counters free of all clutter. Perhaps if it hadn't been so perfect, so neat, I could have truly believed it really had all been a dream, that Sonia was here, that I was just normal Brett once again. The absence of untidiness screamed as loudly of Sonia's absence as had the torn-up house.

I knew what I'd see when I walked into Sonia's room. For some reason, knowing made it worse. The walls were clean, brand-new. The mattress was bare of sheets, but it was no longer stained with blood. The closet door was reattached. There was nothing that spoke of the travesty that had occurred here. Nothing that spoke of the fate Sonia had met. Nothing to show she had put up a fight. Nothing to honor her death, let alone her life.

Without searching, I knew there would be nothing here that could lead me to the vampire. Even if he had left something behind, or if Sonia had found a way to leave a clue, it would be gone, just as surely as she was.

All my fury left in a gush of wind as I sank onto her mattress. The absence of everything brought Sonia's death home in a harsher way than shuffling through our destroyed house would have. No longer did I feel the surety that I could find the vampire, or that I had any hope of making him pay for all he had done. I curled into a ball against Sonia's headboard and watched the shadows on the wall gradually shift positions as the sun traveled its course outside.

"BRETT, sweetie, wake up."

I felt a warm hand on my face, a thumb caressing my cheek. I opened my eyes. The room was awash in a pale orange light. I craned my neck to glance out the window. Sunset. I must have fallen asleep.

"Do you know where you are, Brett?" I turned my head to find Finn sitting beside me. He forced a small encouraging smile.

Did I know where I was? In the room of my dead best friend. In the room of the person who had been my rock. Yeah, I knew where I was.

I managed a nod.

"You scared me to death, you know. You hadn't moved in a couple of days. I step out to the bathroom and return to find you gone and the bed on fire."

A couple of *days*? I had to process his words before they made any sense. "The bed was on fire?"

He nodded. "Yeah. Luckily I didn't decide to read a magazine while I was in the bathroom. By the time I got back, it would have been like a forest fire."

Even as I said it, I felt stupid. "Did I do that?"

He shrugged. "Dunno. Did you get angry?"

I grimaced.

A crooked smile cracked his face. "Then my money is on the partial fire demon setting the bed on fire. What's your bet?"

Scrunching my eyes shut, I muttered, "I'm sorry. I didn't mean to." I forced my eyes to return to his face. "Did you get it out?"

"I'm not a warlock for nothing." He gave me a wink. I could feel he was doing his best at trying to ease the situation—not draw more attention to the fact we were in my dead best friend's room.

I started to sit up, but it seemed like too much effort. I lay back down and closed my eyes. Finn sat beside me, his hand making wide, slow circles on my back. The motion made me think of Sonia and how many times she had sat beside me and comforted me when it seemed the rest of the world was out for blood.

After several minutes, I looked up at Finn. "How did you find me? Do you have a locator spell or something?"

"Did you really think I'd need a spell to find you? I knew where you'd be. However, you kinda took my ride. I had to borrow one from Caitlin."

In a rather awkward fling of my body, I shot up into a sitting position on the bed. "Caitlin's here?"

Finn let out a genuine laugh. "Lord, boy, you should see your face! Priceless. Wish I could have taken a picture to send to Cate to show her what effect she has on men! Not that she'd care, I guess...." He continued to chuckle until he realized he hadn't answered my question. "Oh no. She's not here. She just let me borrow her car."

"Really? That's pretty nice of her." I couldn't picture Caitlin slowing down if she saw me dying by the side of the road, let alone agreeing to allow me in her car.

"Well, don't tell her this, but she's not really all that horrible. I don't think it hurts that she isn't quite as convinced that the Royals are after you anymore."

"She isn't? Why?"

He gave a pained expression. "They don't leave messes. They are very careful to go unnoticed by humans." He motioned to the room. "They never would have left the house like he did."

I followed his hand's arch around the room. "But, Finn, they didn't. Look at it. Everything's gone. It's like she was never here."

He let out a sigh. "That was me. I asked my family to come by here."

"But everything is fixed. The table is back to normal. The hole in the wall, the sliding glass doors, everything."

"We are witches, remember?" He gave me an apologetic grimace. "My folks came down here with Cate and Cynthia and took care of everything. I hated to have to take care of business when you were going through so much, but it wouldn't serve us very well for vampires to be discovered either. Plus, I'm not sure what trouble you could have gotten in if the police had found your place torn up and you gone."

I stared at the floor numbly. It was too much to take in. "So, all her stuff...."

"It's all in my garage, at least the things that could be salvaged. You can go through it when you're ready."

I shook my head, the hole in my chest ripping a bit further. "I don't think I can do it. I can't just go through her stuff and decide what to keep, what to give to her family." I let out a groan. I hadn't even thought of her family.

Finn turned my face to his with a gentle pull. "Hey, you don't have to worry about any of that right now. It's all safe and packed away. It can stay there until the time is right. Your stuff is there too."

"My stuff? What about my room?"

"All at my place."

"But, I live here. I have to—"

Finn interrupted. "Brett. You're not staying here. You can't. For one, you'd drive yourself insane being here where all this misery happened. Plus, the vampire knows where you live, somehow. If you stay here, he'll be back."

Part of me wanted to say *Good, let him come!* But I didn't feel it. I was too tired, too spent. "Fine. Then I'll need to just get a hotel for a bit, until I can find a place."

"You're staying with me, Brett."

I shook my head. "No. Absolutely not. Sonia died because she lived with me. I don't need to add more people to that list."

"Sonia didn't know what was coming, and she didn't have anything to defend herself with." He reached out and took my hand. "I have my powers, not to mention my family. Plus, I'll feel a whole lot safer with a fire demon under my roof who has already burned the vamp halfway to a crisp once."

"Finn, I couldn't even protect Sonia. We both know that I won't be able to protect you either, if the vampire comes around again. Besides, you don't need me. You're just trying to be nice."

He took my hand and held it tightly. "I don't know that, actually. I don't think you've even begun to realize your power. And I'm not trying to be nice." He glanced down at our hands. "I want you to stay with me. No expectations or anything. Just stay until this gets figured out. We are in this together now, and I'm sure there are going to be a lot more questions you'll have about everything."

I watched his thumb slowly caressing the back of my hand and felt his other hand still making Sonia-like circles on my back. "Okay."

CHAPTER TWENTY

THE absence of hate in her eyes didn't detract from her distrust and accusation. It was clear that, even though Caitlin no longer thought I was going to bring the entire Vampire Cathedral down on top of her family, she wasn't ready to forgive me for getting her brother involved in this mess. Nor did I figure she'd decided to trust that a fire demon wouldn't turn wild and slaughter everyone around.

We were in the driveway of her house. I had followed in Finn's truck as he drove Caitlin's car. A few minutes after Finn had run into her house to use the restroom, Caitlin had walked purposefully out her front door. Coming to a stop beside the driver's side of Finn's truck, she stared at me.

I debated whether I should get out of the truck. If she wanted to hurt me or put some kind of spell on me, I doubted being inside would offer much protection, but better safe than sorry.

Cautiously, I rolled down the window.

I could see her battling with the words she wanted to say, probably trying to decide whether she wanted to curse me out or spit in my face. Her voice was barely audible. "I'm sorry to hear about Sonia. Finn says you were really close to her."

Due to the surprise of her cordial words and my throat closing up at the mention of Sonia's name, I simply gave a weak nod.

She narrowed her eyes and tilted her head, like a bloodhound trying to sniff out clues. "Did you really not know you were part demon?"

Apparently sympathy time was over. "I...." My voice cracked and stopped my words. I cleared my constricted throat, trying to push away the thoughts of Sonia. "No," I managed to squeak out.

She cocked her head to the opposite side. "You didn't know about witches and vampires?"

"No."

She leaned in closer. "What do you want with my brother?"

I suppose I should have seen that question coming, but I didn't have an answer. I opened my mouth but closed it again. What could I say?

"Finn thinks you're all innocence and helplessness. You're his new lost little puppy. And maybe you really are as naïve and dull-witted as you would have to be to not realize you're a demon, but that doesn't change a thing." Her words came out in a snarl. "If he so much as gets a scratch because of you, I swear, fire demon or not, I will destroy you."

Her piercing eyes bored into mine. I couldn't think of anything to say, not that I could have spoken if I had.

After a few more intense seconds, her eyes shifted once again, the anger receding. "I am sorry about Sonia."

I tried to nod, but the chasm in my chest made me immobile. Visions of the house torn up and all the blood in the bedroom flashed behind my eyes. In my head, I could hear her screaming as she ran through the house, trying to get away from him.

"Everything okay, Cate?" Finn's voice caused me to jump, bringing me back to the moment.

Caitlin turned casually to look at her brother. "Of course." She took a few steps toward the house, passed Finn, and then turned back around. "Where is he staying tonight?"

I saw a flash of irritation cross Finn's face. "Caitlin, you know very well that he's staying with me." She opened her mouth, but he cut her off. "And he will be for the foreseeable future."

Her gaze left Finn and found me as I watched them from the truck. "It might be safer for him if he stayed here with me. I'm sure the vampire has your scent too, Finn. He doesn't have mine. If he comes looking, this would be the safest place. No sense for Brett to lead him right to you. I'm sure Brett agrees with me." Her eyes drilled into me.

Her pretense of caring about my safety probably even sounded false to her ears. "Don't you, Brett?"

Before I could open my mouth to respond, Finn's hard voice broke in. "Cate, you can be such a bitch. I'm not sure what you're trying to prove, but back off. Brett and I will be fine. Plus, what would all your little girlfriends think if they saw a big, handsome man coming and going from your place? You've got a rep to keep up, you know."

Finn took two steps and pulled open the door. "Scoot over. I'll drive, okay?" As I slid across the seat, he began to step up into the cab, without looking back. "And whatever spell you're getting ready to cast, big sister, I'd think twice."

"Fag," I heard Caitlin mutter as the engine turned over.

Finn began to reverse out of the driveway as he stuck his head out the window and gave her a big wave. "Thanks again for the car, sis!"

Caitlin flipped him off before turning around and storming inside.

WE WERE several blocks away before Finn said anything. I had already zoned out, staring through the window into the night, doing my best to not think about Sonia, to not think about anything.

"So, wanna tell me what happened to my steering wheel?"

I glanced over at him. His hands were smaller than mine, and they were encased by the deep impressions my hands had made. I'd forgotten. "Sorry. Again."

"A little mad while driving I see. I'll have to invest in a fire resistant suit, just in case you get upset with me when I'm sitting too close to you or something." His gaze darted over to my face before returning to the street. "Sorry. I was kidding. It's not a big deal, really."

"Maybe Caitlin's right."

He let out an exaggerated guffaw. "What? Did you hit your head in the middle of all this mess and I didn't know it?"

"Finn, I'm serious! It's not safe to be with me. Obviously, the vampire is after me. He's already killed Sonia." My voice broke again at her name. I held up my hand when Finn started to speak. "There's no reason for him to have to kill you and your family too."

Finn let out a deep breath and set his jaw. "Listen, if you don't want to stay with me, if you would rather be somewhere else, then just say so. However, if you're just worried about the vamp or letting Caitlin get to you, then don't. Just don't. We could argue and go back and forth forever and not get anywhere. Whether you stay with me or not, my family is involved. *I'm* involved. Too late to change that. There's nothing you can do to make it any different."

The uncharacteristic anger in his voice caused me to stay silent. He probably was right. If the vampire was coming, he wasn't going to stop just because I wasn't at Finn's house. Me not being home hadn't saved Sonia.

The anger left his voice. "Do you have a problem staying with me? If you do, it's okay. Just tell me now."

I shook my head.

"Good. It's settled, then. No more discussion."

We drove in silence for the final few miles before he pulled into his driveway. He turned the key, and the engine shut off.

I shifted to look at him when I heard him start muttering. Both his hands were suspended a few centimeters over my hand indentions in his steering wheel. As I watched, the edges of the black vinyl slowly began to creep together, filling in the crevasses, like skin growing over a wound at an extremely accelerated pace.

When the steering wheel looked as good as new, he peered over at me and grinned coyly at the astonishment on my face. "See, no harm done."

DESPITE apparently sleeping for nearly two days at Finn's and again at my house, I was struggling to stay awake as I sipped the coffee, sinking deeper into the sofa in Finn's living room. I looked around, taking in the room for the first time as Finn got something to snack on from the kitchen.

It was a tiny house, nothing overly special or unusual about it. However, it was clean and simply decorated in a way that gave the impression that he'd spent a lot of time carefully choosing the few items that had been incorporated into this home. The ceiling was high and vaulted, and the room was painted in a palate of browns, tans, and a dusty blue. I was starting to drift away in the corduroy cushions as Finn returned from the kitchen.

"You are the sleepiest man I have ever met. You've slept more than half the time I've known you." He grinned at me as he set a platter of pastries on the sleek coffee table in front of me. I assumed they were from his bakery. "Try this one." He pointed to one that had rosemary sprinkled over the golden crust. "It's blue cheese, shredded chicken, and cashews. I made it up. Mom thought I was crazy, but now it's her favorite."

With a groan I leaned forward and reached for the pastry. Considering that I hadn't eaten since Sonia died, I should have been ravenous, but the last thing I wanted was to eat. I didn't think I'd ever be hungry again, something Sonia surely would have said was impossible.

I watched as Finn grabbed a pastry and plopped into the armchair next to the sofa. He took a huge bite, noticed me watching him, and flushed. "Well, how do you like it?"

"It's good. Thanks."

He glanced down at my plate. "You haven't even tried it! Come on, you need to eat."

I eyed the pastry, then returned my gaze to Finn's face, my thoughts chaotic. "How bad is your room burned?"

He chuckled. "It hadn't spread too far, just the mattress and up the wall behind the bed."

I gaped at him. "It spread to the wall?"

He shrugged, unconcerned. "Nothing big. I got the fire out before I left to find you, obviously. I'll fix the rest before we go to bed."

"Sorry." I really did feel badly for setting his bedroom on fire, but my voice sounded flat and detached.

We sat there in an awkward silence. After a few more bites, Finn reached over and snagged a sugarcoated empanada. I noticed him glance again at my untouched plate, and with an effort, I picked up the pastry and took a small bite from the corner. As I chewed, not tasting, I began to think about what Finn had done in the truck.

He had repaired the steering wheel as easily as if he had been simply breathing. I imagined it would be the same when he fixed the burn marks in the bedroom, just like his family had obviously used magic to fix the house. I vaguely remembered Paulette saying something about using the elements to do spells. If everything in the world was part of the elements, then there shouldn't be much they couldn't affect in some form or another. Everything alive is part of the elements. Everything that used to be alive....

I glanced up at Finn so suddenly he flinched in surprise. I was finally awake. "Finn, magic!" As if he could read my mind.

He looked at me questioningly. "Yes?"

"You can do magic!"

His eyes continued to narrow as he tried to understand. "Well, Mom hates it being called magic, which is making something from nothing. She prefers—"

I broke in. "Whatever she wants to call it, you can do magic. You can fix things, like you did with the steering wheel"—my voice rose to a nearly manic level with every word—"like you'll do with the bedroom, like your family did with my house!"

"Okay, sure, Brett. Yes, I can do magic."

"You use the elements of whatever you are working on, right?"

He nodded hesitantly.

"Can witches affect anything on the elemental level?"

"It depends on how much power a particular witch or warlock has, but in theory, yes."

My mind started making connections. This could work. This would work. "Do you have more power if more than one of you is trying a spell?"

"Yeah, generally." His voice took on a wary tone. "Brett, I think I know where you're going with this—"

I cut him off. "All we have to do then is find her. Whatever the vampire did with her body, we can find her. Just do a little locator spell for the vampire."

He shook his head. "Locator spells aren't completely reliable in the best of times. They for sure aren't going to work on a vampire, who's technically dead. Besides, Brett, there is no way to—"

"I'm sure if several of you tried to use it, or maybe even focus on Sonia, maybe since she was alive more recently—"

"Brett, it won't—"

"You could bring her back! Just affect whatever elements have to be tweaked to heal her. I don't know why I didn't think of it before!"

Finn gave me a slow, sympathetic smile. "Oh, Brett, I'm sorry." He shook his head. "That's not how it works. No witch can bring back the dead. Even if we had arrived seconds after, we just don't have that kind of power."

I looked frantically around the room, trying to find something that would help. Then a thought hit me. "Then what does?"

"What?"

"What can heal her? What does have that kind of power? You said there are other magical creatures. Werewolves, vampires. Are their only evil sorts of supernaturals? What about unicorns or phoenixes or… or… or whatever has a good sort of power?"

He put his hand on my knee. Unintentionally, I jerked away.

"Brett, nothing has been given that kind of power. Nothing that I know of can raise the dead." His eyebrow twitched as another thought hit him. "Well, except for angels. They have that kind of power. However, by definition, they are bound to only do what God instructs."

"Then let's find an angel!" Unbidden, I stood up.

A sad laugh escaped him. "Brett, it's not that simple. You can't just go hunt down an angel. It's not like they hang around on street corners. Have you ever seen an angel?"

"Well, how would I know?" I tried to stop the anger in my voice, but I couldn't seem to soothe it. "I didn't know Ricky and Christina were witches, and they've been in front of my face for ages! I didn't know there were vampires, but that didn't stop one from taking me and killing Sonia, did it? I didn't know there were demons and come to find out there's one in the fucking mirror! There might be an angel living right next door. Maybe we should go ask!"

Finn's expression had transformed from concern to one bordering on fear. "Brett, you need to calm down, okay? Breathe." He was standing now, and he held his hands out to me but didn't try to touch me.

"Why should I calm down?" I was screaming now. "We could do something! We could bring Sonia back!"

Finn's voice was a whisper. "Brett, look down. Look at yourself."

I glanced down. My hands were balled into fists in front of me, shaking. I could feel my entire body trembling. Smoke was wafting up from my arms, causing the room to look blurry in front of me. As I watched, my fists burst into flames, vibrant orange and yellow licking at my skin, flecks of sapphire blue at my knuckles.

My eyes caught Finn's, and he gasped.

"Help me." My voice was barely audible, even to my ears.

"Breathe, Brett, breathe. Focus on calming down." Finn moved half a step closer, but stopped just out of reach. "Everything's going to be okay. We'll find the vampire, okay? We'll make him pay. Sonia will be avenged. I promise. Okay? Breathe."

After several deep breaths and letting Finn's words sink in, the fire on my hands went out, and the smoke gradually drifted away. I couldn't make my body stop trembling.

Finn took another step closer. "You should have seen your eyes. I've never seen anything like it. I've never heard of a demon with blue eyes like that."

"Sorry. I couldn't help it."

He reached out to touch my arm but then jerked his hand back. "Still a little warm."

I paced around the room until I was calm enough to sit back on the couch without setting it aflame.

Finn shoved my plate back in front of me. "Here, I'm not taking no for an answer. You need to eat. So eat! Then let's go to bed. It's after eleven, and rest will help."

Too spent to argue, I stuffed huge bites of the empanada in my mouth, chewed, and tasted as little as possible until it was gone.

Finn gave me a little wink as his eyebrow arched. "Good boy. Now, let's go to bed."

Finn's house had to be the tiniest I had ever seen. Within ten steps we were in his bedroom. I could see the kitchen, living room, a bathroom, another bedroom, and that was it. Although it was tiny, it all seemed to have had the same painstaking care applied to it as the living room.

"Oh, Finn." I gawked at the wall above the bed. "I'm so sorry." There was a six foot charred portion from the top of the bed reaching nearly to the ceiling. In parts, you could see some of the insulation inside the wall. The upper half of the mattress was pitch black and scorched thoroughly. It caused the image of the vampire's burned, eyeless face to flash into my mind.

Finn didn't say anything, just walked calmly over to the bed and laid his hands down near the bottom. His lips didn't move as the mattress's fabric began to restitch itself, little threads jumping and then diving from the healthy side, weaving together over the destroyed section. After what seemed like mere seconds, he lifted his hands from the mattress and climbed up to the headboard, which had also been made whole. On his knees, he placed one hand on either side of the scorch mark. Like wisps of smoke, the grayish blue of the wall overtook the fissure, erasing all evidence of my anger.

Still on his knees, Finn looked over his shoulder and gave me a brilliant smile. "See, all better."

It was probably the most amazing thing I had ever seen. No probably about it, actually, it blew away every other amazing thing I had ever witnessed. Between this and the steering wheel, my worldview was definitely being challenged. "Wait a minute, Finn. I just realized something."

He flipped around and scooted off the bed. "And what was that?"

"In the car, I heard you muttering some kind of spell, but here you didn't say anything at all."

"Oh, that." He waved it off. "Yeah, I don't have to say the spell out loud, although sometimes I still do without realizing it."

"So, witches don't actually need spells?"

"Well"—he reddened slightly—"some do. It depends on how much power you have. Everything you call 'magic' involves a spell, a request or demand of the elements. If you have enough power, you don't necessarily even have to say the spell at all, you can just implore the elements, with… with… I don't actually know with what. I've never thought about it. I guess with your heart or mind or something. Sometimes, I slip into saying the spells without thinking, out of habit."

The more he spoke, the deeper his blush became. I couldn't help but grin at him. "It's kinda a big deal that you don't have to use spells, isn't it?"

He shrugged. "It's like Mom said, our family is just blessed with more gifts. It all goes back to demon blood. My family just happens to have its roots enmeshed firmly in the bloodlines of several different demons. Pure chance."

"For a family that owes its power to demons, I sure did scare you all."

"Yeah, I know. Sorry about that, but it's just not the same thing. I don't really know how to explain it. Witches and warlocks somehow get the power of their demon ancestry without all the evil that goes along with it. Most of them do, anyway. There are exceptions."

"Evil witches, you mean?"

He nodded, obviously becoming self-conscious with the topic. "So, do you wanna sleep in here with me, or would you be more comfortable in the guest bedroom?" He gestured to the bathroom. "The restroom connects the bedrooms. It's right through there."

My gaze traveled over Finn's handsome face and down his muscular body. With a twinge of guilt, I realized I really did want to stay in his bed with him. I hated that I felt that way. I shouldn't even be able to entertain such thoughts after just losing Sonia. "Uh, I should probably sleep in the guest room. I'd hate to have a bad dream and set you on fire during the night."

"I'm not worried about that." Finn tried to give me a flirtatious smile but then faltered, probably thinking the same thing I was. "But, if you would be more comfortable in there, that's great. The room's yours as long as you need it."

CHAPTER TWENTY-ONE

"YOU really don't have to do this." Finn dragged his fingers through the dark hair falling in his eyes as he turned to look at me. "There's no reason for you to put yourself through this torture."

"Yes, there is. I owe it to them. I owe it to Sonia." I didn't face him, just kept my gaze fixed on the cars as we zoomed past them on the freeway.

"I can see telling her family in person, but Derek? Why put yourself through this when they weren't even in a relationship? I can call him or something."

"Would you want someone to tell you if I'd been killed?" I glanced over to see his skin flush at the reprimand. A twinge of guilt shot through me. He was just trying to cause me less pain.

"You're right. I would." He shifted gears as he changed lanes, getting ready to merge onto the Hillcrest exit. "You don't really know him, do you? How are you going to know where to find him?"

I couldn't help but grin. "Oh, I know where to find him. Sonia had been wanting him to ask her out forever. Derek's the only guy I'd ever seen her nervous about. He lives pretty close to Rascals, and we've met. He'd come in from time to time."

"To Rascals?"

"Yeah. That should have been enough of a sign for Sonia to know he was interested. Straight men don't like the burgers at Rascals enough to go there without an ulterior motive."

Finn let out a quiet snort. "I bet there's quite a few *straight* men that go to Rascals with an ulterior motive."

"Yeah, well, I'm sure you're not wrong there. Sonia wasn't worried about that. I'd mentioned that possibility when he first came in. I swear that girl has better gaydar than I ever... *had* better gaydar...." Squeezing my eyes shut, I tightened my interlocking fingers until the knuckles hurt.

I felt Finn's warm fingers gently brush across my forearm before closing over my hand. I didn't respond.

Sonia's parents had been on my mind the entire night. If I had gotten any sleep at all, it hadn't been for more than five minutes at a time. Sonia didn't talk to her family every day, but they were still fairly close. The thought of them going about their lives as if everything were normal, expecting to see or hear from Sonia soon, was too much to bear. Sonia had been dead for four days already. How much longer was her family supposed to wait?

Derek. I'm not sure why I was so determined to talk to him. I knew Sonia would want me to, but really, I think it was more for practice before I faced her folks.

I wasn't really sure what I was going to say to them.

I couldn't exactly tell them about the vampire. Sonia's death would be enough to deal with. They didn't need to know the world they lived in was so different than they believed. Even if I thought there was a chance they'd need to know about vampires, they'd just think I was crazy. I'd only met them a handful of times—not nearly enough for them to take my word that their daughter was killed by a mythical creature.

There wasn't even a plausible explanation I could come up with. How do you explain your best friend being murdered four days ago and not telling her parents, not having her body, not even having a torn-up house as proof?

"Do you wanna go into Rascals for anything?"

I looked over at Finn blankly.

"You know, to grab any of Sonia's stuff from there?" He shot a glance at the dashboard clock. "It's about lunchtime. We could get something to eat, if you'd like."

The thought made me shudder. "No. I don't think I'll be able to go there again. I couldn't face it without her." I looked past Finn out the window. The restaurant was already bursting at the seams as the lunch crowd jostled for position on the patio. It seemed irreverent for business to be going on as normal when Sonia wasn't weaving through the customers, delivering beer and flirting outrageously. "She never kept important stuff there anyway. I'm not gonna bother with them. I'd rather have them think she just up and left and never called in. Better than the gossip that would catch fire in that place if they thought she'd been murdered."

"That makes sense." Finn gestured out the windshield with his chin. "You said over there, right?"

I followed his gaze to the small stone apartment complex forming a semicircle around a flower-filled courtyard. "Yeah. That's his Explorer over there, so he's probably home. He lives in the first apartment. The one with the big arch window."

He gave me an inquisitive glance. "Why are you smirking?"

"Oh, just remembering." An honest to goodness chuckle escaped. "From time to time, Sonia would swing past here when we were on our way to a movie or something. She was always hoping to catch Derek at the window without his shirt on."

He rolled his eyes. "I bet you two were always getting into trouble together." Finn pulled into one of the angled parking spots, his truck hanging over both sides of the too-narrow space.

I didn't reply as I exited the truck, accidentally shoving the door into the Accord in the adjacent space as I tried to squeeze out my shoulders and chest.

Finn waited for me at the sidewalk as I managed to finish extricating myself from the vehicle. "Sorry, I didn't realize what a tight squeeze it was."

"'S okay. Parking is always a bitch in Hillcrest."

"Do you want me to stay out here while you talk to him, or do you want me to come with you?"

"No, why don't you come." I joined him on the sidewalk. "However, I think it'd be best if I talked to Sonia's folks on my own."

He just nodded as we entered the courtyard together.

I paused to take a couple of deep breaths before I knocked on his door. I could do this. He wouldn't need as much explanation as Sonia's parents. Just tell him I'd come home and found the house broken into and Sonia murdered. That her family had decided to have a private ceremony. That she had really liked him.

"Brett, you don't have to do this, babe." Finn snaked his arm across my back, and he pressed into my shoulder.

I turned to him, only then realizing a solitary tear was making its way down my face.

He reached up, placed his hand on my cheek, and brushed the tear away with his thumb.

The gesture made me feel strange.

I wasn't used to another guy trying to take care of me. Only Sonia and, before that, Grandma. Somehow the kindness in his handsome face made me want to sit down on the stoop and cry for real.

"Yes, I do." Without planning it, I bent down and gave him a firm kiss on his lips, causing his face to instantaneously flush. After turning, I knocked on the door.

Nothing. After looking for the nonexistent doorbell, I knocked again.

There was no sound coming from inside. I glanced back at his car in the street and then over at Finn.

"It doesn't mean anything, Brett. He could just be out for a walk or sleeping."

Without responding, I reached out for the handle, turned it, and opened the door. Unlocked.

I looked back at Finn. He was beginning to look as nervous as I felt.

Stepping into the apartment, I expected it to mirror the destruction at my house. Chairs overturned, dishes broken, holes in the walls.

Nothing. Everything looked normal. "Derek?" Walking through the living room, I peered down the hallway and raised my voice. "Derek?"

"I don't think he's here, Brett." Finn crossed the room toward me. "I can't sense anyone alive here."

I didn't call his name again, but I did a quick tour of the house. He definitely wasn't there, but neither did there appear to have been any kind of struggle. The bed was unmade. There was dark whisker stubble in the bathroom sink, dirty socks beside the toilet. Nothing to indicate violence or anything to hint at being cleaned up to cover any tracks.

"Hey, Brett?"

I followed Finn's tense voice to the kitchen, my heart rate accelerating slightly. "Yeah? What'd you find?"

He was standing by the sink, an ice cream carton in his hand. He held it out for me to inspect. "Just this. And an empty bowl. The ice cream is melted."

I peered into the soupy grayish-brown mixture and then behind Finn at a blue bowl beside an ice cream scoop and a spoon.

"Whadaya think?"

Finn shrugged. "I dunno. It looks like he left in a hurry or just got distracted."

"Neither of those sounds good."

"I know. But there's no reason to think anything bad happened to him, Brett. How would the vampire know who Derek is, let alone where he lives?"

"What if he tortured it out of Sonia?"

Finn looked perplexed as he gave it some thought. "I don't know. That doesn't really seem to make any sense. He doesn't have a grudge against Sonia. It's you he's trying to get to, and you don't care about Derek."

"Maybe he doesn't know that. Maybe he's just going after anyone I'm connected with at all." Who next?

"I don't think so. Look around. We've already seen what this vamp likes to do. There is nothing here to make us think he killed Derek or even took him. Surely Derek could have put up as much of a fight as Sonia."

"So, what then? You think he just went out to do errands and left the door unlocked and ice cream on the counter?"

"I don't know. That doesn't make sense either."

"Can't you do some spell that tells you if someone else has been here?"

Finn looked apologetic. "I could, but it wouldn't help in this case. It would only tell me if someone alive has been here. There's no way of knowing if a vampire has been here or not, at least not that I know of." Helpless frustration passed over his face. "I'm so sorry I don't know more about these kinds of things. I could be more useful to you." He looked defeated.

"Hey, no. Come here." He took a tentative step toward me, and I pulled him into my arms. After a few moments, I felt him relax as his arms encircled my back and his body formed to mine. "Without you, I wouldn't have any idea how to do any of this. Without you, I'd probably be dead myself. It's me who should be apologizing to you. Without me in the picture, you and your family wouldn't have to be worrying about vampires right now."

He started to protest, but I cut him off. "Let's get over to Sonia's parents. Whatever this means, I doubt it's a good sign. We need to warn them." How to do that without telling them Sonia was killed by a vampire….

"Okay." I felt him nod against my chest.

"Let me just leave a note here for Derek. Tell him to call me. I still need to tell him about Sonia."

Finn pulled back to meet my eyes. "Are you crazy? You can't leave him a note."

"Why not?"

"Brett, what if something really has happened to Derek? At some point, someone's going to come looking for him and find him missing. Does his family live here?"

I shrugged. "I don't know where he's from."

"Well, if they are and they come here, all they will find is a note from you about someone else who is missing."

"Okay, that's true. But what do we do about telling Derek?"

His lips thinned minutely. "I know it sounds harsh, but we don't do anything. If Derek is fine, we will come back by and tell him about Sonia. Let's not jump to any conclusions until we check on Sonia's parents."

Chapter Twenty-Two

Piao and De Liu's home was in Golden Hill, on the southeast corner of Balboa Park. They called it a home. I'd call it a mansion. The few times I'd been there, I had desperately wanted to bring Grandpa. The lavish decadence of their house would have made him nauseous. All he would have been able to see were all the dollars that could have been piling up in the bank instead of used on such wasteful things as top-scale appliances, elaborate crown molding, and imported lamps and rugs.

While De was almost uncomfortably shy, she had always been welcoming and warm when I had come with Sonia. On the other hand, I had never really gotten comfortable around Piao. I never figured out if he had a problem with me being gay or just that I lived so cheaply with his daughter. Sonia swore that he liked me. That he just lived as he had in the old country.

Piao had moved his family to California when De became pregnant with their second child. They had thought the government would give them an exception to the "one-child" policy. That hope had been crushed when they'd found out De was having a girl.

Piao, De, and six-year-old Lake, Sonia's older brother, left everything they had in Shanghai. By the time Sonia was born as an American citizen, Piao had already established Shining Dragon, the jewelry store that would help him and his family achieve the American Dream.

I'd never met Lake. Shortly before I moved in with Sonia, he and Piao had argued over the future of Shining Dragon. Lake wanted to be an artist. Piao told him not to return until he chose to honor his family. There hadn't seemed to be such pressure placed upon his daughter.

"JUST turn up there on Russ Boulevard. Take a left."

Finn gaped at the houses as we drove past. "Sonia grew up here?"

"Yeah."

"Wow." He fell into speechless silence as we drove the final two blocks to their house.

"Right there. We can just park here and then walk through the gate. I'm not sure how to get into their driveway."

"Here? As in, that one?" Finn pointed up the small embankment.

I nodded.

"As in the biggest and nicest castle on the block?"

I laughed nervously. "It's not a castle."

Finn shook his head. "Remember my house? This is a castle." He looked at me narrowly. "You said you wanted to do this on your own. But with not knowing about Derek, I think it would be best if we both go. That okay?"

I nodded.

THE wrought iron gate that led up the walking path to the front door was always unlocked. I closed it behind Finn after we slipped through. As always, everything was immaculate. Gorgeous.

"You know, I don't think we needed to be worried. Everything is the same as always." I looked up the sweeping lawn at the turreted house, its huge curved windows glistening and welcoming. I turned to Finn as we reached the bottom step that led up to the main door. "I don't think I can do this. How do I tell them their daughter is dead? How am I supposed to explain?"

Finn didn't answer. He was looking ahead at the front door.

"What? Do you see something?"

"No. I don't know. Something just doesn't feel right."

"Are they home? Can you sense them inside?"

He didn't answer me for a moment, his honey eyes going unfocused. Finally, he shook his head. "No. Nothing. Not even a pet."

I let out a sigh. "That's actually a good sign. De never leaves home without Sapphire."

Finn looked at me quizzically.

"Her dog." I held my hands out, one about six inches above the other. "She's this little Maltese. They're inseparable."

"Oh." Finn continued up the steps and stopped at the door.

His flat response made the hairs on the back of my hands stand up. I followed him.

He turned to look at me. "It's locked. Do you want me to break in?"

"No, did you try the doorbell?"

His brow furrowed in a worried expression. "I scanned already, remember?"

I looked between him and the door several times. If Piao and De came home, they wouldn't be worried about Finn and me breaking in after they learned why I was here. "Yeah, get us in."

Finn turned away from me and placed his hands around the knob in an almost protective manner. In less than a second, he swung open the door.

Relaxing a little, I looked around the main entrance. Although massive, the entire first floor could be seen from the atrium. The huge, elaborate living room with the glowing cherry floors. The library, which was more like a museum of precious gems. The kitchen, its white marble floor and the onyx granite counters glistening. The formal dining room, with crimson walls adorned with gold leaf dragons cavorting across the expanse.

I turned to Finn, expecting to see him standing in wide-eyed wonder at all the marvels the house had to offer.

"See, everything is fine. Perfect, as always."

When he didn't reply, I followed his gaze up the spiraling staircase that swept above the shining grand piano.

"Let me go upstairs by myself." He turned to me, imploring. "If I need you, I'll yell."

"What is it?"

"I don't know, Brett. I just think I should go up there alone."

Without waiting, I leapt for the stairs, taking three or four at a time.

Finn called out for me, his shorter stride making it impossible for him to catch up.

I paused when I reached the top, not seeing anything out of the ordinary. I had only been to the second story once. There were only three rooms. Over half of the top floor was the master suite—an enormous bedroom, a closet the size of my living room and kitchen combined, and a bathroom that seemed like it belonged at the top of Trump Tower. The other two rooms, which were also huge, had been Lake and Sonia's bedrooms before they moved out. Last I knew, Piao and De had left them how they were.

By the time I entered the master bedroom, Finn was beside me. Again, everything was pristine. The black-and-gold bedspread was tucked tightly, without so much as a crease, into the immense modern bed frame. The sitting area under the bay windows looked as formal and uncomfortable as ever.

"I think you're just worried, Finn. You don't have to protect me. All I was worried about was telling them about Sonia. I never stopped to think that they might be in danger as well."

Finn quietly walked across the bedroom and opened the door into the bath. I followed.

At first, I didn't see him. The oval pedestal bathtub in the center of the room was empty and shimmering in the sunlight coming through the picture window overlooking Balboa.

It was the reflection in the mirrors over the his-and-her sinks. Turning away from them, I barely suppressed a yell as I saw Piao. His thin naked body was crumpled on the floor of the walk-in shower. There were only a few places where his skin was devoid of bite marks and chunks of missing flesh. His blood had dried to a dull rust color between the black stones encasing the shower. His eyes stared at me with a dull, milky haze.

"De!" I turned and rushed from the bathroom. "De!"

Finn caught me by the arm, forcing me to stop. "Brett. Stop. Remember, I already scanned. No one is alive here. Go downstairs. Please. I'll find De if she's here. There's no reason for you to have to see her."

I glared at him. "She can't be dead. He couldn't have killed them all. He couldn't have!"

He whipped his hand off my arm and shook it in the air.

I glanced down to see my hands and arms billowing steam. Looking back at Finn, I expected to see reproach in his eye. "Sorry."

He gave me a sad smile but didn't reach out to touch me. "It's okay. It's okay. You can't help it. Please let me finish by myself."

"No. I'm sorry, but I can't. I have to do it. I owe it to them. To Sonia."

He let out a long breath. "Fine. Which room next?"

The answer was obvious. "Sonia's."

Carefully, Finn reached out and clasped my hand, giving a little wince but not letting go. "Lead the way."

Sonia's bedroom door was open. We walked in.

De lay in Sonia's old bed. Her eyes were wide in frozen terror. One wound was visible on her neck. Two relatively tiny pricks. From her pallor, there was obviously no more blood in her body, but neither was there any blood around her. Her hands were folded on her breasts. Her long skirt splayed out on the bed, arranged perfectly.

Finn's hand tightened on mine. "I'm so sorry, Brett."

My breath left me in a gush. I stood there. Numb. No more terror. No more shock. No more. Sonia was gone. Her parents were gone. Maybe that part was a blessing.

Instantly, I shoved the thought away.

"Let's go."

"Okay." Finn paused before starting to move. "Brett, I think we have to assume Derek is dead too."

"Yeah. I know."

"I'll call Officer Torres. He'll handle it. That okay?"

"Yeah." I started to move, but just before I turned around, I noticed something beneath the bed skirt.

Stepping closer, it was obviously a small pool of blood seeping from underneath the bed. I stooped over, lifted up the fabric, and peered beneath.

Sapphire lay in a tangled mass of blood and fur. Here and there little unsoiled white tuffs stuck out. She looked as if every bone in her tiny body had been shattered.

My knees hit the floor as I dropped the cloth back into place.

Finn knelt beside me, his arms encircling my back, pulling me to him as I began to sob.

Chapter Twenty-Three

DESPITE how exhausted I was from not sleeping the night before and the stress of the day, I couldn't fall asleep. It felt like I lay there for hours. One minute I would start thinking of different ways to track the vampire. Then pondering over how to find an angel. We could bring them back. All of them. As long as I could find Sonia's body.

I'd get so worked up that I'd stand and start pacing the room, only to fall back into bed, twisting and turning. I couldn't believe I was actually thinking about how to track down an angel. Sane people don't try to go looking for angels. Of course, sane people don't normally catch on fire at what seemed to be increasingly short intervals. Sane people didn't continuously find dead people on an escalating basis. There had to be a way around the whole "magic can't bring back the dead" thing.

Such thoughts kept returning me to the fear that I wouldn't be able to figure out how to bring Sonia back. That she had died needlessly and violently, and there was nothing I could do despite all my newfound power.

Not for the first time, I wished so desperately that Sonia were here. I wasn't really sure what she would say about discovering that there are witches and vampires, or finding out her best friend is a fire demon. I was fairly certain she would have loved the idea, probably would have been jealous that she wasn't a part of it. Well, I guess she was a part of it now, wasn't she?

I didn't hear him knock, or call my name as he walked across the room, or feel him climb into bed with me. It wasn't until his arm snuck around my chest that I realized I wasn't alone. I flinched at his touch.

"It's okay, Brett, it's okay." Finn's arm grew tighter around me. "I wasn't trying to startle you. I was just in the bathroom, and I couldn't help hearing you cry."

I was crying?

"Sweetie, you've got to stop shaking. Here, lean back into me. Just let it go."

I hadn't realized I had curled up into a ball at some point and started sobbing. Again. I'd never been a crier before. Since Sonia's death, I didn't seem able to stop. I'd never felt so weak. I ran the back of my hand over my nose. "Ugh."

I felt him lean away from me, heard him rustling with something. "Here." He handed me a wad of tissues.

I blew my nose.

All of the sudden, now that my shaking was starting to come under control, I realized that I was starving. Ravenous. Even more, my skin was crying out to be in the ocean. Diving deep. Lost in the currents. Detached, I figured that was probably a good sign.

I leaned back into Finn as he slipped his right arm under my head to wrap me fully in his embrace. "It's okay to grieve, Brett. I'm sorry if I'm intruding. I just couldn't leave you alone in such agony."

Sniffing, I nodded. "What time is it?"

"We went to bed about two hours ago. It's almost one in the morning."

We lay there in silence for a long time. My body finally relaxed against Finn's. With tender fingers, Finn traced lightly over my chest and stomach. His cool skin felt soothing against mine. Every so often, I would feel his breath against my ear as he whispered how sorry he was and how he wished he could fix everything for me.

After what seemed like hours, my shaky voice shattered the silence. "I don't know how to do this, Finn."

"Do what, Brett?"

"I don't know how to get through this. I don't know how to let her go."

He was quiet for several moments before he gave a response, his voice cracking. "I don't either. You just do. You keep waking up, you keep breathing, you keep putting one foot in front of the other. You fake that you're really living, and one day you'll wake up and realize you're not faking it anymore."

After several more seconds, with his fingernails lightly massaging my scalp, he continued. "And you focus on the good times. You give thanks to God for allowing her to be in your life as long as she was. You ask him to keep her safe and to somehow bring the two of you back together one day."

His answer took me by surprise, serving to distract me momentarily. "You mean like in Heaven or something?"

"Sure, why not?"

"You believe in God?"

He paused as if caught off guard. "Well, sure I do."

"But you're a warlock!"

A small chuckle escaped him, "Yeah, I know. Why does that mean I can't believe in God?"

"Do you think he loves you?"

Another pause. Again, "Sure, I do."

I thought about it for a moment. It was surreal to have this discussion with him. Not only was he a warlock, he was gay. I could just imagine what my grandfather would say. There would be a very special place in Hell for the likes of Finn. And me, for that matter.

My voice was even quieter. "And you're gay."

"Again, yeah, I know." He gave my nipple a quick tug, letting out a soft laugh. "Nothing slips by you, does it?"

"And you really think that God loves you?"

"Yeah."

"What about your family?"

"They love me too."

"No, no. I mean, what do they think about God loving them?"

"Brett, I grew up in church, just like everybody else. We're Methodists."

I hadn't even considered witches and warlocks going to church. I wondered if there had been some in my grandparents' church. "But if we are descended from demons, then how could God love us?"

"Remember what I told you? Don't you know what demons are, where they come from?"

Being raised in church, I didn't think twice. "Sure, they are the fallen angels. The ones that followed Lucifer when he challenged God and was ejected from Heaven."

"Exactly. They are angels. They've made their choice. Just because they procreate doesn't mean that their offspring don't have a say in the matter. We still all have free will." I felt him give a little shrug. "Sure, those closer to their patronage have a harder time with not being evil, but the further away that gets, the less that's an issue."

"And the gay thing?"

"Well, God let me be born a warlock and be born gay. Why would he have a problem with either?"

"Well, if you really grew up in church, then the problems with that should be obvious."

"I said I believe in God, not everything preached from the pulpit. Although the church has good intentions, for the most part, I don't believe that what is preached and God's true nature are necessarily the same thing."

It seemed a little oversimplified, but at the moment, simple worked. I wanted to believe in a God who loved me. Loved me in spite of being gay, in spite of being a demon. In Finn's way of thinking, not in spite of, but maybe because of those qualities.

"Ah, Brett, I'm sorry. I wasn't trying to make you cry again."

I wiped my eyes and awkwardly turned in Finn's arms so we were facing each other. "Kiss me." I held his gaze with mine. "Please."

His eyes grew wide in the dark, then softened. Slowly, his lips touched mine. At first, barely brushing them with his, then with more pressure. His hand came up and cradled my jaw and cheek in his palm as his kisses deepened, his tongue leisurely caressing mine.

I wrapped my arms around his neck and back, pulling him closer to me. His bare chest was covered in a light sweat from my heat.

The passion took its time building, both of us content for our hands to gradually discover each other's bodies, enjoying every touch, every sensation, every kiss. We didn't talk; we didn't need to. Something had changed. We had been through too much, and we weren't strangers any longer. We didn't know all the intimate details of each other's lives, but there was certainty that we had plenty of time for that.

By the time our shorts were off, our faces were both rubbed raw by each other's stubble.

I forgot the pain of the past few days. I didn't forget Sonia, but I also knew if anyone would approve of the unspoken choice Finn and I had made, it would be her. I lost myself in the hardness of his muscles, the softness of his full lips, the slickness as our stomachs slid over each other, in the way his penis felt as it mashed into mine, his low groans, his contented smile as we found our rhythm.

Just as Finn opened the drawer and pulled out a strip of condoms, his cell phone rang from the other room.

Our eyes met in a mixture of concern and trepidation. "I don't have to get it."

"Finn, of course you do. It must be important. It's gotta be past four in the morning by now."

With a sigh, he slid off me and rushed through the bathroom and into his bedroom, the moonlight from the window catching the curve of his ass as he went.

"It's Mom!" he hollered from the other room.

I sat up, my stomach sinking.

He walked back toward the bed, and in spite of what I was certain was bad news, I couldn't help enjoying a thrill from the movement of his naked body as he came closer, the way his penis shifted from side to side.

"Yeah, Mom. We'll be right there.... I know. I love you too."

He flipped the phone shut and looked at me.

"What? What happened?"

"Rodrigo's dead."

CHAPTER TWENTY-FOUR

"Really?" More death.

"I know. I can't believe it." He shoved his hand under the sheets and retrieved his underwear from somewhere near the foot of the bed.

"Finn?"

"Yeah?" He started to lift his leg to slip into his shorts.

I leaned over and snatched them from him. "Who's Rodrigo?"

A confused look passed over his face but cleared almost instantly. "Oh, sorry. Of course, you don't know Rodrigo yet." He faltered momentarily. "*Didn't* know, I guess. Rodrigo is this adorable gay boy who was a waiter at Taberna de las Brujas. He started as a busboy when he was twelve or thirteen. His family is pretty much crap, so we kinda took him under our wings. He kinda became like part of our family."

How much more death? This had to stop. "Oh, I'm sorry, Finn. What happened?"

"The vampire."

"You sure?"

"Yeah, he was killed by the vampire. Mom didn't give me any more details. She just said to hurry to their house. They are calling the whole family together right now. They don't think it's safe to be on our own. They called me first. She was getting ready to call Caitlin."

It would be too much to hope that he'd died in a car wreck or some other inane accident. Of course it was the vampire. What else would it be? I slid out from under the covers, pulled myself over to

Finn's side, and stood up. "I'm sorry, Finn." I slid my hand over the length of his arm. "Will you be okay?"

"Yeah. I will. We all cared about the kid and will grieve, I am sure, but I wasn't anywhere nearly as close to him as you were to Sonia. It's not like that. Right now, though, we can't really stop to think about it. We need to get to Mom and Dad's. If the vamp is coming, we don't want to be caught on our own."

"Finn…." I moved my hands down his waist, and I pulled him to me until our abdomens were touching and our faces were inches apart. "Are we…." My voice trailed off, suddenly feeling self-conscious and stupid, unsure of why I was needing assurance of Finn and my standing.

Finn didn't need me to finish. He put his hand against my cheek. "Yes." He slipped his hand behind my head and pulled me down to meet his lips.

We stood there, arms wrapped around each other, our naked bodies forming one, confirming our decision without words.

At last, Finn pulled away. "We've gotta go, before we fall back into bed and end up getting killed or getting someone else killed. We'll have plenty of time for this later." His warm brown eyes probed mine. "I promise."

PURE pandemonium greeted us as we stepped through the doors to Paulette and Wendell's house. Caitlin and Paulette were yelling. I couldn't tell whether they were arguing or just talking absurdly loud. Cynthia was curled into a ball on the sofa in the sunken living room, sobbing, her body shaking all over. I couldn't see Wendell.

As Finn closed the door, something ran into my legs, nearly taking me out at the knees. I looked down to see a small black-haired boy in yellow pajamas, lying on the floor, the impact with my legs apparently having knocked him down. His red-rimmed eyes filled with tears, and he began to wail at the top of his lungs.

"Saul, buddy, what's wrong?" Finn bent down and swooped the little boy into his arms and brought him up to eye level.

The boy looked into Finn's face, trying to clear his blurry eyes to see who had a hold of him. "Uncle Finn! Don't let him get me. Don't let him get me!" With another great wail, the child flung his arms around Finn and buried his face into Finn's neck, sobs wracking his tiny body.

Finn gave him a squeeze and began rubbing his back, flashing me a sad face. "Don't let who get you, buddy?"

Saul just cried all the louder.

"Finn! Brett! I'm so glad you are here, finally! What took you so long?" I looked over to see a beautiful woman with thick, long black hair cascading over her shoulders. She rushed at us, dragging another boy roughly by his arm.

I felt a quick rush of affection as I saw her. "Christina! It's good to see you. It's been too long."

"Yes, Cariño, it's been too long." Christina rose on her tiptoes and pulled me into a swift, tight hug. I felt her breath tickle my ear. "Told you you'd like my brother, didn't I?" She pulled away and gave me a sly wink with a heavily lashed eye that was the exact same shade of brown as Finn's. Her gaze quickly traveled back and forth, taking in the stubble burns covering our mouths.

Before I could blush, she turned her attention to her brother and pecked him on the cheek. "You wanna know why Saul is in hysterics?"

Without waiting for a response, she jerked the boy behind her and positioned him between herself and Finn. "We weren't going to tell the boys what was going on. Too scary. But *this one*"—she made a dismissive gesture toward the older boy—"overheard me on the phone to Grandma. Why he was up, I don't know." She glared an accusatory glance at the boy before returning quickly to Finn. "And he went and woke up his brother, telling him that there was a vampire coming to suck all his blood. And just now, I caught him chasing Saul around the bedroom using his fingers as fangs!" She ended her tirade with a string of Spanish that I didn't understand.

Finn slid the still-sobbing Saul to his mother. I could see a small twinge at the corner of Finn's mouth, an effort not to grin. Christina noticed it as well. After a warning glare, Finn quickly readjusted his features. He reached out his hand to the older boy. "Come on, Peter. Let's go chat."

"And you just wait until your dad gets here!" Christina bellowed after them. Saul had started to soothe himself in his mother's arms as she turned back to me. Her eyebrow raised in a very familiar fashion. "So, half-demon, huh?"

This time, I did flush. "Yeah, so they tell me."

She just smiled. "I always knew you were a special one."

"I'm really sorry that I got your family involved in all this mess." I faltered for words momentarily. "If I'd have known...."

"Nonsense. Demon or not, there is no way you could have known that you'd somehow get a vampire set on your trail." She shifted Saul from one side to the other. "And I've already spoken to Caitlin." She paused, searching for words. "Ricky and I don't feel the same as her. We've known you a long time. If you were a dangerous, bloodthirsty demon, you'd have killed a lot more of our clientele and ordered a lot fewer tortillas."

I couldn't help but laugh. "Thanks, Christina." It surprised me how much her voiced support mattered to me. "Where is Ricky?"

"He's finishing up at the restaurant. Things with Rodrigo have to be... handled—"

"Brett!" Paulette swooped over, cutting Christina off. "I didn't even see you!" She gave me a warm, motherly hug. "I'm so sorry about Sonia, dear."

Unbidden, I felt my eyes begin to sting. Thankfully, Paulette had already turned to Christina. "Lord help me, I'm going to murder your sister any moment. She's wanting to call the Cathedral. Again!"

"What!" Christina's voice rose sharply, causing Saul to begin crying once more.

"She thinks they will help us get rid of this troublesome vampire." Paulette rolled her eyes.

"Sure they would, and us right along with him!"

Paulette nodded emphatically. "You know Caitlin." She pulled Christina and Saul off toward Caitlin, who was fuming across the room. I looked around, suddenly alone and unsure what I was supposed to do. I glanced at the sobbing Cynthia on the couch and considered trying to comfort her. It only took a second for me to picture how that would go—her looking up into the eyes of the evil demon and going into hysterics. Finn had told me she'd stayed with me for a bit when he'd left. But still....

Instead, I stood by the door and listened to the women arguing over calling the Vampire Cathedral, while trying not to look like I was eavesdropping. It seemed like Caitlin's first response to every crisis was to call in the Royals. Maybe her true intentions were to get rid of me just as much as to get rid of the vampire.

After what seemed like hours, Finn came back into the room. "Peter's asleep now," he told his sister. He noticed me still standing by the door and came over to me. "What are you doing? You don't have to stay in the doorway. Are you okay?"

"Yeah, of course. Just not sure what I'm supposed to do."

"You're not supposed to have to do anything. This is family. Don't worry, even Caitlin will get used to you. It will all be fine. You'll see."

Somehow I doubted that.

"Come on." He grabbed my hand. "Help me get our bags out of the back of the truck. We'll put them in my old room." Before we left his house, Finn had thrown some of the things he'd salvaged from my home into a backpack.

As the door closed behind us, he gave me a quick kiss on the lips and then led me to the truck. The cool morning air felt refreshing on my skin, which seemed hot and dry. It struck me again that this truly was the longest I had ever been without being in the ocean. Just the thought made my skin feel itchy and uncomfortable.

Finn motioned to the east. "Looks like the sunrise is going to be pretty today."

I glanced over. The very edge of the horizon had a golden streak. "Well, I guess things will be safer in a few minutes, huh?"

"Yeah, guess so. That is one blessing. At least he's not a Royal. We'd never have any peace."

As we pulled out our bags, a small red minivan pulled into the driveway directly behind Finn's truck, jerking as it was slammed into park.

For a moment, my heart sped up. Did vampires drive? I glanced over at Finn.

"It's just Ricardo." He gave a little chuckle. "Although it would be kinda fun to see a vampire in a minivan."

"Well, you never know," I grumbled. "Ricky's a warlock in a minivan. What's the difference?"

Finn opened his mouth to retort.

"Hi, boys." Ricky got out of the van. He looked years older than the last time I had seen him. He had huge dark circles under his eyes, and his shoulders were slumped and defeated.

Finn slapped his arm over Ricky's shoulders. "Everything done?"

"Yeah." He let out an exhausted sigh. "Detective Ash came down and took care of Rodrigo. His good-for-nothing family showed up right when Ash had just about finished cleaning up the blood. They were ranting and raving about suing."

Finn snorted. "Who are they going to call? I don't know many lawyers, human or otherwise, that would be willing to sue the Royals."

"Nah, they mean me. They said they told Rodrigo that our family was nothing but trouble and that he should never work for us." He rubbed the bridge of his nose with his thumb and forefinger. "Not one tear. Not one! Not even from that worthless mother of his!"

"I know, Ricky. I know. We'll mourn for Rodrigo. He won't be forgotten." Finn gave Ricky another squeeze and then dropped his arm. "Go on in. Everybody's waiting."

As we followed Ricky inside, I leaned over to Finn and bent down toward his ear. "Could Ricky and Christina lose the restaurant if they sue?"

Finn shook his head. "Nah. Who are they going to sue for vampire attacks? The Royals? Rodrigo's family is trash, and they hardly have any power anyway. They'll just rant and threaten. As soon as they realize we won't give them anything, they'll leave. Probably won't even stay for the service, if I know them."

We dropped our bags inside the door. Ricky had already joined Christina on the sofa, Saul asleep in her lap. Cynthia seemed to have gotten herself under control, as she was now sitting up and blowing her nose daintily. Caitlin, of course, was pacing back and forth in front of the fireplace. As Paulette waved us over to sit on the steps leading down into the sunken living room, Wendell rounded the corner with a huge tray filled with a large bowl, a plate of tortillas, and several small bowls and spoons.

Finn leaned close to me as I sat down next to him on the steps. "Any time there's family drama and Dad has more than a ten-minute warning, he always makes green chili and tortillas. I bet he's been in the kitchen since Christina called Mom."

Within a few minutes, everyone, even Cynthia, had a large bowl of steaming green chili. Between the warmth of holding the bowl and the simple act of scooping up the green chili with the tortillas, things seemed calmer, more manageable.

After everyone had enough time to consume a good portion of their food, Paulette broke the silence. "Ricky, I waited to share the few details I know. I didn't see the sense in telling it over and over again. Now that we're all here, would you mind?"

Ricky swallowed the bite of food he was chewing and nodded. "Sure." Christina gave his knee a squeeze as he took a deep breath before he began. "We had just finished cleaning up around two thirty or two forty-five or so. Almost everyone had left. It was only me and Charley." He glanced at me. "Charley manages the place when Christina or I can't be there. Anyway, I started thinking, I don't even know why, and I realized that I hadn't seen Rodrigo for hours." He paused and shook his head. "Maybe if I had realized earlier, I could have found him in time."

Christina returned her hand to his leg, and Wendell leaned forward, his voice steady but tired. "None of that, Ricardo. This is no one's fault, least of all yours. The only thing that would have happened if you had realized earlier is that Peter and Saul would have lost their daddy tonight."

"Oh, Dad," Cynthia whispered. "Don't talk like that."

"Well, it's true, dear. It's a blessing that Ricky didn't go looking for Rodrigo any earlier." Wendell motioned for Ricky to continue.

"Well, Charley and I went out to find him. Calling his name, looking everywhere around the restaurant. At that point, I wasn't even considering the vampire. I don't know what I was thinking. After we searched everywhere, and I found his car a few blocks away, I realized what had happened. I told Charley to go home, that I was sure Rodrigo would show up." He looked up at me again. "Charley's human. He doesn't know about us." He started to take another scoop of green chili but then seemed to think better of it and let it fall back into the bowl. "After Charley left, I said a sense spell to find him, but couldn't. I knew what I'd find then."

I wondered since he had spoken the spell if he had the same level of power as his in-laws. I set the thought aside with the intention of asking Finn later.

"Sure enough, after what seemed like forever, I found him. He was over half a mile away, in another damned alley. I've never seen anything like it." He shuddered and looked down at Saul to confirm he was still sleeping. "I doubt the fucking vampire even drank from Rodrigo. There was blood everywhere. It was like the walls and concrete had been painted with it. Rodrigo's face and torso was nothing but cut upon cut, some shallow, others deep enough to show the bone. The rest of him was scattered everywhere."

Cynthia's face jerked toward her brother-in-law. "The rest of him?" Her voice sounded like it would break.

"Holy fuck!" Caitlin murmured, earning her a glare from Paulette.

"Yeah. He was torn into probably eleven or twelve pieces. It was like he'd been…." His voice trailed off.

Paulette, for once, sounded as shaken as Cynthia. "In pieces," she repeated as she let out a slow breath and gazed at her husband. "I've never heard of a vampire doing that. Torturing, sure, but never in a way that would waste much blood. What kind of vampire are we dealing with?"

The family continued to discuss details of Rodrigo's death and their different theories about the vampire. Finn filled them in about Sonia's parents and not being able to find Derek. I was grateful that he handled it. The last thing I wanted was to break down in front of the entire de Morisco family.

Gradually, it was all I could do to keep my eyes open. I wanted to hear all that was said. In a twisted sort of way, I couldn't help but be fascinated. It seemed like I was constantly being reminded that I was living in a different world and that I needed to catch on quickly if I had any chance of surviving long enough to be a part of it. Still, all the stress and loss of the past several days was taking its toll. On top of everything else, this much exhaustion was a new experience for me as well. I'd never before felt like I couldn't handle something. Even when I had to leave my grandparents' home, I was sad and lonely, but it had never affected me like this.

Sensing that I was fading, Finn reached out and put his arm around me, and since I was one step lower, my head rested easily on his shoulder. I drifted in and out as the family made plans for the foreseeable future.

It was decided that people could go about their days in a normal fashion, using Wendell and Paulette's home as base. Everyone had to be back at least an hour before sundown and would sleep in their childhood rooms—Peter and Saul in sleeping bags in Christina's old room with their parents. They agreed to use protection spells around the house and to have the men take two-hour shifts throughout the night while everyone else slept.

It was Caitlin's raised voice that finally brought me back to full attention. I turned to see her pointing at me accusingly. "And what about him?" Disgust distorted her lips as she addressed her parents. "Are you really going to allow this to happen in your home?"

"Caitlin...." If Caitlin's voice hadn't already woken me, Finn's warning growl would have.

Wendell held out a hand, signaling Finn to calm down. "Caitlin, watch how you say it, but say what you're thinking, because it will be the last time it will be discussed."

"A lot of good that does, Dad! It's obvious that you've already made up your mind to be suckered in by the demon. You're seriously going to let *it* stay here? Under the same roof with your grandchildren?" Out of the corner of my eye, I saw both Ricky and Christina flinch and begin to speak, but they were also silenced by Wendell. Caitlin continued her rant. "You're fine with *it* sleeping in the same bed with your son? You're fine with your son fucking *it* under your roof? Do you really—"

"Enough, Caitlin!" Wendell's face was nearly purple, and no longer sounding tired, his voice reverberated with fury. "I told you to watch how you speak. If you weren't my daughter and if I didn't love you, I would make you leave—vampire or not. You're correct. This is *my* roof"—he glanced back at Paulette, who was beet red, whether from anger or sadness I wasn't sure—"*our* roof. We will decide who can be under it! There will be no discussion if Brett is welcome or not. The decision was made, and not just because there is a vampire on the loose. He has done nothing to show that he is or will be a danger to any of us. Your prejudice is based on fear and weakness, Caitlin, and you are better than this! Your brother cares about him, and I believe Brett cares about your brother. That is all any of us need to know or ask. That is enough to make him welcome, always. Every one of us is staying here." Caitlin opened her mouth to argue, but Wendell cut her off with a wave of his hand. "No arguments, Caitlin. You are staying too, even if I have to use every element under the heavens to keep you here. You are not going to be killed out of your own petty spite. So, either be cordial and polite or keep your mouth shut and stay in your room!" He finished his speech by pointing his finger up the stairs toward the bedroom.

Her face crimson and on the verge of tears, Caitlin squared her shoulders and marched across the room, paused by the front door as if weighing her options, and then made her way up the stairs.

It was a rather humiliating experience for everyone in the room, and a horrible ending to a hard, heartbreaking day. While I appreciated both Wendell's defense of me and his acknowledgement of how Finn and I felt about each other, I couldn't help but have some amount of sympathy for Caitlin. For a woman of thirty who had so much pride, it had to be debasing to be lectured and sent to her room like a child. Finn must have felt similarly, as he didn't say anything negative about Caitlin as we crawled into his bed, discussing the day before we fell asleep, his head cradled on my chest.

CHAPTER TWENTY-FIVE

THE next day was stressful and equally exhausting. Everyone slept in until the late morning, except for Cynthia, who had left shortly after the meeting, as soon as the sun was up enough for Paulette and Wendell to feel safe about her being on her own. She opened the bakery. Finding this out made me begin to see Cynthia in a different light. She might be timid and scared, but she obviously had a portion of the de Morisco strength that was abundantly evident in the rest of the family.

When I woke up, Finn had already gotten out of bed. He and his mother had a huge breakfast on the table by the time everyone else had woken. Even with the tension from the night before still thick in the air, breakfast was an experience unlike any I had ever had, one that made me long to relive it over and over again. Despite subtle hostile looks from Caitlin and her refusal to speak to anyone, the meal was filled with chatter and laughter from Peter and Saul. Although forced, everyone seemed to do their best to put on cheerful faces for the sake of the children, never discussing the vampire or the plans for Rodrigo's service, which would take place on the day after next.

Growing up, while I knew that Grandma loved me, I'd never experienced this sort of gathering, filled with all the members of the family coming together and showing one another care and concern. Being a part of it made me feel even closer to Finn. I'd been spliced into the de Morisco family with Caitlin being the only hiccup. While I appreciated it and wanted to allow myself to slip right into the role, it made me wonder if I had whatever it took inside to pull off such a seemingly Norman Rockwell existence—if the painter had included scenes of vampires, demons, and witches. I wasn't sure the old Brett Wright had the settling-down gene, much less the newly demonized Brett Wright.

THE next two days were unlike any I could have ever dreamed up. It was somehow decided that I would spend my days helping out Wendell in the costume shop. Finn and Paulette were constantly bringing over different pastries and snacks. I was suddenly thankful for my demon-given metabolism, and wondered how the de Moriscos weren't all as large as elephants. Even Cynthia would pop over from time to time, occasionally giving me an intimidated attempt at a smile, a gesture that made me grateful for her trying to accept my presence and guilty over being the source of so much fear.

Several times throughout the day, Wendell made offhanded remarks about Caitlin, often complaining about shallow things such as her constantly changing hair color and her choices in girlfriends. I got the impression he was used to her popping over from her store as much as the rest of the family, and that their current alienation was taking a larger toll on him than he was willing to admit.

The majority of people who came through the store were everyday, average humans, expecting nothing more than fun, novelty gag-gift items, or wanting to rent a costume for such-and-such occasion. However, every once in a while, after a particular patron left, Wendell would come over and tell me that they were a witch or warlock. He showed me how he had actual magical merchandise spread throughout all the novelty items. Of course, he referred to them as *elemental* materials—still seemed like magic to me. Some of the things were rather obvious after he pointed them out: crystals, herbs, certain rocks, and bones (that I had previously assumed were made of resin or something—not so much). Conversely, there were other things that I never would have thought would be used for magical purposes, such as differing masks and robes, enchanted mirrors, picture frames, small vials of water and sand from different regions, and even some of the packaged snacks that were arranged on a variety of shelves behind the cash register.

I found all the magical supplies interesting, things I never would have imagined, but my favorite part was the customers. After the first couple of people who Wendell told me were other witches, we made it a game. When each person left, he would raise an eyebrow questioningly. I would then take a guess whether the person was human or a witch. By the middle of the second day, I was beginning to have a fairly accurate record. I couldn't place my finger on what it was that made the difference, outside of the fact that all of them were at least a little above the average attractiveness level, but other than that, there really weren't any telltale signs. They didn't move differently or speak differently. There was a wide variety and range in the ways they dressed, and they didn't even treat Wendell any differently than his human clientele did. However, after a while, I began to notice a certain feeling I would get when a witch or warlock would enter the store. It was a sense of suddenly being just a touch more awake, like they radiated a small electrical charge that heightened the sensations around them.

There were two people that came in the second day who I instantly knew were other than human. However, they didn't have the same feeling as the witches who came in the store. The first was one of the most exotic women I had ever seen. She entered the store with her head covered in a shimmering, translucent blue veil. As soon as Wendell noticed her, he went over and locked the front door and removed the open sign.

"Hello, Amalphia." His normally gentle and caring voice was filled with a tone of respect and awe that I hadn't heard from him before.

Before she replied, she stepped further into the store, away from the windows, as she pushed her veil away from her face, letting it fall in folds around her shoulders. Her hair, though long and thick, looked nearly transparent, except for a faint greenish-blue tint. Every plane of her face was angled and pointed, in a way that seemed like it shouldn't have existed in nature, but came together to form a fragile, ethereal beauty. "Hello, Wendell. I trust you are well." It wasn't a question. Her voice made me long for the ocean, and once again, my skin began to feel as if it were ready to crack and flake off.

"Euphrates again, my lady?" Wendell's head did a slight deferential nod as he addressed her.

She shook her head, the motion causing the reflected light from her hair to scatter prisms of color off the walls. "I think the Tigris this time. I don't know what I might be missing. I hope there may be a greater power in the soil from the East, where dawn's light touches first."

I hadn't the slightest clue what they were talking about. I didn't even venture a guess.

Wendell gave another nod, stepped away for a few moments, and then returned with one of the small vials filled with sand and water. The sand in this one was a dark, murky brown color that tainted the water above it. "If this one still isn't what you need, let's try Konar. I really believe it may hold the answer."

"I do not think the source is in Asia, not from the sense I am getting from it, but if this fails, very well." She slipped the vial into the folds of her gown and reached up, once again hiding her features under the veil. In a gentle rush of cool air, she turned and slipped through the door as Wendell reached out to unlock it.

I stood there for a second until he turned around, a distant, dreamy expression on his face.

"Wendell, what was that?"

"Hmm?" He gave his head a little shake, and his eyes slowly slid into focus on my face. "Oh yes. Sorry. What was it you needed, Brett?"

"What was she? She obviously wasn't human. Was she a different kind of witch? She seemed to put you in some sort of trance, and she didn't even pay."

"Goodness, no, she didn't pay. Her kind will never pay. What they do, they do for all of us. Humans included."

"Really? What is she?"

"She's a nymph. A river nymph, to be more precise."

"Oh." That didn't really help. "What's a nymph?"

For a moment he looked up at me in confusion, as if it was inconceivable that I wouldn't know what a nymph was. "I keep forgetting how new all of this is to you. Sorry, Brett. A nymph is similar to a fairy, I suppose. Well, no, not really, but I guess in human terms.... There are wood nymphs, nymphs of the air, water nymphs, like Amalphia. They protect and nurture different aspects of nature."

"There are fairies too?" Every answer I got seemed to only bring more questions.

Wendell just gave a small smile and a nod as he returned to restocking the rack of cheap magic tricks for children.

The other patron who was instantly identifiable as a nonhuman was a giant of a man who came into the store only a few minutes before it closed. I noticed Wendell stiffen and draw himself up before I saw the man. He was easily a head taller than me. While he was massive, it was easy to see he was completely lean, no excess fat on him at all. He radiated strength. More than strength. Every movement was fluid and intentional. It was his eyes, though, that gave him away more than anything else. They were black. I couldn't tell if they were all pupil or if the iris was black and just blended in.

He had only come in a few feet when I saw his nostrils flare. He jerked his head toward me, taking me in with his dark eyes. His top lip curled, and a low, trembling growl emanated from him.

"It's okay, Farvin. He's with me." Wendell took a cautious step out from behind the counter and moved closer to me.

The man's eyes didn't break away from mine. It was everything I could do to continue to meet his gaze without glancing away. However, something in me knew that to do so would be a misstep. "I thought you had more sense, Wendell. You should consider the company you keep." His voice was so low and gravelly that it took me a few seconds to sort out what he had said. "If I had known *you* were what he was talking about...." A disgusted laugh escaped him. "Definitely not your typical boyfriend."

This time, I looked away—sending Wendell a *what the hell is he talking about* glare.

"I vouch for him, Farvin. He's with me," Wendell repeated, his voice sounding more declarative.

The man's gaze finally left me and moved to Wendell. As it did, I felt my shoulders loosen, and tension I hadn't realized I'd been holding escaped. "I'll return at a time when your shop is fit for other customers. I thought to warn you of dangerous choices of those around you. However, it appears to be a family trait."

Wendell didn't respond, but took another step, this time entering the space between myself and the man. After a moment, the huge man turned and left the store in three great strides.

I turned to Wendell. This time I was confident. "Werewolf?"

"Yeah." Wendell nodded as he walked over to flip the closed sign. "Farvin's never exactly pleasant, but he typically makes more sense. I think it's time we gather the family and go home."

"I take it werewolves and demons don't get along so well."

Wendell only gave me a warning glance and then began to close up the store.

IT WAS a new experience, sleeping next to someone. Even in my past "relationships" and dating experience, after sex we would each return to our own houses to sleep. I was surprised how comfortable I was with Finn next to me, his gentle snoring serving as soothing white noise instead of an irritant. He twisted and turned more than I thought was normal, but I didn't really have any reference. It was almost awe inducing to feel him curl up next to me, his body forming to mine, his thick arms wrapping around my chest. After a brief discussion, we decided that neither of us wanted our first time to be under his parents' roof with his family all around us. The tension of knowing his naked body was next to mine and that I couldn't yet take full advantage of it was the only aspect of sleeping with him that kept me awake.

On my two-hour shifts of keeping "guard duty" in the living room, I rifled through photo album after photo album. Some of them dated back as far as Paulette's and Wendell's childhoods. It was amusing to see pictures of Finn as a child and an awkward teen. I couldn't help but laugh at photos of a thirteen-year-old Finn in a lime-green suit and baby-blue cowboy boots at Cynthia's *Quinceañera*. All the other boys around the girls were dressed in black and blue suits. However, Finn's suit matched the sash around Cynthia's dress. That probably helped minimize any shock when Finn had decided to come out of the closet to his family. In addition to intensifying my ache over Sonia and her parents, the photo albums once again brought on the ever more familiar emotions of excitement and apprehension over the possibility of becoming part of a family.

ASIDE from being with and sleeping next to Finn, the evenings were my favorite part of the day, despite the increasing tension as each night grew longer. Each moment that passed was one more that could bring the vampire closer to attacking. However, each was also another moment that he didn't come and everyone was okay.

To have gone from a family of three to living with just Sonia, it was surreal to be in a home crowded with ten people.

There was always noise, always a wait for the restrooms, always some sort of bickering going on, always laughter. I knew if I had to stay here for days on end, I would probably rip my hair out and run away screaming. Given the current turn of events, I would probably end up exploding into a ball of flames. However, at the moment, it was a taste of a life that I had always wondered about but never really thought I would get to experience. I liked it. At least, I thought so.

It was also fascinating to see the inside, everyday life of the de Moriscos, and how what I called magic was as natural to them as breathing. If you weren't paying attention, it would be easy to miss. They cooked and cleaned like everyone else. There weren't brooms floating around sweeping the floor all on their own, and the dishes didn't wash themselves. However, it was a constant when Paulette and Wendell were cooking that a drawer would open and a cooking utensil or different spice would shoot into their outstretched hand. More than once, as the children were playing, they would knock over a lamp or vase, and it would fall to the floor and break. Christina would get on the children for their carelessness, but by the time she had picked up the pieces, whatever had broken once again sat back in its place, whole.

Peter and Saul were the most interesting to watch. Unlike the adults in the family (Ricky not included, I discovered), they were not yet able to cast spells without using words. As they played in the middle of the living room floor, action figures and Legos floated around them amid their soft murmuring. To my great pleasure, the boys let me play with their handheld video games. Somehow, they had bewitched them so the figures rose off the screen in a sort of hologram.

Both evenings after dinner, the entire family, even Caitlin, who had ceased sauntering around like a wounded animal but still refused to speak to me, played games together. The first evening we played old-fashioned board games (Clue, Monopoly, and Life). The pieces moved on their own, guided by a finger or even just a gaze.

The second night, after Peter and Saul begged relentlessly, the family gave in and played hide-and-seek throughout the house. Their twist on the game was that everyone was invisible, both the people hiding and the person seeking. Ricky did not join in this game because he was not able to sustain his invisibility spell without recasting, thus giving his hiding spot away. To his credit, I was impressed to notice that he neither seemed embarrassed nor resentful of the fact that his wife had greater power than he did. He sat on the couch and hollered out good-natured taunts to the person seeking everyone else.

I, of course, hid the traditional way, having to find something large enough to hold my mass while still concealing my bulk from view. The boys, having never played this way before, squealed in delight each time they discovered me hiding behind the clothes in the closet or hunkered down between the washing machine and the wall.

It wasn't until I was the designated seeker that I discovered another aspect of being a demon that I hadn't been aware of.

I prepared myself to not let on when I discovered Peter or Saul. They had to keep chanting to stay invisible, so everyone would tiptoe by them, pretending not to hear them, until enough time passed that the boys would start giggling and be discovered by default. However, without meaning to, I glanced over under the kitchen table as I heard the muttered castings of Peter.

With full intentions of letting my eyes pass over the spot, I found his location and stared at him, my eyes narrowing in confusion. At first I wasn't sure what I was seeing. There weren't any colors, but right at the base of the table, behind the legs of one of the chairs, it looked like the air was trembling. It reminded me of looking through the heat vapors rising off blacktop. I realized the shimmering air was outlining Peter's tiny form.

"Hey! No fair!" Peter gave me an angry face as he suddenly became visible again. "You could hear me!"

Sure enough, Peter was situated in the exact same spot where the air had been displaced. He crawled out from under the table and held out his hand to me. "Tag me! I have to be it now." I held out my hand distractedly, and he jumped up and slapped it. He raised his voice to a shrill yell. "Come on back. Brett found me. He cheated!"

Within seconds everyone had vacated their hiding places and had returned to the living room.

Peter looked up at his mom, his lips in a small, thin line. "He cheated, Mom."

Ricky spoke up before Christina could respond. "Peter, none of that. We don't accuse people of cheating. If you are going to play the game, you know that sometimes people are going to hear you casting. You have to learn how to do it quieter."

"I didn't hear him," I murmured, more to myself than anyone else. I looked up at Finn, my voice returning to normal volume. "Well, actually, I did hear him, but that's not how I found him. I saw him."

"You saw him?" Finn gave me a confused look. "You mean you could see through his invisibility charm?"

"Sorta. I couldn't really see him, just the air around him. It was wavy or fuzzy or something." I looked from him to other members of the family. "Is that normal?"

I saw Caitlin shake her head emphatically out of the corner of my eye. Wendell spoke up. "You could tell he was there without actually seeing him?"

I nodded.

"Really?" Finn took a step back and disappeared. "Can you see me now?" It was a little disturbing to hear Finn's voice so close and not be able to see him.

At first I didn't see him, but as I narrowed my eyes, the same sensation happened yet again. The air around his body seemed to steam and quiver, showing his form. "Yeah. I still can't see you, but I can see where you are."

Finn materialized once again. "Wow, that's awesome. I didn't know that could even happen."

"Must be from the demon blood, huh?" Christina grinned at me cautiously. "I wonder what other little surprises you're going to discover."

Caitlin turned around and left the room.

CHAPTER TWENTY-SIX

SUNDAY dawned with the familiar sense of relief that we had all survived another night without incident. However, the family's mood was heavy and sad. Rodrigo's service was scheduled for noon. Just as they said they would, the de Moriscos had handled all the arrangements over the past two days. Through their planning, I learned there were several businesses that catered to the witch community. Witches and warlocks couldn't go to a human doctor. Not that they got sick or hurt in such a way they couldn't heal themselves with the elements very often, but I guess it did happen on occasion. Likewise, their bodies could not be handled by a human-operated morgue, as they could, if inspected for some reason, give away their true nature.

As they shuffled out of the house dressed in their best clothes, I was struck again by how beautiful the entire family was.

"Are you sure you don't wanna go to church with us, babe?" Finn came over and sat down on the couch beside me as the rest of his family left the house.

I shook my head. "Sorry, Finn. I'm not ready to darken the door of a church just yet, even one that is okay with witches and warlocks." I saw a hint of disappointment that he tried to hide. "I'll go one of these days, soon. Promise. Besides, like I told you, I have to get in the ocean. It's been a week! I've never gone so long before, not even close. I feel like I'm about to crack into pieces."

He gave me an endearing smile. "I could skip church, go with you. We could swim for a while, and then I'm sure we could find *something* else to occupy our time." His hand slowly crept up the length of my thigh.

The thought made me start to harden. I was dying to be alone with Finn, really alone with him, but I shook my head. "I'm sorry, Finn. I would love that, I can't tell you how much I would love that, but I really need some time to myself in the water." I wanted to swim out much farther and dive deeper than Finn would be able to go—I *needed* to. "Is that okay?"

Finn's face fell once more in disappointment, but he didn't try to guilt me into letting him come. "Of course that's okay. You need to get out there. It will help you feel better, work through some things." I knew by "things" he meant Sonia. "Just don't boil anyone, okay?"

"Shut up, ass!" I leaned forward, took his jaw in my hands, and kissed him with as much passion as I could muster. Now that I knew I was minutes from the ocean, my skin was crawling.

His warm chocolate eyes glowed as he pulled away. Not for the first time, I was taken aback by how lucky I felt to have found Finn and how fast things seemed to have fallen into place.

"Is it still okay for me to borrow your truck?"

"Of course. Feel free to melt the steering wheel if you need to."

I grabbed his sides as he let out a laugh. "Oh, you think you're so funny, don't ya?"

At that moment, the loud blast from the van's horn outside broke the mood. In my mind, I could see Caitlin reaching over Ricky to blare the horn. Finn rolled his eyes. "I guess I should probably go, huh?"

"Yeah, sorry." I gave him another peck on the lips. "I'll be ready when you all get back, and we'll go to Rodrigo's service together. That work?"

"Sure." He stood up and headed to the door. "I love you, Brett."

"I love you too, Finn."

HAVING not been in the ocean for longer than ever before, I wasn't prepared for the sensations that swept through me as my toes touched the water. The relief had never been like this. I took two large strides and dove into the surf, my stomach scratching against the sand in the shallows. Within a few quick strokes I was several yards out into the water, deep enough that I could no longer touch the bottom.

My skin felt alive, like it truly had been slowly dying and now was given healing nectar. The tingling that coursed through me felt nearly orgasmic. Each stroke took me farther out into the deep, farther away from everything behind me, the good and the bad, taking me away from myself.

Before I had gone out more than a hundred yards, I found myself surrounded by twenty or thirty jellyfish, their translucent flesh shimmering and undulating in the morning sunlight. I ran my hands through their spiral tentacles as they surrounded me, relishing the pleasurable tingle of them against my skin.

I rose to the surface, took one final look at the jellyfish from an overhead view, inhaled one more deep breath, and dove. I went out farther and deeper, where the shore was no longer visible, where the bottom of the ocean couldn't be seen.

There was rarely much ocean life when I swam out so far. There was a large school of krill, and in the distance I could see a lone shark swimming away from me. It was too far away to see what kind it was, and I wished it would turn and swim with me for a while.

I dove deeper, the water getting cooler and darker. When I looked up, I could see a faint blue light far above me, but it seemed a different world, one that was too distant for me to return. After several more feet, I stopped swimming, letting my body float lazily in the currentless deep, the water cradling me. Wrapped in the protective pressure of the ocean, my mind traveled to Sonia, the loss of her coming to me again. Thinking of her here seemed easier. Somehow it all seemed to make more sense. Not in a way that provided a reason that would suffice for her death, but it felt natural. At least as natural as a vampire slaying could feel. The vampire was the shark, a hunting, emotionless killer. Sonia, a beautiful, exotic fish, unaware the life in which it flourished was about to be invaded and destroyed. It didn't make it right or easy, but it was life. I wasn't able to bring myself to say good-bye, and I doubted I would ever be able to, but I thought I could let go of some of the angst, of the senselessness of it all. Life and love didn't always make sense. Not in the ocean, not on the land.

I hung suspended for what felt like hours, letting my grief flow from me and into the wild water, letting the life so abundant in the sea seep in, reclaiming me as its own.

I'd always been able to stay underwater for extended periods of time. In fact, I usually came up for air because I knew I was supposed to, not because I felt a bodily urge. Like many things, I hadn't allowed myself to dwell on it much. I'd never stayed under for this period of time before. One more demon side effect, apparently. Why couldn't life just go back to normal? Erase everything over the past few days. Erase all that had happened to Sonia and her family. Erase my fucking demon blood, while we're at it.

After a time, I found myself swimming gradually higher, into the warmer water. Three giant rays glided past me on their way back to the shallows, their black skin gleaming like onyx in the shafts of light penetrating the waves.

Before long, I found what I was seeking. Again I closed my eyes and let the ocean do its work.

I sank easily into the strong ocean current as it swept me in its southward journey. In the current, my mind couldn't focus on anything but the ride itself. Nothing could distract from the thrill of the surge. At times I could see things in the distance, formless shapes and blurred colors.

There was no time. No world. Nothing outside the endless flow.

Abruptly, I felt a painful jerk on my left arm. I yanked it free and came to a sudden halt in the water. I swirled around, searching everywhere trying to find what had pulled at me. I couldn't see anything other than a few colorful fish swimming in and out of the kelp forest. However, I could feel it. I could feel its eyes on me, sense it moving too swiftly for me to see. Instantly, I felt stupid. I had been so focused on getting back to the ocean and simply being in the water that I completely forgot about what had been happening every time I'd gone into the ocean alone in the weeks prior to discovering I was a demon.

Having the peace of my world so abruptly shattered, I felt like I had been thrown out of a warm bed and into a brick wall. My anger began to build, and my body began to warm. I closed my eyes, putting all my effort into bringing down my anger. I knew what I was now. I was a demon. A fire demon who could set things ablaze under water. I could control it if I had to, if I wanted to, and right now, I wanted to. I was tired of this. Whatever was stalking me, it was time for us to come face to face. Whatever it was, I was confident it could burn.

I swam a little farther toward the kelp forest in front of me. There were hundreds of small colorful fish darting in and out of the tangles of leaves, as if they had been called out to watch the show. A few of the more daring were swimming out farther, coming toward me.

A light touch ran across the back of my shoulder. I whirled around, my hands grasping for whatever was there. I saw nothing but a flash of gold disappearing into the blue, just like before. I peered into the current, trying to discern any distinguishable shapes. Again I felt something, this time caressing my hair. Without turning, my hand flashed up, grasping, but I got nothing but my own hair. I turned around and swam the short distance to the forest. With my back nearly pressed against the caressing kelp fronds, I looked out at the open water in front of me. The fish began to swim around me, at times darting in to rub their sides against my skin and then dashing away again.

As I peered out, trying to make out some shape, something recognizable, the flash of gold darted in front of me again. It seemed only a few feet away. After a second, it flashed again over my head. There was something about it that made me think it was some kind of tail, but I couldn't be sure. I couldn't make out any shape. It was more just a feeling or a sense that it had to be a tail of some sort.

Cautiously, I stretched out my hand. Even as I did so, I realized how idiotic the action was. I didn't know what this thing was. Could it take my hand off with a clean bite? Could it drag me to the deep, to where the pressure was too great? Could it—

It grabbed my arm and jerked me forward a few feet. Without warning, I burst into flames, a ball of fire that seemed to encircle me several feet on every side. I made the inferno continue as I tried to adjust my eyes to be able to see through the flames and into the blue.

I thought I saw another flash of gold zip around me, but I couldn't be sure. It could have just been the flickering of my flames. I turned myself around within the fire, trying to catch it behind me. There was no spark of gold, no flash of fins.

What I did see cut through me.

Part of the kelp was inside the fireball with me, quickly being devoured. It took several seconds to realize what I was seeing, but when I did, the flames instantly went out, a sinking feeling overtaking the center of my chest.

Forgetting the monster of gold, I swam forward, shame washing over me. A huge portion of the forest was destroyed, empty murk where moments before life had flourished. Even where the fire hadn't touched, everything was scorched, simmering gray vapor wafting up toward the surface. I couldn't see any fish. I was sure whatever fish had been caught in the fire had been completely consumed, and the rest had hopefully managed to dart away before they were boiled by the heat.

Heaviness came over me as I looked at what I had done. How much I had destroyed in a matter of moments.

For the first time I could remember, I felt like I didn't belong in the ocean.

As an afterthought, I remembered the creature that had been toying with me. I looked around. I didn't see anything, nor did I feel its presence like I did before. Whether I had frightened it away or it had been devoured by the fire as well, I didn't know. At the moment, I didn't care. I wished it would come. Come and drag me away to whatever demise it could dream up.

With a final glance at the forest, I turned my eyes up and began to swim. Up through the inky soot and vapor from the dead and dying kelp. Up to the surface.

Chapter Twenty-Seven

By the time I returned to the de Morisco's house, I only had fifteen minutes before they were scheduled to pick me up. I wasn't sure how I was going to make myself get through a funeral. The only funeral I wanted to go to right now was my own. Bitterly, I thought how excited I had been to be in the ocean again, how it had made everything seem right. I never dreamed there could be an event that would make me wary of returning to the sea.

I had just gotten out of the shower and was toweling my hair when I felt a hand cup my ass. "If it wouldn't ruin this suit, I would pick you up and carry you in the bedroom and…." Finn's voice trailed off as I turned and met his eyes. "What's wrong? I'm sorry we're early. Take more time if you need."

"No, that's not it." I lowered the towel and began to dry my chest and abdomen. "Swimming didn't go so great."

Finn's face fell even further. "Oh, I'm sorry. I thought that would really help you sort through everything."

"Yeah. Me too."

"What happened?"

A picture of the dying kelp flashed through my mind, followed by the thought that I still had to get ready for the funeral. "I'll tell you later. It's too much right now." I finished drying my back and legs, stepped into the bedroom, and started putting on the clothes I had laid out on the bed. I didn't own a suit, so I resorted to a white button-down shirt with gray cargo pants. "Church go okay?"

"Yeah. Same old, same old."

I looked up at him. "Really, they didn't say anything about Rodrigo?"

"Rodrigo didn't go to church with us. The funeral won't be in a church. None of ours are."

I thought about asking what he meant, but I couldn't find the strength or the desire to care that much at the moment.

Hurriedly, I stuffed myself into the clothes, ran some product through my hair, joined Finn and the rest of the family in cramming ourselves into the minivan, and headed to the funeral.

THE drive took about forty minutes, and by the time we arrived, Saul had been crying for over half the way. I was feeling so restless and closed in that I concentrated only on breathing and not bursting into flames and taking the entire family with me. Finn tried to put his hand on my knee, but I swiftly shrugged away from him. It was enough that I felt like we were playing sardines. I couldn't handle any more contact. For a moment when I saw the hurt in his face, I wondered if he would be able to handle the moodiness that came with being with a fire demon. Of course, I had always been moody, so maybe I was just blaming it on my demon side. Then again, I had always been a demon. I just hadn't known it. I quickly let the train of thought slide away and returned to focusing on maintaining control.

When we all managed to extricate ourselves from the prison on wheels, I was taken aback by the beauty surrounding us. I wasn't sure where we were. I had never been here before, and I prided myself on knowing every inch of the California coast, at least the view from the water.

We were on a lush cliff. To the rear was a forest of evergreens. We walked about a quarter mile to join a group of others who had already gathered close to the cliff's edge, under a lone old, twisted willow. Beyond that, the rocky coast and the sea filled the horizon.

The sublime beauty of the cliff lifted my mood instantly. I looked over at Finn by my side, my eyes wide.

"I know," he whispered, smiling at the expression on my face. "Pretty amazing, isn't it?"

I let out a stream of breath in response. "Where are we? I've never been here before."

"No, you wouldn't have. It's a place specifically reserved for us, for witches and warlocks, at least for those of us that are fairly local. There are other locations spread throughout the world, of course, not just here. Places of spiritual significance for us. We have all our funerals, weddings, baby dedications, anything of consequence, here. It's enchanted. Humans, and even most other supernaturals, can't find this place, unless brought here by a witch."

"Wow." I looked around again, the exclusivity somehow making it seem even more beautiful. "Are you sure it's okay for me to be here?"

Finn smiled sweetly at me. "Of course it is. You're with me. Now come on, let's join the rest." He took my hand and led me the rest of the way to the willow. My moodiness at not wanting to be touched forgotten, I willingly intertwined my fingers with his.

I would have thought a group of witches and warlocks gathering in a sacred place would have been wearing robes or gowns or something magical looking, maybe even pointed hats. However, the fifty or sixty people who were here were all dressed in everyday suits and nice dresses. They would have fit in at any church or business meeting.

As we walked closer, I peered over the crowd's heads to see where the casket was, see if there was a grave that had been dug. All I could see was a small wooden bowl, intricate carvings covering every surface, nestled in the grass. As the thought formed, I glanced around once more. If this was the place where all witches were buried, the cliff should have been covered with headstones. I couldn't see any, which was good if they had weddings here as well. That would seem rather morbid.

By the time we were ten feet away, a quiet, lyrical murmuring met my ears. The group gathered around the willow was chanting or singing. Maybe casting spells. I couldn't tell. We joined the crowd, and the de Moriscos joined the singing, Paulette's voice a touch louder than the others, haunting and melodic. Whatever they were saying was in another language, one that I had never heard before.

Before Finn joined in the chanting, he raised up to put his lips to my ear. "I'm sorry. I should have taken the time to explain what all is going to happen. Are you going to be alright with everything?"

I nodded. Truth be told, I was a little apprehensive of what was going to occur, but something felt right here. I could feel an undercurrent of sadness, but the greater sense was of peace and rest. This was how I normally felt in the ocean. I let myself sink into the stream of emotions flowing from the crowd.

"I told you his family wouldn't even show up!" I heard Caitlin hiss behind me, momentarily disrupting the peace.

Cynthia's voice cracked with emotion. "Be still, Cate. It doesn't matter. *We're here.*"

Gradually, the chanting song grew strong as other latecomers joined in behind us. When it seemed like it would go on without end, everyone stopped in unison, the last note reverberating in the air.

I felt Finn give my hand a squeeze, and I glanced over at him questioningly.

"Just remember that everything will be okay. Just keep hold of my hand."

Confused, I nodded and looked back toward the willow and gasped. There was a small fire that seemed to be consuming the roots of the tree, growing at a rapid pace as it began to devour the bark higher up. After a few moments, however, I realized that the tree wasn't being harmed, and that the fire was beginning to take on solid form.

Gradually, the shape began to morph into a figure I could make out. As the flames died away, a woman stepped into being. She was unusually tall, angular, and wispy. Her shimmering, sheer gown was a bright yellow that seemed to move on its own despite the absence of a breeze. Her skin was a shining white. The most striking thing about her, however, was her hair. It was a brilliant orange, almost red. It was piled in a mass of uncontrollable curls atop her head, with tendrils whipping around her face and over her shoulders, looking too heavy for her slender neck to support.

Before I could fully take her in, I noticed the ground at her feet begin to quiver, as another form began to take shape. Within seconds a woman had formed from the earth, her skin a deep, dark brown, her hair the color of moss, flowers seeming to bloom from the tangles.

I tore my gaze from the women and looked at Finn. He just grinned and squeezed my hand. As he did so, a swift breeze rushed through the crowd, spinning and twisting around the two women, causing their gowns to whip around them frantically. Neither woman moved to adjust their clothing or hair. They stood serenely, their gaze traveling from person to person in front of them. When the gust gave way, there was a third woman standing with them, every bit of her nearly translucent, only having a little more substance than a ghost might. She was beautiful like the others, but her crystalline eyes shown with wildness the others lacked. A chill ran down my spine as her gaze met mine before she looked away dismissively.

"Only one more," Finn whispered. "Watch your feet."

"Watch my feet?"

Before he could answer, I felt the ground beneath us grow soggy. I glanced down. Just as it felt like my feet were going to sink into the earth, the ground solidified and was dry. Beside the three women, a spiral of water rose in the air, ribbons of it twisting and turning, weaving in and out of itself. The water took shape, and I recognized the woman instantly. "Amalphia," I breathed.

Finn glanced at me in surprise and nodded in affirmation.

In unison the women spoke, their voices at once sounding like a torrent, a storm, and yet conveying a sense of naturalness and motherly femininity. "From the fire is born the spirit, and into the fire, the spirit returns. From the earth is born the body, and into the earth, the body returns. From the air is born the soul, and into the air, the soul returns. From the water is born the tears of life, and into the water, the tears of life return."

Every hair on my body stood up, and I felt my skin tingle—the power radiating from the four women was a palpable force. I had no doubt that, had they wanted, they could have destroyed every person on the cliff, me included, without having to blink.

"A child of the elements has been slain by one who is a child of the night, a child of death. We welcome his return to his creator, to light. His passing marks the birth of discovery, the dawning of knowledge, the unveiling of truth, the first step in fulfillment of freedom from slavery."

I felt Finn stiffen beside me. I tore my eyes away from the women and glimpsed his confused, almost scared, expression.

"We offer our child back from whence he came, and we offer him to you." In a tangible silence, their voices ceased. They circled around the wooden bowl on the ground and lifted their hands heavenward. As they did, the bowl rose into the air until it was floating, even with the tips of their fingers. It hung suspended for several moments and then gracefully lowered back to the ground. At first I didn't notice, but where the bowl had been hovering, there was now a swirling gray mass.

"Rodrigo," Finn whispered beside me.

"Huh?" I didn't take my eyes from the scene in front of me.

"Rodrigo's ashes."

Oh. Although I had never met him, seeing his remains made me feel an ache in my chest for Rodrigo, one that compounded my wish that I could give Sonia such an otherworldly memorial.

With the women's hands still raised, Rodrigo's ashes rose higher, until they were level with the top of the willow, where they began to flatten out until they took the shape of a huge smooth disk spinning in place.

"Back from whence he came." The women's voices rang out suddenly, causing me to jump slightly. With their words, the ashes began to spin faster and faster. As they did so, the gray transformed into brilliant silver, shining and sparkling in the midday sunlight.

"Back to you." The silver disc spread out and lowered itself to engulf the congregation of witches.

"Breathe deep." I heard Finn instruct over the sound of the wind whipping the silver around us.

Without thinking, I did as he told me. I closed my eyes and drew in deep through my nose, filling my lungs with air. As I did, I felt some of the silver ash rush into me. For a moment I felt light-headed and was then filled with a feeling of such intense love that it caused my heart to hurt nearly as much as the loss of Sonia.

My eyes flew open. I couldn't see anything besides the swirling silver around me.

The women's voices rose in one final outcry. "Back to his creator."

At their words, an explosion of air blasted from the center of the group, sending the ashes out in a huge arch. They rained down onto the earth, covering the grass, trickling down the edge of the cliff, carried out to sea by the wind. I looked at the women just in time to see the redhead holding a small tongue of flame in her hand, gazing at it as a few of the silver ashes sparked and twinkled as they were consumed.

Without any other words, without a farewell, the women left in the reverse order they had come. Amalphia sank back into the earth, as it grew moist beneath our feet before returning to its dry state again. The translucent woman with the fury in her eyes dissipated into the air and departed in a rush of wind. The woman of the earth stepped around the redhead and quietly slipped into the willow's gnarled trunk. The final woman once again raised her hands to the sky and was engulfed in a torrent of flames, bathing everyone in a gust of heat.

As one, the crowd murmured, "Rodrigo," in a prayerful voice, turned, and broke into smaller groups as they walked away in silence.

The ride home wasn't nearly as stressful as the ride there had been. Everyone seemed caught up in their own minds. Even the children were still and didn't fuss or complain. The silence wasn't isolating like it so often can be. We were all bound together in our shared experience, and it was enough to simply breathe.

THE peaceful feeling continued when we arrived at the house. Finn and I sat on the sofa in the sunken living room, and the boys curled up together in Wendell's recliner, fast asleep. Some of the family had gone to make food for a barbeque they were planning for later in the afternoon, but Ricky, Cynthia, and Caitlin joined us, lounging in scattered locations in the living room.

I hated to break the silence, but I had so many questions I couldn't contain them any longer. My voice sounded harsh and strange after so much time without speaking, even though I tried to whisper to

Finn. Caitlin grimaced. "So, those women, they were all… nymphs? Right?"

Finn nodded. "Yeah. How did you know Amalphia's name?"

"I met her in your dad's store yesterday. She came in and bought some sand or something."

Finn pursed his lips. "Really? Still?" He gave a small shake of his head and then turned to look at me. "So, what did you think?" His eyes twinkled.

I thought for a second, trying to find the right words. There weren't any. "It was unbelievable. Maybe the most amazing, beautiful thing I have ever seen."

"Yeah, no matter how many times I see it, it never loses any of the wonder."

"You've done that before?"

Finn smiled sadly. "That's how it is for every passing. It never changes. It's how we send our loved ones on to wait for us." He grinned at my gaping face. "You should see the weddings. You'll flip." He let out a little laugh.

I couldn't imagine anything more amazing than what I had already seen. "What was with his ashes changing color?"

Another smile lit up his face, and he sighed. "Oh, I wasn't surprised by the silver at all. Not with Rodrigo." He noticed my confused face. "Sorry. Everyone's ashes change color when the nymphs offer them up. It depends on where your greatest power lies. If a person's greatest strength is in spirit, their ashes are always silver. Rodrigo was always so sweet and tender, always in tune with how others were doing. Always trying to help people and make them happier."

"What color would you be, since you and your family have power in many areas?"

"Already planning my death, are you?" He leaned over and whispered in my ear, "Just kidding, babe."

Caitlin made gagging sounds from her place sprawled on the floor.

"Shut up, Cate," Ricky scolded, before he looked over to me. "Even witches who have several different areas of strength always have one that is more dominant. The ashes will correspond with whatever that power is."

"Yeah," Finn agreed, "a person might not ever know what their primary strength is, they all might seem the same, but there's always one that is stronger."

"Would my ashes change color?" I hadn't even been thinking that. I wasn't sure where the question had come from.

Finn and Ricky looked back and forth between each other. At last Finn offered an apologetic look. "Sorry, sweetie. I've never seen the passing of a demon. I don't know how that would go. Plus, the only thing that can kill a demon is another demon, so I doubt there would be much left to turn to ash after another demon gets done."

"Yeah, but we don't know if that rule applies to me." I sure didn't feel indestructible when I was swimming earlier that morning.

"True. Which is why we're worried about the vampire. If we were one hundred percent certain of your heritage, there would be no concern of him being able to kill you. As it is...." Finn looked uncomfortable. "Can we talk about something else? I don't really wanna think about you dying."

I wasn't really sure how I felt about the subject, to be honest. The idea of being killed, especially by another demon, didn't sound good, but neither did the prospect of living forever with everyone I loved dying around me. "Why did you have me breathe in Rodrigo's ashes?"

"Didn't you feel a surge of love after?" Cynthia piped in, surprising me.

I nodded, afraid my voice might startle her back into silence.

"Well," she continued, "that was Rodrigo. His gift was spirit, love. It's our way of keeping those we love with us. Rodrigo is a part of us now, a part of you. His love will always be within us."

"Wow. That's kinda cool, actually." I couldn't help but feel cheated that I had some of Rodrigo with me but none of Sonia.

Finn broke in, "If his major force had been fire or air, you would have felt a heat go through you or a cool gust of air."

Surprising me yet again, Cynthia spoke up once more, looking to Ricky and Caitlin. "What was up with the nymphs talking about the discovery of truth or whatever and that thing about slavery?"

"The birth of discovery, the dawning of knowledge, the unveiling of truth, and the first step in the fulfillment of freedom from slavery," Finn quoted. "Yeah, I have no idea. That was crazy."

"That was unusual?" I questioned.

"Completely." Wendell stepped into the room from the kitchen. "The passing ritual never changes, but those lines have never been spoken before. I don't know what they mean, but the nymphs offered us some sort of prophecy today. It had to be."

Caitlin spoke up, this time with no sarcasm in her voice. "But why Rodrigo? Why would his death be the start of some life-changing prophecy?"

Wendell shook his head in wonder. "I have no idea, daughter. I don't know if the prophecy is dealing with things that will happen in our lifetime, sometime soon, or if they were foreseeing things centuries from now."

"It has to be centuries from now." Ricky looked toward his father-in-law. "There aren't any races that are still in slavery."

Caitlin laughed bitterly. "The vampires have made all of us slaves."

Wendell shook his head. "No. Just because they are called Royal and people are afraid of them doesn't mean we are slaves. I don't believe that is what the prophecy was about." He turned and looked at me before continuing. "There were times when certain races were enslaved. Both werewolves and fairies were captives of both vampires and demons at one point or another. Other species died off entirely due to slavery, like dragons and manticores."

Cynthia shuddered. "I hope you're right, Ricky. I hope it's centuries from now. Prophecies always mean change, and change always means war."

Chapter Twenty-Eight

"How do you want your burger done?" Wendell turned and looked at me over his shoulder, holding the spatula in midair above the grill.

"He's a demon, Dad." Caitlin's voice sounded playfully sarcastic, but I was certain I could hear the insult behind the humor. "How do you think he wants it done?"

Instead of rising to the bait, Wendell kept his eyes on me. "Brett?"

"Rare, please." I felt my face flush as Caitlin gave an "I told you so" nod to her father.

"Brett, dear. Would you please help me carry out the chips and drinks from the kitchen?"

"Of course, Paulette."

The afternoon's relaxing melancholy had given way to the bustle of the family getting ready for their barbeque. Finn and Ricky had taken the boys into the small strip of woods that ran behind the de Morisco's neighborhood to play war with water guns. The rest were getting everything ready. Christina was helping her mother make potato salad and coleslaw, while Cynthia was setting the picnic table with a blue-and-white checkered tablecloth and paper plates.

I stopped just outside of the kitchen as Christina was leaning toward her mother, whispering, "Mom, I'm not really sure we should have a picnic today. It seems a little overcast, and with the vampire out on a rampage and all...."

"Nonsense." Paulette waved away her concerns. "It's not even six yet. We have a few hours until sunset, and whoever heard of a vampire out and about because it's cloudy. I refuse to let this worthless piece of trash interfere with us living our lives any more than I have to."

"I don't know, Mom. I just have this feeling…."

Paulette looked up from the head of cabbage she was shredding and saw me hovering in the doorway. "Come on in, Brett." She motioned to a cabinet in the rear of the kitchen. Christina suppressed an annoyed look and turned back to whatever it was she was chopping on the counter. "All the chips and soda are in there. Just grab a variety of each, and that would be perfect. Thank you, dear."

I loaded my arms with an assortment of chips and sodas and quickly returned to the backyard.

Just as the food was being loaded onto the picnic table, Finn and the others arrived, all thoroughly soaked.

Outside of the ones at school and church, picnics were a relatively new experience for me. Grandpa had always struggled with allergies, and since he didn't enjoy being outside, no one else should either.

The food was great, and once again, Peter and Saul helped fill an afternoon that could have been caught up with conversations about funerals, prophecies, and vampire murders with giggles, stupid jokes, and a rather rousing belching competition. Caitlin won. Go figure.

The past couple of days were the first time I had ever spent any extended period around little kids. It was so fun to watch Finn interact with his nephews. It was clear they both worshiped the ground he walked on, and from the way Finn carried on, the feeling was mutual.

The sun finally came out from behind the clouds after dinner had been cleared away. Wendell and Ricky retired to the living room to watch a game on television, while Finn and I helped clean the dishes.

As I bent down to pick up a dishtowel I'd dropped, I felt a gentle tug on my back pocket. I looked back to see little Saul standing behind me, his eyes huge. "Mr. Brett, can you and Uncle Finn play hide-and-seek with us in the woods, please?"

Christina hollered over her shoulder without turning around. "Peter! If you want to play with Finn and Brett, you come and ask yourself. Don't put Saul up to doing your dirty work for you!"

After a couple of seconds, Peter sauntered into the room, hands stuffed deep in his pockets. "Well, can they?"

"I don't know. You'll have to ask them." Christina continued doing the dishes.

Peter looked up at his uncle. "Well, can you?"

Finn looked over at me and grinned. "Want to?"

"Sure. I'm always up for a game of invisible hide-and-seek when I can't be invisible."

"Yay!" Saul gave a little jump as he clapped his hands vigorously. "I'm gonna hide in that big rotted tree!"

"You're not supposed to tell where you're gonna hide, stupid!" Peter rolled his eyes at his brother.

This time, Christina turned around, her wet finger flicking water on Peter's face as she shook it at him. "Don't call your brother stupid, or you can spend the evening in your room." She turned to Saul. "And no, you're not going to hide in that old tree. It's likely to fall and crush you."

Saul's face fell.

"Cate." Christina looked over at her. "Will you please go and hide with Saul? Hide-and-seek in the woods is not appropriate for a five-year-old, and I don't trust these two goofballs"—she gestured to Finn and me—"to not get bamboozled by my little monsters."

Caitlin glanced at me with disdain and then down at Saul, who was now tugging on her little finger. A genuine smile escaped, something I wasn't sure she was capable of. She bent down and picked up Saul. "Sure, why not? It's you and me, cowboy!"

Saul let out a shrill cheer.

WE PLAYED several rounds, and I had been caught three times already, so I was "it" yet again. I counted to one hundred and then turned around and headed back into the woods. We had set the boundaries as anywhere you could still see the house. It seemed to make sense but had turned out that, since the house was situated on a slope above the woods, you could see it from nearly everywhere. The hiding places were endless.

There was still a good hour until sunset, but the sun was exceptionally intense, and I was sweating more than I normally did. I wiped my brow with the back of my forearm. I had discovered on the previous rounds that it was harder to discern the outline of the hiders' bodies in the woods than it had been in the house, due to all the differing colors and patterns.

I had been searching for two or three minutes when I was able to make out the shape of Caitlin and Saul crouching between a large boulder and a hawthorn shrub. Since there were two of them, they were easier to find, not to mention that Saul had a hard time not squirming. I'd caught them two other times, so I let my eyes travel over them and continued searching. Finn had yet to be caught by anyone, so I was determined to find him.

I went farther into the narrow woods, wishing even though I couldn't be invisible that I could at least manage to not sound like a wild boar crashing through the undergrowth. After a few minutes, I was nearing the other side, which was shared by another housing area. Glancing behind me, I realized I couldn't see the de Morisco house. I'd gone too far. I turned around and started to head back the way I'd come.

"You looking for the boy? Or should I have gotten the good-looking one to get your attention?"

The voice caused me to stiffen in surprise. I felt my skin crawl. Even though I hadn't heard his voice before, I knew who it was before I turned around.

He stood there, less than twenty feet away, his back pressed against a cottonwood tree, his arm wrapped around Peter's neck, the boy's head twisted at an awkward angle.

Again I was struck by how normal he looked. He didn't appear overly powerful, his thin arm relaxed as it coiled tighter around Peter's throat. If I didn't already know, I would have made the fatal mistake of lunging at him, thinking there would be no trouble in ripping the boy from his grasp. "Let him go," I growled. I instantly felt the heat course through me. My hands began to tingle.

His eyes traveled down to my fists. With a grin, he looked back up at my face. "I wouldn't suggest that." It struck me how his voice sounded like an everyday man's. I'd expected something deeper, more sinister. "I'll snap his neck before your fire gets halfway to me."

Tears were pouring down Peter's face, and his bulging olive eyes burrowed into mine imploringly.

I took a few calming breaths, trying to stop the shaking and regain control.

"That's it. Don't stress yourself out." He gave a little laugh. "As you can see, as I'm here right now, the only one you'll kill is the brat."

In the shock of seeing him here, moments away from killing Peter, I'd forgotten about how I had left him the last time. Forgotten the charred, eyeless face that had glared down at me.

Other than his smooth skin being an ashy gray, he looked the same as I remembered. His hair was back, full and red. His eyes were....

His eyes. They pulled me toward him. I wanted him to touch me, just for a moment. One touch was all I craved. I needed him to touch me. Be inside of me again. Feel his fangs plunge into my neck as he sank into me.

Peter sobbed, breaking the vampire's hold on me. I shook my head, trying to shake away the disgusting thoughts. Anger surged afresh—both at what he was doing to Peter and how he was controlling my desires. I heard the vampire chuckle again.

I focused on Peter, my eyes holding on his as I stepped forward.

"Don't come any closer, not yet." The vampire grabbed Peter's hair with his free hand and jerked his head backward so his throat was exposed, the two punctures above the hollow of his neck now evident, blood trickling downward. "I've already tasted him. I'll finish the snack before you can get over here."

I stopped moving once again, still keeping my eyes on Peter, fighting every urge to look up at the vampire. I didn't know what to do. I couldn't even think of options. From everything Finn had told me about vampires, I didn't doubt that he was serious. I was sure he could either suck Peter dry or break his neck before I could get so much as a spark out, especially since I didn't know how to control the fire. The scene in the ocean replayed in my mind. It had seemed so easy, so natural in the water. I saw Peter engulfed in the flames, like the fish, like the kelp. What good was my strength, my power, my fire? I was useless to save Peter. I couldn't even begin to think of how to proceed. I cursed myself for not practicing or trying to learn how to use my gift.

Keep him talking. I had to keep him talking. Surely Finn would realize soon that something was wrong.

"What do you want, vampire?"

"What do you think I want? Don't act like a fool. Surely you're not as dumb as you are pretty."

I tried another tactic. Maybe it wasn't really a tactic. I just couldn't stop myself from asking, "Why Sonia? Why did you kill her? She wasn't involved."

He let out a deep, sensual groan. "Oh yes. Sonia. Gorgeous. She was the most fun I've had in months. Delightful. So full of life, so full of fight. So full of blood."

"Why Sonia?"

"Because I wanted to."

He paused, and I risked a glance up, trying not to meet his gaze.

"You sure you want to keep asking those types of questions?"

I glanced down at my hands. They were trembling again, steam rising off my knuckles.

I growled in frustration. "What do you want? Why are you hunting me? You're obviously not a Royal, so—" I stopped dead and looked up. The sun was still out. A swift glance at the vampire showed he was standing in the shadow of a cottonwood, but still, the sun was out. "You *are* a Royal." I could hear the defeat in my voice. If he was a Royal, I was sure the rest were out in the woods too. It was only a matter of time before they arrived. The best I could hope for was that they would settle for me and leave the de Moriscos alone.

"No." He gave a small jerk of his head, his smirk growing. "Maybe you really are that dumb. I'm not a Royal."

"You have to be. You're out in the daytime."

"Wrong, again, pretty boy." The mockery in his voice went all through me. I longed to tear him to shreds.

"If you're not a Royal, then what do you want?"

He paused for several moments. I decided he wasn't going to answer. When he finally spoke, his voice was so quiet I could barely hear it. "I want to know what you are."

"What?" Surely I hadn't heard right.

"I said that I want to know what you are!" he screamed.

Sonia died because he wanted to know what I was? That's all? I felt my stomach sink. I felt like I was going to be sick. "I'm a demon. A fire demon."

The vampire tightened his grip, and Peter gasped. "Lie to me again, and I will kill him. Don't try my patience. You are no demon."

Without thinking, my eyes flashed up to his. "I am too. Part demon, anyway. Half fire demon, half human."

He searched my eyes, his own darting back and forth rapidly. I didn't feel his pull this time. "No. I have tasted human, I know it well, and I have tasted demon, on the rare occasion." His lips curled into a snarl, showing the length of his fangs. "You may be demon. You may be human. But you are something else as well. What is it?" He was screaming again.

"I don't know! Why do you think I'm something else? Why does it matter?"

He sounded half-crazed. "Why does it matter? Look around you, you fool. You said yourself that I am out in the daytime. If I'm not a Royal, what does that tell you?" He didn't wait for me to respond. "Your blood did this! Your blood! I drink from you, and I can be out in the daylight. In the shadows, yes, but in the daylight, nonetheless!"

It was my turn to yell. "Fine, it was my blood. Big fucking deal! Good for you! What do you want?"

His voice grew cold, filled with sarcasm, with disgust. "What do I want? I want more, of course. If a small draft can do this"—he gestured to the lengthening shadow around him—"then the rest of you can complete it. I will be the same as a Royal. I will walk in the sun."

"The rest of me?"

"You truly are an idiot. Of course the rest of you." His voice took on a singsong, mocking tone. "That means I'll drink the rest of you, and yes, you'll die without your blood, stupid little boy—demon or not!"

I glanced around. It seemed impossible that Caitlin and Finn weren't here yet. It had definitely been long enough, and there was no way they hadn't heard all the yelling.

The vampire's voice rose again. "Well, what will it be?"

"What?" I asked stupidly, still looking around.

"Will you give yourself to me now, or do I need to keep drinking those you love until you give up?"

Sonia flashed through my mind. Her blood covering the bed, the walls. Her beautiful laughter in my ears transforming to gut-wrenching screams as life was sucked out of her. Her eyes staring into mine as she died. Alone.

The vampire's face blurred and then disappeared entirely. All I could see were the flames. I could feel the fire expanding out further from me, rapidly becoming a blazing sphere.

Throwing myself backward, I stumbled and fell to the ground, the crunch of the leaves barely registering before they were consumed. Like a crab, I scurried back on my hands and feet, imagining Peter engulfed in fire.

Despite my fear, I couldn't release myself. The thought of Peter being harmed by me only increased my fury. Instead of lessening, the flames grew hotter, their white and blue spreading from me. I could barely see the flickering orange as it ignited the vegetation that hadn't already been destroyed.

The grief that had been such a constant torment over the past week was kerosene to the blaze. Fury, terror, and anguish gushed forth from me. For the first time, my body felt at risk of being devoured by my fire. My skin was hot. Dry. Blood pounded through my head, through my body, threatening to boil forth, ripping me asunder.

Throwing myself off the ground, I screamed. It reverberated, resounding on itself within the sphere of fire. It was the scream of an animal. Of anger, rage. Of a demon.

The scream continued as the flames died.

At last silence fell.

My mouth closed, my throat aching.

My eyes opened, and I saw the earth, scorched and blackened, under my feet. Small flames lingered here and there, still feeding on some random particle that had survived the extermination. As if viewing from afar, I saw myself, my naked body steaming. Muscles rippling and trembling from the exertion. Fists clenched, knuckles white.

"Are you done?"

It took a moment for my eyes to focus. When they did, they found the vampire yards away, a bored expression on his face. Peter, tears streaking through black soot, was still ensnared in the monster's grasp. His strangled breathing reached my ears. He was now dangling from the vampire's hold, his feet unable to touch the ground.

They were no longer by the cottonwood tree; it was a charred skeleton between us. In some fucked-up reality, Peter owed his life to the vampire's speed in escaping my outburst.

"I asked if you're done. Your little display was quite entertaining. And, as much as I enjoy seeing a hot naked man screaming, you are wasting my time." His gaze wandered slowly up my body.

I was empty. There was nothing left. I looked back at Peter, the blood running more rapidly down his strangled throat. "You'll let him go if I let you drink me?"

"Yes."

I glanced around once more. A picture of Sonia flashed through my mind, of Finn. There was nothing else to do. "Fine. Let Peter go."

"Not until I am done with you."

"No. No way. As soon as you're done with me, you'll turn on him."

"After you, why would I give a shit about the ounce of witch blood in him?" The right corner of his mouth curved into a sinister smile. "What choice do you have?"

He was right. What choice did I have? If the others hadn't come yet, then who knew how long it would take. Even if they did come, what did I expect them to do? If I couldn't set him on fire, what chance did they have?

"Fine." I crossed the yards of smoldering earth between us, not looking at the destruction. I kept my gaze on Peter. Only Peter.

He held out his hand signaling me to walk slowly. Peter's eyes were closed, but I could see the rise and fall of his little belly. He must have passed out.

Within a few more steps, I was there. I looked into the vampire's eyes, partly hoping that he would make me want him again, make it at least a little pleasurable. He didn't.

"Lean close, and tilt your head to the left." His voice was quiet, reverent.

I did as he asked. Within a second, I felt his lips on my throat, giving me a kiss. Without any more warning, his fangs sank in, fire instantly rushing through me. A strangled scream escaped me. The pain was unbelievable, like he was running pipe cleaners through my veins with every draft of my blood.

His hand reached around to the left side of my face, pulling himself deeper into me. He moaned in pleasure as I felt myself grow weaker. The weaker I became, the less pain there was.

It seemed that half-demons were capable of dying, of being killed by something other than another demon. I almost smiled at the relief of that knowledge.

When I was sure the end was mere seconds away, I opened my eyes, refusing to leave this world in the dark.

There was a burst of wind, and I was soaring through the air, the surroundings blurring as I flew past them. I heard an enraged screech and voices shouting. My voyage through the air came to an abrupt stop as I slammed into something solid and everything went dark.

Chapter Twenty-Nine

"Caitlin! You've got to calm down! Seriously!"

"I'm sorry. He's bleeding, Finn! What if he doesn't wake up?"

This time, I didn't have any problem knowing where I was when I came to. Everything rushed back in a second—the vampire, little Peter. The fire. I opened my eyes carefully. The only reality I was having a problem accepting was that I was alive. I had known I was going to die… was seconds, if that, from death. Yet here I was, blinking into the red setting sun.

I tried to sit up, but as soon as I lifted my head, the charcoaled trees began to spin, and I crashed back down into the crunch of ashes of leaves and shrubs.

"Cate, you're a witch, for crying out loud. Heal his neck. I'll be right back." I heard him take several rushed steps, and then his face was over me. "Brett, baby, how are you feeling?"

I groaned. "How's Peter? Is he… is he okay?"

"Yeah. He's got a bite and he's unconscious, but I think he'll be fine." His eyes grew momentarily soft. "Thanks to you."

"Thank God!" I shut my eyes, his face spinning above me. "What happened? Where's the vampire?"

Caitlin ignored my question. "He's gone, Finn. He ran off. I doubt he'll be back right now, but still, we need to get out of here."

I started to get up, but nausea rolled over me. "I don't think I can do it, Finn."

"I'm not surprised. You've lost a lot of blood. I was afraid we were going to be too late." He glanced over toward Peter and Caitlin. "Hold on, okay? I'll be right back."

He was only gone a few seconds. "Okay, Peter's conscious, and Cate's gonna carry him back. We sent Saul back to the house when we realized what was happening, so the others should be coming soon. Not that they could have helped hearing."

"You sent him by himself? What if the vampire doubles back?"

His face darkened. "There wasn't another choice. We couldn't have him there with us. What if the vamp got him too?"

"But, Finn...."

"Brett, enough. We did what we had to do, just like you did. Let's get going."

"I can't, I told you. I feel like I was hit by a car."

"Well, you hit a fairly good-sized tree and snapped it in half, so that's not too surprising. And, if you'd let me finish, I wasn't going to try to get you to walk. I can levitate you back."

"Levitate?"

"Yeah, just like Mom did that first night. Of course, you probably don't remember that." He grinned at me playfully. "You get knocked out a lot, don't you?"

"Ever since I met you."

He bent down and gave me a firm kiss. "I'm so glad you're okay. Thank you for saving Peter. I love you."

"I love you too. Can we go now?"

He laughed. "Sure." He slipped off his shirt and draped it over my nakedness. Without saying a word, he placed a hand a few inches above the skin of my chest.

I felt myself rise into the air. It was like I had strings threaded all over the top of my body and something was pulling them up, stretching my skin. As I began to move, my nausea increased, and I stifled a gag. "Finn, I think I'm gonna hurl. I don't suppose there's anything you could do about that, is there?"

"Oh yeah, sorry." His other hand rose and stopped right above my forehead. Instantly, the nausea vanished, as well as the sensation that the world was spinning on a tilt-a-whirl. "Better?"

"Much, thanks."

I watched as the tops of the trees drifted by overhead, the branches shifting from blackened to lush, the sunset casting a rosy hue over the leaves.

BEFORE we had gotten halfway back, the others found us. Saul was chattering away happily, like he'd just had a great adventure. Finn floated me the rest of the way as his family peppered him with questions.

When we reached the house, they wrapped me in a blanket and propped me into a modified seated position on the sofa. Paulette began spooning leftover green chili into me, assuring me that it would initiate my body replacing the lost blood. She hadn't stopped crying since we arrived back at the house. "I'm so sorry that we can't do any more than speed up the process. We can't make something from nothing, you know." She wiped at her swollen eyes. "I should have listened to Christina."

Cynthia had attempted to help my bone marrow produce more cells to alleviate my blood loss. It seemed my body was resistant to being manipulated. One more lovely demon attribute.

"It's okay, Paulette. Between Finn taking away my dizziness and you healing the bite wound, and the green chili, I guess, I am feeling a lot better." I really was. I assumed part of it was also due to the demon blood and its healing powers. Cooling off in the shower as Finn had rinsed me off and getting in clean clothes had helped as well. I figured at this rate, I would feel back to normal by morning.

The rest of the family was gathered around us in the living room, Finn seated beside me, his hands cupping my right one. Christina had a newly healed Peter sleeping on her lap, and Caitlin had Saul in her arms. He was chattering incessantly, retelling her every detail of his journey back to the house on his own.

In between bites of green chili, I peppered Finn with questions. "How did you and Caitlin get us away from the vampire?"

His hands squeezed mine roughly. "We did a knock back spell simultaneously. I focused on you, and Cate focused on Peter, making sure he landed safely."

"A knock back spell? Using air, I take it?"

He nodded. "Yeah. It was the only thing we could think of. We were afraid if we used fire, we would either burn the two of you at the same time, not that it would hurt you, or the vamp would just finish the job before trying to put out the flames."

"I think he would have." I tilted my head toward Paulette as she fed me the last bite of the green chili and slid the bowl onto the coffee table. "What took you so long? I thought you would have heard all the yelling."

"Sorry about that. We were there for a long time, still using our invisibility. Unlike demons, apparently, vampires can't see through it. Or he just didn't notice."

"Well, what the hell were you waiting on?" I couldn't stop the irritation from creeping into my voice. The thought that they had been watching while the vampire sucked the life out of me was inconceivable.

Finn's face darkened as he blushed. "Babe, we knew it was the only chance we had. The minute we cast another spell, we would become visible. We had to wait until he was biting you, when he closed his eyes. Otherwise, he would see us and kill you or Peter. We didn't know what else to do." He glanced at Caitlin. "Actually, I made the call. Cate wanted to charge in and rescue you both immediately, especially after you set everything ablaze. I was afraid. She was probably right. I hate that you had to go through that. Hearing you scream was unbearable." His bloodshot eyes looked close to tears.

Shame flooded me. "I'm sorry, Finn. I think you're right. Anything else and he would have reacted." He turned so his eyes were looking into mine. "Thank you for saving my life. I thought it was over." Finn started to speak, but another thought hit me. "If you were there, then you heard what he said he wanted, didn't you?"

Finn nodded.

Caitlin cut in, this time with no animosity in her voice. She looked back and forth between her mother and father as she spoke. "He told Brett that he wasn't just a demon. That he is something more. He wanted to know what he was."

"More than just part demon?" Wendell looked at me with a mix of curiosity and wonder, or maybe it was fear. I couldn't tell.

"Yeah," Caitlin continued, "he said that after drinking Brett's blood the other night he could be out in the daytime. He made it sound like he could only be in the shade or something." She looked over at me questioningly, and I nodded. "He said that he believed if he finished drinking Brett's blood he could be like the Royal Family, walk out in the daytime."

Wendell continued to stare at me. "I have never heard of such a thing. I don't know of any race that supposedly has blood that allows vampires to walk in the sun." His eyes left me momentarily to look at his grandsons. "One thing is for sure, Brett. There is something special about you. I don't know what destiny has in store for you, but I am thrilled that my family gets to be a part of it with you."

Once again, guilt washed over me. "Without me, the vampire would never have come into your lives at all."

It was Christina who contradicted me. "You didn't make him show up in Old Town that night. It was pure chance. And without you, I would have lost one or both of my sons tonight. Whatever it is that you are, you are a gift from God, and I am forever in your debt."

HOURS later, after endless discussion and speculation over what other race could make up my mysterious heritage, Finn and I went to bed. I was already feeling good enough to walk up the stairs without much effort.

Before I had finished undressing, there was a knock at the door. Finn was in the restroom, so I rebuttoned my jeans and answered it.

Caitlin stood there, taken aback by my shirtless state. "Oh, sorry. I didn't think that... I should've waited."

"It's okay." I chuckled. "It's not like you haven't seen me in less clothes lately. Finn's in the restroom. I bet he'll be out in a—"

"No. It was you I wanted to talk to."

"Oh." It seemed the surprises were not going to stop today.

She wiped a fallen strand of her spiky hair out of her eyes. "Listen. I can't say that I'm completely okay with you. I think having a demon here is risky, especially now that we know that there's even more about you that we don't know."

I couldn't believe she was doing this now. Of all times. "Caitlin, I don't know what I am either. I'm not going to hurt anyone." Unbidden, a picture of the smoldering kelp forest rose in my mind, of what could have happened to Peter, and I wondered if I were making promises I might not be able to keep.

She raised a hand to cut me off. "What I'm trying to say"—her eyes darted to the ground—"is that.... Well, I just want to say thank you. We saw what you did. You could have walked away, let the vampire have Peter. You didn't have to give yourself to him. You don't even really know Peter, and...."

"I would never—"

She raised her hand again, her eyes meeting mine. "You saved Peter's life, and you didn't have to. Thank you. I can't tell you how much I love those boys. Finn could do a lot worse than you." With that she turned and walked off toward her room.

"Wow." Finn spoke from behind me. "For Caitlin, that was like she just wrote a sonnet in your honor."

I closed the door and turned around. "Yeah, I guess so. I'm sure that wasn't easy for her to do."

"Well, that's the least she should say."

"Still, that was nice of her."

Finn was draped only in a large white bath towel, and as he stepped toward me, he let it fall to the ground. He glanced beside me, and the candles on the nightstand ignited, filling the room with a warm glow. I felt my breath quicken at the sight of him. I was also aware of my cock beginning to rise with arousal. He was beautiful. Still damp from the shower, his thick muscles glistened in the flickering candlelight. Within a couple more strides, he was in front of me, his chest pressing against me.

I looked down at him and gave him a crooked smile. "Are you wanting something, Mr. de Morisco?"

In a husky voice, he whispered, "I love you, Brett. I want you." His hand curved on my hip. "Now."

I glanced around, as if his family were suddenly going to appear in the bedroom with us. "Here?"

"Yeah, here."

"What about your family?"

"I don't care. I can mute the sounds so they won't leave the room. Even if I couldn't, it doesn't matter. I love you. I want you." He pulled away to make it easier for him to meet my eyes. "Is that okay?"

For a split second, fear shot through me, telling me to run before it was too late, before I lost whoever it is that Brett was. As I looked at his beautiful face gazing up at me, the fear faded away and was replaced by a feeling of contentment. "Yes, more than okay."

He pulled my face down to meet his. Our lips met in a long, tender kiss, arms wrapping tightly around each other, relishing the feel of skin touching skin.

The kiss grew in intensity and passion as I felt him grow hard against me. Without taking his lips from mine, he unbuttoned my jeans, slid the zipper down, and released me into his hands.

Finn pulled back from the kiss and looked down at my penis. He caressed up the shaft, then wrapped his fingers around my girth. "I've been dying to touch you like this."

I pushed my pants the rest of the way down and kicked them off as we fell together onto the bed.

He released his hold on me to slide his hands tantalizingly up my stomach, lingering over each rise and divot of the muscles. The movement raised my T-shirt over my chest. I reached up and pulled the material over my head.

He sighed as he watched me above him. "I love you, Brett. I never dreamed I'd have someone as wonderful as you."

I searched honeyed-brown eyes, unsure what I was looking for. Confinement, maybe. A cage. All I could find was love. Adoration.

"I love you too, Finn." I brought my thumb down to trace his bottom lip. He was such a strange mix. His face and body were so thoroughly masculine—hard, chiseled, strong. Yet, even though I'd seen his inner strength as well, there was something about him that seemed so fragile. The complete love shining in his eyes was unabashedly genuine. Despite him being the older of us, I felt like I was responsible for taking care of him. Making sure he didn't get hurt. The combination of his beauty and tenderness was simultaneously terrifying and enticing. "I've never known anyone like you, as good as you. As sincere and beautiful."

He pulled me down, his lips taking mine. I let my body meld into his as he urged my weight to roll beneath him.

Seeing him above me, the candlelight flickering over his golden skin, was more proof than anything else I had seen that convinced me I was no longer in my safe little familiar world. I ran my hand over the wide plane of his chest and then wrapped it around his back, crushing him to me. Already the coolness of the shower had been replaced by a sheen of sweat over his skin, and we slid against each other.

Even though I wanted it to last, my hips were thrusting against him of their own accord. I followed the divot of his spine down, flicking my finger over the slickened skin between the rise of his ass checks.

Finn arched upward toward my touch, causing my finger to slide lower. I brought my left hand from the back of his head and began to squeeze the tight muscles of his ass. He let out a long, low groan as I shifted from massaging to using my fingers to spread him wide.

"I wanted to make this last longer, Finn, but I want to be in you now."

His triceps flexing, he pushed off from the bed and rose above me once more, the motion forcing the top half of my finger into him. He clenched tightly around my finger, and I keened in expectation.

Precum was already running down the length of me. Seeing it, Finn smeared it over the head of my cock and began using it in long, slow strokes as he began to ride my finger. "Good. I need you in me. We have all night. We can take it slower in a bit."

Letting out a hiss between clenched teeth, he lifted himself off my finger, his strong thighs going taut as they straddled my waist. Without leaving the bed, he leaned over, fishing for the jeans he'd removed before getting into the shower.

The motion caused the muscles of his back to bunch, and I raised my hand to trace their hard contours. "God, you're gorgeous."

The compliment caused him to laugh self-consciously. He started to rise back up, having retrieved the condoms.

"Wait. Don't move." I pulled myself from beneath him and rose to my knees. Tracing his body with my hands, I moved behind him, taking my place between his legs, enjoying the view of his kneeling form.

Again I spread him wide, this time using both hands, exposing him to the candlelight.

At my touch, he shuddered and arched his back further.

I traced his entrance with my thumb, then lowered my head and gave a slow swipe with my tongue.

He pushed back against my mouth with an eagerness I hadn't expected. Finn was so sweet that I'd expected him to be passive in bed. My erection hardened to the point of pain as I realized I'd been so wonderfully wrong.

Finn reached back between his legs and grabbed my cock, not bothering to disperse the precum before he began pumping.

In response, I shoved my tongue inside of him, relishing the immediate clenching of his muscles around me. Flattening my tongue to stretch him out, I was rewarded with another groan and another push against me, driving me deeper into him.

Already he was working me to the point of climax. Before I could warn him that he needed to slow down, he pulled away, pivoting on the bed.

He rose up on his knees, his body aligned with mine. He reached up, grasping the back of my neck and pulling me down to his lips. His tongue sank into my mouth, as always tasting like the spices he wielded at the bakery.

As we kissed, his hands moved over my back with firm, confident strokes. I continued to massage his ass, flicking at his hole, until he shoved onto me once more, pulling my head even lower with the motion. Gingerly, I eased the tip of a second finger into him. A gasp escaped between our lips, and he settled into the rhythm once more.

His hands left my back and I could feel him struggling with something. I didn't break our kiss until he leaned backward, again forcing my fingers deeper inside of him. Continuing to thrust up and down on my hand, he arched back further, leaving a space between our bodies. With one hand he placed the condom on the head of my cock. With the other, he rolled it down the shaft.

He glanced up at me, concern replacing the passion for a moment. "Does it hurt? I should have gotten larger."

I shook my head, unable to make my voice work. It did hurt, the tightness of the lip of the condom cutting into the base, pulling at the loose skin of my balls. All it did was intensify the sensations.

"Good." He lifted himself off me once more and lay back on the bed, guiding me to him, using my cock as a leash. "Then I need you in me."

I had never had a night that seemed to last so long, a night that I wished would go on forever. Finn had been right. There was plenty of time to take things slower. A couple different times, as it turned out. One second I was burning with lust, and then the next so completely enraptured with Finn that it was all I could do to not simply stare in wonder at him. I'd always assumed that I wouldn't be able to find love and lust with the same person. It was overwhelmingly heady.

I AWOKE, the darkness outside the curtains confirming it was still the middle of the night. Finn's deep breathing tickled against my hair as he slept on my chest. Gently, as not to wake him, I ran my fingers through his dark hair, enjoying the moment to watch him without being observed. He truly was beautiful, and even in his sleep he radiated a serene kindness. I felt at home with him nestled against me. As much as I had felt at home with Sonia, more. Safe, even.

CHAPTER THIRTY

FINN DE MORISCO

My skin boiled and blistered. The steam was like knives cutting into my skin, seeping through my pores, infecting my body. Try as I might, it was impossible to drag in a speck of oxygen. It was as if my chest had been filled with gravel, collapsing my lungs. Claws raked at my brain, on the inside of my skull.

I tried to scream. Tried to rage at what held me in its grasp. To curse it to Hell.

Curse me to Hell? To Hell? Soft, sinister amusement cut through the torment of my mind. *Surely you can do better, be more original.... Why not try Heaven? Curse me to Heaven.*

I flailed about, my body thrashing and twisting, unable to have any effect on the invisible restraints.

You are a lion who believes himself a newly weaned cub. I could almost hear the curve of smile in the tone. *You are mine. You paint this picture in your head of who you are, but you know better. You know who you are. You know you are mine.*

This time, a strangled protest escaped my cracked lips.

That's it. Get angry. Break your bonds. It should be so simple for you. Like straw. Be the man you are meant to be. Be the warlock you are. Be mine, as you know you should be.

My stomach dropped as I hit the bed. Lying still, I made sure I was alive. It felt like I had free-fallen a thousand feet. Commanding my pounding heart to calm, I opened my eyes.

My bedroom. My bed. Just another dream. With each one, the voice got clearer. The heat hotter. The fear more consuming.

I'd never had nightmares before. Never. Not even as a little kid. Now, I was beginning to dread going to sleep, waking up covered in sweat, twisted in sheets. Why did this have to start right when I was able to sleep with someone? Brett! He was going to leave me just for continuing to kick him in his sleep every night.

Turning to apologize, again, for waking him, I reached over to lay my hand on his chest—my mind already transitioning from my grief to sex.

Only the divot on his pillow met my advances. I glanced over, saw the glow from under the bathroom door, and sank back into the bed with a sigh.

Every night, the same thing. Well, nearly the same. Each night seemed to get more intense. More real. Every night since The Square.

I knew who it was, what it was. Not specifically, I guess. I didn't know its face, its form, but I knew. The presence. Whatever had held me in its clutches that day, breaking my ribs, leading me to The Square. Each night, it seemed closer. Clearer.

Why it wanted me, I had no idea. I just knew it wanted me. I had a nagging feeling that it didn't just want a snack, a new play toy. That would be bad enough. It didn't want to consume me. It wanted me. Whatever it thought I was, it wanted me.

I'd almost told Cynthia several times, but I just couldn't bring myself to worry her, and I knew she'd feel guilty for her part in enabling me to go. Brett had enough to deal with. Telling Mom and Dad wasn't an option either. They didn't need to know I'd gone to The Square—much less that I'd brought back a little traveling companion. Probably not so little.

Anger flashed through me. I hadn't worried about it tonight. It was a violation that anything could invade this night.

Being with Brett was even better than I had imagined. Not just the sex. Not just the feel of him, our rhythms matching, his face as he came. I didn't feel worthy of him, but I could see us together. See our lives as they wove into one. See us together for good. It wasn't a crush or infatuation.

Sex I was familiar with. Even love. At least, I thought I was. The thing I thought was love seemed cheap and flimsy next to Brett.

I returned to the light under the bathroom door. I didn't see a shadow moving about. Couldn't hear the flow of water.

Maybe he'd passed out on the floor; maybe he'd hit his head on the tub as he fell. It had been stupid to initiate sex the same day he'd lost so much blood. Selfish.

After throwing back the covers, I slid out of bed and rushed to the bathroom. Anxiously, I gave the briefest of knocks, not waiting for an answer, already imploring the lock to allow entrance. There was no need. The door swung open easily.

Squinting against the abrupt brightness of the bathroom, I took a step toward the tub. There was no blood. No body. No accident. No Brett.

Stupidly, I looked around the tiny bathroom, as if expecting Brett's huge form to be tucked away in a corner.

Confused, I stepped out of the bathroom, continuing in my attempt to find Brett hiding someplace.

A hole in my stomach opened, and I fell through. I knew what had happened. I knew I wouldn't find him. Still, I looked.

Careful to move as quietly as possible, I left the bedroom. Not bothering to check the other bedrooms, I slipped downstairs. The living room and kitchen were dark. Flipping the switch, light flooded the room. No one. There wasn't any indication that anyone had been here since we'd gone to bed.

I leaned against the table, staring blankly out the window, the glow of the streetlight soft through the sheer curtains. Even though I knew the truth, I argued against it. He wouldn't leave. Not with a vampire attack only a few hours before. Not with all that had transpired. Not after being with me.

Being with me. The thought was a blow to my gut. He'd left because of me. Because of us. No matter what I'd felt, no matter what I thought he'd felt. I was the reason he was gone. It was me he didn't want. I'd pushed too much. I hadn't been good enough. We'd moved too fast.

Still, choosing to face a vampire over staying with me....

The clock shone red from the microwave in the kitchen. It was a little past three thirty in the morning. We hadn't been asleep all that long.

I couldn't let him be out in the night alone, or even in the daytime now, it seemed. I had to find him. Had to bring him back. Even if he didn't want me, he had to be safe. I simultaneously chided myself, knowing that as much I wanted Brett to be fine, I was mostly motivated to disprove that I was the reason he'd left. The voice from my dreams taunted me. According to him, I wasn't a good enough warlock. I was weak. Apparently the same was true for the man I was as well.

Hurriedly, I slipped into a pair of sweats and a tank, went back downstairs, and slid out the door. All the cars were still in the driveway. He hadn't stolen one this time. He'd just gone for a walk. That's all—a walk. I was turning into Caitlin. Overreacting. I might as well have thought of calling the Cathedral. He'd not given me any indication that something was wrong. I'd fallen asleep to him telling me how much he loved me, that he couldn't believe how he felt about me. Still, to go on a walk at night when you're vampire bait…. It didn't add up.

Luckily, my truck was parked on the curb, so I didn't have to deal with being blocked in the driveway by Ricky's van. I slipped behind the wheel, but paused before I turned the ignition. I realized I'd been preparing to go to Sonia's. He was walking. He couldn't have gone that far. The thought threw me off. Then where?

Part of me felt guilty for what I was about to do. That I was invading his privacy, infringing on him in some way. I shoved it away. I'd worry about that when there wasn't a vampire in the picture. For now, it was time to find him.

Closing my eyes, I focused on Brett, picturing him in vivid detail. Unlike the first time I'd tried to find him this way, his image came to me instantly. Not simply his form, but the man he was beneath his skin.

Unbidden, he took shape as he had in the forest. Naked, his body shimmering in the midst of the fire. The reflections of the flames glinting off the sweat as it poured off his rigid muscle. Short blond hair whipped about as if in a windstorm. Otherworldly blue eyes alight in fury.

Desire and hurt swept through me in equal measure. Let it be some other reason, some other desire than to simply be away from me.

You shame yourself. You hurt over something you want, something you want to choose you. Mocking, the sneer disrupted my concentration. *All you need do is take. It is in your power. Will it. He will be yours.*

My eyes flew open, and I whipped my head violently from side to side. This was the first time I'd heard his voice outside of my dreams. My dreams! That's it. That's all this was, just one more dream. I was asleep.

This is beneath you! I demand you stop! The voice filled the cab of the truck, its reverberations hurting my ears. *Be the warlock you are, not a sniveling little coward hoping everything is just a bad dream!*

"Shut up!" My fist slammed into the stereo, the faceplate cracking.

Ah, I thought I felt breath on my face at the exhale, *that's more like it. Rage is what you need to be yourself.*

"Shut. Up." I winced at the sound of my teeth gritting.

I closed my eyes once more. This time, I brought the night's events to mind easily. Brett lay beside me in bed, his arm under my head as his open hand moved in lazy circles over my chest and stomach. Brett. The sound of his whisper as we lay after, our bodies slick with sweat. The smell of his breath as he drew closer to kiss me again. The feel of his desire for me pressing into my hip as he wanted me again.

And there he was. I could feel him. Feel him moving. Feel his angst, his confusion. He was farther away than made sense, but I didn't question. I knew I'd found him. The engine whined and lurched forward as I used too much force on the starter and slammed the gas.

IT HAD been years since I'd been to La Jolla. Never really liked it. The only redeeming thing about the place was the cliffs and the cove of seals. The rest might as well have been an attempt to recreate an exclusive little Beverly Hills. I didn't remember ever seeing the place at night before. Every house had spotlights illuminating the walls, transforming them into little Californian castles. Each one gaudier than the next. At least Sonia's folks' house had been vintage, not some modern attempt at grandeur.

Brett was near. Even if I'd been a warlock without much power, I wouldn't have needed a very strong locator spell to find him with the torrent of emotions pouring from him.

I'd only been on Torrey Pines Drive for a few blocks when I knew where I'd find him. I let the invocation fall from my mind, Brett's essence fleeting, leaving me empty. Pulling the truck halfway off the street, I shut it down and exited.

Typically, entering a graveyard, even in the middle of the night, wouldn't faze me. However, knowing a vampire was potentially close by should have raised my heart rate more than it did.

Even without my power, it only took moments for me to find him.

The grave still looked fresh, the strips of sod over the mound not yet having time to blend with surrounding grass.

Brett sat in the middle of the new sod, less than a foot away from the headstone. His head lowered, his broad back slumped, causing him to resemble a fallen giant.

I almost put my hand on his shoulder, sinking down beside him. I stopped myself. Feeling like an intruder, I broke the silence. "Brett?"

He turned, his strained blue eyes slowly rising to mine. He looked neither surprised nor excited to see me. His deep voice was flat. "I'm sorry if I scared you."

Scared me. Understate much? "How did you get here?"

"Hmm?"

"How did you get here?" Why was I asking? Like it mattered.

"Oh. Taxi."

"Taxi? From the house?"

His slouching shoulders rose and fell in what was most likely meant to be a shrug. "Yeah. I walked till I got to the main road and found one."

"And you came here. To the graveyard?" Obviously.

"Yeah."

"Why?"

He didn't look back at me, just continued to stare at the carved stone.

Marvin Alexander Wright
1934–

His death date had yet to be engraved.

Easing myself down, I sat perpendicular to him.

I waited for him to answer, to cry, to get angry, to say anything. He didn't. He sat there, a strange mixture of apathy and seriousness on his face. After a few moments, I reached out and placed my hand on top of his thigh. He didn't move away.

"Did you need to talk to your grandfather tonight?"

He looked at me out of the corner of his eye, and his lips twitched into a remembrance of a smile. "No. Even if I did, this would be the last thing he'd wanna talk about."

"Probably not too big on vampires and demons, huh?"

Impossibly, he slumped even further. "No. Not about that." He started to say something more, but then stopped, his dirty fingers raking through his hair. "I don't know why I'm here." He let out a long breath. "I mean, why here? Why would I need to see him? It's not like I looked for his approval or guidance when he was alive. Why should I now? Why would it matter what he thinks?"

My chest tightened. "What do you need his guidance about?"

His blue eyes met mine briefly before darting away.

"Oh." As I feared. The tightening gave way to wrenching. I removed my hand from his leg. He didn't try to stop me.

He sat there, his gaze traveling back and forth between the headstone and the damp grave he was sitting on.

"Listen, Brett." I hated the catch in my voice. "I'm sorry if I'm freaking you out, if I told you I love you too fast." The sound of him telling me over and over how much he loved me just hours before echoed in my mind. "I wasn't trying to—"

"No. No, don't do that." He swiveled his body around to face me, reaching his hand out to take mine. "This isn't about anything you did wrong. Really."

My eyes narrowed, trying to see deeper into his. He didn't look away or try to hide. "Then what?"

"Finn, I don't know." His left hand dug through his hair again, this time leaving a trail of dirt on his forehead. "I'm all over the place. So content one minute, then scared shitless the next. It's all of it. The demon shit. The vampire. What happened in the alley. Sonia." He motioned to the gravestone. "Even this, so it seems."

He paused, catching his breath. He looked so distraught. Broken. It was nearly impossible to comprehend the fact that he was a demon when all I could see was this broken, unearthly beautiful man.

His blue eyes found mine, and he held my gaze somewhat desperately. "It's just that, I think you want me for forever. I look at your family, how perfect it is...."

"Are you kidding? Please don't think like that. We are so far from—"

"I know. I don't mean like that. I know you fight. I know you've all got your own issues." He couldn't suppress a grin. "I mean, look at Caitlin."

"Well, see—"

"Still. Your family is... well, it's just that. A family." He leaned closer, as if asking me to understand. "I don't think I have that in me. I've never really wanted that before. I don't think I can be who you want me to be."

"You haven't liked being a part of my family the past several days?"

"Yeah, of course I have. It's been amazing. Strange, but amazing."

"Well, then, see, you do have it in you."

He gave his head the smallest of shakes. "I'm afraid I don't. I don't want to cause you pain, babe. I don't wanna be the reason your family faces vampires. I don't wanna be the reason you all fight. I don't wanna be the reason you'll hurt later."

As much as I tried, I couldn't keep the desperation out of my voice. "But, you said you love me. More than anyone. More than you thought you could."

"And I do." He reached his other hand over my hand until both of his enclosed mine in their large, warm grasp. "I never thought I'd love anyone like I love you."

"That's how I feel about you."

"I know." He sounded as if the thought made him sad.

"Brett, what do you want to do? Do you want to end this already? Is that why you left?"

His eyes shot heavenward, and he let out a ragged sigh. "I don't know, Finn. I don't know how to do this. It's too much. Everything is just too much. I do love you. So much. I think that's part of the reason I'm freaking out right now. I have no idea what to do about that."

I leaned forward, allowing him a fraction of a moment to pull away. I pressed my lips to his. When he didn't try to pull free, my hand slid behind his head, drawing him closer.

The kiss was soft at first. No pressure. No more than my lips touching his. "Please, don't throw us away. Not yet." I hadn't meant to say anything. Hadn't meant to break the kiss.

He pushed in closer, the softness of his kiss giving way to need, to demand. His lips almost hurt as they crushed mine. An agonized groan escaped him as his tongue slid into my mouth, pushing deep, filling. His demand increased until his weight was on top of me, his hard body pushing me into the soft mound of dirt, reminding me we were on his grandfather's grave. For less than a heartbeat, I considered suggesting we move away from the grave. I shoved the thought away. Who cared where we were?

Rising up, he looked around as if wondering how we'd gotten there. His eyes returned to mine, a confused, haunted sheen over them.

"Please, Brett." I couldn't help pleading again, even as I despised myself at the sound. He was too important. What I had with him was too important. "Don't throw us away because you're confused or scared. Please."

Darting back and forth, his eyes continued to search mine. I didn't know what they were looking for.

"Please, Brett."

He hovered above me. Neither of us sure what he would choose. After a brief eternity, he nodded.

"Yes?"

He nodded again. "Yes."

This time, I felt my lip split as his kiss pressed into me, his tongue forcing itself so deep I wasn't sure I'd be able to breathe. His hands tore in desperation at my clothes, his mouth never releasing mine. His eyes opened to stare into me before closing again.

He had my clothes off, my naked back chilled by the damp dirt of the grave, before ripping his shirt over his head and beginning to tear and fumble at his belt. With a brush of my hand, his jeans disappeared. His solid, bare body crushed me further into the moist earth, his searing skin instantly eradicating the cold.

"Brett, I love you." I pushed his face from mine to look in his eyes. "I need you to not give up on us because it's scary, okay? I love you."

He gave a fierce nod. "I'm sorry I'm struggling with this. I love you too."

"It's okay. Really. We'll get through it. We have to."

The palms of his hands slid up my chest in response, traveled up my arms to secure my hands over my head, and my knuckles scraped the headstone.

"I love you, Finn." The moon behind his head silhouetted the outline of his arms and back as he held me in place, making him appear carved of stone. "I need you in me. Now."

It took me a second before I realized what he was asking. I managed a nod.

Without any other warning, his body arched downward, impaling himself on me. He cried out, a loud animallike call, his eyes wide with pain.

I waited as he hung there, suspended, letting himself grow accustomed to my girth. His warmth surrounded me, even hotter than his skin. Hot enough it seemed like it should hurt, should burn. It didn't. I gasped as he tightened around me.

Another guttural groan escaped him as I pulsated inside of him. Before he began to rise up on me to begin the ride, he held my gaze. "I won't leave you. I love you."

CHAPTER THIRTY-ONE

BRETT WRIGHT

"I STILL say that we have to keep living our lives. We can't just hide in here forever."

"Wendell, that's exactly what I was saying yesterday to Christina, but then we almost lost Peter"—Paulette glanced over at me sitting on the other side of the breakfast table—"as well as Brett."

"That's right! We have to be careful." There was a tremble in Cynthia's voice, but her jaw was set determinedly. "Plus, things have changed. We didn't know the vampire could be out in the daytime. Now we do. And who knows how much stronger he is now that he got to drink more of Brett. He could be outside right now, just waiting for us to separate."

"Now, let's just take a step back. We don't know that Brett's blood has anything to do with it. That's the vampire's theory, not ours. Who knows what actually happened. Maybe he could always be out in the daytime as long as he stayed in the shadows. Maybe he just discovered it by accident after he bit Brett that first time." Wendell, usually so confident, seemed like he was trying to convince himself more than anyone else.

While I liked what he was saying, his words didn't sit well in my gut. They didn't feel true. "What if he's right? What if my blood makes vampires able to be in the sunlight? If that's true, with how much he took from me yesterday, Cynthia is probably correct."

"Who has ever heard of a species that makes vampires able to walk in the sun? Do you really think they would have been able to keep that a secret? Even if there were such a race, if that had been known, I guarantee the vampires would have hunted them to extinction by now. Either from the lone vampires, all trying to get that power, or from the Vampire Cathedral, so that the others wouldn't be able to have the same ability as they do."

"But Dad"—Finn wiped his face, dusting off the crumbs that had gotten stuck in his stubble—"what if they didn't know? What if this vampire is the first to discover it, or what if whatever other blood is in Brett has never been combined with demon blood before. How would they know?"

Wendell shook his head. "Spoken like someone who hasn't lived long enough. There isn't much that is new to the world, Finn. If it is his blood, I can guarantee that he isn't the first of his kind. And if he isn't, then I can also guarantee, if there is power in his blood, the vampires would have known of it centuries ago. And again, if that was the case, the Royals would have taken care of that situation. They wouldn't want the other race of vampires to pass for a Royal."

The table fell silent, all lost in their thoughts and worries. Before we went to bed the night before, it had been decided that they were going to take the morning off. They weren't going to open their stores or restaurants until they were ready. No one set alarms, and everyone just slept until they woke up on their own. The only ones still asleep were Ricky and the boys. Everyone else seemed to wake up at nearly their normal time, so before long, they were in the kitchen making breakfast. It seemed that, in the de Morisco family, everything, good and bad, revolved around food.

Luckily, no one had been awake when Finn and I returned home. It hadn't seemed they even noticed we'd left. Having cast the guard spells, Wendell lay sleeping on the couch. We slipped past quietly, and since we belonged in the house, the magic guards didn't alert him. I was thankful they weren't aware my fear had led me to have Finn leave the house and risk facing the vampire.

I was a torrent of emotions. I was terrified of my choice but was somewhat surprised when I realized I was glad to be back. Glad I was still with Finn. With his family. Even though every aspect of this life scared me, it also felt right, peaceful. Even sitting here was a challenge. One minute fear spiked through me, the next wave after wave of guilt. For involving them in this. For leaving Finn in the middle of the night. For not simply being able to relax and enjoy what I'd discovered in Finn. What was wrong with me?

I had been extremely nervous to face the family as I left the bedroom. Finn had told me I was just being silly, that it didn't matter. If anyone had heard Finn and I having sex during the night.... If they'd noticed we'd been gone.... I was the only one who blushed as they said good morning. If they noticed that Finn didn't go more than a few seconds without reaching for my hand or touching my shoulder, they didn't let on.

Part of me still wanted to book it for the door and not stop running. The other part wanted to drag Finn back up the stairs and devour him again.

"Well, I think we have to look at the worst case scenario." Caitlin put her chin in her hands, both her elbows resting on the table.

"Of course you do, Cate. What else would you think?"

She gave Finn a dirty look but continued as if he hadn't spoken. "We have to assume that there is some kind of power in Brett's blood, that the vampire can now be out in full daylight, and that he is waiting for the moment he deems is best to attack again. If that's not the case, then no harm done, we are prepared."

"Wait, hold on." Christina, spoke up for the first time this morning. She had been rather downcast. Nearly losing your child the day before would probably do that to anyone. "You just made a good point. Let's say that Brett's blood really does have the power to make them capable of being in the sun. With how much the vampire got yesterday, why are we assuming he is still waiting to attack? Why would he need to?" Her lips slowly curved into a smile, relief beginning to fill her face. "He's been after Brett this whole time. I bet that is why he went after Rodrigo, trying to find him. Brett already gave him what he wants. Why would the vampire be hanging around here waiting for us? He would be off somewhere else, living it up in the sun. He's probably at the beach snacking on surfers!"

Far from being comforting, her words caused a heaviness to cover my chest. I hadn't considered anyone outside of this household. Thanks to my blood, I had just opened a whole new world to the vampire. Now there was no time of day when he couldn't feed. What if he attacked a hospital or school?

Finn squeezed my leg. I looked over at him. He gave me a questioning eyebrow raise, and I shook my head. Even if my concerns were valid, the family had enough to worry about without me adding to it.

"Sorry to burst your bubble, there, Christina." There wasn't sarcasm in her voice. Caitlin obviously didn't want to cause her sister more worry over her kids. "But that's not the worst case scenario."

"Come on, Cate. Do we really have to do this?"

"Yes, Christina, we do." Caitlin lowered her arms to a folded position on the table and squared her shoulders. "We're not going to keep the boys safe by telling ourselves a pretty little fairy tale." The idea that the picture of the vampire killing a bunch of surfers in broad daylight was a pretty little fairy tale seemed a little bit of a stretch to me, but I didn't think it would be such a good idea to interrupt. "The worst cast scenario is that whatever change his blood causes can't be completed unless the vampire drinks it all. So, there's every reason to assume that he will be coming back, and will keep coming back until he finishes Brett off. There is also every reason to believe that he is probably stronger now and maybe doesn't have to hide in the shadows as much as he did yesterday."

Finn's harsh voice caused Cynthia to jump and let out a little squeak. "So, what do you want, Cate? You want to send him an invitation to come over this afternoon to finish the job?"

Caitlin looked nearly as surprised at her next words as I was. "No." She paused and then gave a little shudder. "No. That's not what I'm saying at all. We just need to be prepared for the worst. That way we don't accidentally lose anyone in this family. Brett included." Her eyes met mine but flashed away instantly.

Christina looked at her sister, a mix of frustration and desperation on her face. "Well, then, what do you suggest? How do we stay safe?"

"We stay together. Between us, our power can hold a vampire long enough to finish him off."

"And how do we find him?"

She shrugged. "He knows where we are. He'll find us."

Wendell shook his head and leaned forward, his weight supported by his elbows causing the table to lean toward him. "Caitlin, we can't all hole up in here. We all have businesses to run, and there is no guarantee he is going to come back."

"And there's no guarantee he isn't, Dad. How can we take the chance? If we split up, he can pick us off one by one. Brett's the only one whose fire can hurt the vampire enough to make him back off."

"Caitlin, listen. We can't—"

I broke in, unsure of what I was going to say until my words met my ears. "It's me he wants, not you, and he's going to keep coming until he gets me. I'm not comfortable using your family as bait so we can catch him." Finn started to interrupt, but I squeezed his leg to silence him and kept going. "We need answers. If it really is my blood that is doing this, then there has to be a way to find out what I really am. I didn't just appear from thin air. Obviously, my grandparents aren't my biological family. I had to be adopted. I had to be created from something, and whatever that something was, it's probably still out there somewhere. If I can figure that out, maybe that will give us the answers to help us know what to do with the vampire. Maybe I have some type of power we don't know about yet, something that would help us kill him." I looked at Caitlin. "And, you're right. I do have the power to stop him from killing me. I did it once, and now that I know at least part of what I am, I bet I can do it without nearly dying in the process. So, if I'm not here, you won't be in danger."

Finn finally broke in, unwilling to stay silent any longer. "Absolutely not! You weren't with Sonia or Rodrigo, and that didn't stop him from killing them, so you can't use that as a reason to go off on your own."

I looked at him imploringly. "We have to do something. *I* have to do something. We can't just sit here and wait for the next attack. And the only thing I can think to do is get information so we know what we are dealing with."

"Fine, then. Where do we start looking?" He obviously didn't expect me to have an answer.

I didn't expect to have an answer either, but suddenly I knew where to start. I just knew. "My grandma's house."

"Why? You said yourself that she couldn't be your real grandmother."

"I know, but if they adopted me, there have to be papers somewhere. Maybe they could give us a place to start looking. Parents' names or an orphanage or social worker or something."

"That's not a bad idea, actually."

Finn glared. "Dad! Come on. You can't be serious."

Wendell gave his son an apologetic grimace. "I don't know what else to do besides sit here and wait, and no matter how hard we try to stay together, at some point, he'll be able to get one of us alone and use us against Brett again."

THE family spent the day inside the house, the boys bouncing off the walls. By dinnertime, everyone was so on edge and irritable that we all ate in the living room with the television on. Something Paulette informed me was never done.

Finn assured me that as long as the rest of the family stayed together in one room, even if the vampire showed up, they would be able to keep it away with enough defensive spells that he wouldn't be able to do anything to them.

MUCH to Finn's disappointment, I headed to my grandmother's house at nine o'clock that evening. Much to my frustration, Finn came with me.

Grandma had gone to bed at eight every night for as long as I could remember, and was one of the soundest sleepers I had ever met. She normally was asleep within minutes, so I figured an hour was more than ample to let her be lost to her dreams before we broke in.

Finn wanted us to just go knock on her door and ask her about the adoption. I couldn't. It had been too long since we had spoken. I couldn't just show up on her doorstep claiming I was a demon and demand to know why. She was already worried enough about my soul. I didn't need to give her any more reasons to hurt. She had been through enough. Her daughter running away (if there ever was a real daughter, not just some made-up girl to make me feel like I belonged), her grandson being gay and having to watch as her husband kicked him out of the house, then to only have him die of cancer a few years later. No. I couldn't bring myself to hurt her more, nor did I think I was brave enough to face her and "come out" as a demon.

We parked several blocks away from her house, afraid the engine and lights would wake her up, no matter how sound a sleeper she was. As we made our way through Torrey Pines, constantly looking over our shoulders for the vampire, I was overcome with déjà vu. It had only been a little over a week since I'd hidden behind the garage and spied on her and Judith Jones, but it seemed like it had been years. So much had happened. Sonia had died, I'd discovered I was both a demon and something else, I'd met vampires, witches, werewolves, and nymphs, and I'd met a man I loved and who loved me. Once again, that thought caused my heart to skip as I remembered how brief a time it had been, no matter how long it felt.

"I thought you said it wasn't that far away?" Finn's whisper brought me back to the present.

I looked around, the darkness and shadows confusing me for a second. "Oh shit. Sorry. I got lost in thought. We passed it a couple of blocks ago. I didn't notice."

His eyes narrowed and his hand stretched out to grasp my arm. "Babe, are you okay? I'm worried about you. We can do this tomorrow. Let's wait until you're better."

"No, I'm okay. Really. Just a lot on my mind. Sorry." I turned and headed back the direction we'd just come, motioning as I did so. "Really, come on."

He followed, still looking concerned. I needed to get myself together. Focus on one thing at a time. It was enough that I might be moments away from discovering what I really was, for better or worse. Everything else I could stress over later.

Within a few minutes, we were standing in front of her door. With a flick of his hand, Finn caused the light over her "God is Love" doormat to sputter out, hiding us in the shadow of the overhang separating us from the moon.

Finn's whisper was so quiet I had to think for a second to comprehend what he asked. "Do you have a key?"

I shook my head. "No. Grandpa took it when he kicked me out. I thought that you could"—I wiggled my hand—"you know. If I break it, it will make too much noise. Plus, I really don't want to do anything to Grandma's house."

"Of course. I just assumed you had a key." He stepped forward and placed the first two fingers of his right hand on the doorknob. There was a faint click, and with a turn, Finn pushed open the door.

We stepped into the dark house and closed the door quietly behind us. It took a few seconds for my eyes to adjust, and I looked around the room. Just as I assumed, nothing had been changed. Grandpa hated for things to be moved around. He felt that if things were good how they were, there was no reason to mess with them. I figured Grandma hadn't wanted to go against his wishes after he died.

"Where should we start?"

"The only place I can think of would be in Grandpa's old office. If the papers aren't there, then I don't really have any other ideas. What if he put them in some safe-deposit box somewhere?"

Finn tilted his chin. "Let's just hope he didn't." He waited for me to move. "Well, lead the way."

"Oh, sure." I wasn't very good at this breaking-and-entering thing. Not only did it feel wrong to be coming into the house this way, it was unnerving to be back in the home I grew up in. Back in the room where, the last time I had been in it, my grandfather had been yelling, calling me names, and condemning me to hell—which he didn't even believe existed anyway—with my grandmother sobbing in the background.

I led Finn down the hallway, motioning for him to be extra quiet as we passed my grandma's room with her door cracked open. The very last door led into the office. We stepped through, and I shut the door silently behind Finn.

"Oh my God," Finn breathed. "This is unreal." He walked toward the far wall, which consisted entirely of windows.

One of the few areas where Grandpa had been willing to splurge was his office. All the walls were a deep mahogany wood, and large stones surrounded the door, the floor-to-ceiling bookshelves that ran along the walls, and the windows. It felt a little like stepping into a castle that had a large modern desk and huge squishy leather chairs in the middle.

I joined Finn at the glass wall.

He looked up at me, his eyes twinkling teasingly. "Do you think we'd wake up your grandma if we took a few seconds to have sex here? This is crazy beautiful."

He was right. The office was on the back of the house and looked over the cliff. On either side of the window were trees, but beyond that, you could see nothing but the jagged rocks that dropped off into the ocean, which stretched on endlessly, the moon shimmering on every rippling wave.

I leaned down and kissed him, letting our lips meld together.

Just as he pulled me tighter into him, I pulled back. "Finn, we gotta do what we came here for and get out. I'll call Grandma later and ask if she minds if we have hot and heavy gay sex in front of the window of Grandpa's office."

He snorted. "Ass." He gave me another quick kiss and let go of my waist. "Fine. Get to it. Where do we start?"

My gaze ran over the room. I'd never spent much time in the office. This had been Grandpa's space, and Grandma and I rarely interrupted him when he was in here. "I guess with those." I pointed to the middle of the room. "You wanna take the desk, and I'll take the file cabinet?"

"Sure." Within a couple of steps, he was seated at the desk and pulling on the center drawer. After trying two others, it was clear they were locked. He motioned toward the file cabinet. I went over and pulled on the top drawer. It didn't budge. Finn stood, and after a light touch of his hand on each drawer, I was able to open them and begin to sift through the papers. He returned to the desk and went through the same procedure.

Within twenty minutes, Finn had already gone through the entire contents of the desk, finding nothing except a picture of a gorgeous dark-headed girl. "Yeah, that's Jessica. She was my mom, or so they told me. I'm wondering if they just made her up so I wouldn't ask questions about being adopted since they were so old."

After finishing with the desk, Finn joined me at the filing cabinet. Despite Grandpa being ridiculously organized and neat, he'd devised his own filing system, complete with codes and symbols. This didn't surprise me in the slightest. In addition to being frugal to a fault, he had always been convinced that other people were going to try to get access to his finances and business dealings. As I couldn't tell what any file was about from his tiny slanted scrawl across the top, each one had to be inspected to determine if it could be helpful. Each of the eight drawers was packed so tightly that it was difficult to even pull an individual file from the group. I didn't want to make a mess or make it obvious that things had been moved if Grandma came in to go through the files one day.

It was a mind-numbing process, and after an hour, we had only finished with the second drawer, finding nothing other than paper after paper dealing with receipts, tax returns, and business contracts.

A gasp from behind us caused me to jump, dropping the file in my hands onto the floor, papers scattering everywhere. "Brett, is that you?"

I turned around to see a small, fragile frame in the doorway, a gun trembling dangerously from shaking outstretched hands. The moonlight cascading in lit up Grandma's face. Her eyes narrowed and darted back and forth, attempting to see our faces, which I realized were silhouetted with the light from behind us.

She took another quavering step toward us. "Brett?"

"Yes." My voice cracked. "Yes, Grandma, it's me, Brett."

"Oh thank God." Her face glistened as tears began to trace down her cheeks. "Brett," she breathed out reverently.

The shaking of the gun increased, the muzzle vibrating awkwardly.

"Grandma? Do you wanna put the gun down?"

She looked at the gun in a shocked manner, as if unsure of how it had gotten there. "Oh Lord Jesus." She quickly dropped her hands and lowered the gun to the floor as if it were a serpent getting ready to strike.

As soon as she was erect, she took several steps toward me, her arms wide, and wrapped me in her embrace, her head nuzzled below my chest. She began to sob so hard that I thought her body was going to shatter if she didn't stop shaking.

"Grandma, it's okay. You're safe. I'm sorry we scared you." I caressed her small head, her gray hair soft and thick.

She cried harder. "Oh, Brett. I'm so sorry. I've missed you so much. You shouldn't have gone." She let out another sob. "He was wrong. I hate to speak negatively about his memory, but he was wrong. I was wrong."

I felt my tears begin to burn behind my eyes. I pulled her closer and held her as she cried. "It's okay, Grandma. It's okay. I'm fine. I'm here now."

After several minutes, her trembling began to subside, and her breathing started to return to normal.

"Here"—I led her across the room to the huge sofa—"why don't we sit."

She sat down, never letting go of my hand. "Oh, Brett. I'm so glad to see you. I've almost called you a hundred times. I've even seen your house. It's so cute." I felt myself cringe at the mention of the house. She gasped again and looked at me, her eyes huge. "Oh, and your Grandpa. Oh, Brett, he's...." Her voice fell away as more tears overtook her.

"I know, Grandma. I know." My hand covered hers. "I was there."

"Really?" She smiled. "I knew you would be. Somehow, I knew you would be. I'm glad you were there. That means so much."

Finn tried to take a step quietly but accidentally scrunched some paper beneath his foot, causing both of us to look up in surprise.

I had momentarily forgotten about him, about why we had broken in, about the possibility that there was a vampire waiting for us outside or tormenting his family back at the house.

Grandma looked from Finn back to me. "Is this your... your *friend*?"

I paused, unsure of how to answer. "Uhm, yeah, he is." I looked up at Finn, and he gave me an encouraging smile. "Grandma, this is

Finn de Morisco, my boyfriend." I hadn't spoken the word aloud, and it felt weirdly good, though I hadn't pictured ever saying such a thing to my grandmother.

She took a deep breath and let it out slowly. With a firm nod, she stood up, offered a hand to Finn, and smiled warmly. "Nice to meet you."

Finn took her hand, offering a smile of his own. "Nice you meet you as well, Mrs. Wright. I'm so sorry about your recent loss."

Her smile faltered for a second. "Thank you, dear. And, please, call me Beverly." She gestured to the armchair next to the sofa. "Have a seat, please." She sat back down and looked at me. "I'm sure you're not here for the fun of it. Why don't you just tell me what you need, Brett? You know I'll help you anyway I can." She made a pained face. "Are you needing money, dear?"

I shook my head emphatically. "No. No, of course not. I would never steal from you."

"I know. But, what do you need?" She reached out and took my hand. This was the grandmother I knew. The grandmother I loved. The woman who was strong enough to face anything. The woman who would rather know the truth, no matter how hard it would be to hear.

I glanced over at Finn, giving him a questioning look. Now that she was in front of me, all the questions I had wanted to ask her seemed impossible to put into words.

"Go ahead, Brett." Finn nodded encouragingly. "I think she can take it."

"Take what?" Grandma looked at me, her eyes once again large with fear. "What's wrong, Brett? Just tell me, please. I don't think I can handle not knowing. Whatever it is can't be worse than this."

"I'm not so sure of that." I closed my eyes, unbelieving that I was actually getting ready to tell her. I didn't think there would be anything harder than having to tell her I was gay. I'd been wrong.

"I'm a demon, Grandma." I blurted out the words, and I couldn't take them back. I cracked my eyes open, looking at her cautiously.

After another deep breath, she met my eyes. "I know, dear."

There was nothing she could have said that would have shocked me more. She could have told me that my grandfather had spent the last two years as a drag queen and I wouldn't have felt more surprised. "You what?"

She nodded. "Yes, Brett. I know." She waved a hand. "Well, I didn't know demon, necessarily, but I knew it was something, and demon had crossed my mind."

"You mean they told you I was something else besides human when you adopted me?"

It was her turn to be confused. "What?"

"Well, from whoever it was you adopted me. What did they tell you I was?"

"Why in the world would you think you were adopted?"

I cocked my head at her quizzically. "I'm not?"

"Well, of course not, sweetie. You're my grandson, through and through."

I looked over at Finn, who shrugged, and turned back to Grandma. "If I'm not adopted, then how do you not know what I am?"

She glanced down at the floor, tears once more filling her eyes. "I don't know how to tell you this, Brett. I don't think it's best if you know."

Finn spoke up, his voice gentle but urgent. "Beverly, I know this is probably a lot to take in, but I think you appreciate directness." She gave him a nod, and he continued. "This is going to be hard to believe, but here's the bottom line: there is a vampire after Brett, and by extension, my family. We don't know why, but he thinks there is something about Brett that makes him special, something he wants. For us to figure out a way to keep Brett safe, we need to know where Brett comes from."

Grandma looked at me, back to Finn, and then back to me once more. "Vampire?"

I nodded. "It's the truth, Grandma. It's been a really crazy week or so."

"I had no idea." She touched my face with her fingertips. "Are you okay?"

"Yeah, I'm okay. Thanks to Finn and his family, but I won't be if we can't figure out what is going on, why he wants me so badly."

I could see her battle internally. I had a good idea what was going on behind her eyes. I was sure that whatever she wanted to say, Grandpa had forbidden her from ever speaking it out loud.

Her eyes hardened and she looked up, taking Finn and me in at the same time. "Your grandfather wasn't always like he was, you know. He used to be such a sweet, gentle man. There was nothing he wouldn't do for me. Everything I ever wanted, he got for me." This didn't sound anything like the man I knew. "That all changed after I became pregnant with Jessica."

"He didn't want kids?" I guess that would explain why he seemed so resentful of my existence.

"Oh no. He did, but he knew that Jessica wasn't his. We'd tried for so long. We'd given up the hope of ever having children. The doctors said it had something to do with his testosterone levels." She let her words sink in as I gaped at her wide-eyed. "He'd gone with the church for a three-month business trip to Japan. When he left, I wasn't pregnant. When he got back, I was."

She was right; I didn't want to hear this. "You had an affair?"

She slapped my hand. "Lord, no, child. You should know better! I loved your grandfather with all my heart. That *never* changed, even after he did." She took a final deep breath and then plunged ahead with her story. It came rushing out as if once the flood gates opened, there was no slowing it down.

"It was here, at the house." She motioned out the window. "Down there, beneath the cliff, actually. Marvin and I always walked down by the ocean right after sunset, every single night. I continued to walk even after he left on the business trip. It made me feel closer to him.

"Marvin had been gone almost two weeks. I was down by the ocean, just sitting there, enjoying the sea and stars, imagining Marvin out there looking up at the same stars. Silly, I know." Up until this point, she had been keeping constant eye contact between Finn and me, but now she looked down at the carpet, her voice growing quieter.

"I felt a sudden burst of heat behind me, and everything lit up for a moment. I turned around, expecting to see a fire or something. I don't know what I thought, maybe a falling star that I hadn't noticed, or something equally as stupid. There was a man there. He was huge, larger than you, Brett. He was naked, and he was the most beautiful person I had ever seen. He had long black hair and skin as white as moonlight. For a moment, all I could do was stare at him. I've never seen anything more beautiful in my life, not before or since." Even in the dark, I could see her cheeks flush.

"He took a step toward me, and that's what snapped me out of it. I turned and ran. I don't know if I was screaming or not, but I just knew I had to get away." She shuddered. "I doubt I made it even ten feet before he had me. He whirled me around and shoved me to the ground. I couldn't do anything. He was so very strong. He clamped his hand over my mouth, and then he... his skin felt like fire...." She broke off, tears flowing once more. "After... he left. Just disappeared."

"Oh, Grandma." I couldn't believe this was the same woman in front of me. How could such an atrocity have happened to her? Who could have been willing to hurt her so badly? "I'm so sorry. If I'd had known, I would have—"

She cut me off. "I'm not even close to being done, and if I don't get it out, I never will." She looked back up at me, her tears already gone. "By the time Marvin returned, I was showing. The baby grew fast. I was a mess. I had a fever the entire time. I couldn't stop throwing up, not ever. I didn't even leave the house.

"I'll never forget Marvin's face as he saw me, the pain. I'll never forgive myself for that pain. I told him. I told him that it had to have been something not human. I even said demon, I think. Of course, I said lots of things. Lots of ignorant guesses. I had no idea what he had been.

"Your grandfather never believed me, I don't think. Of course he didn't believe the demon part, but I also don't think he ever believed me about the rape part either. Of course, Marvin being Marvin, didn't want to hurt me or shame me. He told the world that the daughter was his. That Jessica was his. He never questioned me about that night again, never accused me again, but he was never the same, never able to really look at me again." Her voice got even quieter. "Never able to make love to me again."

I reached out to her, but she looked up, her eyes fierce. "I'm not done yet. Wait!" She looked over at Finn this time. "Jessica. I tell you, you've never seen a prettier baby, a prettier child. By the time she was eleven, she looked like a grown woman, and there was never a more gorgeous woman to walk this earth, I promise you. Nor was there one more mean or evil. From the time she was little, she was setting things on fire. Why, when she was seven, I bought her a little cocker spaniel puppy, hoping that she could learn to love something beside herself. Learn to care for something. She hadn't had that dog for more than two weeks when it was burned to death. Poor creature.

"We tried everything. Even therapy, which Marvin was so against. We tried boarding school after boarding school. She kept getting expelled. Nothing worked. Every year she got worse, every year more cruel. I'll never repeat the things she said to Marvin and me. Never.

"In a last effort to bring the family together, I convinced Marvin to take us all to Mexico. I thought maybe a family vacation; we'd never taken one before. I thought maybe time away, someplace beautiful, someplace new.... I don't know what I thought. I was desperate. I was such a fool.

"Our first night there, our very first night, I got up and saw that Jessica was gone. She wasn't in her bed, not in our room. I didn't wake Marvin. I just left, determined to get her back before he woke up. Even though she looked full-grown, she was only thirteen. She couldn't be by herself."

She shook her head, a look of disgust on her face. "I found her at the beach, in the ocean. Having sex with some man. Well, at first I thought she was with another woman. The person on top of her had such long white hair. I yelled at them. The man looked up. I honestly don't think he was human either. Maybe it was the moonlight, but his skin looked like pearls. It was shiny and sparkled. As soon as he saw me, he somehow flung himself backward into the ocean. He just disappeared into the ocean, I tell you. I stayed there for a while with Jessica, and he never surfaced again. I don't know if he drowned or what, but he didn't come back. It was like he swam away.

"Jessica was so angry at me. I'd never seen her like that. She hit me and I fell. She stood over me. She had fire coming from her hands. I swear she did. I thought she was going to kill me. She screamed and cursed at me, but the fire went out, and she ran off.

"She showed up a few hours later, before Marvin woke up. I didn't tell him, at least not then. Of course, Jessica ended up pregnant, and I had to tell him anyway. It was the final straw for Marvin. He didn't say anything, nothing at all. He just looked at his lying wife, making up stories about a man from the sea, just like she had made up about a man of fire on the beach thirteen years before.

"Jessica's pregnancy was nearly as rough as mine had been, and much longer. It was thirteen or fourteen months until she finally gave birth, to you, obviously, Brett. That night, after she gave birth, she left, just ran away. I've never heard anything from her since."

CHAPTER THIRTY-TWO

I COULDN'T help but laugh as we walked back into the de Moriscos' house. I jumped in surprise when we walked through the door and Wendell, Christina, and Caitlin were sitting at the table, staring at me, their eyes huge with anticipation. The rest were asleep in various locations around the room.

"Good grief, you guys." Finn rolled his eyes as he shut the door behind him. "It's past one in the morning. Why aren't you sleeping?"

Caitlin gave him an eye roll of her own. "Gee, Finn, I wonder."

"Well, it didn't stop the rest from sleeping."

"Okay, cut the small talk and just tell us what you found out." She turned from her brother and looked at me. "Did you find the adoption papers?"

I shook my head. "No. We didn't."

Before I could say anything else, their faces all dropped as one, the small glimmer of hope in their eyes vanishing.

"No, it's not like that. There aren't any adoption papers to find. There aren't any at all."

Wendell looked up inquisitively. "No adoption papers? You mean you found out where you came from?"

"Yeah, we did." I pulled up an empty chair and sat down, Finn claiming the one beside me. "Grandma woke up and caught us going through Grandpa's office."

Finn tipped back in his chair, folding his arm behind his head. "And she nearly shot us in the process."

A groggy voice spoke up from behind. "Shot you? Good gracious, are you alright?"

I turned my head to see Paulette get up from the sofa, bleary-eyed, and make her way to take her place beside Wendell.

Finn instantly lowered his chair back into its correct position. "Yeah, Mom, we're fine. Beverly realized it was Brett before she took our heads off."

Paulette gave a sympathetic sigh. "Poor woman, waking up in the middle of the night discovering someone breaking into her house after her husband just died. Probably scared her to death."

"I think we almost did, but Grandma is tough." I pictured her at the door kissing us good-bye, her tears flowing, promising she'd keep us and Finn's family in her prayers. Making me swear I'd keep checking in so she'd know I was okay, and offering my old bedroom back to me—an offer Finn and I had yet to discuss. "Tougher than I ever dreamed, actually."

I let my voice trail off, lost in thought again. While I hated to discover my heritage originated in rape and a troubled teenage mother, it felt comforting to know that the woman I had always called grandmother was indeed my real grandmother. It also gave me solace to have some understanding of what my grandfather had been through, and be able to see why he had been so resentful of me. After learning what he had faced and how he had never betrayed my grandmother, I felt like I could possibly begin to forgive him for his emotional neglect and hostile demeanor.

"For crying out loud, Brett. Tell us what you found out. It's not like we've been sitting here unable to sleep for the fun of it!" Caitlin's tense voice brought me back to the present.

"Oh, sorry. I've got a lot on my mind."

"It's okay, dear, take your time." Paulette smiled at me encouragingly.

Caitlin grimaced at her mother. "Like hell. I'm about to come out of my skin. Tell us what you know so that we can decide what the next step is."

Finn leaned forward over the table. "Chill out, Cate. It's been a rough night."

I started in before a sibling war broke out. "That's the thing. I don't know if what we found out is that helpful. We got the story, but no real answers."

I went through everything Grandma had told us, the rape, my conception, how she wasn't sure about who my father was, and how she didn't even have any confirmation on what had assaulted her until this evening.

They sat there in silence when the story was done, everyone sifting through their thoughts and theories.

Wendell was the first one to offer his opinion. "I'm glad for you that you have the comfort of knowing that your grandmother is who you knew her to be. However, it would have been more helpful, in a way, if there had been adoption papers with a name or a place we could go to get more information. Right now, all we know is already what we figured out. You're part demon and part something else."

"Didn't you say something about your grandmother calling your father a man from the sea?" Christina's voice rose in excitement, and she looked like she was on the verge of an epiphany.

"Yeah. I did."

"Well, what if…." She looked down at the table suddenly, her voice lowering in embarrassment. "What if he was a mer?"

Caitlin snorted loud enough to cause Ricky to mumble in agitation as he turned over in his sleep in the recliner. "Okay, Christina. He's a mer! And maybe we can all ride unicorns to get away from the vampire."

Christina knotted her eyebrows and glared at her little sister, but didn't say anything.

In a kinder voice, Wendell addressed Christina. "Well, we should look at every possible angle, we don't want to miss something, but I think we can safely rule that out." He rushed on, as if afraid his words would bring her to tears, which from what I had seen from Christina seemed doubtful. "But, it is helpful to rule out as much as we can. It will help us get closer to finding the truth."

I looked around the table, and it seemed everyone else was following this conversation and not experiencing the same confusion as I was. I almost let it go. I was getting tired of constantly needing clarification on everything, but then I remembered how much was at stake. I realized that this was no time to worry about looking ignorant. "I'm sure I should probably understand this, but, what's a mer?"

"A mermaid, dear," Paulette replied. "Or in this case a merman, I suppose."

I glanced at Christina, unsure of why she had been so nervous to offer it as a suggestion. "Well, that makes sense, doesn't it? A merman would be a man from the sea, just like Grandma said, and that would explain why he didn't come back to the shore. He just swam away in the ocean." I felt a thrill of excitement at the thought. It probably wouldn't make it much easier to find him, but at least we had a starting place.

"No, Brett, dear. Your father couldn't have been a merman." Paulette looked at me tenderly, as if breaking the news that the man I had always thought was my father turned out to be someone else. "The mer are fairy tales, legends passed down in both human and witch culture. Probably originating from sightings of sea nymphs."

I thought back to Caitlin's sarcastic response, and I turned my head to her. "So, there aren't such things as unicorns either?"

She gave me a look, as if I wanted her to tell me there was no Santa Claus, and shook her head.

I couldn't really see what the big deal was. If there were witches, demons, and fairies, it didn't seem such a big stretch to think there could be mermaids. Two weeks ago, I would have said that vampires were a myth too, and, boy, was that ever wrong. "What if there are mers? What if you just have never seen one?"

Wendell shook his head. "There aren't mers, Brett. It's not going to help us to start searching for things that don't exist. We've got to do everything we can to find out what your father was, since that's the only chance we have at figuring out how to deal with this vampire.

Your grandmother calling him a man from the sea only tells us that he and your mother were in the ocean at the time of…. Well, when you grandmother found them."

I looked back at Paulette. "What about a nymph? You said that the myth of mermaids probably came from people seeing sea nymphs. Maybe my father is a sea nymph. Something about this feels right. I've always loved being in the ocean." I cocked my head, considering the nymphs at the funeral. "Are there male nymphs?"

"Yes, there are. However, nymphs can't procreate with any other species, at least not successfully."

My hands started trembling in my lap. I glanced down, seeing the faintest trace of steam beginning to form. I glanced over at Finn to see if he'd noticed. He had his head in his hands, propped up on the table. I started my deep breathing. I was beginning to feel like a woman practicing for labor, constantly having to focus on my breathing in order to not burst into flames. It was so frustrating to constantly have more and more questions, more and more that I didn't understand, and instead of getting anywhere that would have answers, only being offered solutions that were really dead ends or other questions.

"I've been thinking." Finn sat up and gave me a wary look, as though I might not like what he was about to suggest. "Maybe we are coming at this from the wrong angle. How are we going to find someone when we have no clue what they are? What if we tried to find Jessica?"

I gaped at him, momentarily speechless. "What?"

He rushed ahead. "Well, she would probably have more of an idea of what species the man was who she had sex with in the ocean. She might even know where to find him, or at least others like him."

Finding my mother had never occurred to me. Not once, as weird as it may sound. Even as a kid, knowing that the subject of my mother was firmly off-limits, I didn't think much about her. She was an object of shame and pain in my family. She had always seemed dark and terrifying to me, more the stuff nightmares are made of rather than fantasies of a mother who would return to me one day and tell me how much she loved me and how hard it was for her to have to leave.

"How would you suggest we find her? Even Grandma hasn't heard from her since my birth. She's been gone for twenty-three years. Who knows how much she has changed since then. She'd probably be unrecognizable."

There was an excited note that Wendell couldn't suppress. "Actually, considering she's half demon, I doubt she would look any different from the picture you saw. In theory, having that much demon blood should make her nearly immortal. I've heard stories of demons removed as far as five generations away that live for thousands of years."

It seemed the connection formed with everyone around the table the same instant as it did with me. I felt my stomach drop as his words sank in, and I glanced around to see every eye on me. We had discussed the implications of my demon heritage on my longevity, but it hadn't been quite as real as it was at the moment. "So, that would make me one-fourth demon. I'm only two generations removed."

Wendell nodded slowly. "I can't explain it. It doesn't make sense with anything I've ever heard before. By all accounts you should be nearly as violent as a full-fledged demon—at the very least somewhat deranged and psychotic, as we've stated many times. I've never heard of a person so close to their demonic heritage that was able to function in society, let alone be the type of person you are."

Finn looked back and forth between his father and me, as if searching for answers. "According to his grandmother's story, he's half of something else too. Maybe whatever blood that is counteracts the demonic effect. One more reason to find his mother."

"I've never heard of anything powerful enough to temper the power of demon blood, other than continued distance through the bloodline, and if—"

I cut Wendell off. "So, does that mean I am going to live thousands of years?" With all the people in the world desiring to live forever, it seemed strange that such a thought would fill me with a dread I'd never experienced before.

Wendell didn't seem to be picking up on my emotional state. He grinned broadly at me as he replied, "I would only assume so. At least there's some good news mixed in with all the bad, I suppose."

I looked over to see Finn staring at me. I could see fear building up behind his eyes, but he forced a smile and looked away.

Oblivious, Wendell kept on. "I think Finn might be on to something. If we could find your mom, we might have a chance of figuring out how to get rid of this vampire problem."

I saw Paulette staring at Finn, her face sorrowful. "I think it's time for all of us to turn in. This is nothing that can't wait till tomorrow, and it has been a long, emotional day. Finn and Brett, why don't you two head on upstairs? The rest of us will be fine down here."

Wendell looked over at his wife. "I'm not so sure that's a good idea. It's best if we all stay together."

Paulette looked Wendell square in the eyes and stated firmly, not glancing over at us, "Finn and Brett, go on upstairs to bed, dears. Sleep well."

FINN and I got ready for bed without a word, both of us averting our eyes from the mirror as we brushed our teeth.

We kept our sweatpants on as we slipped into bed. We lay there for several minutes, the darkness a heavy blanket suffocating the room. I started to speak several times, but I was clueless as to what to say, what I should say.

"So." Finn's voice cut through the room, the tension still palpable. "Are we going to talk about it?"

"Sure. We can, I guess." I felt him shift on his side of the bed, turning his body to face me. I lay where I was, staring up at the ceiling.

His hand reached out and lightly traced over my stomach. When I didn't respond, he pulled his hand away. "Thousands of years, huh?"

"I guess so."

"Kinda scary, I would imagine."

"Yeah. Kinda." I wanted to turn to him. To offer him some kind of comfort, some type of assurance, but my body refused to move. How could I offer what I didn't understand?

The silence returned momentarily, the absence of voice and touch becoming a physical pain.

After several minutes, I felt Finn's hand slip into mine. "Please look at me. Talk to me."

I turned to him, his glistening eyes cutting through my heart. It was hard to believe my heart still felt enough to be cut. "What do you want me to say, Finn?"

"I just want you to talk to me. I want to know what you're thinking."

I clamped my mouth shut, but then it exploded. "I'm thinking that everything is fucked up. That's what I'm thinking! I'm a demon, and I'm sorry if I'm supposed to know how to handle that after a few days, but I don't! I'm sorry I'm scared of you. Of us." I sat up in the bed, my body beginning to tremble. "I'm thinking Sonia is dead, and I'll never see her again. I'm thinking that everything I've ever known isn't real. I'm thinking I'm not going to die for thousands of years!" My voice rose. I was sure I was probably waking up the rest of the family downstairs, but I couldn't bring myself to care. "Hell, maybe I won't even die at all. Who knows what my father was. Whatever he was, maybe they can't even be killed. I could be there when the world fucking implodes on itself in a billion years. Maybe I'll even survive that, just floating out in space with a bunch of fucking cockroaches for the rest of eternity!"

Finn had sat up when I did, and he drew himself closer and pulled me to him, wrapping his arms around me. I tried to pull back without hurting him, but he wouldn't let me go.

The steam began to pour off of me. Any second, I knew I would burst into flames. Finn's skin probably felt like it was smashed against an oven. Again, I saw the destroyed kelp forest, saw the boy at the beach, remembered how close I'd come to killing Peter. Distantly, I heard him murmuring something, probably some trite thing to make me feel better.

After a moment, I felt my skin cool, like a soothing cold gel had just been lathered on my body.

I looked down and then back up at him in surprise. "I didn't know you could do that."

"I didn't either. Don't know why I didn't think of it before."

He held me for a long time, his body conforming to mine, his legs wrapped around my waist and our heads resting on each other's necks. In wave after wave, he sent the cooling energy to wash over my skin. My breathing returned to normal, and I calmed and started to grow tired.

"I'm sorry, Finn. I don't mean to be angry or distant. I'm just freaking out here. I don't know who I am."

He tightened his arms around me. "It's okay. You don't have to apologize. You're not supposed to know what to do all the time. You don't even have to know who you are all the time. I know who you are."

"Who am I?"

"You're a good man. You're smart and caring. You're brave. You're strong and you're going to get through it. You're going to figure it out. You're the man I love."

I felt my throat constrict, his words causing comfort and a tinge of panic simultaneously. One issue at a time. Just one. "Thousands of years, Finn. Thousands." A bizarre sensation of claustrophobia flooded through me.

He pulled back and took my face in his hand, refusing to let my eyes look anywhere else. "We don't know anything for sure yet. We have no idea where this is going to lead and how long it will take to find all the answers. And, I promise you this. We *will* find the answers." He gave a determined look, one that most other times I would have found adorable. "I hope you caught that. *We*. No matter where this leads, I will come with you. I will help you figure it out. You're not alone, and if we find out that you really will live thousands of years or whatever, that doesn't change anything for me. Nothing. I love you, no matter if you're a… well, no matter what it turns out you are. No matter how long you might live, I will be with you as long as you want me to be."

Again, his words caused a surge of mixed emotions. Between the threat of eternal life and seeing forever in his eyes, I felt a suffocating mantle descend over me. "I don't think I can do this, Finn."

Finn's eyes widened, the pain behind them evident. I hated doing this to him. His voice was scratchy. "Do what?"

"Any of it. All of it. It's too much. It's too much for me."

He took my face in his hands again. "We've been through this. Do you love me?"

My heart twisted. Something had happened between us, and even though we'd been together for just over a week, we were a unit, one, and it killed me to hear him questioning my love for him, for him to question me, even though I couldn't blame him—even though I questioned it myself. "Yes, of course I love you. More than I thought I could ever love anyone." My heart recognized the truth of the words even as I said them.

"Do you know that I love you?"

"Of course I do."

"Then that's all that matters. That's all we need."

CHAPTER THIRTY-THREE

"Do you have to do anything to get them to show up?" I glanced around, the full moon making it easy to see in the forest, yet also giving it an eerie ambiance.

"Not really, just a little demon blood as an offering."

My head jerked toward Finn before I realized he was kidding. "Whatever."

He let out a soft chuckle. "No, we won't have to do anything, they will just know we are there. And would you stop looking around? You're creeping me out."

"Your mom would kill me if I let the vampire get you because I wasn't paying attention."

He shrugged it off. "I'm not as afraid of vampires as I was, at least as long as you're with me. I don't see how he could do much to us right now. There's no one he could capture for a hostage, and you can set the fucker on fire, so what's there to be worried about?"

"He could take you for a hostage. What could I do then?"

Finn ignored me and kept walking toward the cliff. "Come on. We're almost there."

After spending the day watching the de Moriscos place temporary protective spells on their businesses, it was decided that Finn and I would begin the search for my mother. Wendell thought the best place to begin would be the nymphs, and although I wasn't sure how they would be helpful, I couldn't help but be excited about seeing them again. I was already starting to get used to seeing Finn and his family casting spells all day long. They were like normal everyday people who were really talented or something, but there was no denying that the nymphs were far from human, something I still couldn't believe actually existed even though I had seen them with my own eyes.

When I had expressed confusion over why Finn's family hadn't placed spells to protect themselves from the vampire before, I was informed that such invoking of the elements to provide constant supervision and protection drained the life force of everyone and everything within a close proximity. If they weren't careful, such spells could easily kill or severely weaken anything living (other humans, plants, or animals) around them. It wouldn't hurt the ones it was cast to protect, but they didn't feel right taking the chance of harming others who weren't giving their consent to give of themselves. However, they figured that Finn and I wouldn't be gone for very long, and as they were going to work shortened days and then gather once more at the house, they felt the strain on others would be a minimal risk until we returned.

Before Finn brought us back to the cliff, we stopped in La Jolla to see my grandmother. She was thrilled to see me again so soon, but was in tears by the time we left when we told her that the reason we wanted to borrow a photo of Jessica was to hunt down other demons that might know her. Despite her fear over my safety, she asked me to tell Jessica that she loves her, when and if we found her. Before we left, she once again brought up the possibility of me living with her again. I wasn't used to having other people's emotions and happiness depending on me. Now I had both Grandma and Finn wanting me, needing me, to be with them, and there wasn't an option that didn't hurt someone. It seemed like it should be enough to have to worry about vampires and long-lost demon mothers without having to think about crushing the people I loved. Apparently not.

"Okay, take my hand."

I looked down at Finn's outstretched hand and slipped my hand into his. As every time before, the touch of his skin on mine made it a little easier to breathe, easier to believe that things might actually work out.

We stood there, a few feet from the ancient willow, the sea stretching out before us, a glittering endless jewel in the moonlight. The smell of salt on the breeze called to me, momentarily making me want to run to the edge and dive off, plunging into the water below. Just as every other time I had lately longed for the ocean, the memory of the kelp burning and dying drove away the impulse.

"Are you okay? Do you not feel like doing this?"

"Huh?" I looked over at Finn's concerned face.

"You look like you're going to be sick."

"Oh." I shook my head. "I was just thinking of the other day in the ocean." He squeezed my hand. "No, I want to be here. I want to do this."

I felt the change in the air the moment it started. The sizzle of electricity, the surge of power. Maybe it was because I had seen it once before, maybe it was because I was so thrilled to see it again, but the entrance of the nymphs appeared to take mere seconds this time, each one seeming to arrive just as the previous one had taken form. Before the blaze of the first had extinguished, the smell of freshly turned earth reached my senses as the wind whipped my shirt about my chest, and the ground grew sodden and dry once again, and Amalphia stood before us.

Out of the corner of my eye, I saw Finn's head lower reverently to his chest, and I followed his lead, though it made me nervous to take my eyes off the four women.

It was the translucent one, her eyes riotous, whose sweeping voice addressed us first. "Child of the elements, what is of such importance that it requires you to seek our attentions?" Her eyes flickered to me, narrowing, before turning back to Finn. "And what reason do you have to bring the child of the fallen into our presence yet again?"

"Peace, Ventas. He is still a child of ours." The torrent of red-orange curls moved on their own, dancing against the wind, as the nymph formed from fire placed her hand on the shoulder of her agitated sister.

Ventas shrugged away, her eyes flashing to me again, causing a chill to pass over my normally sweltering skin. "Not a child of all of us, Cenera. He could lead to folly."

"And he could lead to freedom, as you know." The dark-skinned woman's voice was gravelly and sultry. "A child of one is a child of all."

Amalphia, her voice yet again bringing an ache for the sea deep within me, addressed the earthen beauty. "Well spoken, Jordskote. Especially true since he is a child of two."

I knew they were discussing me, but I couldn't make sense of most of the conversation. I could tell Ventas wasn't as comfortable with my demon blood as the others, but beyond that, I was clueless to their meaning.

Ventas spoke again, turning her attention to Finn, and what little patience she had was gone. "Again, I ask, what brings you, and why is he here? He is no witch."

I was impressed with the mix of humility and strength Finn exuded as he met her gaze. "We require your guidance, honored nymphs. The safety of my family is in jeopardy."

"Your family is in peril due to the fallen one you bring before us." The wind rushed around us, making it hard to stand. "Cast him out, and your family shall be spared."

I saw Amalphia begin to speak, but Finn's voice rose, determined and strong. "He *is* family."

Finn's even glare was focused on Ventas, and he didn't see the sorrowful look Amalphia gave us as she stepped forward into Ventas's path. "What is it you require, Finn de Morisco?"

Finn bowed his head at his spoken name. "We need direction, my Lady. A vampire is tormenting my family, and we think that knowing his heritage"—he motioned to me—"could provide us with the answers we need to defend ourselves."

Jordskote stepped forward, her nearly black skin glistening a wine red in the flickering of Cenera. "We cannot tell you the path Brett Wright should take. The way of nature is to grow with the help of the elements, not surge forth from nothing."

I looked into her black eyes, shocked and humbled that she knew my name.

There was no animosity as she addressed me. "Yes, I know your name, though the path you may choose is not yet clear, despite the destination being set."

"We are not the fates, children." Amalphia looked at us lovingly. "We cannot give you the answers you seek, only help guide your direction."

"We will be thankful for whatever you deem appropriate to give us." Finn stood, his head bowed. Despite being used to such otherworldly experiences, his demeanor of confidence and clarity both surprised me and endeared him to me even more.

Cenera flashed into flames and was standing before me, crossing the space in a heart's beat. She held her hands out toward me.

I looked at her hands and then at her face, uncertain of her intention. Cautiously, I stretched out my hands and placed them in hers. At her touch, both of our bodies were swallowed in flame. I heard Finn gasp and call my name, but it was as if he were miles away, in a universe separate from mine.

Her glowing yellow eyes searched mine lovingly. "You are a child of mine, dear one. As you know, there is another who has more of a right to call you child than I. The time for her to speak is not yet upon us. Ask what you will."

My voice seemed lost momentarily as I was consumed in the dome of fire encompassing us. Tearing my eyes away, I turned back to her. "Do you know my father? What he is?"

She gave me a sympathetic smile, her teeth brilliant and shining in the reflected light. "Alas, I cannot tell you what you do not know. That discovery shall come in its natural time."

I couldn't help but feel frustration at her answer, the flames around us growing taller and hotter.

She looked around and grinned in what seemed a proud way. "You will have to learn to control your power, my child. Fire is a mighty force and can move obstacles and create room for growth, but it can also consume."

"What could you have to offer if you can only tell me what I already know?" The tone of my voice gave me pause. I needed to remember to whom I was speaking. I had no trouble believing she could take away my concern of living for eternity.

Her smile didn't falter; she only gazed at me patiently. "I can offer you guidance. Ask me the question that brought you here, Brett."

My mind went blank. What question had brought me here? I needed to know what my father was. That was all I needed. All that mattered.

"Nature moves in gradual steps and motions, not in giant leaps. Even the greatest, most uncontrollable fire starts out as a spark."

Inconceivably, her words made sense to me, and I remembered our plan. How we were going to find my father. "I need to find my mother. She would be a child of yours as well, I think. Her name is Jessica."

Cenera nodded, her smile faltering momentarily. "Yes, your mother is a child of mine, but more a child of the fallen than are you. Her presence, however, is not what you require."

"Then what do I require?" This all seemed so pointless. It seemed like the nymphs had the answers to all our questions, but were refusing to give them to us.

"One of the fallen will guide you. One of the fallen shall take you by the hand. One of the fallen will offer you the answers you seek."

My heart leapt at what seemed like a direct answer, at least direct as far as the nymphs were concerned. "How do I find… this demon?"

"Be sure before you choose. He will take you to the path that leads to enlightenment, but before you embark on your journey, you will pay a price."

"What price? What will I have to give?"

"It is not what you have to give, but what you choose to give."

"What is it?"

As if not hearing me, she continued. "I give you my blessing. You will assist in the unveiling of the truth, but the path you choose to fulfillment is up to you, not set in the stars or the elements." Her eyebrows rose questioningly. "Remember that."

I nodded my agreement, though I had no idea what she meant.

She leaned forward and pressed her burning lips to my forehead. As she pulled back, she released my hands, and the fire around us sank into the earth.

Finn started to rush forward, but Jordskote held out her hand to stop him.

Cenera turned to the other three nymphs. "Come, sisters."

They circled me, one on each side. "Kneel," Amalphia whispered.

I knelt. As I did, each one placed a hand on my head, Ventas waiting until Cenera gave her a warning glare.

They began to chant in the language I had heard at Rodrigo's funeral, their voices blending in a soothing yet terrible song. I wasn't sure what they were doing, but I expected to feel something. Some knowledge. Some type of power flow through me. I felt nothing.

As their singing ended, Cenera motioned for me to rise. Her voice was quieter than before, calmer. Sad. "The path to the fallen is within you." At her words, a miniscule heat sparked in the center of my chest. "When you choose to seek him, you shall find him." She looked as if she had finished speaking, but then her eyes met mine once more. "I bid you warning one final time. The choices you believe have no other option, in truth have many different paths that will take you to your chosen destination. Do not act out of rashness or fear."

She didn't wait for a response, and in a rush of wind and fire, scent of rain and earth, they were gone. Finn and I stood alone on the cliff, the night suddenly moonless and cold.

WE PULLED into Wendell and Paulette's driveway. Finn unbuckled his seat belt and reached for the door handle.

My voice surprising me, I reached out to his arm. "Wait. Please. Can we talk in here for a moment?"

The ride back had been silent, both of us lost in our thoughts, shaken by our encounter with the nymphs. The entire time, my spirit felt heavier and heavier. I didn't want to do what I was about to do, but I didn't see any other way. It was what was best.

He turned around in his seat, giving me the classic Finn de Morisco raised eyebrow. "Sure, what's up?"

I stared at him. My voice not wanting to speak. Refusing to speak. I can only imagine what my face must have looked like.

"What is it, Brett? What's wrong?" Finn's voice had taken on a panicky edge that wasn't there before, as if his core recognized what was happening before he did.

I held his golden brown eyes with mine for a moment, trying to memorize their beauty, their kindness. After an extended glance out the window, trying to find strength, I fixed his eyes again with mine. "I have to leave, babe."

He balked, giving his head a minuscule shake. "Leave?" His voice was tiny, beginning to quaver. "Where do you need to go?"

"Away, just away."

"You mean for a while. To figure out whatever it was the nymph told you?" His eyes pleaded with me, tears already beginning to spill.

I shook my head. "No, sweetie. I mean I need to leave."

"Leave *me*?" His voice broke.

I nodded. "Yes." I hated myself for the pain in his eyes. The pain I was putting there.

"We've done this already. We can get through this. We can."

I shook my head, my heart withering as I remembered my words, my promise that I'd stay. I'd meant it.

He looked down at our hands, which had somehow found each other, tears falling on them. His head shot back up. "You've stopped loving me?"

How could my heart keep breaking like this? Surely it would stop at some point. "God, no! I love you. I love you more than I ever thought I could love anyone. I love you more than anyone in my life!"

His brows knotted in confusion. "Then why are you leaving me? I don't understand!"

I searched around the truck, as if there would be an answer waiting that I could give him. "I can't do it. Like I tried to tell you in the graveyard, it's just not in me."

"What? What's not in you?" There was an edge of anger that had crept into the desperation.

"I know I'm going to leave sometime. I have to figure out who I am. What I come from. I might as well leave now, before it will hurt worse."

"You don't have to leave me to figure out who you are, where you come from. I'll help you."

I started to speak, but he rushed forward desperately. "Or, you can find out on your own, if you don't want me with you. I will wait!"

I shook my head again, my tears starting to fall. "No, Finn. I just have to leave. For me. It's not because I don't love you. I do. Please believe me, I do. But, I just have to go. I can't be the man you need. I can't be the man you build your forever with. Hell, I don't even know what kind of man I am, if I really am a man."

"I do! I know what kind of man you are! And I love you. You love me. I know you do. That's enough!"

"No, babe." I shook my head, my eyes briefly leaving his. "No, Finn. It's not. It's not enough."

His shoulders slumped as he looked at me, his eyes empty and dull, Finn gone from them.

We stared at each other. Stared endlessly. With a final squeeze of his hands, I leaned forward, pressed my lips to his, and then slid out of the truck. "I'm sorry. I love you. I'm so sorry." I was at the end of the driveway before I looked back. His silhouette showed through the back window, hunched down, curling into a ball in the front seat, shaking with uncontrollable sobs that reached my ears.

With a groan of agonizing pain, I threw myself forward and ran. My legs pounded the ground. Somewhere in the back of my mind, I wondered if I was crushing the pavement under me. I ran and I ran. I ran until I crumpled into a heap on the side of the road, my body convulsing with sobs of my own.

CHAPTER THIRTY-FOUR

SOMETHING wet and cold kept pressing against my cheek. I swatted it away, but after a moment it would be back, leaving a cool wet mark where it had been. My eyes flew open when I felt whiskers brush my lips. A pair of huge, moist, chocolate eyes were mere centimeters away from mine. I jerked my head back, only to hit it on whatever I was lying on.

Before I could move further, the overwhelming odor of dead fish rushed over me as the chocolate eyes moved upward, giving way to a wide, fanged mouth that let out a mournful growl.

I scampered backward on my elbows and wiped the slimy spittle from my face. Looking back at what had accosted me, I saw a harbor seal gazing at me, its head cocking from side to side like a dog.

I groaned. "Oh, hi there. You nearly scared the shit outta me." It took a few more lumbering steps, pulling itself toward me, its face invading my space again, its nose poking my chin.

In confusion, I looked around. I was on a beach, less than ten feet from the surf. The sun was high in the sky and beat down on us. Taking another look around, I saw that I was alone with the seal, nothing else on the beach outside of a couple of tiny crabs scurrying about.

Another rough poke from the seal against my neck and everything rushed back. The nymphs on the cliff. Finn in the truck.

Finn sobbing.

Finn.

My breath caught, the hole in my chest that never closed overtaking the rest of me, leaving me empty and weighted down. Before I realized it was me, I exhaled a deep, pain-filled moan, pulling my knees up to my chest and burying my head in my arms.

In a sympathetic gesture, the seal growled, low and gravelly, its flippers draping over my feet.

I let my hand fall onto its slick, smooth head. It shifted its weight, pushing against me.

I couldn't remember a time I had ever felt so lost. As the thought occurred to me, it seemed rather ludicrous. In the past several days, I had learned I was a demon, I had fallen in love, my best friend had been murdered. Still, sitting here on the beach, a sensation of utter vacancy washed over me. What was I doing? What had I been thinking?

I made a motion to stand up, the seal shuffling a couple of feet away. I needed to go back. Tell Finn I was an idiot. Beg him to forgive me.

Then what? Feel loved and less guilty for hurting him? Freak out when I see forever in his eyes again? Wait for a few weeks or months until I can't take the pressure any more and then leave again? Maybe wait until we discover together what type of monster I really am so he can see I'm not the man he needs anyway, and then leave?

I fell back to the sand. No. I'd done the right thing. It was the right thing. It had to be. Grandpa always said "the right thing to do is never easy and it always hurts." A snort broke from me as a picture of his old, bitter face came to mind. *Well, Grandpa, I'm sure you'd love this. Your fagotty demon grandson, alone and sobbing on a beach. You'd just smile and say you told me so, huh?*

I'd tried to ignore the feeling the past couple of days, but it had continued to grow. I think I'd subconsciously known I was going to hurt Finn. I knew I wasn't going to be able to be the man he thought I was. Not the marry-me-forever kind. Not even the I'm-a-human-with-a-soul kind. It was right that I leave. Right that I hurt him now, hurt us now, before more time passed. Before I might not be able to walk away.

I looked out at the sea. The water was perfectly smooth, the only movement the gentle surf meeting the shore. That was where I should be. Get lost in the waves, lost in the depths. All my answers were there. I knew it as surely as I knew anything. I could leave the demon behind. Leave the people. They all wanted too much from me. They wanted me to keep them safe from vampires. Wanted me to love them. Wanted to die on me. Wanted to leave me alone.

Even if the sea didn't have any answers, it had water. Endless water that I could search for the eternity I had in front of me, and maybe never discover all there was to discover. Endless water that didn't have any expectations.

I stood up again, frightening the seal that had almost made it back to me. Without looking around, I slipped out of my clothes, letting them stay where they fell.

Two giant strides and I was in the water. It had crept up past my chest when, once again, the vision of the desecrated kelp forest flooded my mind, stopping me dead in my tracks.

The sea did have an expectation of me. Not to kill it. An expectation I couldn't keep.

My body longed to dive beneath the surface, to swim until time ended. I couldn't. I couldn't let myself disappoint Finn. How could I do anything different to the ocean, the only thing I loved as much as him?

Feeling something rub against my chest, I looked down. The seal was paddling in front of me, its jovial eyes pleading with me to swim. To play. I stroked its head again. "I'd only hurt you, buddy." I gestured out to sea. "Go. Go find your friends. Play with them."

Without a look, I turned and headed back to shore.

Unwilling to completely leave the comfort of the sea, I stopped when the water reached my calves. I lay down in the surf, the easy waves covering me and then pulling away again.

I couldn't be with Finn. I couldn't be in the ocean. I couldn't live in Sonia's house. I couldn't stay with Grandma, leading the vampire to her.

What was I supposed to do? I knew there was nothing left for me. Not in the human world that I knew, at any rate. Demons shouldn't be part of the world, shouldn't own their own homes, shouldn't fall in love and get married.

So, then what? I had an eternity in front of me, literally. On the bright side, it might only be a few thousand years. As if there was a difference.

The water momentarily submerged my head again, stroking my hair, kissing my skin. My eyes closed, allowing me to get lost in the ebb and flow of the sea. Its rhythm soothed the hollow ache within me.

Cenera's otherworldly face filled my mind, her fiery hair dancing as if in the waves, her voice echoing. *The path to the fallen is within you. Choose to seek him.*

I sat up. The fallen. The demon.

On the cliff, the thought of facing a demon was about as appealing as rolling around in raw meat and throwing myself into a lion's den. Now, however, nothing could sound any better.

It was a no-lose situation. The demon would either kill me or lead me to my mother, who would also probably kill me.

Perfection.

I stood up and turned back toward the shore. I had only taken a step when I saw movement to my left. Turning, half expecting the demon to have found me, I saw a couple holding hands, stopped in their tracks, staring openmouthed at me.

Remembering that I was naked, I looked down at myself and then back at the couple. Without knowing why, I let out a wild laugh and flipped them off, walked over to my clothes, picked them up, tossed them over my shoulder, and walked off the beach.

THE instant my toes touched the grass at the edge of the beach, the spark that Cenera had placed in my chest the night before ignited once more. It took me by surprise, causing me to halt and hold my hand over the spot, momentarily thinking that I had burst into flames again.

Whatever the nymphs had done, it seemed that this fire was my key to finding the demon. I wondered if it would lead me to any demon, whichever one was the closest, or if there was a particular demon they had in mind. I wasn't sure how many demons there were wandering around San Diego, or California for that matter, but I hoped there would be one close. Then I realized I really didn't care. There was nothing else I needed to do. There was no one waiting for me. There was no place I had to be, and, according to Wendell, I had at least nigh on a couple thousand years to locate a demon that could help me find my mother. I had time. Plenty of it.

Why did I want to find my mom, again? The necessity of it all escaped me at the moment. I had never needed or wanted her before, why now? I had to intentionally dig through my memory to come up with the answer.

The vampire. The vampire that might still be stalking me. Stalking Finn, his family. However, I doubted the vampire would still be after the de Moriscos. From everything I had been told about them, vampires weren't stupid. He would know I was no longer there. He'd come after me.

Let him come. I'd welcome it. Maybe the vampire had been right. Maybe being drained of blood really could end the life of a demon.

No sooner had I felt a second's thrill at the thought of the vampire taking me, than I remembered Sonia's bedroom. The blood casting a gory sunset on the wall. To my surprise, there must have been a small portion of me that wasn't as dead and hollow as I thought.

I couldn't let the vampire take me. Regardless of my apparent death wish, Sonia had not called death to her. I had to avenge her. He had to die for ending a life that brought such light to this world.

To do that, I needed to find my mother, find out what my father had been. Find the answer to what the vampire desired from me so much, and in so doing, hopefully find the key to his destruction. After that, maybe I could find another vampire to finish the job he had started, if this demon didn't do it first.

As if waking from a dream, I realized I was surrounded by a small crowd of people. Some pointing and talking to each other in hushed tones. Others, taking pictures with their cell phones, or videoing me. An older woman in the center of the group, who looked shockingly similar to my grandmother, was frowning and shaking her head in disgust.

Following their eyes, I glanced down at my body. I was still naked. I looked up at them, and, for an instant, I considered giving them the same response as the couple on the beach. Realizing that I was being stupid, that continuing to walk around naked would only hinder the process of locating the demon, I bent down and slipped my legs into my shorts and pulled them up. I tugged the T-shirt over my head and stuck my feet into my flip-flops. Once more appropriately decent, I looked at the crowd around me, once again started to flip them off, but then caught the disapproving gaze of the grandma. With an annoyed grumble, I pushed my way through the crowd and started walking.

AFTER several hours of walking, it had become apparent that the nymph-given fire was little more than a magical homing device.

That's right, Paulette, I said magic. Magic, magic, magic. You can call it whatever *natural* word you want, it's still fucking magic.

Most of the time, the flame remained a steady burn in my chest, but occasionally, it would decrease to barely an ember, and I would turn this way or that until it started to smolder once more. Other times, it would flare up and I would gasp or clutch at my chest in surprise and pain. I assumed that meant I was going the right way, so I would adjust my path until the flame seemed like it really would set me on fire. After a few feet in the new direction, it would return to its homeostatic steady warmth.

I continued walking the rest of the day and well into the night. I would stop here and there to rest for a moment or find a partially secluded tree or bush to relieve myself. Sporadically, I would stop in at a grocery store or street vendor to get something to eat. My normally heightened appetite turned voracious with mile after mile of walking.

The first place I stopped, a small gas station, I chose a few microwaved burritos. I took them to the counter and reached into my back pocket for my wallet. It wasn't there. I could see it in my mind, sitting on the dresser beside Finn's bed. Without giving the clerk a second look, I scooped up the burritos and walked calmly out the door as he bellowed at me and threatened to call the police. Over burritos. After everything else, I doubted minor theft of crappy mass-produced food was really going to be my undoing.

After that, though, I was careful to slip things into my pockets or waistband. Truth be told, I relished the feeling of having the salesperson know I was taking their merchandise and didn't care, but I knew excessive shoplifting would be a distraction that could impede the rate at which I found the fallen one. Even though I had eternity, I couldn't help but want to just get it over with.

It surprised me how I didn't feel human anymore. I didn't look at the store clerks or other people strolling through the streets as people. Well, I guess I did. They were people. I wasn't. I didn't know what I was, but I knew I wasn't one of them. What did their petty, simple lives matter in the scheme of things? They were going to go to work, come home, eat something, maybe fuck someone, fall asleep, and then do the same damn thing the next day, until they died.

That night, when I started nodding off while I was walking, stumbling over roots of trees, cracks in the sidewalk, things that weren't even there, I ignored the dimming of the fire in my chest and found my way back to the beach. Curling up on a rock at the edge of the waves, I fell asleep, the ocean climbing and receding over my legs as I slept.

I didn't dream of Sonia. I didn't dream of Finn. There were no witches, demons, or vampires. There was only emptiness that was occasionally overcome by the dark currents in the deep.

THE screeching of sea gulls woke me a little after dawn. I opened my eyes to see scores of their white faces peering stupidly at me, their beaks open in a ceaseless cacophony. Thrashing my arms in the air, I stood up, scattering the birds back to the sky. As I did so, something cut into my foot, causing me to stumble back onto the rock, slicing my hand on something else as I reached out to steady myself.

Glaring down at my bleeding hand, I saw a partially shattered sea urchin. A glance showed the same fate had befallen another of the black, spiny creatures, crushed beneath my foot. Getting up once more, carefully, I discovered the rock was completely enveloped in hundreds, if not thousands, of thorny urchins that had arrived while I slept.

Making my way off the rock as meticulously as possible, I still trampled several others of the tiny animals, each one taking its revenge on my hands, feet, and knees. Reaching the sand, I inspected the twenty or so cuts on my body. Each one stung sharply, the salt on my skin increasing the burn.

In the back of my mind, a picture of Finn's handsome face rose. With no more effort than an invoking thought, he would have healed each slice, making my skin as good as new, if not better. One more piece of evidence before the jury. One man good, pure of heart, loving. The other a thief, an incinerator, not even a man. I was right to leave.

Before I had a chance to feel his absence, I shoved him roughly from my mind and started out toward the spot I had last felt the warmth of the nymph-fire the night before.

I walked the rest of the day, having to stop and rest more frequently than I had the day before. My wounds burned and itched more with every step I took. At times, I feared their ache would overshadow the burn in my chest, causing me to lose my way, but the tiny flame continued to burn, guiding me ever further.

Around noon, I swiped a tube of Neosporin from a pharmacy. It seemed to cool the ache for a few moments. However, the relief fled as soon as I started out again.

Night had fallen, and I was preparing to head for the beach to sleep once again, urchins and sea gulls be damned, when the fire within blazed white hot, taking the breath from me. I stood there, clutching my chest, doing my best to breathe before I passed out.

Sucking in insignificant amounts of air, I glanced around. I was less than a mile from Tijuana, and to the west I could see the ocean. Other than that, there was nothing around besides a few rocky cliffs. No houses or buildings of any kind.

Still, the fire hadn't burned like this before. I knew this wasn't a little you're-getting-warmer-keep-going tingle. This was the real thing. The fallen one was close. Here. Still searching, I couldn't find anything that could give me a clue as to where the demon might be.

Seek him and you shall find him. Surprised I had enough faith to pay any attention to Cenera's words, I closed my eyes, focusing entirely on the firestorm within me.

In blindness, my arms at my sides, my feet moved forward. Each step made the inferno increase. Every so often, the pain would lessen and I would adjust my direction.

Several minutes later, I felt the softness of the grass beneath my feet give way to a crunching, uneven surface. I was at the cliff's edge. Eyes smashed shut, every ounce of my being centered around the swelling agony within me, I made my way down the steep jutting surface, crab-walking with my hands held out behind me, gradually making my way down.

I didn't stumble or slip. Though my breath was coming in short wheezes, my body was guided by the heat within. After what was probably twenty or thirty feet of a zigzagged diagonal path downward, the fire in my chest exploded through my body, every fiber of me turning white-hot.

Then it was gone. Completely. Leaving only the empty shell.

My eyes opened, and I looked around. I was probably still a good ten or fifteen feet from the base of the cliff, the ocean beginning a few hundred yards out. I saw nothing that would give any hint of housing a demon.

With a feeling of the *monster's behind me, isn't it*, I turned around. Nothing. No demon, no portal into Hell, not so much as a little buzzing fairy.

I looked up to the star-filled sky in frustrated desperation. The fire was gone; there was nothing left to guide me. I was three-quarters of the way down some stupid cliff just outside of Mexico, and the only halfway demonic thing in view was me.

If the vampire showed up, he could have me. Screw Sonia's revenge. He could have me. He could send me to her.

Seek him.

"What does it look like I've been doing?" The sound of my voice startled me. It sounded dry and unfamiliar. I didn't remember the last time I had spoken. Oh wait. Yes, I did. To Finn.

Seek him.

Letting out a growl, I glared at the cliff in front of me, *seeking*. I couldn't see anything that looked remotely like an entrance or a path that led anywhere. I looked behind me and down. Maybe if I got to the bottom of the cliff and looked up I could see something clearer, the whole not-seeing-the-forest-for-the-trees kinda thing.

Seek him.

The next time I saw her, I was going to strangle that crazy fire-girl, maybe give her some fire of my own. With a furious yell, I smacked my fist against the rock face.

Instead of slamming into the rock, my hand passed through it as if through air. Unexpectedly losing my balance, I fell straight into, straight *through*, the side of the cliff. I landed with a loud crash on the ground, the air once again knocked out of me.

Taking a second to regain my bearings and my breath, I pushed up with my hands and stood, shakily putting out my right hand to steady myself on the rock. My eyes met his as I looked over from where I stood. They were copper, and they sparkled in fury as he stood up to attend to his intruder.

CHAPTER
THIRTY-FIVE

IDIOTICALLY, my first thought was of Finn. How we had guessed it might take weeks before we found the demon, even after the nymphs' help. We'd been wrong. About everything, it seemed.

Second, I felt the demon was the most beautiful thing I had ever seen. There was no other word for it. He was beautiful. So much that it physically hurt to look at him. He was easily seven feet tall. The pure mass of him seemed to fill the space, every inch of him bound in lean, bulging muscle. Framing his incensed copper eyes, his golden hair fell sleek and straight over his squared jaw and past his extensive shoulders.

He was so obviously otherworldly that the straining white T-shirt and carpenter pants he wore seemed ridiculous. He should have been wearing a shimmering white robe, regal ivory wings jutting out from his back, a halo over his gorgeous face—which was probably the look he'd been accustomed to before relocating to earth.

"It has been ages since I've had the pleasure of ending the life of another fallen." His full lips curved wickedly into a crooked smile. "Why has God seen fit to give me such a gift?"

His voice was deep and rumbling but caused a sense of warmth and well-being to wash over me, conflicting with the intention of his words. I stared at him. Despite myself, wanting him to come closer, to touch me, to speak again.

He grimaced in distaste. "A lover of males. Vile, despicable habit." He sneered in my direction. "I would have preferred a challenge, the potential to be destroyed myself. You will be a bore."

How did he know I was a demon? And how did he know I was gay from a glance? The way I was looking at him probably gave it away. His eyes drew me to him as much as the vampire's had.

He let out a growl and took a step toward me. "You dare compare me to a vampire? To a filthy parasite leaching off of God's most failed creation?"

I shook my head. How did he…? He could read my thoughts!

He rolled his eyes, which at any other time would have struck me as funny. "Yes, I can read your thoughts and make you think or feel anything I desire. And your thoughts are as dull and void of depth as any human's."

He closed the gap between us, causing me to look up to see his face. Again, I felt like I should be terrified, but I couldn't make myself be. A feeling of safety continued to flow over me.

"Is it fear that you want to feel instead? Would that make you more interesting?" He gave a genuine smile this time. "That can be arranged. The sound of a lover of men's screams is a very pleasing experience. However, before we get to that, tell me—you did not just stumble into my dwelling by chance. What would bring such a pathetic excuse for a demon knocking at my door?"

I waited for him to read my thoughts, to spout them back at me.

He gave another impatient eye roll. "I want to hear you speak. If I choose to listen to your mind again, I will. I am hoping the act of you speaking will be more amusing than your thoughts."

He stared at me. The anger never left his eyes, and yet the pleasant, homey feeling never left me either.

"Well," he boomed, "why are you here?"

Without choosing to, I began to speak. "The nymphs gave me the ability to find you, to find a demon. That's how I discovered where you are."

He took a step back, his eyebrows knotting. "Nymphs sent you?"

I nodded.

"Why?" His voice took on a quiet, concerned tone.

"To help me find my mother."

At this, he threw back his head and roared with laughter. "To help you find your mother? Are you a lost dog that needs to suckle?"

I didn't answer him, just continued to stare.

After his laughter died down, he gave me a long, inquisitive look, as if trying to decide what he was supposed to do with me. It seemed the mention of the nymphs might have changed things. They were powerful, but I hadn't imagined a demon being afraid of them.

His eyes flashed and the safe feeling fled, giving way to nervous trepidation. I figured that came directly out of me, a feeling I wouldn't need any help from him to conjure.

"That's right. I will let you feel what you should feel, you repugnant half-breed! You dare assume that I feel fear? Fear of the nymphs? I might as well be afraid of you."

The peaceful feeling was gone, but neither was I terrified. He was intimidating, and I knew he could destroy me with a flick of his hand, but I couldn't bring myself to care. With any luck, that was exactly what he would do.

He gave me another curious look and relaxed back to his original seated position. "You are more interesting than you appear to be at first glance. You do not fear death?"

I shook my head, my voice so quiet I was surprised he heard it. "I welcome it."

"I doubt that." His lip twitched. "Still, there must be true demon in you after all."

I didn't give a reply, and we remained, one sitting, one standing, staring at each other. After several moments, it began to seem less likely that he was going to kill me, which seemed par for the course lately. Finally, the silence seeming rather ridiculous, I spoke up. "I'm here to find out about—"

"When I am ready to answer your questions, I will tell you. Until then you will remember your place."

Neither apologizing nor forcing my hand, I let my mouth shut and resumed staring.

He motioned to what appeared to be a chair close to him. "Sit. We shall talk."

As I walked over to the chair, I took in the room for the first time. To call it a room didn't seem quite right. It was more of a dwelling. Everything seemed to be formed from the rock of the cliff, as if it had grown naturally from it, each piece smooth and fluid. If I hadn't known it was a demon's lair, I would have found it beautiful. Outside of the nymphs themselves, this was the most obviously magical thing I had seen. There was no mistaking this for human creation.

There didn't seem to be any source of light, yet the rock gave off a warm glow, the various colored striations of the stone swirling and flowing, giving the feeling of being surrounded by a melding mixture of caramel and honey. There was nothing soft in sight. No pillows or blankets. I didn't see a bed either, for that matter. The stone rose up from the floor to form a large table and three chairs, of which we occupied two. The other structure was what could only be described as a bookcase, the rock having formed a curved mound that streamed in and out to take the shape of shelves. There were hundreds of books on the shelves and scattered throughout the room, the only aspect of the dwelling that gave any indication that humanity existed. As I sat down at the table, I noticed what he had been reading when I entered. My eyes widened as I realized it was a Bible.

In a grimly serious voice, the demon smiled wryly. "I enjoy Genesis. While it can't come close to capturing the true experience, it is pleasant to review my past work. I will never forgive him for soiling it with the stain of human beings. What a waste!"

"Your past work?" He couldn't be serious. "You helped create the world?"

An insulted look came over his face. "Of course. I was the one to impart the wishes of God to the angels of creation. Whatever I spoke was done."

That didn't make any sense. "How did fire help you with that?"

He gave me a quizzical look. Then I became aware of a probing teasing at the back of my mind. "Fire demon! You take me for a worthless angel of battle? Do I look like a *servant* to you?" His voice increased in volume with every word he spoke. "Do not begin to bring me down to a level equal to your heritage!"

"You're not a fire demon? Don't all demons use fire?"

His copper eyes burned red as he addressed me. "I am Pensatus, a herald angel. An angel of proclamation." His chest swelled. "I do not need fire. I impart the words of God. I know every desire and craving, every thought, every sinister notion." He gave a chuckle. "Many, I put there myself."

"You impart the words of God? A demon?"

He sneered. "Of course not. No longer do I do the bidding of God. I am the servant of no one."

I shook my head. None of this made sense, not that it needed to. I just needed an answer, not a lesson on demonology.

He let out another growl. "This will be done at my leisure. Not yours."

When I didn't respond, his voice returned to normal. "Ask me about yourself."

Talking to him made less sense than trying to get a straight answer out of the nymphs. "I want to know where my mother—"

"No!" His face flushed. "I said about you! We are not addressing your quest yet."

Warmth began to flow into my hands. This was getting ridiculous. Demon or not, there was only so much more of this I could handle.

Pensatus looked at my hands and, without waiting for me, began. "You are part fire demon. You come from a line of warriors. Nothing more than glorified slaves. You have immense strength and the gift of flame, but your kind was nothing more than the watchdogs of God."

I knew, despite his obvious power-trip reasons for explaining, that this was what I'd been waiting for, what I'd been seeking—what the de Moriscos had been seeking. For having wanted so desperately to understand what I was, what it meant to be a demon, I now couldn't even pretend interest in his words, even though I knew I should feel it. "That makes sense, I suppose." It seemed for all his self-proclaimed importance, Pensatus wanted nothing more from me than a pair of ears to listen to how wonderful he was and someone to bully around.

"Be careful with your thoughts, weak one. You shall find your death wish granted."

Threats, always threats. My grandfather. The church. The vampire. Now a demon. I was over it. He could kill me, he could answer my question, he could throw me out, but I was done with this inane conversation about angel hierarchy. "If you were so intent on killing me, why are you considering answering my questions?"

"The nymphs have never sent something with a soul to me before. I want to know why."

For the first time, his words gave me real pause. "I have a soul?" I asked quietly.

He leered at me. "It wafts out of you in pungent waves. Even the fragrance of the demon within you can't disguise it."

Finn had been right about something.

"Why did they send you to me?"

I started to speak, but he cut me off. "Besides your desire to find your mother."

I looked at him blankly. "That's it. There was no other reason. I need to find my mother so that I can find out what my father is. Then I can take revenge on the vampire who is stalking me."

He scoffed. "The nymphs wouldn't care about a solitary vampire, nor a quest of revenge. Why else did they send you?"

Shaking my head, I shrugged. "There isn't another reason. That's it."

"It's in your blood to be a servant. Even now, you are doing the nymphs' bidding, and you don't even know it." He chuckled. Closing his eyes, he paused as if concentrating intensely. "You didn't heed the fire nymph's counsel either, did you?"

"I didn't?"

"You made rash and selfish decisions. You didn't care what they said. You would have still chosen the easy way, regardless." He laughed again. "Not that I would have you make any other kind."

My heart sank at his words, though I didn't know to what he was referring.

His eyes opened, his gaze locked on mine. "Ask."

After a moment's hesitation, I began. "Where is my mother?"

His lips curved into a suggestive grin. "Jessica?" At the look of surprise on my face, his smile deepened. "Oh, yes, I know Jessica, though she goes by another name now. I know her well. I've known her many times. Though the servant's blood in her veins is beneath me, her fire can be most… tantalizing."

He probably hoped his words would disturb me, and maybe they should. But she wasn't a mother to me. She was just another demon, a means to an end. What should I care how she chose to occupy her time? Was I supposed to be offended that my hateful mother wasn't a virginal prude?

"Where is she?"

He grinned again. "Not here, though I wish she were."

"Can you help me find her?" His hard eyes bored into me.

"Why are you asking me about her when you could inquire about the issue for which you seek her?"

I reframed his words in my head, trying to make sense of them. "You mean, you can tell me what my father is?"

"Yes, I can. I won't. But I can."

The steam began to waft up from my fists again and rose between us like a wall of fog. "I'm tired of this game, Pensatus. Answer my questions or don't. Kill me or don't, but let's finish this."

Instead of looking irritated like I expected, he only seemed to be enjoying himself more.

"There is one thing I have yet to tell you about being a herald angel."

I couldn't suppress a roll of my eyes. He chose to ignore it.

"I knew of the downfall of mankind before it occurred. Indeed, I knew of my own, but I chose my own destiny."

I considered his words, trying to decide if he was telling me anything of importance or not. "You mean you know the future."

He gave a noncommittal shrug. "Before the fall, yes. Everything from the instant of creation to the end of time." His voice quieted. "As a demon, though, my sight is more… limited."

"Good for you, Pensatus. Why are you telling me this?"

Another small chuckle escaped his lips. "I also should tell you that if anyone else spoke to me in the tone and manner which you chose, the pain I would inflict would have them begging for death. In your case, however, the events that are in store for you this night are better than anything I could contrive, so I shall let nature take its course, inflict my revenge for me."

A chill crept over me at his words, but I shook it off. "There is nothing left for me to lose, Pensatus. Nothing that the fates can take from me, nothing left for God to steal, and definitely nothing left for you."

He smiled at me. A smile that almost seemed sweet, almost. "How wrong you are, little slave. How wrong you are."

"Fine. Whatever. More heartbreak. More pain. Big surprise. Are you going to tell me about my mother or father or not?"

He ignored me. "I still am not clear on why the nymphs would send you to me. Maybe they have a sense of humor after all, though I find that hard to believe." He wiped a strand of gold hair out of his eyes. "However, since they did, I will give you this crumb, not that you need it—your heart will shatter before the rise of the sun." He must have heard my thoughts, because he interrupted himself. "Yes, it is already broken, but not entirely, not yet. When it is, go to what calls you. Your questions will answer themselves."

I stared at him. My anger increasing by the second. "Seriously. That's it? All the effort to find you? For this?"

He smiled broadly, this teeth gleaming. "Go."

"You've got to be kidding. This is ridiculous! More damned riddles. You're no more of a help than the nymphs! All I need is—"

"Go!"

I was outside, on the cliff, the night wind cool around me.

I erupted into flames.

CHAPTER THIRTY-SIX

IT WAS well past midnight by the time I calmed down, my body feeling unusually cool as the air dried off the moisture left by the steam.

After screaming and ranting and pounding on the suddenly solid rock, I scrambled to the top of the cliff and took off running, fury consuming me. By the time I calmed down enough to take in my surroundings, I was miles away from the demon's cave. I wasn't sure where I was. I was in a residential neighborhood. The houses were modest but clean and kept up. In a few of them, a light shone from a window or a front porch, but most were cloaked in darkness. The occupants slept, unaware that a seriously pissed off and possibly deranged fire demon was on their street. Oh, I'm sorry, *slave* demon, apparently.

I realized, without warning, that I was once again starving. As a bonus, I also realized that the quickest way to solve that problem was to raid someone's kitchen, since I didn't see any convenience stores handy. The thought of breaking into someone's house sent a thrill through me. A flash of shame erupted from somewhere inside. I was acting like some juvenile punk trying to get his mommy and daddy's attention. I shoved the notion away. I was a demon. I finally felt like one. Be what I am.

Turning slowly in the middle of the street, I looked at the houses, taking in their details. At first, I thought I should try the largest house, assuming that the bigger the house, the more food they might have. However, at this point, I was more focused on the excitement than the thought of whatever food might be available.

Still debating which house had the most promise, I noticed a movement to my right. A figure stood leaning against a light post. It was the vampire. His red hair gleamed in the incandescence. Even from this distance, I could see his skin was fully back to normal. Apparently my blood had healed whatever injuries had been lingering. Of course, who knew how many victims he'd taken since he'd fed from me in the woods outside of the de Morisco home.

I took a few steps toward him, then paused, my fists already clenched and steaming. There was no chance this was coincidence. None. I met with the nymphs, then the demon, and the vampire just happens to show up. After I ran for miles, he just shows up? Yeah, right.

The nymphs had said there were many paths to the same destination. At least that's what I thought they'd been saying.

So I was meant to be here right now. With him. Whether it was orchestrated by the nymphs, the demon, or God himself, I didn't know or care. This was what I'd been waiting for—I'd avenge Sonia and make sure Finn and his family were finally safe. Then I'd go try every possible thing I could think of to test my immortality.

The vampire smiled. His thin lips were tight against his fangs. He still hadn't moved, content to lounge against the post. He was filthy, dirt caking his clothes and newly healed skin. I couldn't fathom how he had made me believe I wanted him. Maybe it was just my hate of him, but I didn't think I'd ever seen anyone more revolting.

His green eyes flashed, locking onto me.

Desire flooded through me. The fire from my hands extinguished, and I took another step toward him, feeling my cock harden down the leg of my pants.

The vampire's gaze turned away slowly, drifting down my body, his smile growing in satisfaction as he took in my arousal.

At the absence of his stare, shame replaced my attraction, swiftly followed by fury. Again my fists erupted, flames licking up my forearms, singeing the sides and sleeves of my T-shirt. This fucker was going to die, even if I had to gouge out my eyes to accomplish it!

I tensed to rush at him, but he raised his finger to his lips in a shushing motion. It was so unexpected that I paused in confusion.

His gaze met mine again, this time allowing me to be desire-free. With a jerk of his head, he motioned to the house behind him.

Following his gesture, I looked at the house. There was nothing special about it. It wasn't the largest or nicest on the block. Nor did it seem to have anything wrong with it. The only light was a flickering glow in one of the first story windows.

I did a double take as I turned back to the vampire. He was no longer there. Only the barren light post illuminating the curb remained. I twisted, looking all around, expecting him to descend on me. Despite the flash of fear at the thought, I wished he would. I was fairly certain I'd be able to explode into a ball of fire on command.

Nothing.

Continuing to turn in the middle of the street, I finally decided he wasn't getting ready to attack. I looked back at the light post and then the house he'd motioned toward. Had I just fallen for the oldest trick in the book—motioning somewhere to distract the enemy, then running away? Maybe he'd gone into the house and wanted me to follow.

For a second, I discarded that idea. No way was I following a vampire into a strange house. Then I remembered I wasn't the man I used to be. A vampire couldn't kill me, or so I was becoming ever more certain. I could burn the fucker without a thought. And, oh yeah, I didn't care if I lived or died anyway.

Not confident in the choice I was making, I snuck to the rear of the house. There was a security light over the back door as well, but it was flickering on and off sporadically.

Stepping into the pulsating yellow light, I reached out and grasped the door handle. It wasn't broken. Maybe vampires had unlocking spells like witches. A picture of Finn simply requesting the door to unlock for him flowed into my mind, and once again I shoved it away. Without any more effort than it takes to snap my fingers, I twisted the door handle and heard a grinding snap. The door swung open under my hand's weight.

Laughter drifted to my ears from the open door. I paused and turned my head toward the noise. More laughter followed by an increase in volume and someone shouting about a new car dealership by the airport. The television.

Feeling stupid, I stepped inside the dark hallway. After shutting the door behind me, I quietly took a few steps forward, letting my eyes adjust. Ahead, I could see three doorways. Two dark, one with a glowing light pouring from it. I crept forward as quietly as possible. I came to the first dark room. It was closed off with a door, but I didn't see any light coming from underneath. Quietly, I peered into the room. A small bathroom. Empty.

Moving on, I glanced into the second dark room. A stainless steel refrigerator peered back at me from the other side of the room.

Continuing down the hallway, I made my way to the final doorway and peeked through. The television glowed, an infomercial promoting a revolutionary new stain remover screeching loudly. Other than the solitary lamp beside the couch, there was no other light. In the glow of the lamp, lolled back onto the sofa cushions, was a sandy-colored balding head of hair. Sleeping. Although how the man could sleep with the television screaming like that was a mystery to me.

My gaze traveled over the rest of room. No one else there. No vampire waiting to jump out. Maybe I really was losing my mind. The vampire hadn't wanted me to come in here. He'd just run away, and I was stupid enough to fall for it. Still, I had to be sure. I crept to the rear of the sofa.

Running my hand over the seam stretching the length of the back of the sofa, I made my way around, slowing down as I reached the end and turned to face the man.

Uncertainty washed over me as I looked at him. Was I seeing things? As I took another step forward, my heart sped up, a feat that shouldn't have been possible. Another step and I was no longer confused. I knew what I was seeing.

The man's white shirt was awash with red. It ran down his arm and soaked into the couch. Following the trail of blood back up, I saw the gaping, ragged holes glaring at me from his throat.

Even with the proof in front of me, I couldn't accept what I was seeing. There was no feasible way the vampire had come in here and killed the man in the few seconds it had taken me to get from the street to the back door of the house. Yeah, he was fast. Fast enough I hadn't even seen him run from the street, but not this fast. Surely.

Sweeping the room, I saw a staircase running up the far side of the living room. He was still here. He had to be.

Without thinking, I ran up the carpeted stairs, three at a time, and stopped abruptly at the top. There were only two doorways off a small hallway up here.

Slowly, I made my way to the first doorway and peered in, expecting something to smash into my face. For his fangs to come flashing out of the dimly lit room. A cold sweat broke out over my skin as I took in the bedroom.

A lanky woman lay sprawled across the bed, her feet tangled in pale blue sheets. Her long, limp, mousey-brown hair lay matted in blood, covering the bite marks in her neck. Her dull eyes stared at me as her head hung upside down from the edge of the bed. This didn't make sense. Something was wrong. The vampire had not done this in the past two minutes. Still, he had to be here. Had to.

My unease spiking, I turned from her, cutting off her empty gaze. One room left. One more room and I'd have the vampire. One more room and it would be over. Either way it turned out, it would be over. One more room.

With less caution, I walked to the final room and stepped through the doorway.

Once again, the sight before me only caused confusion, making me unable to process what I was seeing.

I didn't see the redheaded vampire. There weren't eyes that called to me or tried to make me do their bidding.

Instead, there was long black hair hanging in curtains over the face of what appeared to be a small girl.

The girl's feet lay in tangles of sheets, just like her mother's, but her body arched upward, supported by the vampire's arms. Blood dripped from beneath drapes of ebony.

Sensing my presence, the vampire's head snapped up, her violet eyes flashing at me. *Violet eyes!*

Shoving the lifeless girl back onto the bed, causing her to bounce and then slide to the floor, the vampire came at me with such great speed, I didn't even see her move. One moment she was by the bed, the next her hands were wrapped around my throat and pulling my head toward her.

My brain shouted to shove her away. Get away from her. Set her on fire. But I couldn't. I couldn't move. Couldn't budge. Every synapse of my brain was consumed with only one thing.

"Sonia?"

The vampire's head jerked backward, her flashing fangs arching away from my throat as those violet eyes snapped to meet mine.

It was her. True, her eyes shone more violet than ever before, a strange glint in them. Her perfect lips were curled in a snarl over her fangs, but it was her. It was Sonia. My heart gave a leap of joy as I whispered her name again, and then it crashed. As the image of the man on the couch, the woman in the bed, the destroyed child lying on the floor severed my elation. My heart ripped. Whatever had been left of it died. I had thought it was dead before, but there was no mistaking it this time. It was dead, as surely as the child at our feet. As dead as Sonia was. As dead as she should have been.

Our eyes held each other momentarily, each searching the other.

With a force that sent me crashing into the wall across the room, she shoved me from her, tearing from the bedroom, her long black hair whipping around her as she fled. Before I had even finished hitting the floor, I heard the door downstairs slam against the wall as she made her escape.

Sitting in the mess of broken toys I had landed on, for what must have been the billionth time in the past week, I sobbed. For Finn, for the pain I had caused him. For the life he hoped we would live together. For Sonia, for her death. For her having to die again one day. For me. For everything I had become. For everything I would never be.

THE sun was beginning to peer through the pink lace curtains when my weeping finally ceased, at last truly leaving nothing in its place.

I stood up, pushing a gray stuffed elephant out of the way with my foot, and walked to the side of the bed. I looked down at the girl. She had been probably six or seven years old. Thick blonde lashes rested on her pale cheeks. Only the cavernous fissures in her throat and her chalky pallor destroyed the illusion of sleep.

Cocking my head at her, I was sure I was supposed to feel something. Pity. Outrage. Irony, maybe? Nothing. I felt nothing. Without another look at the girl or her slain parents, I made my way out of her room, down the stairs, and out the front door that was swaying gently in the breeze.

EPILOGUE

It wasn't the prophecy of the nymphs or the fortune telling of the demon. It definitely wasn't God. Nothing led me. Nothing except myself. It wasn't a thought or a decision. It just was.

By the time I walked onto the sand that was barely beginning to warm, there were already a few people milling about. An old man with a metal detector. A few joggers. A couple of ditzy girls already beginning their day of tanning.

The water was up to my knees when it occurred to me to take off my clothing. I slipped my sandals off, using the sand beneath my feet as leverage, and let my pants and shirt fall into the water and go where they would.

Wading out into the surf until I could no longer touch the bottom, I dove beneath the surface. Within four or five strong strokes, I was far away from where anyone could follow.

I was over a hundred feet below when I felt the presence. The eyes were watching me. I couldn't see them, but they were there. As before, my skin began to tingle. The water bubbled around me.

With another stroke, I sank deeper into the sea, leaving my fear and my fire behind. Whatever it was, whatever its intentions, it was time.

I waited, turning around slowly over and over again. I couldn't see anything. There was nothing alive around me, not so much as krill or plankton. I was alone.

Refusing to move, I stayed where I was, neither rising nor falling. This would be my resting spot for eternity if that was what nature had in store. I couldn't imagine much better.

I couldn't see the light of the sun from the surface above, so I gradually lost track of time. There was no use for time here. Not in the darkness and coolness of the deep. There was no use for anything.

It might have been hours. It might have been weeks. Gradually, I became aware of the presence once more. I would feel it come close, think I felt something graze my skin, only to turn around and find nothing. The presence would leave, only to return sometime later. After several of these interactions, they became commonplace, and I no longer turned to see what had touched me. I didn't prickle with anticipation when I felt it draw near. Whatever it was, it was part of the deep, just as I now was.

When I saw something in the distance, I thought I was seeing things, an underwater mirage. However, the harder I looked the closer it got.

Gradually, it took on form, getting closer, darting away once more, and then cautiously creeping forward yet again.

At last it swam up to me, pulling up even, and traded its horizontal swimming position for an upright one to match my own. We floated there face to face. Our eyes locked on each other, communicating volumes without so much as a word or a thought.

His long, white-blond hair swirled around him, at times brushing against my face. His shining pearl-white skin shimmered even in the absence of the sun. His glistening orange-golden tail occasionally flicked its flared fins to remain in place.

After every nuance of him had been forever burned into my mind, he stretched out a hand toward me and gave a slight motion with his long, willowy fingers. With that, he turned and began to swim away.

I followed.

AUTHOR'S NOTE & ACKNOWLEDGMENTS

As I sit here thinking of everyone to thank, I am overwhelmed. Submerging was finished three years ago. Over those three years, I fought countless times to get both *Submerging Inferno* and *The Shattered Door* published. Now, here I am: *Shattered* has been published for several months, and *Submerging* is next. Men of Myth book two, *Rising Frenzy*, is already finished, and I'm getting ready to begin book three, *Clashing Tempest*. What an amazing feeling to know that by the beginning of 2014 all four books will be in publication. I am so grateful for my dreams finally beginning to come to fruition, and I am so thankful to all those who have stood by and supported me through this journey—for those who remember when I kept talking about all the books I was writing for all those years (rock star dreams) and who are still here now that I can honestly say that I'm a writer. I thank God for this gift and letting there be a lift under my wings.

First, thank you, Reader. Thank you for taking a chance on a new gay fantasy series. Thank you for wading into this world with me. I hope you enjoyed this first step into the lives of these men of myth. Get ready, it's about to get stormy.

Elizabeth, thank you once again for being the one to say yes and seeing worth in my words. I am forever grateful and in your debt.

Anne Cain—You are magical. Thank you for the beautiful cover. It's stunning and captures Brett perfectly.

Desi and the slew of editors—Thank you, thank you, thank you. You'd think after three years of editing the damn thing, I would have had zero mistakes for you to find, not the hundreds that you uncovered. Desi, you've made me a better writer. There's no higher praise than that!

Trevor—I'm thanking you first of all the people who've been in my life for years, for it was you who first said, "Why don't you write what you read?" Well, here it is! Pure fantasy.

Chad—You're second because I wouldn't have had the courage to try if it hadn't been for you. You believed in my writing more than anyone I'd met up to that point. Your love inspired the first part of Submerging. The heartbreak inspired the rest. Thank you for your continued belief in my dreams and changing my life. This book is fully dedicated to you.

Sonia—I love you. Thank you for being "my little sister." Know that, even though I am the world's worst corresponder, I hold you dear and love you with all I am.

Joel—Thank you for creating the awesome Men of Myth badge! Thank you for lending your passion to mine, and for your loving friendship.

Michael "Mouse"—Thank you for also believing in my writing and your editing and feedback of *Submerging*, even though fantasy just isn't your thing.

Stephen—As I said in *Shattered*, you weren't around when *Submerging* was written, but you were there when I rushed home to tell you I had a publishing contract. Thank you for believing in my dream and supporting me through all the submissions, book signings (I'm pretending there was more than one), and self-promotions. Most of all, thank you for your love and walking through the beautiful and dark times with me. I love you!

Kevin—You will always be on the thank-you list, even though you don't read, for being my best friend and letting my tears and laughter be yours and allowing me to give you the same gift.

To my family—My mom and dad. My wonderful brother, Trenton. My treasured nephew, Gavin. While my words are not what you would have me write, thank you for your love and being the most consistent and sustaining people in my life! I love you all so very, very much!

Patrick—As always, cuz. We dream, and we fly! I love that we are both beginning to soar. http://www.patrickalancasey.com/

Cheryl—Thank you for your support over the last few years. Coming into my classroom before our days begin, checking on both my heart and my writing. Your strength and humor are legendary. I will never have a blue cheese olive without thinking of you.

Dunkyn and Dolan—My beautiful corgis, my little men. I love you both so much! Dunk, without a doubt, you've been the most loyal man of my life. Thanks for sharing your life with me. And, yes, Dolan, I love you too—now quit licking me!

With so much love and gratitude,
Brandon

Don't miss what happens next in

Coming soon to
http://www.dsppublications.com

PROLOGUE

Finn de Morisco

"NOT enough?" My voice cut through the heavy silence that filled the cab of the truck. It was abrasive, the sound making the moment seem more real. I lowered it to a whisper as I turned to look out past the driveway, searching the dark street beyond.

"Our love wasn't enough?" He wasn't anywhere. The solitude of the neighborhood suddenly made the street I'd grown up on sinister and oppressive. I couldn't find any trace of him. I whipped around, hitting my left elbow on the steering wheel, and looked out the driver's side window, expecting to see Brett standing there. Waiting to tell me he'd changed his mind. That he couldn't walk away after all.

Nothing. Only the sidewalk that led to Mom and Dad's front door, illuminated by the porch light only a few yards away. "I wasn't enough."

Of course you weren't enough. Haven't I been telling you that for days? You're a sorry excuse for a man, let alone a warlock. Can't even hold on to your demon of a boyfriend.

I ignored the berating voice that filled my mind. I wasn't going to let it intrude into this moment. Even if what it said was true.

Turning back, I stared at the steering wheel. Why had I fixed it? I should have left Brett's melted handprints, a testament to him. A memorial. I wrapped my fingers around where his imprint had been.

It didn't matter. He'd be back. He had to be. He'd just been freaked out by whatever it was the nymphs had said to him on the cliff. He had every right to be. It hadn't even been two weeks since he'd been attacked, since his best friend had been killed. He just needed some time.

He loved me. He'd be back.

No he won't.

A motion caught my attention. The front door of the house opened, spilling light in an arc over the yard.

Before I could see who it was, I jammed the truck into reverse and slammed my foot on the gas. Once out of the driveway, I paused just long enough to tap the break and switch to drive. Just long enough to hear Mom's worried voice carry through the night. Just long enough for my tears to start to fall again.

I was over two blocks away from the house before I had the sense to begin to look for Brett again. Still, there was nothing in the pools of yellow light that fell from the street lamps. There weren't even other people wandering around the neighborhood. There was only me.

How long had I lain there curled up in a pathetic ball in the seat of my truck, alternating between sobbing and utter disbelief? Ten minutes? Twenty? How far away could Brett have gotten in that amount of time?

I just needed to find him. To reassure him that he was going to be okay. That we were going to be okay. That as long as we loved each other, everything was going to work out.

And how many times did you have to do that in the two minutes you and the demon played house? He didn't love you. He felt sorry for you. He tried to leave you nearly every second you were together. He just kept wussing out because he didn't want to make you cry. He finally grew a pair, didn't he? That's more than I can say for you.

"Shut up!" My arms jerked as I screamed, pulling the truck to the right and popping the front tire over the curb and onto the sidewalk. I overcorrected, driving into the oncoming lane before getting control once more, tears streaming harder as I continued to rage at the voice. "He did love me! Brett loved me. He loves me. You'll see. He'll be back any moment. He'll be back at Mom and Dad's before I return. Maybe he's already back at my house, just waiting."

The voice didn't reply, just issued a long, satisfied laugh.

"He loves me."

I drove a few more feet, until I was exactly halfway between two light posts, allowing most of the truck to be cloaked in shadow. I'd already wasted too much time. I should have followed him as soon as he walked away. I'd only confirmed what he'd said, that love wasn't enough. At the first chance, I'd let him down. He just needed to know I wasn't going to give up.

The nagging feeling kept returning. At first I'd thought it was the voice when I'd felt it as Brett shut the door of the truck.

This time was different.

RISING FRENZY

I'd heard it in his voice. Seen it in his eyes. This wasn't like his other moments of panic.

That sensation was harder to block than the voice. I wished the sensations were from whoever taunted my mind. It would have made them less true.

I pushed them away again.

A locator spell. Of course. All I needed to do was focus on him. I'd found him easily enough in the graveyard the other time he'd left.

I removed my hands from the steering wheel and placed them in my lap. My fingers ached from the strangling grip they'd held. I closed my eyes, trying to block out everything else.

As soon as Brett's face rose in my mind, a searing pain cut through my chest. A mixture of emotional and physical agony so intense it took my breath away.

Yes, so powerful. What a mighty warlock you are. Can't even do a locator spell.

Again, I shoved the voice from me, doubling my efforts to bring Brett into focus. See his beautiful face, feel his turmoil.

Starbursts of white light exploded behind my eyes, my brain experiencing a sort of massive brain freeze.

I sat there, managing nothing more than dragging in deep, shuddering breaths. Even that felt like too monumental a task.

Finally, the pain ebbed, and my pulse began to slow.

"You're doing this, aren't you? You're making it where I can't find Brett."

If you're such a great warlock, I wouldn't be able to do such a thing, would I?

"Why are you doing this? Let me find him."

He doesn't want to be found.

Another rush of those feelings returned, not brought on by the voice, though confirming its claim. Brett didn't want to be found. He didn't want me.

I should go home. To my home, not Mom and Dad's. Brett wasn't there. The vampire wouldn't be coming. Maybe Brett would show up if I were at home. I shook myself. He wasn't going to be at my house. Not tonight. He'd be back. He had to be. We were meant to be. I just needed to have faith. Let him take his space. I didn't need to suffocate him. That wouldn't help.

You could make yourself forget him. Or cause him to feel all the pain you feel. I bet even a useless lump like you could pull that off. I'd help.

The suggestion was so out of the realm of possibilities I couldn't even respond for several seconds. "I'd never hurt him. Ever. And I don't want to forget him. I could never do that. Plus, he'll be back."

I looked up at the stars, dim through the dusty windshield. He was out there. He was struggling and hurting. He was afraid. But he loved me. Loves me. Brett loves me.

He'd be back.

RISING FRENZY

CHAPTER ONE

Finn de Morisco

Four Months Later

"SHUT up, Caitlin!"

"I'm not going to shut up!" Caitlin flung the door closed, making the frame tremble and sealing us in my bedroom. "I don't care if Mom and Dad feel too bad to tell you to grow the fuck up. Christina and Cynthia can whimper away about how heartbroken you are. Don't fuckin' care! Get out of the damned bed, pull on your big-boy pants, and get to work!" Her red face clashed with the current cotton-candy color of her spiky hair.

I turned away from her, pulling the white duvet over my ears. "You're the last person in this family who has any right to cast stones. Go away."

The blinds, of their own accord, shot up to the top of the windows with a clang, and sunlight flooded the dark room. I buried my head deeper under the fabric.

She growled from the opposite side of the room. "Don't think the covers won't be next."

"So desperate for a man you're turning to your own brother now?"

Her voice lowered. "You know, your lesbian humor used to be much sharper. And with as much weight as you've lost, there's not much to see anyway. I'm going to count to five."

I sat up, anger flaring. "Really! Count to five? Screw you, Cate! Try it. I'll have you knocked back and frozen to the wall the rest of the day."

She crossed her arms. "I wish you would. Some sign of life would be encouraging. Any sign of life."

I glared at her, then flopped back down and burrowed once more. "Try it."

The bed shifted as her weight sank next to my back, and her arm came to rest on my shoulder. Her voice was suddenly low and soothing. "I'm worried about you, Finn. Really I am."

"Whatever, Cate. This strategy change doesn't become you. Go back to threatening me like a six-year-old. It suits you better."

"I *am* worried. You never go in to help Mom and Cynthia at the bakery. You don't eat. You come home in the late hours of the morning, if you bother to come home at all."

"You don't even live here. What do you know?"

"It's not like it's a secret." She removed her hand. "If you want to spend the rest of your life at a bathhouse, the least you could do is learn to be sneakier so it's not rubbed in Mom's and Dad's faces all the time."

"Bathhouse?"

A guttural scoff escaped her. "So, you're back to being Mr. Innocent, huh?" I felt her weight leave the bed. "Fine, pretend. At least start helping out with the stores. Even if it doesn't make you feel better, your family needs you right now."

Sitting up once more, the covers pooling at my waist, I turned to face her. "Again, Catlin, you're the last person who should judge. How long were you out of commission when Alice, or whatever her name was, left? Six months? More?"

I swear I could hear her teeth gritting.

"Allison. Don't pretend you don't remember her name. And that was different."

"Different. Really? How? Are lesbians entitled to more grief time than the rest of us?"

"Because we'd been together over five years, you selfish little brat. How long were you and Demon-boy together? Not even enough time for bread to mold. That was barely worthy of being classified as a hookup, let alone a relationship!"

Without even a twitch from me, the door slammed open and Caitlin hurled through. Judging from the sound before the door shut her out, there was a Caitlin-sized hole in the drywall.

CAITLIN got what she'd wanted. There was only so long I could lie there and seethe. Not that getting up had changed much. If anything, the motion of moving around only increased my agitation. Even driving wasn't helping soothe me. I pulled onto the Five, cutting off a Honda Civic in the right lane.

RISING FRENZY

I'd have given anything to have Caitlin's tirade not echo my own thoughts. I wished I could just dismiss them as my sister being her normal, bitchy self. While that might still be true, it didn't negate what she'd said.

For weeks after Brett left, I'd been thoroughly heartbroken. Several times a day, I'd have panic attacks where I'd have to teach myself to breathe anew each time. I searched endlessly. For Brett. For the vampire. For any clue at all. The voice allowed me to use every spell I could think of, and still I couldn't locate him.

Even the nymphs were no help. Only Amalphia showed, and she simply waxed philosophical about choices and the paths our lives take being fluid. Whatever.

Nothing. I'd found nothing. It was like he had vanished.

At first, I'd been consumed by the fear that the vampire had found him and killed him. Then the fear moved to him harming himself. Chances were his demon bloodline made him immortal, but maybe if he were determined enough....

Then the fear turned into anguish. I quit being afraid he was in danger. The truth was he'd left me. Whatever he was facing, whatever nervousness he'd had, it was me he'd left. Me that he deemed not good enough. My family droned on and on and on about how it wasn't me, it was him. I'm such a great catch. How could he not love me? The problem had to be in him, in the demons he faced. Demons he faced! Demons! Mom actually said that, with no irony at all. Demon. I wasn't even good enough for a demon. Yeah, yeah. I'm such a great catch. Such a great guy. So sweet. So handsome. So strong and dependable.

He left. The bottom line is he left. Me. He left me. He didn't want me. That lovely realization hurt me more than the fear that he was dead. That he was out there somewhere, simply happy and relieved to be away from me. I wasn't sure which I was more ashamed of—that he was glad to be away from me, or that the thought hurt worse than the idea of him being dead.

If I started to forget that, even for a moment, the voice jovially brought it all rushing back.

Anguish turned to anger. Anger. That's where I've stayed. Anger and apathy. The sequel to Jane Austen's *Sense and Sensibility*.

My family had no idea what to do with me, and rightfully so. I have no idea what to do with myself. I honestly don't think I'd ever really been angry before. That was Caitlin's role. I was the anti-Caitlin. Now I make her look like a novice.

What makes me the angriest? Even more than knowing I wasn't good enough for him, not even good enough for a breakup involving more than ten seconds in the front of my truck before he booked it? That I loved him.

Really, truly loved him. Still do. The fool. I love him. And Cate's right—there is no way I possibly could. We knew each other for eight whole days! Eight! I even know how many hours. I've counted. I went from "hello" to "be the father of my children" in eight days. Now, four months later, I've let eight pointless days ruin my life. Cate's right about another thing. I need to grow up. Wish I knew how. How to stop hurting. Stop being angry. Stop being numb. Stop loving someone who threw me away.

I don't remember talking to myself before Brett, but I do now. I narrate my pathetic life. Have entire, in-depth conversations with myself. Hell, I even have them with Brett. And the voice, of course. Everyone wants me to talk to them, just get it all off my chest.

If I got any more off my chest, it would make vomiting seem subtle.

I slammed the gear into park and was out of the truck before I'd even realized where I was. Didn't pause when I figured it out, though. Of course this was where I'd end up. This was where I always ended up.

It surprised me they'd concluded I was spending my time in the bathhouse. The thought of Caitlin discussing me at a bathhouse was revolting enough, but my mom too? I wondered which would freak them out the most. Me wasting my life at a bathhouse or here? It's a pretty safe bet the bathhouse would be the sunnier option.

The voice that greeted me as I entered The Square didn't even faze me. Sometimes when I walked alone at night in Old Town or did my nightly haunt of Brett's grandmother's house, or any other time at all, it bothered me. But not here. The voice was at home here.

Welcome back, sire. The sarcastic sneer no longer caused my hackles to rise. *It didn't take long between visits, did it? What's wrong now? Your family make you angry? Might have to go back to work? Another boy break your heart?*

I passed Gifts without looking in. I knew that witch would be watching. She did every time. She always knew when I was here. Just a few more moments and I'd be able to shut out the voice. I'd been getting better at it. See, Caitlin, I have been doing something productive over the past four months.

Shut me out? Why, that's just hurtful. And here I am, simply trying to help you become the man you were born to be. Help you to embrace the power inside you. Let your anger start to—

Talking about Brett to my family wasn't going to happen, but I really wished I could ask my father about the voice. I no longer thought it was a figment of my psyche. It was real. It belonged to something or someone here in The Square. The blistering fire that accompanied it in my dreams seemed less like an illusion as well. Telling Dad about the voice would be harder than talking to him about the supposed bathhouse, and that was never gonna happen.

Crossing over to Hemlock Street, I cast a glance over my right shoulder. Sure enough, there she was, her sour face watching me from the window of Gifts. As before, she neither looked away in recognition of being caught staring, nor offered any acknowledgment of any awareness of me.

Without a response of my own, I turned back around in time to throw open the door to Bar and slip inside. The red light radiating from behind the glass bar fell over the few patrons, giving them a unifying washout of color.

The blonde barely spared me a glance as she handed a froth-laded tumbler over to a rotund witch. "'Sup, Finn?"

"Same as ever."

I took my place on the barstool at the end. I couldn't see the front door from my vantage point, but I could see nearly every other inch of the narrow space. My gaze slid over each figure. At first, this new little paranoid, hypervigilant twitch of mine was rather exhausting, but now I kinda liked it. A new second nature. I'd never realized how much was really going on around me until I sat back and started looking. I never would have noticed the odd tremor in the hands of the witch Marina served or the spill of the vodka on the counter as she lifted it to her lips. Was she nervous? Scared? On her way to passing-out drunk?

I might have missed Marina's habitual covert glances at the clock on the wall, judging to see how much more time until her shift was over. It was this longing act that had let me know Marina wasn't as hard or tough as she played at being. She wanted to leave her job early, just like everyone else.

Even the gorgeous redhead in the corner would have escaped my notice before. She held her boyfriend's hand across the booth but kept her attention focused on me. Be happy where you are, sweetheart. Wrong tree. Wrong time. Wrong guy. Wrong everything.

The massive hulk that seemed to appear from thin air at the back of the bar would have caught my notice even if I hadn't been paying attention. He was the definition of tall, dark, and handsome. Handsome in a serial killer kind of way, but handsome nonetheless. The last thing I'd been looking for in my men lately was sweet or tender. Judging from the sneer on his face, this one was right up my alley. It seemed that I wasn't the only one observing the surroundings. The man's dark eyes swept over me as he took in the room, then returned to meet my stare head-on. His eyes grew darker—in anger or passion, I wasn't sure. With any luck, both.

I began to get up, but a hand grasped my wrist. Jerking away, I tore my eyes off the man. Before I could get out the curse words that were on my lips, Marina slammed down a frosted pint. "Don't even think about it, Finn." She wiped up some of the foam that had flowed over onto the bar. "He's nothing but trouble."

"Trouble is fine, especially packaged like that." My gaze flickered to where he'd last been. He was now seated a couple of stools down from the large witch. He drummed his fingers on the bar. "I think he's in need of service."

She rolled her eyes. "Not hardly. He's probably just trying to make the room stop spinning. Although you'd think he'd be used to it by now." She glanced over her shoulder, gave a chin thrust in way of greeting, and turned back to me. She lowered her voice, but not enough to keep others from hearing. "I wish we didn't have to serve humans in here. Disgusting." She shrugged. "Gotta keep the buffet line going in case a vampire or someone wants a snack."

"*He's* a human?" I gave him an incredulous look. His eyes were still drilling into me.

"Don't let the packaging fool ya, sweetie. He's just a Happy Meal in four-hundred-dollar loafers."

"Really? I would have guessed demon. Or at least part. He's huge."

"Nope. Just biggie sized." She leaned in conspiratorially. "I'd forgotten your thing about demons."

A sigh escaped. "I never should have told you about Brett. Not sure what I was thinking."

"I'm not sure what you were thinking either, but I'm sure glad all the waterworks have stopped. That was getting pathetic."

"Wow. Thanks, Marina. Your support is overwhelming."

Another shrug. "Well, it was. Just because you're one of my favorite new regulars doesn't mean I'm gonna sugarcoat the truth. Hell, you're lucky I like you at all. Neanderthal over there's been coming a lot longer than you have, and I won't say more to him than the price of his bill. And he's here for days at a time. You just pop in and leave again."

"He's in here days at a time? You let him sleep at the bar?"

Marina gave me an icy glare. "For all your heartbroken, angsty anger and your random hookups, you're still nothing more than a Boy Scout, aren't you? Of course he doesn't sleep at my bar, the piece of filth. Who said anything about sleeping? That's the last thing he's doing back there."

"Back there?" I looked around her to the shadows at the rear of the bar where I'd first noticed him. "The bathroom."

"For fuck sake, Finn, not the bathroom. In the back room. I keep waiting for you to ask to go back there, but, as I said, too much of a Boy Scout."

RISING FRENZY

The witch put her trembling hands on the bar as she leaned forward. "Can I go? I've always wanted to try the back rooms."

"Seriously, Devinia. You? In the back rooms? You know there are standards."

Fury flitted across the witch's face. Her hands began to tremble more violently as her vodka tumbler rose in the air, spinning, gradually picking up speed. "You let a human—"

"And for what fucking purpose, do you think, you old cow? You really wanna take his place?"

The old witch's eyes bulged.

"And if you break one of my glasses, I'll make sure you get to see the back rooms, and I get to pick. They could use you for a long time in Restaurant." The spinning tumbler returned to rest on the table, and Marina filled it once more. "Shut up and drink. And know your place."

Looking back and forth between the back of the bar and the man, I let her words register. Raising my brow, I looked at her. "What's in the back rooms anyway?"

"I'll let you discover it for yourself."

"Is it safe?"

"Fuck, no." She let out a sharp laugh. "Well, actually, I guess it depends on your perspective. It's safe for you."

"It is?"

Marina patted my hand like she was talking to a child. "Isn't The Square always safe for you?"

I didn't know how to answer that. Nothing had ever happened to me here, but I would never apply "safe" as an attribute of The Square. I glanced at the man again. What had he been doing back there for days? He was still glaring at me. His loss. The back room sounded much more interesting than some huge drunk guy. No matter how good-looking he was.

"Can I go back there?"

She nodded. "Yep. All you needed to do was ask."

The witch glared at me.

"Knock it off, Devinia. Maybe in your next life, you'll ascend to a higher life-form. Come back as a slug. I'll let you in then."

"Remind me not to get on your bad side, Marina." I raised my mug and downed the remaining beer.

"Remind yourself, Finn." She gave me what she probably thought was a kind smile. "Maybe some time in the back rooms will help put all this demon-lover crap to rest and you can move the fuck on."

With a noncommittal grunt, I left my seat and rounded my corner of the bar. I could see the witch's hand-tremble increase as I came closer. With a thought, I froze her hands where they were. Her hate-filled stare intensified, but she knew better than to try another spell.

Tall, dark, and handsome watched as I came closer. On second thought, it wouldn't hurt to have company, someone who at least knew their way around the back room. Maybe I could talk this guy into being my tour guide.

I've got something better for you than him. You're gonna love it. Promise.

The voice threw me off, and I paused stupidly beside where the man was seated. He stood up, towering over me. Maybe even taller than Brett had been… is… was… whatever.

Before I could even open my mouth to inquire, the man's hand shot out and encircled my throat. He lifted me off the ground and slammed my back into the bar. My body bent so my legs dangled in midair, and my eyes met his bloodshot, unfocused gaze as he leaned over me.

"One more look from you, you fucking little faggot, and I'll bury this in your skull. Got it?" I heard the click of a switchblade being released and felt the point puncture my ear. "Be doing the world a favor to get rid of one more faggot wetback who only wants to—"

His throat opened up into four parallel gashes, and blood sprayed onto my face, filling my mouth and stinging my eyes.

The witch's screams pierced my ears. In pure panic, I flung myself away from the man, which only took away my support and left me to crash to the floor.

Spitting and gagging, I pushed up onto my knees and used the backs of my hands and sleeves to get the blood out of my eyes.

His body crumpled to the ground with a wet splat that made my stomach churn.

Through the stinging blood, I could see the ragged slices in his throat, four wicked grins mocking me from below his bulging eyes. "I'm so sorry. I didn't mean to. I've never done anything like that. I didn't even know my power could do that. I'm so sorry. So sorry."

"Finn"—I felt Marina's hands under my arms, trying to pull me up—"what are you talking about? What the fuck are you sorry for?"

I jerked away from her, returning to the man's dead stare. "I didn't mean to kill him!"

"I killed him." The voice was like gravel, deep and low and not at all soothing.

RISING FRENZY

I followed the voice. Behind the man's body was a pair of black cowboy boots. I followed the dark denim pants up to a stained, muscle-filled wifebeater, then to a wide, square face. "What? Who are you?"

"I said, 'I killed him.'" He raised his hand, and my eyes involuntarily tracked the motion. Furred hand with long, talon-like claws. I returned to the man's face.

"Werewolf."

The man didn't acknowledge or deny. "He was not allowed to harm you."

Marina placed a hand on my shoulder. "I told you that you're safe at The Square."

Photo by David Schmidt
Ink by Aries Rhysing

BRANDON WITT resides in Denver, Colorado. When not snuggled on the couch with his two Corgis, Dunkyn and Dolan, he is more than likely in front of his computer, nose inches from the screen, fingers pounding they keys. When he manages to tear himself away from his writing addiction, he passionately takes on the role of a special education teacher during the daylight hours.

Website: http://www.brandonwitt.com
Author Facebook page: https://www.facebook.com/brandon.witt.author
Twitter: https://twitter.com/wittauthor

Coming Soon: Book Three

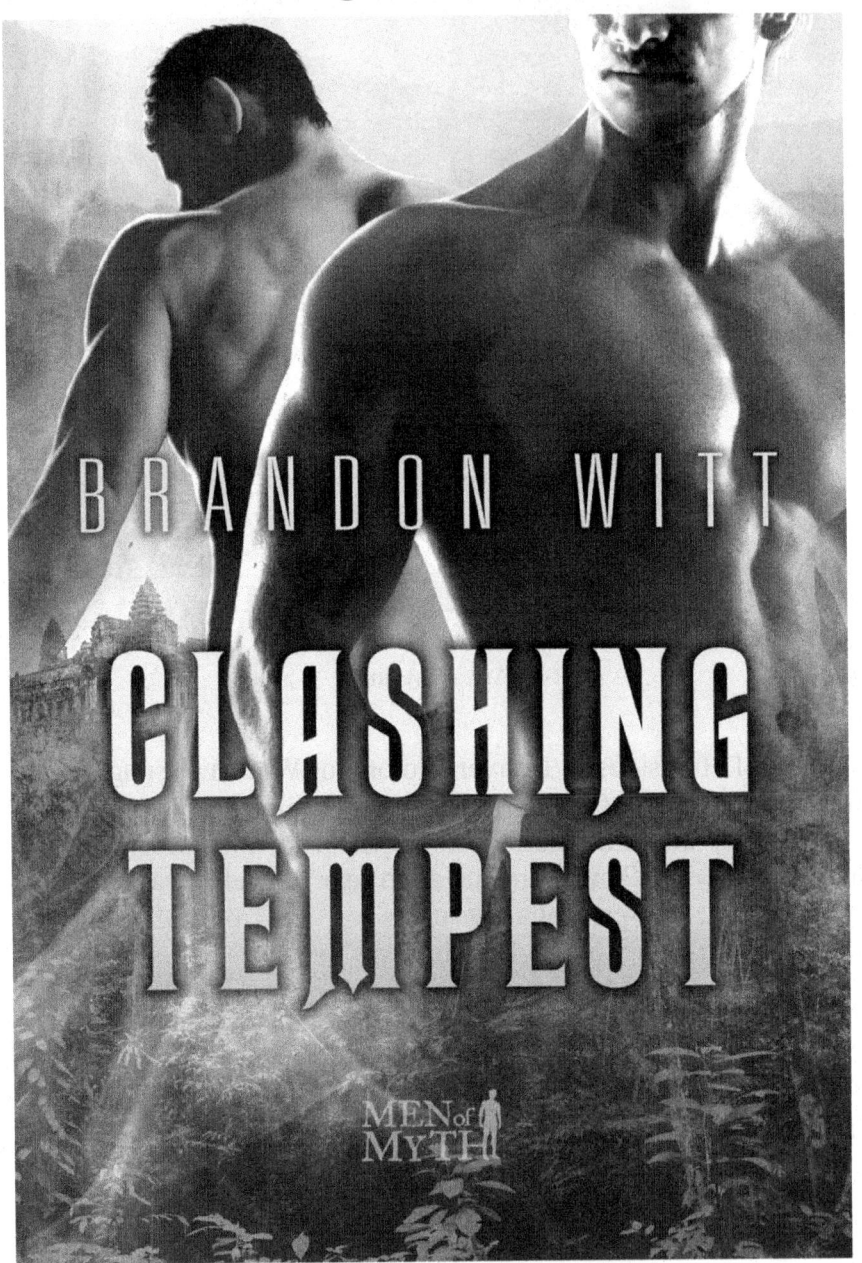

http://www.dsppublications.com

Also from DSP Publications

Third Eye

By Rick R. Reed

Who knew that a summer thunderstorm and his lost little boy would conspire to change single dad Cayce D'Amico's life in an instant? With Luke missing, Cayce ventures into the woods near their house to find his son, only to have lightning strike a tree near him, sending a branch down on his head. When he awakens the next day in the hospital, he discovers he has been blessed or cursed—he isn't sure which—with psychic ability. Along with unfathomable glimpses into the lives of those around him, he's getting visions of a missing teenage girl.

When a second girl disappears soon after the first, Cayce realizes his visions are leading him to their grisly fates. Cayce wants to help, but no one believes him. The police are suspicious. The press wants to exploit him. And the girls' parents have mixed feelings about the young man with the "third eye."

Cayce turns to local reporter Dave Newton and, while searching for clues to the string of disappearances and possible murders, a spark ignites between the two. Little do they know that nearby, another couple—dark and murderous—are plotting more crimes and wondering how to silence the man who knows too much about them.

http://www.dsppublications.com

Coming Soon

'Til Darkness Falls

By Pearl Love

A malicious deception…. An ancient curse…. A timeless love….

Brian Macon is a worn-out homicide detective whose job and life hold no meaning until he meets a gorgeous German man who turns his world upside down. Alrick Ritter has a poet's soul, a master cellist's skill, and a sniper's deadly accuracy, and though constrained by sinister forces to be a killer-for-hire, Alrick wants nothing more than to be with Brian. Helpless to resist the call of their hearts, Brian and Alrick begin a cautious affair, keeping secret the reality that places them on opposite sides of the law. But an ancient danger threatens to destroy their love.

Three thousand years ago in the burning sands of ancient Egypt, Prince Rahotep and his devoted slave, Tiye, were robbed of their lives, betrayed by a powerful woman's mad hatred and the cruel humor of an evil god. Now, destiny has reunited the lovers, joining them in an unquenchable passion even as a twist of fate casts them as potential enemies. Will Brian and Alrick be able to overcome the centuries-old curse to secure the love that should have always been theirs?

http://www.dsppublications.com

Coming Soon

Desert World: Book 1

Desert World Allegiances

By Lyn Gala

Livre once offered Planetary Alliance miners and workers a small fortune if they helped terraform the mineral rich planet. People flocked to the world, but then a civil war cut the desert planet off from all resources. Half-terraformed and clinging to the edge of existence, Livre devolved into a world where death was accepted as part of life, water resources were scarce and constantly dwindling, and neighbors tried to help each other hold off the inevitable as the desert fought to take back the few terraformed spaces.

Temar Gazer claims to be the victim of water theft. His claims could be a simple misdirection intended to help him escape a term of labor after his criminal prank caused irreparable damage to a watering system. However as the only member of the council arguing against a short-term slavery sentence for Temar, Shan Polli can't escape the fear that something darker is happening. The more he investigates Temar's story, the more he finds that his world is not as free of politics or danger as he had assumed. Together, Shan and Temar must get to the bottom of the conspiracy before time runs out for the entire planet.

http://www.dsppublications.com

Also from DSP Publications

Willow Man

By John Inman

Woody Stiles has sung his country songs in every city on the map. His life is one long road trip in a never-ending quest for fame and fortune. But when his agent books him into a club in his hometown, a place he swore he would never set foot again, Woody comes face to face with a few old demons. One in particular.

With memories of his childhood bombarding him from every angle, Woody must accept the fact that his old enemy, Willow Man, was not just a figment of childish imagination.

With his friends at his side, now all grown up just like he is, Woody goes to battle with the killer that stole his childhood lover. Woody also learns Willow Man has been busy while he was away, destroying even more of Woody's past. And in the midst of all this drama, Woody is stunned to find himself falling in love—something he never thought he would do again.

As kids, Woody and his friends could not stop the killer who lived in the canyon where they played. As adults, they might just have a chance.

Or will they?

http://www.dsppublications.com

Also from DSP Publications

Eagle's Blood

By A.J. Marcus

Brock Summers is a Colorado Parks and Wildlife Officer who loves his job and takes it very seriously. When he discovers a video of golden eagles being shot and learns of a nest in trouble, not even a blizzard can stop him from trekking up the mountain in an attempt to rescue them.

When Brock returns with the one eaglet he manages to save, Landon Weir, the local wildlife rehabilitator, patches up the bird and the injury Brock suffered during the rescue. Though they have been friends and colleagues for years, they discover a shared passion for protecting wildlife and vow to work together to protect the majestic birds from the criminals preying on them. It isn't long before another video of eagles being killed comes to their attention. They must face inclement weather, a dangerous mountain, and armed poachers if they want to ensure the eagles'—and their own—survival.

http://www.dsppublications.com

Also from DSP PUBLICATIONS

Infected: Prey

Infected: Book 1

By Andrea Speed

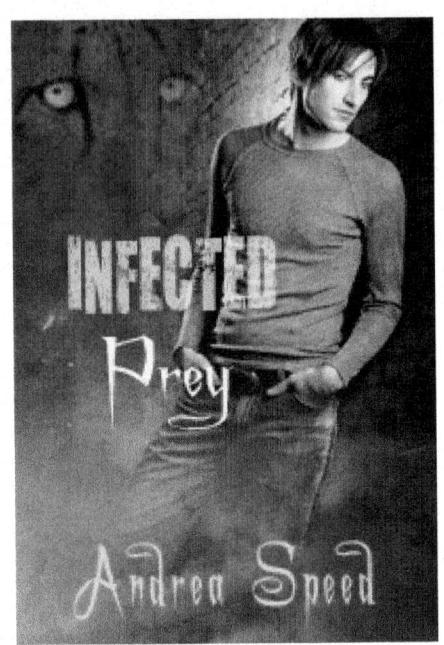

In a world where a werecat virus has changed society, Roan McKichan, a born infected and ex-cop, works as a private detective trying to solve crimes involving other infecteds.

The murder of a former cop draws Roan into an odd case where an unidentifiable species of cat appears to be showing an unusual level of intelligence. He juggles that with trying to find a missing teenage boy, who, unbeknownst to his parents, was "cat" obsessed. And when someone is brutally murdering infecteds, Eli Winters, leader of the Church of the Divine Transformation, hires Roan to find the killer before he closes in on Eli.

Working the crimes will lead Roan through a maze of hate, personal grudges, and mortal danger. With help from his tiger-strain infected partner, Paris Lehane, he does his best to survive in a world that hates and fears their kind… and occasionally worships them.

http://www.dsppublications.com

Also from DSP Publications

Erasing Shame

By Yeyu

The son of a Han traitor who had let the Xianbei Mongols invade the borders, Jiang Shicai swears to restore his family's honor, hoping to better the Hans' lives through peaceful means. He believes violence is never the answer, but to gain respect, he finds himself fighting for the Xianbei.

Ten years later, an annoying but handsome playboy, Dugu Xuechi, arrives as the incompetent new military inspector of Shicai's region. Shameless, irresponsible, and obnoxious, Xuechi tests Shicai's patience almost every second. Despite their mutual dislike, Shicai finds himself drawn to the capricious man, especially when he sees the resemblance between Xuechi and his deceased best friend. Yet Xuechi's self-destructive behavior and refusal to accept help require attention that distracts Shicai from his goal for peace--and it doesn't help that Xuechi is Shicai's strongest political opposition. Haunted by a childhood promise he never had the chance to fulfill, Shicai must choose between his feelings and his values.

http://www.dsppublications.com

Lightning Source UK Ltd.
Milton Keynes UK
UKOW05f1330050317
295819UK00001B/290/P